All of a Sudden

All of a Sudden

JOURNEY TO THE DARK

Saman Bareen Ashraf

ALL OF A SUDDEN
JOURNEY TO THE DARK

This is a work of fiction. All of the characters, names, incidents,
organizations, and dialogue in this novel are either the products
of the author's imagination or are used fictitiously.

iUniverse books may be ordered through booksellers or by contacting:

iUniverse
1663 Liberty Drive
Bloomington, IN 47403
www.iuniverse.com
1-800-Authors (1-800-288-4677)

ISBN: 978-1-4917-5259-3 (sc)
ISBN: 978-1-4917-5260-9 (e)

Printed in the United States of America.

iUniverse rev. date: 11/05/2014

CHAPTER 1

+≈ Journey to Dark ≈+

I

About ages ago, a grief-stricken thing happened on this tiny piece of earth. It happened so when the earth people prospered in enmity. There was a thirst of blood. To dominate other became obligatory for every leader in their secular religion. A man left the other man alone in dark. The time had come when the survival had been hard and a man could not find solace anywhere. Murders, accidents, suicide attacks and the else like became a common building block in the everyday living. Nothing was bothering. The price of man became the smallest currency note. The massive use of technology and science reduces man's will and the greed for wishes became higher and higher touching the surmounting heights equivalent to the skies. What happened at the time that brought man to the Past? He had deprived of all his facilities and the freedom. Thus, a man got the punishment of his crimes. The more powerful and the strong people assaulted the Earth. Living in space on a small planet, scientists could never be able to discover, there were treacherous people. They were just like men with more power. They were more intelligent and wise. They were beautiful with extraordinary beauty and talent. The difference in their physical appearance was that they were having a sun sign on the back of their right hand and it remained hot like a coal. They were planning to beat the earth from ages but could not get any opportunity to have fulfilled the desire and, at last, on one day, the man gave them the chance. They came loaded with unseen and outthought weapons. Men gathered and fought bravely. They used modern and high range guns, helicopters, tanks and weapons of every type but could not succeed. Those people called as Sunasians captured men and their belongings. They deprived them of their essentials. The invaders did not spare men and started their tyrannies and so the Earthmen could not struggle for freedom. They killed all the outstanding, talented and the brilliant people of the earth. They threatened the Earthmen to leave the land or they would not be able to see their existence on the earth.

The poor, fragile people where could go? Some people rushed to the seas and the deserted islands but they found the people from a drop of water, a little piece of land and brutally slaughtered each and everyone. Some requested for mercy but Sunasians did not spare anyone. Hence, a time came when they had been in one of those endangered species in their own scientific language and on one day, the Omnipotent and the Omnipresent, Almighty Allah took pity on the silly people of the earth and sent a help in the variety of a man. He called himself as a Sunasian. He was looking kind-hearted and had a great love for humanity. The feared, unlucky people gathered and were questionably staring the tall, healthy and the graceful old man. He addressed the Earthmen,

"O People! I am Alberic. I have been from Sunasia. Although, I am a Sunasian but I

have respect for your people. I have come for you people. You must cooperate with me. Instead, I should say you must trust me. These people have come to the Earth with the latest technology. You had been having superman, Spiderman and the batman in your fantasies but they were having them in their real life. Now they have come here in search of a small ball shaped, err... err... err I forgot the name. I am so sorry. I really forgot the name but for what I have come to the earth is the reason that I want to take you to the Sunasia what have been vacant now. No one lives there. We shall start a campaign to convince Sunasians for our survival and both the nations of the two different worlds shall live together like brothers. There would be the atmosphere of goodwill, friendship, sacrifice and peace.

You have the punishment of your crimes. You have the lesson of your life. Now as far as I view the lash of hardships and sufferings should have an end. I am a simple man, a simple human and a simple existence. Nothing is complicated in my formation and yours. I have been thinking as an independent being and your minds have been under my control due to the troubles you have faced and due to the pains revealed to you but still I am giving you the time to think. The plan of moving

will be decided at your final decision. You are to choose one path either to rely on Sunasians or to search for the superior fate. Now, I would like to move. I shall be backing tomorrow hoping for the best decision. Good Bye".

In the meanwhile, a small car appeared, the door opened itself and the old man moved to the car.

"Listen man!" A voice from the crowd came. The old man turned with a smile at his face. "I think we have no time to think. A day to think and a generation is lost." The man burst into tears. "Please take us with you. Please!" The old man had almost been knelt. "They killed my son and now I don't want to loose my daughter. They dragged my wife, my sister and my mother. She is the only left." The man pulled a little girl's hand and grabbed her in his arms. "Please take us with you." The man was crying.

The car's door had closed itself. The old man looked to the mob for their decision. Nothing he could see except tears and nothing could he hear except sobbing.

"What do you say? Should it be done today simultaneously?" The old man thundering voice echoed in the open air.

"We respect your love for us man, but it is hard to trust you. To go with you will be like facing a new trouble." One of the women with a cruciform tied around her neck spoke elegantly.

"What do you think stupid lady, to let us be slaughtered?" The man roared with rage. The woman furiously opened her big black eyes and quietly stepped back without the defensive words. The crowd remained silent for some moments and the people stared one another waiting for the other to speak but there was no sound.

"I am giving you one day for the final decision. I'll meet you tomorrow." Alberic moved to the car whose door opened itself. As he stepped into the car, the door closed after him and the car flew into the sky without having any wings or feathers. The mob started scattering after the car looked to them like a small dot into the skies.

The whole day and the whole night, people continued thinking about their fate. Some people preferred to die on their earth and some decided to save their lives. Thus, the day came when the people said goodbye to their sweet land with tears. All of they gathered in a big van, which flew into the skies after loading their luggage with them. The planet situated in the lane of Asia to the right of the sun was a hot planet. The weather was so unpleasant for the Earthumen to live in that their population came under a big devastation of fatality. Due to the hot weather, many people died of brain stroke. It was an upsetting situation for Alberic. He prepared some tablets with the help of his country people for the earth people to maintain the temperature. After a few years, people managed to live on Sunasia. They struggled and prepared modern tools and weapons.

Now, let us return to Sunasians. They were happy at their success that they had killed each earthman. They captured the land and started ruling independently without any hurdle or obstruction.

A man is egoistic by nature whether he is poor or rich. He cannot bear his personals in the hands of the others for a long time. Even his conscience has died, but one day it wakes him up. Therefore, like a human nature, earthmen had never accepted their defeats. They were living independently at Sunasia but still the wish to go back to their land was upbringing day by day in their hearts. They had learnt a great lesson of their lives. They had suffered the doom before the doom. Now, they decided to step back to Earth to snatch their right. Fully prepared Earthmen, one day attacked the Sunasians. Equal in power and wisdom the two nations' swords collapsed. Sunasians had been stunned to see their most powerful leader along with the Earthmen. Electric shocks and the bombs were colliding. The war continued for more than a century. Neither Sunasians had been retreating and nor the Earthmen had the decision of loosing. During the great battle, a harmonious event took place, what faded the desires and wishes of both the nations. By continuous use of the electric weapons, these sources began to reduce and at the end the main electric laboratory, where Sunasians had gathered their all types of the resources of the world destroyed by undistracted use of modern machine equipments. The whole world dipped into the dark. It returned to the dark ages where a man learnt to light the fire. The modern weapons, tools, cars, buses and else perished. The science from its peaks drowned into desperation. Earthmen had deprived of their needs and their dreams were distorted. They had been helpless. All of they rushed to their flying cars but their cars were unable to move. Alberic was in a serious trouble. His campaign had failed and his dreams smashed. He was a rebellion and so he did not want to confront the Sunasians. Sunasians had been more than the Earthmen. They arrested Earthmen and locked them in their prisons but they could not find Alberic. None could know about Alberic. Sunasians had been maddening for finding Alberic. The contented idea for Earthmen was that Sunasians could never kill Alberic because he knew the secret of the luminous circle ball and its use. At the end of this, the bright reign of light was covered by the dark. The works of AL beruni, Marconi, Edison, Darwin and Albert Einstein, hence, removed by brutal phase of humanity.

Sunasians had succeeded in dominating Earthmen and they punished Earthmen brutally. They hung some at the burning fire and the other in the cold weather to die of heat and cold. Rest of those who saved became servants to their services. Sunasians believed in no Supreme Power. They had their own religions. Some worshiped their dead ones, some hairs of white tigers, and some worshiped unicorns. Therefore, they forced the Earthmen to do so. The poor people were punished for their disloyalty. They spoke Latin, all their scriptures and holy books, according them were revealed in Latin for their Lords favorite language. At last, they were able to speak English with a French accent, Urdu, Chinese, Arabic and the other languages to some extent. In between the small world of two nations, English became the mode of communication. All the, mosques, temples, churches, holy places and the memorial buildings destroyed and burnt. Those who tried to rebel against the powers of rebellions were slaughtered at the spot. The Earthmen had remained with a distorted future and a desperate fate. Sunasians conquered the area of Earth from North America to Atlantic Ocean.

. The progress of the helping machines had disbanded as the animal carts replaced the smoke eliminating vehicles. At last, the grieved people of Sunasians showered some mercy on the Earthmen. They gave a little piece of this tiny Earth to the Earthmen to live as slaves. Despite of the domination, Sunasians had still been having the serious problem to find Alberic who knew all about the luminous ball. Most often, the leaders of the Sunasians had been in the Round Table Conferences and their main subject of the meeting was Alberic. The presidents came, went, changed, died and the years went by. Slowly and with time passing, few of the Earthmen had been successful in gaining higher posts, but still Sunasians were rulers and the Earthmen had been calamity-stricken prisoners. Few people rebelled and went to the hidden places where they could prepare for a new battle. All the nations of the Earth joined hands together and promised to struggle together. Many people went to find the luminous ball but some were died and some were lost in the dangerous valleys. The time was passing by. Earthmen's anxiety was being aroused for the freedom day by day. They wanted a land where they could live their own life. Every eye was having a hope that was fading in some with the passage of time and kindling in others with the time.

II

It was not a war but a quarrel between the young King of two hundred years and the two young men of twenty-five years. Escaping from the prison of the cells, they were caught and surrounded by the groups of Sun's Forces. The young king laughed off at their failed attempt. Both of they nervously saw the Suns forces in yellow uniforms and the rays of sun shaped at their caps. Their hands at their reigns were circling the two armless young men. They slid back but hit by the horse circling around. King raised his hand of the sun and they seemed to be feared. The animals were hidden in their dens at this last time of the night. All the assaulters took out their swords and the fugitives had nothing to encounter, all they could do to hold their breathe, close their eyes like a pigeon and to recite the last sacred words to relieve their souls in heavens. They gripped hands of each other firmly.

"I thought of giving you a one more day to live, but you did not deserve to live for ten years. Hell..., damn..." The King held his crown down with sun rays emitting and glistening form it. One of them looked to the glimmering crown, as the structure impressed him every time when he saw the king. The king lifted down the crown and sneered. "My queen would be glad when he would hear of the two rebel fugitives and I've arrested and slaughtered them on the way." The young handsome king laughed. "Before you could be able to start a new campaign for being a king, I think the earth should be cleared of you illegitimate men." King permitted the black muscular executioner. Without wasting any time, he lifted up his sword, growled and the sword reached their necks.

"Stop," The king shouted himself. "Before you could die, I want to inform you about one particular matter. You see this crown," The king showed them the glimmering side. "Look, very patently, it will be replaced by an earth sign now, to make our steps fixed and to make the foundations stronger and stronger. *Luguolo Lemma* (Kill them)" King sneered and screamed as they saw a spear briskly pinched into his heart in a single blink. Both of they were stunned and the men of forces filled with rage and revenge. In the second blink, they saw the two more men cold in their footsteps. In a few minutes, they saw all of them down and a spear hanging in the cloth of his left arm. They looked around and saw two young boys of fifteen years aiming at the forces, as they saw him, he ran away. They were two and both of they were running after one another as the fear of the revenge to be taken by the prisoners. They looked around, all of the men were dead and the murderers were running away smashing the rustling grass under their feet, crossing the bushes and leaving the trees behind. One of the prisoners standing in between the horses stepped to the king taking his last breathes. He saw him closely. The spear directly hit his heart.

"W... what are you doing?" The other prisoner keenly looked him and he just shook his head as he quietly entered his hand in the cloak of the king. Raza removed the thrust spear in his cloth.

"Peter, look at this," Raza called him loudly as he quickly ran to him. Raza had held a spear in his hand thrust into the green gem. "The spear did not enter the king's heart, it entered this gem," Peter thoughtfully looked it. "But the king *Vasilios Bacchus* is dead," Peter frowned at the exposure of Raza. His hand jerked at once as they heard a tiger's rage as they were squatting in the jungle of Sundarbans in Bangladesh.

III

She was a tall woman with curved features displaying suppleness, softness, smoothness but wickedness. She had narrow lips, long aquiline nose, pointed jaws and a diamond face shape as she opened the big black eyes with red rims in them. Holding the bowl of blood in the hands of the nearby fearful maid, she threw blood at the two of the elephant red tusks stuck by the wall with precious gemstones sticking at the either sides of these. The rituals completed after prostration. She leaned and stood up. The maids went away holding back the bowl. She was a very tall, beautiful and gentle queen. Her long hairs touched her back and the people of earth would call them the snakes flung/Flinging all around the head until her back. When she would go out at a visit to the people of Earth, the children would flee in danger at either side to avoid from the biting of the snakes. After the natural death of her mother queen and the father queen, she left going on such visits and marrying his man, she stayed in the palace and remained concerned for people of her state. After the maid had gone wiping the red blood of the tusks, she went to her most sacred and lonesome ritual of which she was the only follower in her religion. She released the curtain and underneath was a round and oval mirror covered by tan colored wooden borders. The mid of the mirror quivered and soon a muscular tall strong man appeared standing between the lions and talking to them gleefully. In the meanwhile, a new image replaced the previous one. The small dwarf queen and the dwarf king were addressing their nation. Soon she saw a new scene, of falcons striking the bamboos hardly at the earth. They were inaudible but visible, as the bamboos stroke the earth with emotions and bravery, her heart trembled and she clutched her fists in fear and frenzy. The next was more horrible. A dazzling fog covered her mirror and she could not see anything. Soon, she saw the white foggy shade moving. A horn came to the sights and the black shinning eyes with expressions of purity and extreme mysticism. In the fogs, she saw a snake hissing and the dark smoke enhanced the mirror. At the instant, she saw a smiling, gorgeous and pretty queen with elegant butterfly eyes, long slender nose and elegance in her posture. Jealousy conquered her heart. Smile of excitement dominated her lips as she saw a man's face covered in hood.

"Have a nice day, my queen," The man roared in his heavy ghastly voice.

"It's really good to see you but listen," Queen said fervently.

"Yes, say, say my queen," The man's heavy voice echoed in the room.

"You know, my intentions are to rule the universe. I can't even find my life yet."

"Do as I say you, queen"

"*What?*"

"Remember, enhance injustice, provoke men and women for adultery and fornication, and fill their hearts with lust and malice, for this is the one thing the foundation of our religion. Listen I am superior one as I speak a superior language. I'll remain forever and one day I'll be the Lord and you would be my lady."

"Yes I know you are the Lord forever."

"This is a challenge for what I was banished from the heavens." The queen released the curtain as she heard someone running into his sacred space.

The next moment was stunning for her as she heard her king had been dead. Mummifying the body of the King, after few days of the funeral the queen sent his men after the fugitives.

IV

He was dead. The tigress was dead. Her newly born cubs were lying near her stretching their limbs. They looked to the sharp paws of the beast. Its cubs were opening their eyes. The tigress died of a natural death and the rage they heard was the last rage, a defense for its cubs instead a last rage. The running boys were again back to them. They witnessed the two men with a surprise and foolhardy boys looked directly the lion and one another. The armless men hearing the rustle beyond them abruptly gazed back with fright hoping for the new attack and assault. However, nothing was so. They were the two innocent angels who survived their lives. They tried to run but both of they grabbed their hands firmly.

"Who are you?" Raza was asking a boy whose eyes showed bravery. He was remarkable in his trait of taking aims.

"I... I... did not mean to take your friend's life. The spear hit him just due to a jerk. Instead, I wanted to help you two people." He was bravely facing the man, his elbow still grabbed in hand of Raza. His face beamed with the courage of the boy. "You were looking a prisoner by your dresses." The boy looked from head to toe, his white dress and a number 1234 written at his chest pocket. "So, I've saved you," The boy told him. "Where is 1233?" The boy asked. The face of the man knelt with grief.

"He was executed a day before I ran." The boy nodded wisely. "What's your name?" Raza asked him.

"Shiva, I live in west Bengal, came to Bangladesh with my friend venturing the jungle" Peter grabbing the other one was standing calmly staring at them and listening to their chat.

"Didn't your parents stop you entering this furious jungle?" Raza almost reprimanded.

"No, I've no parents. Sunasians slaughtered them and my uncle sold my sister because we had nothing to eat. I don't know where is she, whether she is alive or not?" Shiva replied curtly. "Can I ask about you?" Raza left his grabbed hand and stabilized the falling crown of his hand. Shiva gazed his act as the beauty of the crown mesmerized him.

"Well... I live in Subcontinent." He took a deep breathe to relief himself. "I lived, but shifted to South America when I heard they are making Asia their official abode and the cells of prisoners. He is my friend Peter, a Christian, he lived with me." They embraced one another.

"And he is my friend Oliver, a Christian," Shiva introduced his friend who was standing behind him while they were taking aims.

"Where are your parents, boy?" Peter asked the Oliver.

"I've a mother and my father is sweeper in the royal palace of princess in Agra. People call 'em a rebellion for he's servin' Sunasians. Therefore, this is the reason why ma family is safe. I've one sister n one brother. They're studyin' in good schools ov Sunasians'." Peter knitted his brows.

"The first meetin' was really a fabulous one. I'm hopeful that we'll make a good bond together." They heard another rage of tiger. They looked fearfully to one another. The crown fell down.

"At the back of the tree," Shiva shouted. The two men quickly hid at the back of a thick stem of the sundari tree. Shiva slid back and estimated the medium of voice. He slid back a little, courageously looked all around, and took aim through the bow. He turned, the tiger pounced at him, he left the arrow at the instant, and the tiger fell down coming near to him. The paws of the beast scratched his shirt when it fell down as the blood pierced out with small cuts. The tiger moaned and it was dead. Raza clapped after seeing the courage. Oliver ran to him, who was gazing the dead lion, the two friends smirked to look one another. Their eyes beamed, their lips curved they gripped hands firmly. The two men stood behind them staring the dead lion. The bond started with a campaign. Shiva went with two men at a journey leaving his friend spying under the reign of Sunasians'. The grand palace of the King was glistening with the shine of proud, glimmering with the success and laughing off at him with arrogance. His father made way for him serving the Sunasians, and his father hopeful for the loyalty he would devote to Sunasians and from here, the story begins when he is married to a beautiful girls of his dreams Martha. They had a son, a beautiful baby wept and smiled in their cradle. He had to marry his sister with the prime minister for the survival of his son who gave birth to daughter. The queen was outraged as she was not on tenterhooks of such imprudence, but witnessing a sun sign at the innocent soft hands of the crying baby, her fury alleviated, as she seemed a pure Sunasian now.

CHAPTER 2

An Invitation

I

The sky was clear on that day. No signs of rain were evident as before. A lonely kite was flying in the mid of two solitary pieces of clouds. His eyes deep into the sky moved down to his mattock and he struck it hard by the soil. The sweat was dripping down his head and crossing his chin to the neck. Turning his index finger round he cleaned the little flow of sweat and gave two more strikes to soil by mattock. He looked back to his field where the crows had moved down and were eating his delicious vegetables. He left mattock and rushed to the fields shouting. "Away! Away!" His hands were also waving as if to beat the crows. "You tiny monsters, how can you destroy my fields?" The crows with his rage had run into the skies and he stopped at the bank of the fields. He was panting and staring into the sky. Unconsciously running after the tiny crows, he had smashed his own fields. He was a man of thirty-five years and was the lonely property owners among Earthumen, a richest man among earth people. At a corner of the town, he had a solitude fine-looking house. Being a landowner he was seen working, sloughing, cutting and harvesting his own fields with his wife and a son. His wife, an elegant woman of thirty-two years looked out of the window while she was beating the eggs. She smiled slightly and moved her eyes to the stove. The man had returned to the same place abusing the crows. She again looked out where his husband was busy in digging the land. The sun was moving slowly to the heights and the night had said goodbye to the dawn since hours. At the drooped branch of a mulberry tree a sparrow chirped greeting morning. The woman was quietly busy in preparing breakfast. It was a peaceful place where not any signs of inhabitants nearby were. Turning the stove off, she moved out of the kitchen to the dinning room with the breakfast tray in her hands.

The man had been digging the soil studiously as if finding something and had to search it today. He was to do or die. "Mr. Oliver!" His mattock stopped in the air before hurting the ground. He looked back following the medium of sound and saw a bulky man shouting his name waving an envelope in his right hand; the man was running to Oliver. "Huh!" He exclaimed and threw the mattock down. "I's expectin' fa somethin' funny now." He murmured as the bulky man had reached him. "Decided to fin' it?" The bulky man said.

"None of your business," Oliver turned his back to the bulky man and saw again into the skies where a kite had been still flying. The man took off black hat from his head under his arms.

"Well! Not in a good mood." The man said ignoring his rudeness and looked to the envelope. He moved it to Oliver.

"I'm not 'ere to make you laugh or to tease you any way! I've something for you." The man continued.

"Look at this kite. Wilson!" Wilson followed Oliver's hand what had raised into the sky. "It's so high. It reminds me of my future. When I was a child, once I grabbed this kite and it bit me and it flew away leaving me hurt. Why does it fascinate me till now?" Oliver stopped lost into the thoughts.

"Well! This is a nice philosophy. Anyways, it fascinates you because it is in the heights where you can't grab it again." Wilson replied normally.

"Oliver, Move your eyes back and down to me. There is a letter from the King." Wilson said making Oliver to turn.

"What?" Oliver turned with a scream. "What are you waitin' for, you fool!" He said and snatched letter from Wilson. Now they were facing one another. Oliver was staring the sun sign pasted at the front of the envelope.

"Yes, the sun is very beautiful. Now open it." Wilson mocked. Oliver ogled and moved to the front of the house with mattock in his hand. He turned back as he realized Wilson stepping after him. "What're you lookin' at me? Thanks fer the letter." Saying this he quickly moved to the house leaving the mattock. Wilson stood there with a smile.

"I'm worried about it." Oliver said as he entered the house. Martha who was putting the tray on the table moved her face up and tensed to see Oliver's worrying expressions.

"What happened?" She moved to her and took the letter from his hands. "What so worried? It is of the same kind, you receive it weekly. It can be any order, any new visit." Martha tried to calm her. In the meanwhile, Oliver had moved to the table pouring tea into his cup. "I don't think it's worrying. Did you open it? Did you read it?" Martha had also reached him.

"Afraid to open n afraid to read," Oliver took two to three sips of tea without looking her. She pulled the wooden chair and sat in it.

"Fine, I'll open it now." She removed the sticker of pasted sun sign from the front and opened it. "Kin' a letter," Martha opened the folded piece of paper and started reading it.

"Mr. Oliver Beckham! I am so glad by your visit to the island near Havana and I am thankful to you for bringing the new sapphires and the diamonds that can be helpful in making us powerful and stronger. I am glad to have such an Earthmen in my reign. I would like to welcome you in my regime and be a part of my nation, Sunasian. I would prefer to you to follow my customs, traditions and my lords if you wish to be. There will be no compulsion if you do not wish. I have arranged a good dinner for you and tomorrow at 6pm I will be glad to see you in my palace for dinner."

Regards *King Vasilios Benigus*

"Oliver!" Martha shouted in excitement. "It's so good. You will've the dinner with the king. For the first time in a history, an Earthman's been going' to take a dinner along with the king." Oliver was shocked after listening to Martha. He took the letter from Martha and started reading it again as if not going to believe. Martha poured tea in her cup.

"Dinner will start at 6 pm. Nothing botherin', just prepare your dress, your shoes and brush your hair until that time. King is dyin' to see you dear!" Martha was too much excited at the success of her husband.

"Stop, Martha! Isn't it strange?" Oliver folded the paper thinking something. "How will you feel eatin' at the table a tasty meal while Max is standin' at the corner of a street with a piece of cooked meat in his hand where a kite came and it snatched it from 'em?" Oliver stared in Martha's eyes to know her answer whereas her smiling lips came back to their normal state. "He is hungry, he is too much hungry." Oliver continued. "No body is ready to share his meat piece with him because everyone has the last one. They are also dyin' to eat." "Stop it. Oliver." Martha stared in astonishment. "Why are you spittin' this nonsense? What do you think? Can I leave my son like that? You are insulting me as a mother." Martha had been gloomy.

"No, no dear! I did'nt mean this to you. You know! My father did'nt die of a brain stroke; somebody murdered him. Later on, where was my mother gone? I really had no idea. They just beat me and threw me in front of my house. I was callin' my mother but I could not see her anywhere. Every corner of the house was quietly tellin' me the story of brutality." Oliver closed his eyes with fear. He could hear the screams only.

"Oliver!" Martha peacefully spoke putting her hand at his trying to console him.

"I'm with you." Martha lovingly said. She smiled as Oliver opened his eyes.

"And than I found you." Oliver smiled.

"Can you imagine? How would I feel eatin', when my people would be dyin' of hunger?" Oliver moved his hand to the pancakes.

"What people? What hunger?" Martha stared her with amazement. "We are not hungry, neither Max nor me."

"I am talkin' about Earthmen. They are hungry." Oliver took a bite of pancake.

"Earthmen," Martha screamed. "They're not yours. Are they? The people do not even bother to come 'ere to see you. You care for them. They even killed your father. They call you a rebellion. They hate you for you're with those who brought you up. You told me this, only this."

"No." Oliver spoke in. "They didn't kill him. They are the Sunasian."

"What?" Martha shouted. "Every time, you're relating the story of your father's murder to Earthmen. Why...? To get the sympathies of the ruling nation..." Martha had been furious with rage.

"No, but to've their trust... so I can ruin their government as they ruined my family." Oliver finished the pancake and his discussion. He stood up and moved to the exit door.

"Goin' where?" Martha who had been stunned after listening to the story rushed after him. "Today is off. I think no working day." Martha put her hand at the handle of the door.

"Yeah, I need some fresh air to make me calm." Oliver said and moved his hand to the door.

As he opened the door, both of they saw bulky man standing at the door.

"Ahem! I'd been waitin' for the answer." Mr. Wilson pretended.

"I know what're you waitin' for?" Oliver looked embarrassed.

"Then what're you looking at? Give me the way." He said boldly and before Oliver will give him the way, Martha rushed to the door.

"No, No, Mr. Wilson! I can't afford cooking a goat." Martha was looking more embarrassed.

"And I can't afford going back." Oliver and Martha looked helplessly to one another as Wilson moved in the house boldly making the way between both of them.

II

In the roar of winds
I can feel my anger
In the skies so high
I can see my grace
In the days of the past
I cannot forget the moments lost
That had given my nation
The passing time so harsh
In the water of the seas
And the trees with cool breeze
I can give with zeal and zest
My nation time of peace and rest
It would be happened one day
You will see a time of gay
When the sun will be puzzled
To shine bright into my eyes

MS

"Impressive. Isn't it?" A little girl said after reading the poem on a piece of paper in the hands of other boy.

"Yeah, it is. Who will have written it?" The impressed looking boy said.

"Look at this." The girl put her finger at the end of the poem.

"It is M...S...." The boy narrated the written words thoughtfully.

"Stupid! Frank, I can also see this." The girl snatched the paper in her hands and started looking at the end of the sign. "But what would've it been meant?" The girl enquired.

"Mary! I don't know. I'm not a sign recognizer." Frank snatched paper from her.

"Hey, Hey give me the paper." Mary was trying to take it back and Frank was cunningly moving it up and down to save from Mary's hands. As he was teasing, someone else snatched it from Frank's hands from back.

"Salam, hi how're you friends?" The new boy with a wooden stick about three feet stood at a distance from them and started gazing the paper turning it up and down.

"Abdullah, how good to see you?" Frank excitedly rushed to hug him.

"It's been so many days since I saw you. It's really good to see you." Mary's eyes widened happily.

"Hey who wrote it? It's good." The knitted beads of the writer with black ink at small piece of paper impressed Abdullah.

"MS" ... "Is he she or he?" Abdullah asked delightfully.

"I think "he"." Frank abruptly replied.

"And I think "she"." Mary tried to make Frank's answer wrong and stared triumphantly into Frank's eyes.

Abdullah roared into laughter. "And I think both." Abdullah replied boldly with smiling eyes. "I got it."

Abdullah attended them. "I know who is she?" Both of they looked to Abdullah.

"Look, she is she. I told you she." Frank told Mary victoriously.

"Who," Mary scowled Frank and looked to Abdullah for his answer.

"She's... is ... my aunt." Abdullah seriously replied.

"Your aunt," Both of they spoke at once.

"Is there any such thing at your house?" Frank asked.

"You nevea talked about your aunt." Mary confused as she squinted her eyes.

"I'm joking, you idiots, If it has been of my any aunt then I think she'd not have been so careless." He moved the paper to Frank. "Let's play friends." Shouting this he ran to the street to gather other children. Mary and Frank with a piece of paper also ran after him. Soon a large group of children had gathered in the street. They were pushing, pulling and running after one another. Busy in their games they were not aware of a new boy who had reached there and was finding something on to the ground.

"Hey Max! How good to see you? Come on join us." One of the girls from the mob of the children shouted. Max only replied with a smile. One of the boys grabbed her and now she had to take the turn. "No, not my turn, I's just talking to him." The girl tried to defend by pointing to Max. "To whom, Bimla" Abdullah reached her to ask as he was panting.

"There, Max." Bimla blamed Max for her carelessness. "Hi, every body," Max just waved with a smile.

"Why're you 'ere? There're no your friends 'ere. They live beyond the red line." Abdullah disdainfully informed him.

"Yeah, I know. But I've some friends 'ere as well like you, like Mary, Frank, Bimla..." "We're not your friends." Abdullah spoke in before Max could complete.

"You're a rebellion's son. We can't make you a friend." One of the girls from the mob replied.

"What brought you here?" Abdullah scowled.

"Err... Err... err; I lost a paper 'ere a few hours ago." Max told his purpose of being here.

"Well! Who're you?" Abdullah scowled.

"I think your aunt." Mary giggled putting her right hand at her lips. Frank also smiled. The mob stared Mary for making fun of their leader.

"Sorry." Marry apologized smilingly.

"Is it this one?" Frank showed him the front of the paper.

"Yeah, this one," Max rejoiced to see his paper unconsciously moved to Frank, but before he could reach Abdullah snatched it from Frank.

"Catch it, if you can." Abdullah challenged and the paper started moving from one hand to another.

"Don't do this. Give it back to me." Max was shouting helplessly after them.

"If you could get it then we'll stop calling you a rebellion but if you couldn't then you know." Abdullah made a face at him. The children enjoyed Max's helplessness for half an hour. After a great struggle of snatching the paper, max could not succeed. Sitting at one side of the road and the twenty children sitting arbitrarily at the other side of the road were looking badly tired. Abdullah and his friends were staring Max smiling triumphantly and Max was looking dementedly to them.

"End of game now friends," Abdullah loudly announced "Second part would start tomorrow." Abdullah laughed loudly with his pals.

"What's the end?" A boy from the crowd loudly enquired.

"A rebellion's son," Abdullah answered and laughed.

The whole crowd shouted with him. "A rebellion's son, a rebellion's son, a rebellion's son," Max ignored the crowd and set off to house way leaving the crowd shouting after him.

"I think I am a rebellion, but for what they call me the rebellion? I've not done something bad for their sake. What is this all about? They are snatching my rights." He had been doomed. Lost in his thoughts he reached the entrance door of his house. As he opened the door, he heard the roars of laughter of Mr. Wilson. The little boy with chubby cheeks had a different accent as compared to his parents for he was studying in the institutes of Sunasians.

"Good mornin', Mr. Wilson", Max said closing the door behind him.

"Hey little boy, mornin'," Mr. Wilson excitedly moved to Max opening his arms wide hugged him and lifted him up in his arms. Max was likewise excited to see his big friend. "Wilson, why do you not take me to the nest? I asked you a hundred times." Max asked him and grabbed some of his hair firmly in his hands. "Hey, hey, little creature," Wilson shouted as if feeling too much pain. "I'll take you today. I promise. Now jus' leave my hair." Wilson requested like a small child suffering the extreme pain.

"Ok, I spare your fault." Max ordered and left his hair disheveled.

"Hey, looked like a king." Wilson appreciated him.

"My son is a king." Martha moved from her place to Wilson. She took Max from him and left him on the floor.

"He'll be." Oliver came from the room and caressed his hair. Max smiled to see his father.

"Dad," Max innocently addressed Oliver. Oliver attended to Max. "What is a rebellion?" Max continued his enquiry. Oliver was astonished.

"A rebellion is one who goes against the rules of a society." Oliver answered.

"Is he a good person or a bad?" Max asked another question abruptly.

"He is a bad person for some and good for some." Oliver stood up from the ground and moved to the dining table.

"Can a rebellion be a well-wisher?" Max asked another question. Oliver smiled and took an apple from the basket. "Yes, he can if he is a good rebellion." Oliver answered normally.

"Stop this, Max." Martha was looking irritated. "What are you talking about? "Everything is fine. You have not taken your breakfast yet. Now it will be brunch." Martha held Max's arm and moved him to the dinning table. Max took his chair. Martha put a pancake in a plate near him. "Open your mouth." Martha cut a piece of pancake; put her left hand under his chin as he fixed his canines into the pancake.

"You will be the king. One day, my prince." Martha lovingly kissed his forehead. Max smiled thankfully at his mother's love.

"Can a rebellion's son be a king?" Oliver's apple stayed in the way before going into the mouth at Max's question.

"What do you mean?" Martha was stunned.

"They call me a rebellion's son." Max complained.

"Who," Martha looked worried.

"They..." "Let them call." Before Max could complain after "they", Oliver spoke in. "If it is so, then you are surely the son of a good rebellion." Oliver dropped the apple back into the basket and stepped to the room.

"Ok, son, see you tomorrow. Martha, it was a tasty meal." Greeting both of them, he looked to the bedroom door. "Hey Oliver, buddy, see you any other time. Bye. Don't forget the tomorrow visit."

"Bring Bill with you tomorrow; else don't come in my home." Max again ordered him seriously. Wilson roared into laughter. "Say well wishes to Mrs. Wilson." Martha elegantly sent message to her friend. "Yeah, yeah sure lady, Bubye every one" Wilson opened the door waving his hand and moved out.

"My son," Martha pulled a chair and put it near Max. "Why are you talking like that?" Martha touched his cheeks.

"Like what?" Max was playing with a plate while talking to her mother.

"The questions like that, rebellion, well-wisher... all that," Martha asked him.

"They call me the rebellion's son. They don't like to play with me. They hate me." His mood was changed. The gloominess had dominated his smiles. "They even snatched my paper." Max was complaining, as his bold voice was looking dim than before.

"No," Martha put him in her lap. "You're a good rebellion's son. Let 'em speak. Be friendly with 'em, whatever they speak. Let 'em do what they do." Martha tried to make her calm. "Today, I'll play with you." Martha smilingly said.

"But why do they not play with me? Am I not a good boy?" Max asked putting his head in his mother's lap.

"You're good." Martha caressed his hair. "You'll be the change one day. You'll rule the world, one day and all of they'll admire you. I bet." Martha encouraged him.

"Will it happen, when sun will be puzzled to shine bright into my eyes?" Max whispered.

"Yes." His mother whispered in his ears. Having the warmth of her mother's lap, he did not know when his eyes started closing itself and soon he had gone into a deep sleep.

CHAPTER 3

⊰ Royal Dinner ⊱

I

Margaret was knitting a shocking pink colored pullover sitting on a plastic sheet. She pulled a blue colored thread from a woolen circle and added a new design to the pullover. Turning the knitting needles, rolling them one above the other she was too much involved in her crafts skills. She did not know when the clock had struck 12 am and when it had been 12 pm of the next day. The children were quiet and busy in their studies. They were not too much involved in the studies as their mischievous eyes were staring one another for finding the chance to escape from the studies. Looking stealthily to one another, they expressed the wish through their mischievous eyes.

"Be attentive to your notebooks." Margaret strictly advised them. "Surely, I want a good result and good remarks." Margaret added words to her strictness. All four of them helplessly looked to one another. "Look to your books." Margaret again ordered and all of them looked down to the books. She stood up from the place and moved to the table where a large number of pullovers had placed over one another. Margaret took a deep breathe and started counting the pullovers picking them one by one. "Enough are these." She murmured with excitement. Mary sitting at the bed was trying to find her best pullover from the back of her aunt. "Aunt," At last, her curiosity could not stop her from speaking. "Yes" Her aunt replied rearranging the pullovers.

"Which one is mine?" Mary asked staring the pullovers sorting out the best one for her.

"Which'd you like?" Mary turned to her with a smile.

"UM... mm... Mm... That one the pink one, you put at the last." Mary pointed to the sweater placed at the end of the table.

"Hey, it's so nice." Saira appreciated her choice. "That's really the best one." Saira deliciously looked to the sweater.

"Ok, it's yours." Margaret moved it to Mary. Mary excitedly moved down to the bed and grabbed it quickly.

"Be calm. No one is snatchin' it from you." Saira commented.

"I know, but I can't trust when you're here." Mary answered her seriously.

"I think, you mind it, I was just kiddin'. Mary," Saira apologized. Mary gave a big smile and giggled. "I know." She said and started wearing it.

"Hey how is it lookin' Saira?" asked Mary.

"Looking cute," Saira answered with her smiling face.

"Now which one'd you like Saira?" Margaret turned to Saira.

"Me," Saira's smile widened more with excitement. "Um .., mm... me, the blue one will be the best." Saira's eyes rested at a fancifully designed blue jumper.

31

"Such a magnificent choice, It has two sides. Look," Margaret turned to Saira, showed its inner black side outward, and smiled.

"Hey, it's really cool." She jumped down the bed with an excitement and grabbed it from Margaret. Therefore, Saira did it like Mary. She wore the sweater with blue side and then with its black side. "That's too warm." Saira was interested in its formation, style and warmth.

"Lady Margaret", Saira called her who was busy in packing the sweaters.

"Yeah, sweetie," Lady Margaret answered without looking back.

"You are elegant and so are your hands. That's really the best gift of this winter. Missing my mother," Margaret shockingly looked back to Saira who was looking gloomy. She moved to her and loved her.

"I'm with you here. Sweetie," Margaret caressed her long black hair touching her back lovingly. She wiped her tears falling down her cheeks. "Be brave, I don't want to see you like this wearing my pullover." Margaret tried to make her laugh. Her big black eyes smiled and her innocent laughter fluttered in the room.

"Ahem...em, where is mine, Lady Margaret?" Abdullah spoke in as Saira's laughter came to rest. "And mom, where is mine?" Frank was also not willing to loose his right.

Margaret looked to them with a slight laughter. She turned to the table and picked two packets.

"These are for you. Can I forget the sons like you?" she threw the sweaters to both of them and they caught them as they reached them flying. Without being late, they tore the packing into the pieces and took out their required object. Both had been of the same grey color with same black horizontal lining. They were happy with the matching and their bond of friendship had been stronger.

"Ok, now turn to your work all of you, Saira and Abdullah, quick. You're to go back home. Your Granma will be arriving soon." She turned to the table and started picking up the pullovers one by one. Children had been busy in finishing their work. Putting the pullovers safely in the cupboards, she heard horse's hoofs outside his house. She looked back and her eyes had been widely opened with fear. Children also looked frightfully to Margaret. Hearing horse's hoofs outside the house could be nothing more than a summon of death. Margaret swallowed hardly. After a few minutes, the door knocked.

"Don't worry, I'll see them." Abdullah jumped from the bed and emotionally moved to the door. Frank followed him in the same way. Margaret rushed after both of them and grabbed both of them instantly. "Come back both of you idiots." She pushed them to the inner room. "All of you move under the bedroom inside the room." Margaret hurriedly ordered them and the girls followed the boys. Entering the room children hid under the bed. Lady Margaret closed the door firmly after them. The door was constantly being knocked. According to her expectations, it should have been broken, but nothing happened brutal. She picked her steps up and slowly moved to the door. Opening it at a snail's pace, she was astonished to see the upcoming visitor.

"Yew," She exclaimed. "What brings you 'ere?" The upcoming woman was giving a loving smile.

"How're you Margaret?" The woman asked. "If you don't mind, can I come in?"

"Who can stop you? By stopping you, I'm not willing to invite my death." Margaret scornfully spoke and gave her the way to come. The woman with a little boy moved after her, she was fully dressed as if going to attend any ceremony.

"Why're you behaving like strangers to me?" Mrs. Oliver asked her in frenzy.

"I was a stranger to you. It was not you, but your husband's sister who had been my friend. But she stung." Margaret scornfully replied her as she sat in a futon besides her.

"She didn't, Margaret. You're wrong in your perceptions." Mrs. Oliver tried to make her understand the right situation.

"Don't show me your sympathy, Mrs. Oliver." Margaret rudely replied.

"I know I can never be right for you." The little boy was just staring the two ladies.

"I don't want to show myself to be right to you, Martha, you know." Margaret carelessly answered.

"Listen." "Be quick Martha, we are to leave soon." Before Martha could complete her words, she heard her husband.

"Go, your husband is calling." Margaret moved his brows to the door.

"Ok, fine, I'm leaving. I'm going to the royal dinner. I'm leavin' Max 'ere with you." Martha knew that Margaret would not answer. She left Max and moved out banging the door after her.

"It's been too late." Oliver said and held her hand to help her move into the carriage. The coachman pulled the reins of the horse and in no minutes, they had reached the king's palace.

"Marvelous", the words slipped from Martha with stunned expressions after taking into account the pomp and show of the palace while Oliver was busy in coordinating with the other Sunasian who had arrived at the same time to join the royal dinner. Martha hardly swallowed.

"Why the prime minister chose Oliver's sister when none of her ladies are less than anyone?" Martha thought zealously. The lights were showering in the skies. As she saw more keenly into the skies, she saw the big black butterflies holding bunches of red roses moving from one place to another. "Wow... Unbelievable," her blue eyes were opening with fear and astonishment. "No way, how could it be?" She was murmuring. "From where did they come?" Martha's steps moved to the end of the second step of the six feet horizontal stair. She was lost in the sight. "Is it heaven?" The dark was all around the palace. Hardly one or two of stars could be visible in the skies. Some of the big stars of golden, silver, shinning pink and shinning purple colors had hung around the palace without any assistance. They were shinning and fading at the same time. His face was lifted high into the skies and she was moving to the skies to touch the stars. She was pacing slowly lifting her hand up slowly. She couldn't know, her foot slipped at the end of the stair. She screamed and before she could fall into the deep tunnel down, someone grabbed her firmly. He was a six feet man and she fell into his arms.

"Are you all right lady?" The man asked her grabbing her arm. In the meanwhile, Oliver had reached hearing the scream of her wife he left the greeting and ran to her.

"Thank you man," Before Martha could answer, Oliver say thanks and held her Martha's hand. He took her away from there. Martha had come into the senses. She looked again into the skies. The stars were laughing at her. Martha scowled at them and she presumed they were laughing more.

"Are you fine?" Oliver asked her but she had been lost into skies. "It's so fascinating." Martha answered. Oliver looked to her and followed her eyes. He saw the stars. "It's all the hallucination." Oliver told her and pulled her to the gate. "Hallucinations," Martha knitted her brows in amazement. "How could it be?" She again raised her sights to the skies. "Marvel, marvelous," She was murmuring repeatedly. Soon their steps touched the inner hall of the palace. Now something new held her breathe. It was the palace with gold lining all around the carpet. The curtains covering the windows had been sparkling like diamonds. Their shine had illuminated the palace, as there did not seem the need of the light here. Her six inches heel had been immersing into the velvety carpet. The couples were moving up and down the stairs. She was just following Oliver, as she did not know where to go. As she climbed two to three steps of the marble stairs, she started stepping back.

"Oliver," She only said and Oliver observed her backward movements.

"I'm to go back. I can't join them. It's hard." Martha was looking too much embarrassed. A diamond stone was glistening near the table reaching the third step and piercing through the holes of the stairs at its both sides. "King wants to see both of us." Oliver convinced her to move. "Bah... I don't want to see that selfish king. I'm missing Max." Martha tried to turn back.

"NO, nobody is 'ere now to leave you back." Oliver said and Martha looked to him. "Oliver, it's hard too much.

Doesn't the palace made you astonished?" Martha slowly asked.

"Yeah, it did me, when I came here for the very first time. It aroused my hate for the King. However, I still had to move after 'em because we're his slave. He'll slaughter us." Martha swallowed.

"What about Lilly," Martha asked him.

"I'll ask from the king today." Oliver said and held her hand to move her up to the stairs. Martha resisted looking at the either sides. At last crossing more than twenty steps with changing courses, they had reached the required place. The women had decorated with jewels from head to toe and none of the men had his index finger without a gold ring at what a sun was shimmering, but gems in between the sun had been of different colors. They were busy in chatting and gossiping with one another. None had been aware of their arrival. Some saw strangely that what the Earthmen had been doing there but seeing the King's letter with a sun sign at its back they had to be quiet. They hated Earthmen so much that they wished to kill them, but this time the sun sign stopped them. Both of they were looking confused. The throne was empty until yet. Oliver and Martha sat at a soft cushion placed at the sofa nearby.

"Why are they staring us?" Martha whispered in Oliver's ears.

"Because we are Earthmen," Oliver answered.

"Ok, fine." Martha realized the reality.

"When the royal dinner will start?" Martha again questioned.

"When the King will come," Oliver answered. The hall was crowding with people.

"I am feeling hungry." Martha shared her problem.

"Yeah, me too," Oliver bit his lips and looked four men nearby chatting and laughing with some drinks in their hands. None of the server came to serving them. Looking at their hands, they came to know of their identities. At last, after a few hours of waiting anxiously the announcer announces the King's arrival. The curtains at the entrance of the room were removed and the king with his wife entered with a graceful smile at his face. King's gown was covered with yellow jewels all around her borders. It was hard to identify her face among the shine of the jewels. King with his sarcastic and arrogant smile moved to the throne. The people made the way and bowed as the king passed by. So did Oliver as King passed by him. At the end, King took steps and reached the stage where a throne had placed. He turned proudly and queen did the same. The people were waving their hands and praising the King with their laudable words.

"May you live long?"

"May the king have nine lives?"

"May the king be king forever?" The slogans like that had been being raised.

The king waved his hand with a smile and sat down.

"Me think my people are hungry." The king proudly told them their problem.

"O yeah," The people assisted the King's smile.

"Let the feast begin." King ordered and the dinner had been ready o be served. AT the tables, the edibles were being decorated and the drinks were being served. Everything was new for both of them, as they had never eaten. They hardly tasted some of the meal. Everything was more delicious and tasty. Martha observed that the same tall man who saved her was staring her time and again. She ignored many a times and it had been hard for her to stay there. She held Oliver's arm and took her at a corner as they had finished their dinner.

"Oliver," She whispered, as they were moving in between the crowd hitting the people sideways. The Sunasians were rubbing their dresses as Oliver and Martha would knock them.

"Yeah, what," Oliver replied in the same tone.

"I can't see Lilly here." Martha asked her.

"Yeah, me too, I was also findin' her." Oliver asked her.

"Ask the king. He'll listen to you." Martha told her the solution. Oliver tried to search the King among the crowd. The king came into the view of Oliver. During the dinner, the King did not bother to look at Oliver. He was busy talking to his own people. Oliver climbed at the table nearby and tried to be the centre of attention of the king but King was looking too much busy in enjoying her chat.

"Excuse me man! Would you please be in your limits?" A server came with a tray in his hand and disdainfully ordered him. Oliver without being late jumped down and moved to Martha.

"He is not even lookin' at me." He told Martha.

"Did forget that he called you?" Martha asked her looking out for the King. "Where is the king?" Martha continued his discussion without having any reply from him.

"There, with the minister," He turned his face to the right side. It had been 12 am they almost wasted in the hall trying to talk to the King and ask him about Lilly but all in vain.

The people had started going back. The problem for them was to go back as the royal conveyance had arranged for them for their arrival and so something should have arranged for their departure as well. Both of they were standing at the corner of the dinning hall where the moon could be seen shinning.

"I think, we should move now," Martha said him tiredly.

"Yeah, I think too," As both of, they moved to stairs the same tall man came in their way. They looked up to him.

"Can I help you?" The gentle voice tried to help them who was staring Martha now. Martha looked to Oliver.

"No way, nothing like that," Martha swallowed and looked to Oliver. "Let's move Oliver" She said and ignored the gentle man. As they stepped near the stairs, someone called them.

"Mr. and Mrs. Oliver Beck hem" Both of they turned back. A man was standing jeweled all around. "I have a message from the King." Oliver's face disappointment changed to some gay.

"Yes, what?" Oliver anxiously replied and so Martha was excited.

"The king had been too much pleased to see you here. He has arranged a cart for your departure and it is ready waiting for you." Man smiled professionally.

"Thanks," Oliver said thanks and both of them ran down to the stairs. The gentle man looked at the messenger strangely.

As both of they had reached outside the palace, Martha looked up, there were no stars and no butterflies. She looked down to the tunnel. There were horribly big silver snakes shinning. Her eyes opened with a fear and she quickly rushed to the carriage.

II

All around the city, the next day people were gossiping about an Earthmen visit in the palace. The King had strictly forbidden abusing an Earthmen like Oliver and his family. The Royal throne was ready for the King and the general staff had been anxiously waiting for the king to come and to discuss about yesterday arrival of an Earthmen at the royal dinner. The announcer as usual announced the King's arrival and the people of Sunasia started taking their positions. Those who were standing sat down and those who were sitting took their right positions. The King with his queen holding a furry cat in her right arm moved to the throne. All the members stood up and bowed. King with his dignity, grace and proud sat on the throne and looked all around the palace. After the King had seated, the people lifted their heads up and moved to their esteemed seats. King smiled to see the dubious faces of his people.

"My people, I think I have no time to waste as I am to discuss other states of affairs. Just to inform you... I am appointing a new person in my general staff and that will be of the chairperson of the foreign trade of the west. It will be a good addition in that our trade schemes would be improved and our trade goods would be exchanged more quickly." The queen was caressing her cat and seemed unaware of the King's address while the staff was attentively listening to the King. The King stopped to look back to her queen who gave him a lovely smile and the king started again. "We are giving one post to an Earthmen." As king said these words, the crowd gave a sudden cry of "No, no, no".

"Stop," The King, raged like a tiger.

"I know about your fears, I know about your worries", The King started politely.

"But listen men, he is the man most trustworthy and I want you to cooperate with that man, because I trust him." Saying this he moved his hand to the right side where a maid of five feet came and she gave a golden plate to the king covered with a yellow cloth. King picked up the cloth piece and put it at a side.

"Look at these," King ordered and the general staff bamboozled to see the shine of the diamonds and the sapphires. "I have not spent the years of this Kingship in waste." King's anger was raising now. "That I shall need your suggestions, Let us join hands with Earthmen. I could not trust an Earthmen but now I can." King said and moved to the throne. Queen was busy in caressing her big white furry cat. Another maid came and she gave a glass to the King to drink. "Now I shall listen to you and any careless comment can cut your heads off." King ordered strictly. Prime minister stood up. He moved and bowed.

"My lord, with due respect, I shall start, have mercy on me, whatever you said was not wrong. We have always respected your decisions and we shall always respect it." King pleased at the obedience. "My majesty, we are ready to join hands with the Earthmen as we are also feared of the dark planet." Prime minister bowed again and moved back to the seat. "Ok, now I am sitting here waiting for my guest." King sat with the queen.

"What guest?" The gentle man stood up from the seat, bowed and then tried to say something.

"I am happy to hear you, Mr. Erastus. I think, both of you will make good bond during the journey." King took glass of wine and sarcastically took one sip.

"What?" Adrastus was shocked to listen. Her eyes and mouth had been widely opened with anger. "I'll never go with an Earthmen." King's smiling lips came back to rest and the expressions of anger covered his face. King threw the wine glass to the right where a maid had been standing. The crystal glass broke into pieces and King stood up with red face. Queen was also looking nervous for he knew the King's anger and rage.

"Mr. Adrastus! You are going with him and he will be your leader during the journey." King ordered with dignity and sarcastically smiled. The concierge rushed in. He was panting.

"My majesty, he has come." The concierge bowed before the king. King's anger vanished.

"Call him in." King ordered. King moved back to his seat and Adrastus moved back to his seat himself. Oliver came in confused. King welcomed him with a smile. He stood at the carpet in between the courtiers.

"I think I didn't do anything wrong my majesty," Oliver swallowed hardly.

"Listen man, we have called you here for some announcement. In front of the meeting at this time, I wholly announce that from now own the chairperson of the trade would be Mr. Oliver Beck hem." King announced. "Mr. Adrastus will coordinate with you." King said and stood up from his throne. Queen also followed her like a dog wagging its tail.

"Both of you follow me." Adrastus and Oliver followed the king. Crossing the stairs all of they reached at a new room completely dark. One of the servants had been following them according to the King's order.

"Light the room." The servant lit up a candle and put it at the table. The queen had just changed the course with its cat in the way. The servant put candle at the center of the table. Both of they standing at the other side of the table gazed the king sat at a wooden desk and pointed both of them to take their seats in front of him.

"Look! I am sending both of you on a journey to Singapore to bring more diamonds and sapphires. In those diamonds and sapphires, there is hidden a sapphire which is fatal to the lord of the dark planet. As you know, he is also the one who want to rule this land. He wants to make the people more astray." They were attentively listening to the king as known about the dark planet their hearts feared for some instances.

"Oliver, you will lead Adrastus to the mines or hills whatever has it been and both of you will bring that deathly gem to me. It is campaign and if you will succeed Oliver your nation will get equal rights as us." Oliver smiled excitedly as his dreams seemed to him to be fulfilling. Adrastus looked disturbed, as an Earthmen had given superiority over him and the one who had been in one of his rivals since the royal dinner. "Now you have been given the time and both of you can decide according to your plans." King stood up and moved out of the dark secret room.

"How is your wife?" Adrastus asked staring the flickering flame of candle. Oliver stunned to look.

After hearing the news of Oliver's improved grade, there was a hurricane of rash words and curses for Oliver in the atmosphere. None of the Sunasians was willing to accept an Earthmen to be in the general staff members of the Sunasian. Wherever any listened to the news, the things fell off the hands, jaws dropping with surprise and jaws twitching in fret.

"Has the king forgotten about the fugitives?"

"Would we obey him?"

"He is the cunning rascal."

"How could the king be so disloyal?"

The superior standing of Oliver was disliked by the Earthumen too as they call him a rebellion who was favoring the Sunasians who had killed their loved ones and daily the Earthumen had been their victims.

The general political members of the state joined their heads together and started pondering on the decision.

"I am not going with him and he will lead me. Me...?" Adrastus proudly announced among the members of the general community. It seemed he had not believed the decision of the king. "How could the king do this to me? He roared at me due to that worm." Adrastus cussed scornfully. The anger was being flushed from each feature of his face. He was restlessly roaming around the round table around what the leaders were sitting. Everyone was seriously listening to him and all the expressions were obviously in his favor. "How cunningly he has won the King's heart?" Adrastus moved to window and gripped it firmly trying to stop her anger. The iron bar of the window broke by the insistence of his hand.

"Listen Adrastus, we are to move him away. The Earthmen will tear us into the pieces. They are more cunning and more intelligent. Their ancestors have taken their first breathe in this atmosphere. They know more and gradually they will overcome us." Prime minister was in a serious tension.

"Just give him some money and say him to take his wife and child from here." The treasurer suggested.

"Wife," Adrastus smiled and turned to them. "To move the wife is not the solution Sir," he smiled sarcastically and grabbed a glass filled with yellow drink. He took one sip and moved his eyes to them. "Cut his head off." He scornfully grounded his teeth that his nacres proliferated and glass in his hand seemed to be broken and he threw it on the floor. The glass broke into piece with a sharp noise. "I shall kill him." Adrastus raged.

"Listen Adrastus that is not the solution." Treasurer dissuaded him.

"Then money is not the solution." He tried to make the treasurer answerless but he only smiled for he knew the real problem. "What do you think that he will be quiet after taking the riches when he knew the secret place of the diamonds and the sapphires?" Treasurer kept silent for Adrastus had given the perfect and the most solid reason. "And I don't want to loose his wife." Adrastus remarked. The room quaked by the chortles of the men.

"So this is the reason." Prime minister stood up and stood by his right arm. "Why didn't you tell me before?"

Prime minister was laughing. His heart was twinkling like a new lover and his lips were making a curvy shape.

"It's really hard task. His wife will not be for sale." Treasure laughed off the matter.

"It's serious." Adrastus was looking sturdy and her seriousness had taken place over his friendly expressions.

"As far as I think, he is a very honest man and he will never be misleading by the money. He knew the secret of the diamonds and the sapphires. If he wanted he can grab them all but he did not." Treasurer mentioned the serious point.

"So, the only solution is to kill that man, to cut his head off." Adrastus said and looked to the setting sun. His black eyes were thinking subtly about the plan.

"Hey, Mr. Abrahamus, What about yours?" Treasurer took a sip of coffee and asked him sneakily.

"I threw as I was fed up?" Prime minister carelessly answered.

"and what about the baby?" Treasurer asked another question as all of they had been taking the meal. Adrastus was quietly listening to both of them and the other people were busy in eating their feasts.

"She is mine, no doubt. She has a suns sign at her hand and she is my daughter." King replied carefully.

"So, you accepted something." Treasurer smiled and took another sip of his drink.

"Hey what about you Adrastus?" Treasurer attended him.

"What?" Adrastus carelessly answered more attentive in chewing his piece of meat in his piece of meat.

"When will you make her trash?" Treasurer seriously asked.

"I think never." Replied Adrastus with a loving smile.

47

"Hey, hey he is a true lover." Treasurer raised a slogan by lifting his right arm up and closing his fist. The room trembled by their chortles and they were merry making, hooting and taking their dinner.

All of they had drunk too much as their black royal uniforms with white stockings had been wet. In stitches, they spent the night and during the mid night, they returned home with their eyes dimmed in the stinks of drinks.

III

"Everything is possible, if you want it to do." Oliver was staring the fork; he was rolling in his fingertips. Martha, quietly looking at her, after a few seconds, he looked to Martha. They were taking a memorable dinner. Max was sitting nearby Oliver munching the almonds coated with honey. He was enjoying the tasty feast and was looking careless about the discussion going on but inwardly he was listening with great interest each word.

"Martha, you can't imagine my condition at the royal palace. For the first time I stepped into his courtroom. The courtiers stared me strangely and sneered. Their glance told me that they were not willin' to accept me. I was totally confused and before I could faint..." Oliver stopped and took a piece of cutlets in his mouth. "His smile encouraged me up, the vagueness of the room was obvious to me after his kind smile. I hardly encouraged lookin' up to his tall posture. I could not believe he was the same King who ignored me in the whole party. Was he really the same? It was hard for me to believe. He looked to me dignified for his venerable behavior and nobleness. He was showing great love for Earthmen." He looked to Martha for first time while narrating his story. "King was happy to see me. He announced me as the chairperson of the trade among his courtiers. He took me to the room where even the prime minister was not permitted to join." Oliver told the story. "It seemed he has trusted me. It was hard to believe." Oliver laughed. "But I had to believe. He told me the secret of something he was talking about any dark planet. I couldn't get it but it was really anythin' imperative to him. He asked me about the trade visit and I am goin' to Singapore with Adrastus the next week." Oliver was looking too much excited.

"Next week!" Martha hardly said. "But it's so soon and so far." Martha was scared and astounded.

"Yeah, it is." Oliver did not care for her situation. "but it's beneficial and when I'll be successful in filling up the King's wish he would be happier and he'll grant us the equal rights. I would be closer to him and he will trust me more. None of the Earthumen would hate me and not any of the Sunasian would sneer me." Oliver smiled at his daydreams and his smile widened thinking of his dazzling future. Martha smiled. "Martha, no need to worry," Oliver continued. "I want to see the lights of earth to illuminate like this flame of candle." He pointed to the flickering flame of candle. "Martha," He continued after some time. Martha was quietly listening to her and Max was busy in eating and eating. "Before going on a visit I want to address the Earthumen."

"They won't listen." Martha abruptly replied and took a spoonful of rice.

"I want your help please." Oliver pleaded and put his hand at her hand.

"Please Oliver," Martha started dissuading him. "Why are you talking about this when you know they are not good to me and not to you? They will never listen. Even they do not like to talk to Max."

"Listen me Martha, You are liked by everyone. You are kind, you are winsome lady. Everyone loves to talk to you and now they will to listen to you. I want your help, please don't rebuff." At last, Martha had to be convinced and he was ready to help Oliver in gathering the people. Martha was looking satisfactory but she had been greatly worried about her and her heart was testifying the upcoming danger. She wanted to cry and to farewell Oliver forever but a little hope was kindling in her mind. She saw to her son who was playing with an empty plate.

"What a pity? When he joined Sunasian's institution, he hated him and when he came back home and tried to play with Earthumen; they hated him because a rebellion's son can never be well-wisher. Now again he had joined Sunasians despite of their arrogance. He was hanging in between the sky and the earth. Thousand of thoughts were knocking the consciousness of her mind. The future of his son Max, the gathering of Earthumen, their rejections and their sense of sneering Oliver, he was to go next week and she was to do it in this week. She gripped her head firmly and closed her eyes with fear. Max was busy in playing with the plate and a fork and Oliver was just thinking about his new visit. The night passed by.

Next day, Max was spending his second day in the institution. The students did not talk to her as the hate for the earth people had fixed firm roots and had turned into a thorny tree. The teachers hardly talked to him. He sat at the end bench of the class and did his own activities. The peers did not care to attend him and he was remained in his enjoyments. Mostly he was writing something and sometimes he went out the bushes to see them. There were the different religions of the children among Sunasians. He went to religious institute, which mostly remained vacant. Only in the morning time, there had been the chorus and students of different religions stood in front of their respective Statues. Those who worshipped the tusks of the elephants stood in front of the two slantwise tusks, those worshipping hair of white tiger stood in front of the statue of a back of the tiger, and some of them had been the worshippers of the unicorns. They stood in front of the statues of the unicorns. Passing by the statue of a white tiger enclosed in the glass-case he laughed. "How could a tiger have white hair?" He laughed at his own thoughts. The lab attendant daily observed him but he did not want to create a fuss with him. He did not even want to talk to him. Martha gave him special time in his studies and she helped him in every field. Max's progress studies were outstanding and it had been hard for the teachers to believe it. The behavior of the students was rude to him. Often he was seen sitting at the back of the bushes writing something fuzzy. He was the only one who could understand his own words. The students and teachers overlooked him. He was a good singer too. He wrote his feelings on some piece of paper and sang them like cuckoo. At the back of the bushes, he was singing his new sonata.

In the roar of winds
I can feel my anger
In the skies so high
I can see my grace
In the days of the past
I cannot forget the moments lost
That had given my nation
The passing time so harsh
In the water of the seas
And the trees with cool breeze
I can give with zeal and zest
My nation time of peace and rest
It will be happened one day
You will see a time of gay
When the sun will be puzzled
To shine bright into my eyes

He sang it with great rhythm, rise and fall. As he opened the eyes after completing the symphony, he heard a huge round of applause. The girls and boys standing all around smiled what made him pleased. Completing his song he was looking gloom as the upcoming departure of his father was tormenting him. He moved away from the mob that was appreciating him and admiring his voice. He moved to other ground and sat near the tower of a unicorn. He was silent lost in the deep thoughts when a girl of his age sat near him. She was dressed in a black gown around what the jewels had been embedded and among the jewels, she was sparkling like sun. She put her bag down and started staring him who was staring the soil. The girl standing stepped some distances away, took out a catapult from her bag and aimed his nose. It struck hard but at the right place.

"Ouch, ouch," he stood up squinting his eyes and held his nose.

"Hi Max," She started carelessly and put the catapult in his bag. She was looking stupid, Max was looking more stupid than her rubbing his nose, and his eyes were flabbergasted to observe such bluntness.

"Ha… ha…a … hi," He hardly spoke, still rubbing his nose.

"I am Bellatrix Abrahamus, follower of unicorn. You also? I guess." Bellatrix tried to guess pointing his index finger to the unicorn standing at his back.

"No, Nops, really," Max replied rudely without looking at her focusing at the mob eating lunch.

"O, I guessed wrong." The girl's lips made a round circle and she knitted her brows keeping an eye at him. "Ok, fine, you would not be." The girls ignored her wrong observation. "I am junior to you." Girl told her.

"So, what can I do?" Max scowled and answered wearily staring the mob in front him.

"O, I hate that scowl." The girl pointed to her forehead. Max looked to her and saw sun sign at her hand. The sun sign made her confused. "I just want you to sing with the choir in the school party." The girl continued boldly.

"No, no, no." Max shouted and stood up.

"Why? Why…? Why?" The girl asked in the same tone and she stood up.

"Because, each word of my symphonies depicts my people, their feelings, their emotions and their desires. They are my people and they will rise like my voice one day." Max was looking sad.

"Who are your people? Aren't they we?" The girl scowled in anger.

"No, I'm an Earthumen."

"What?" The girl shouted.

"Don't try to be so innocent. Everyone knows here." Max picked up his bag and moved disregarding his presence.

"Max, Max, Max" Bellatrix called her. Max did not listen. "Hey, there are your papers." The girl shouted more loudly. Max's steps stopped, he turned and rushed to the girl but he was to ground his teeth in anger where the girl was smiling boldly with empty hands. "I am sorry Max. I think, I am teasing you. Be our voice and you will have everything you want. I do not say you to sing in our favor but why not sing a song of friendship for both nations." Bellatrix had suggested her very strong idea to ponder on. Bellatrix looked in to her eyes. She was dazzling child just like any baby princess. Her last words along with the innocence, her face inspired Max.

IV

What feared Martha that no one would listen to her, but something unexpected happened on the appointed day, many of the people had gathered in the dinning hall of Oliver to listen to Oliver. Mrs. Wilson helped her like a good friend. Now she was helping Martha in serving the hall crowded with the listeners. The guests were being served the soup and the tea and were gossiping. Mrs. Oliver went to Margaret to serve the soup but she refused to take it. The most of the topic of discussion was the abuses about Oliver.

"He has just gathered to make us jealous about his grade." On of the chubby man predicted. The person surrounding him spoke yes with him and stared Martha. There were the discussions about the market matters, about the improved grade of Oliver and many others were the centre of topic of the discussion. With a jerk the main door opened and Oliver entered.

"I am sorry, I am late, my people," Oliver said and moved face the people from the front. The people ignored him. They were looking more interested in the soup instead of Oliver. Oliver faced their front. No one was bothering to look at him.

"Listen," He shouted. Mary sitting in the lap of Margaret attended her to Oliver. She looked to Oliver and again started chatting to the woman nearby. He called them three times but none did listen. He saw Martha helplessly who was humiliated to apprehend the position with a big iron empty tray in her hand. She threw the tray with force onto the ground. The sudden overpowering noise created that some of the people moved their heads down and put their hands on their ears.

"Listen to us people" She shouted at the peak her voice.

"Listen to the beautiful lady," One of the men from the audiences said smilingly and all of they quietly looked to Martha.

"My dear people," Oliver started his speech. The eyes shifted from Martha to Oliver.

"I am not the one you do think." Oliver continued. "I am accompanying Sunasians just for you. I work at their

55

palace just for you. King has made me the head of trade. This is not my success but the first step of your success." The crowd was quiet and attentive. "My, people, you will witness one day, when Kings Neck will be in my grip and his blood will quench the thirst of your revenge. My person, my heart is filled with love for you. I hate myself because you hate me and I will love myself if you will love me.

Be political. Follow me; my way as I've made the way through the palace, you should...."

"Shut up, you rascal," Before Oliver could complete his words; a hard trashcan with a comment from his left side came and hit his face. Women and men chortled and mocked. Oliver held his face and was embarrassed. Oliver was stupidly staring the public and Martha was badly confused. The situation was hard to believe for both.

"What are you waiting for after much...?" Before the man could complete his words, the crowd roared into laughter.

"Probably waiting for another one," Another hard shoe and a rather big from the previous came. Oliver subtly sat down but inopportunely, it hit Martha.

"Ouch" With an impulsive cry of pain she held her head. Mrs. Wilson standing among the crowd repressed her lips with fear. She was feeling pity for Martha. Oliver without being late rushed to her.

"You should tell us to bring tomatoes and eggs with us." One of the women shouted and the room was in stitches.

"Tomatoes are soft and the shoes are hard, you fool lady," One of the men laughed off. The public was in stitches. When Oliver was in view of Martha's head one of the shoe struck his back. He was in fury but was vulnerable.

"Let's move." The crowd one by one moved out cursing the couple. Mrs. Wilson was standing stunned. The room had been empty in no minutes. Mrs. Wilson looked out of the window the crowd chattering flushed with anger. She moved to them. Oliver moved back to the window. "I am sorry Martha, I couldn't help." She hugged Martha sitting near her and both of they burst into tears. Margaret was standing holding hand of Mary.

"Let's go Mary." The manners hurt Margaret too.

CHAPTER 4

⊹⊱A Journey with the rival⊰⊹

I

Adrastus was staying a night at Oliver's home before the appointed day of the travel. Martha did not go in front of her even for the one time, as she had been aware of his unlawful way of staring. She hated that man since the royal dinner. That man had been sleeping with Max in his bedroom. Max was gazing his long legs crossing the border of the bed.

"Is he a giant?" His mind whispered.

"Or a wizard?" The man had been fast asleep and Max was observing his black coat and white stockings while the sleeping man was enjoying his night dreams in snort. Max was not happy to sleep with that man in the room. Oliver came to visit his son and Max predicting his father quickly closed his eyes. Realizing that Max has slept Oliver with a smile came out.

Martha was rearranging the pots in the kitchen when Oliver entered. Oliver took a glass from the basket and poured water in it from the gallon nearby the table. Martha overlooked Oliver and started cleaning the sink with a piece of cloth. She was rubbing hard and hard as if trying to forget something. A crowd of emotions had gathered and conflicting in her mind obviously appeared at her face. Taking the last sip of water, she looked to Martha who was putting cutlery in the cabinet.

"Hey, what happened?" Oliver looked to her and put glass into the basket. She did neither give any answer nor did she look to Oliver. She was looking depressed and her lips had been quieter than before. "Hey lady, can I have your words?" Oliver made her attentive again. Without any answer, she went out of the kitchen and picked up the laundry gathered near the chair. Oliver went after her.

"Ms. Martha, Is everything all right?" Martha mood was looking too much off.

"Everything is fine." She answered moodily and closed window of the lounge. "I am feeling sleepy." Martha said and moved to the bedroom. Oliver followed her. The candle flame was flickering. Oliver sat in a chair near the bed.

"What has happened, Martha?" Oliver asked softly to release her depression. Martha sat at the other side of the bed with her back to Max.

"Nothing," She replied offhandedly. Oliver was depressed for her. "I went there to meet Lilly... to see her daughter. I couldn't have any news about her since her daughter was born. Neither had I seen her with the prime minister. If she wasn't alive, her daughter should be there in the lap of someone." Martha said and touched the flame with her index finger.

"You know, at the dinner children were not permitted."

"Yeah, I know." Martha moved her face a little to Oliver. "but the wives were," She defended herself.

"You know, I tried to talk to the king." Oliver said.

"And he didn't even bother to look at you. He just disregarded us. He degraded us. It was the only thing he was wanting and it was the only idea he wanted to show you your importance." Martha was trying to show her the real phase of life as she was saying and looked back to Oliver.

"No, he didn't want this, Martha." Oliver tried to defend the King. "He has made me the chairperson of the trade due to my good act. One day you'll see I'll take that throne and I'll rule the Sunasians. There, I'll show them the real face and they'll take the way to their land." Oliver tried to make her comfort.

"Oliver, I, too much worried." Martha's tears started to fall down and she did not look back to him.

"About what?" Oliver asked by twisting his body little to her.

"Why is this man going along with you? Last time you went alone and you brought these diamonds and sapphires with you. What is his job now?" Martha enquired.

"He will just be a helper. This time we need a sapphire to work against the dark planet." Oliver explained her reason.

"The dark planet?" Martha frowned, as she had no idea about the dark planet.

"Yeah, there some people who want to destroy this land. That sapphire is a sapphire is something a remedy. King knows it better, me not."

"But why the king is sending you with that ill mannered giant?" Martha cussed the man disdainfully. Oliver roared in to laughter.

"Shh shh shh, be slow." Oliver smilingly put his finger at his lips.

"Oliver, do not go. My heart fears." Martha looked up to the sky.

"Hey, hey Martha, don't do this. Don't discourage me. I went alone the last time too and you said the same words to me. Now I request you to pray for me again. I'll be fine and I'll be back soon." Oliver consoled her and moved out without looking at her. Martha stood up, wiped her tears and went after her. The moon had been peeking through the window. Oliver was staring outside the window. Martha stood near her and the night went by.

When the first ray of sun entered the house, Oliver was moving out of the room with his giant friend and Max.

"Goodbye dad," Max said and waved his hand. Martha was peeking out through the window. As she had been away from her sights, she said her goodbye with tears. Oliver had not the nerve to look back, therefore he did not look back even for one time. He went on a straight road with the luggage of the journey. Both of the men did not talk to one another. They had only two horses with them to cover a long journey. Oliver and Adrastus were walking along with their brown and black horses respectively.

"Your horse looks too much attached to you." Adrastus patted his horse and started the discussion. Oliver smiled and looked his horse walking systematically with him.

"Yours too," Oliver admired his horse.

"Yeah, it looks faithful to you too," Adrastus glanced Oliver who was in good spirits.

"Yeah, its mother had grown up with and now I have it. It knows me since my childhood. It's familiar with each habit of mine. It loves me and I love it." Oliver narrated the story of his horse gleefully. Adrastus laughed off.

"More than your wife?" The man taunted. Oliver looked to him. His expressions were stiff and he who were thinking, as a joke did not like it to talk about his wife. Oliver ignored his undignified talk. He kept quiet. Once again, they started the quiet journey.

II

Mrs. Wilson a bulky woman just like her husband was eating apple standing at a shop of fruits. The shopkeeper was stunningly looking at her. She finished the apple and threw its unpalatable part at the dump of the trash nearby. Touching some apples, she picked another apple and started tasting it disregarding the shopkeeper. He was noticing her.

"Mrs. Wilson, you have eaten five apples until now. The shopkeeper grounded his teeth in anger.

"I taste yet, man," Mrs. Wilson ignored his fury utterly. She rubbed the apple by her red coat and again started to eat. She finished the apple in some minutes. Throwing its rotten part, she moved her hand to another apple.

"Hi, Mrs. Wilson," She heard a sweet voice after her when she was inspecting the apples. The shopkeepers in the shops pointed to one another with their brows and chuckled. Martha observed the situation but she ignored. Mrs. Wilson looked to her left where the woman had stood near her.

"Hey, dear, how are you?" Mrs. Wilson hugged her lovingly. "What about Oliver? Has he been back?" Mrs. Wilson continued after separating from her.

"No, he's not." She said gloomily and put the basket at the table.

"Oh, don't worry dear. He'll be back soon." Mrs. Wilson slap lightly at her back. "There'll be some special campaign." Mrs. Wilson took a bite of another apple. The shopkeeper had to leave her and attended to other customers. She faced Martha for the discussion. "Did you see the black shadows the last night?" Mrs. Wilson mouth was full of apple pulp and she could hardly speak. Martha's eyes opened with fear.

"Were they really?" She was considering it a hallucination but it was real.

"Everyone believed and you're still in doubt, silly," Mrs. Wilson carelessly told her. He had not told about it to Oliver and now he was realizing, he had done a big mistake.

"I thought it a superstition." She explained.

"But it isn't." Mrs. Wilson told her.

"Hi,"

"Salam,"

"Namasty,"

They heard the innocent gallant voices at their back when Mrs. Wilson picking up the bucket and Martha was staring her. When they turned to look back, Mary, Frank, Abdullah and Bimla had moved away without listening their greeting.

"Hey, hey good morning, waslam, namasty," Mrs. Wilson made a loud cry and Martha could only smile.

"These are not are tasty Mr." Mrs. Wilson threw apple onto the table and moved to the other shop.

"Give me the money of seven apples, you chubby," The shopkeeper was shouting after her. She looked back and gave a furious look.

"Jus keep your mouth quiet, flimsy," Mrs. Wilson abused her and looked to other stall. The children were enjoying the matter. In stitches, they turned their faces forward. They were running after one another, enjoying their impish manners, throwing their papers at one another and the other was picking them up. Their innocent chortles were imprinting in the atmosphere when they saw a kite moving to them. All of they immediately sat down.

"O, it's a kite." Bimla pointed back.

"Yeah, it is," Abdullah held her hand and let her to move forward.

"Hey, did you see the black shades last night?" Mary remembered the topic at the sight of the kite.

"They were very strange." Frank assisted her discussion.

"Yeah, they were." Bimla spoke.

"I can guess they were vultures. They were just roaming around, probably trying to find any dead victim. I mean, searching for their food." Abdullah elaborated looking to the cattle grazing the field and the shepherd who was herding them with a long bamboo stick.

"Yeah, somewhat, like that," Frank supported Abdullah's conception.

"How peaceful is it?" Bimla took a deep breathe as she felt a great relief standing amidst the grass. She opened widely her hands and took more breathes.

"The sky was terrific." Mary continued ignoring her liveliness. Frank and Abdullah were listening and pacing with her while, Bimla was standing with her eyes closed. "My body was shivering at the first glance and I had the nerve to look again." Mary continued.

"Mom did not let us to go out. She saw and was weeping." Frank told another event.

"Hey, hey listen, let me take with you," Bimla opened her eyes and rushed to them. They three laughed and stopped to take her.

"We didn't know we missed you in the way." Mary mocked.

"Just enjoying this area, how peaceful is it?" Bimla was looking impressed.

"What did this mean?" They resumed the discussion and ambled. "What was their purpose? Who were they?" Abdullah continued and made them to think.

"Whatever were they? They were dangerous. They were really heart-rending." Mary shared her views. Abdullah looked to the sky. It was clean and clear. Bimla and Mary moved to the bed of roses and examined the flowers to choose the best one to pluck. Frank momentary looked at the girls and stepped afar Abdullah looking to the sky following Abdullah. A sparrow was flying in the sky with song played by its beak.

"Let's find some place to sit." Frank suggested. Abdullah moved his eyes to Frank and visually accepted his decision. Both of they quietly looked around.

"There," Frank pointed to a tree at his left side. It was wide tree with its boughs drooped down. Frank moved to the tree and Abdullah followed him quietly glancing the girls busy plucking the flowers. They sat down and opened their papers, a wooden pen and a black inkpot of terracotta. They soaked the sharp pointed tip of their pencils into the pots of black ink and wrote down on the papers. Soon the girls also joined them and threw their papers and the materials near them. They looked to them and laughed as they had fixed flowers in their right and left ears and were

65

waiting for their praise. Now all of they four were writing an essay on their likes and dislikes as had the lecture been delivered by Margaret.

"You know, I'm too much interested in knowin' the institute of the Sunasians." Bimla broke the silence.

"They'll nevea let us toe to enter." Abdullah answered and they laughed.

"Why no someday go and visit their institute?" Bimla again shared her wish.

"Are you prime minister?" Frank answered without looking at her. Bimla made a face and again moved her eyes to the paper.

"Max can help us." Mary sparklingly suggested.

"I don't need any help." Abdullah moodily answered.

"Me too," Frank answered looking at her notebook. Both the girls looked helplessly to one another and again distracted to their home works.

"Save you" Abdullah shouted at once. All of the three looked to him.

"Why, what happened?" Mary was astounded as there was no danger near them.

"Look," Abdullah pointed forward. "An elephant is coming." Eyes opened with fear both the girls looked back and Frank looked forward. There, Mrs. Wilson was coming. They laughed off.

"Look out, Abdullah" Mrs. Wilson shouted and sprinted to them.

"O, a stampede," Abdullah again spoke nonsense. All of they laughed and Abdullah looked up. This time, he was to scream. A big black vulture was flying over him to his head. It came very close to him, gripped him by the shoulder and flew.

"Abdullah" Mrs. Wilson shouted and ran faster with a bucket of apples hanging in her left hand. The children stood up with fear and ran after the vulture. Mrs. Wilson could not run because she was bulky but it was the time to run. She did as fast as she could. She was looking funnier and funnier but it was not the time to mock. Frank picked up a pebble and hit the vulture. The vulture screamed fiercely and rose higher. Abdullah was screaming with fear in the paws of the vulture. Mrs. Wilson rushed after him but hit by stone protruded in the way and fell down. Without being late, she stood in no minutes and aimed the vultures with her apples. Frank, Bimla and Mary also took apples from Mrs. Wilson's basket and took aims. They attacked hard and the vulture could not rise high. It felt pain and it threw him down. Abdullah fell down and fainted simultaneously. Mrs. Wilson picked him up in his arms and ordered Mary, Frank and Abdullah to pick up the apples.

III

Reaching near the hills, they ambled down their horses and hiked up the hills. The journey was still quiet.

"Your horses' hoof is injured." Adrastus again started the discussion for the horse. Max immediately looked to its horse hoof. It was all right. He had been irritated.

"Where? It is not." He replied bitter normally.

"But it is. Look at its gait." Adrastus again started.

"What happened to its gait?" Oliver looked down to the horse with a slight scowl at his head.

"It is not walking enthusiastically." Adrastus again mentioned the fault.

"It will've been tired." Oliver replied ignoring his irritating behavior,

"Yeah, it has been and so are my toe and my horse." Adrastus told him and sat at the ground. Oliver stopped.

"Why not take rest for one night and let the horses to be full." Adrastus suggested.

"To be full ov (of) soil and sand?" Oliver sarcastically answered.

"No, we will find something." Adrastus carelessly answered and lay on the ground. He put his hand at his eyes.

"Remember, we're to reach the sea to day at every cost. The ships would be waiting for us." Oliver strictly dissuaded him.

"What do you think?" Adrastus slowly moved her arm from his eyes, preset his elbow in the Albericy surface, and stared him. "I shall listen to you. King has made you my leader and you have become." Adrastus looked like furious tiger into his eyes.

"I' m not ordering you, what's hurting you. The point is that the black forces are going to hurt us. It's not about you, about me; it's about both of us." Oliver left reins of the horse and sat near him.

"You go, if you care. I damn care for this." Adrastus again faced the sky and closed his eyes.

"Listen Adrastus, we're to do it together. Both of we'll be rewarded." Oliver persuaded him.

"I have no concern. I just want one thing." Adrastus told him without looking him.

"What?"

"It's in your house." Adrastus plainly told him.

"What's it?" Oliver was confused.

"I want your..." The horse neighed before he could complete his words. Both of they looked to Adrastus's horse. It was neighing for none.

"Tired of the stay," Adrastus stood. He rode the horse. "I am going back and better for you to move back." Adrastus said and his horse trotted.

"Ok, go, I'll see the matter." Oliver stood, moved to his horse, and rode it. His horse walked, trotted, cantered and galloped. Listening to horse hoofs striking hard, Adrastus looked back changing the direction of his horse. He took out his arrow, fixed it in his bow. His horse trotted and cantered as he took aim of Oliver and it hit his left arm. In a fury, he took out the second arrow and again took the aim. Before Oliver could turn, a second arrow wounded his back. He fell down from the horse and could not see his assailant. His faithful horse turned and galloped to his opponent. He neighed lifting his hind limbs he ambled to the assailant in a fury. Adrastus was smiling triumphantly holding the bow and the spear in his hand. The horse was galloping. He took another aim and smacked the horse's shoulder. Its gallop turned gradually to a walk. It looked up with a tear to Adrastus. Adrastus took another aim and it hit its other shoulder. The horse had been badly wounded. It fell down helplessly. Adrastus moved his arm back to take another arrow but his arm waved in the air. There was no arrow left. He moved down the horse and paced to Oliver disregarding the horse who was taking its last breathe. Oliver's eyes were closing. He could hardly see his foe. Everything was obscure to him. Adrastus beat him hard with his foot. He impulsively turned to right with pain. Adrastus squatted and took spears from Oliver's case fallen near him and subtly put them in his case. He overlooked him and moved to his horse ignoring the slight cries of pain passing by Oliver and the horse. In this lonely place, he could not see any existence. He rode up his horse, ambled the hills and started his campaign to Singapore. Oliver was fading. The sun was shinning bright.

"Max," He mumbled with pain. The innocent smiling face of his son grabbing Wilson's hair appeared in his mind.

"Martha," He mumbled and this time her wife was smiling with him in his fields. The life had defeated him and death was conquering. All the fascinating dreams smashed like his fields. He stepped alone in this brutal world and was returning alone. His eyes were fainting with pain. The scenery around was fading with his fainting eyes. His shoulders paralyzed and soon his eyes closed and so of the horse.

IV

My father is a man so grave
Why do I feel his disgrace?
One day the stars will show you
The hidden sacrifice how know you
The damped faces, the melting hearts
Will be healed by him
You will see his well-being
He is not the same you do think
You will see
You will see
The time is passing now
The people asking me it is done how

Everyone says I have a deadly foe
I'm so sweet how he can grow
The time is passing now
You will see one day

Max recording symphony in the skies opened his eyes; he felt his cheeks wet unknowingly how deeply he had lost. Martha was standing behind and Max was unaware of his presence. Max stared into the sky.

"Max" Martha softly called and put her hand at his shoulder. She impetuously moved his face to her.

"How are you, dear?" Martha sat near him. "Didn't meet your mother since morning," Martha pulled him near her and he put his head in her lap. She kissed his forehead. Max smiled.

"I'm not fine, mom. Why my heart is beating fast?" Max shared his worry. Martha looked worried.

"Why what happened dear?" She put her hand at his heart. Observing the fast rhythms her eyes were astonished. Max lifted his head up and gazed the fields.

"Missing dad, I wish he could be here and both of we shall sow the seeds and the harvesting time will come and I'll help him like always." Martha smilingly caressed his hair. "When will he be back?" Max continued.

"After one month or it can be more, it's a long journey. It'll take time." Martha told him.

"O, it's so far." Max stood up with a depressing face and took two to three steps to the field.

"Listen Max," Martha called from back. "Sit 'ere with me," Martha continued. Max moved back with a disheartening face and sat near her again.

"This's for you." Martha opened her closed fist where a chain was glowing like sunshine. His eyes opened with wonder.

"Wow," He exclaimed. "From where did you get it?" Max asked her incredibly.

"I bought it for you." She opened the locks of the chain and did it around the neck of his son.

"Keep it away, I'm not a girl." Max moodily answered and Martha had to laugh.

"This's not for any girl but this's for you." Martha locked it around his neck without caring for his resistance. She moved the chain completely inside her shirt.

"Don't show to anyone. Sunasians'll grab it, otherwise." Martha made him frightened. Max nodded. "Let's go in and take breakfast." Martha continued. Max stood up and moved into the house holding her hand. Max rushed to the table and Martha locked the door. As she turned after locking the door, it knocked.

"Who'll be?" She murmured and Max had taken his chair filling his mouth with sandwiches his mother had made. Martha opened the door as was shocked to see Mrs. Wilson holding wounded Abdullah. Frank, Mary and Bimla were standing on either sides of Mrs. Wilson.

"Is he Abdullah?" Martha worried at the vista. The children nodded and Martha gave them the way to enter. She closed the door when all had moved in. "How did it happen?" Martha asked as she moved after them.

"A vulture attacked him." Mrs. Wilson carefully laid Max at the carpet putting his right hand under his head after looking for no bed. Martha moved to him. The blood was dripping down his head and a small wound was at his lips. He was fainted. The dress at his shoulders torn to shreds. Martha tensed. "How cruel?" She mumbled and bent to examine him more closely.

"What happened?" Max after realizing the situation came near him with a piece of sandwich in his right hand and stood besides her mother.

"He's wounded, a vulture attacked him." Mary informed him. The children were quietly standing around Martha and Mrs. Wilson.

"I couldn't find Dr. Shahab. He just needed a bandage." Mrs. Wilson looked to Martha. Martha touched his forehead and examined the wound at different angles. After examining it, he touched his lips and pressed them to make the cut apparent to her.

"What're you looking at? Just treat the boy," Mrs. Wilson as she felt the wastage of time restlessly asked her.

"Bring my medical box." She pushed Max slightly with her hand. He abruptly turned and brought a wooden box with him. Martha grabbed it and opened it quickly. She was cleaning the blood all around the gash of forehead.

"Go to the chairs." Mrs. Wilson ordered them as all of they moved to the chairs with a basket of apples. Martha was carefully bandaging the little boy. Mrs. Wilson moved after the children. She held her basket from Bimla and sat at the carpet. In no times she yawned and slept. The children could not giggle as their friend was injured.

"How did it happen?" Max broke the ice after looking her mother.

"It was a very black creature, a big one than normal," Mary created suspense and Max felt the story interesting.

"He is my best fellow. I'll kill that devil." Max flushed with anger.

"He doesn't like you." Bimla told him and wiped his tears.

"I know," Max gloomily replied.

"How do you know?" Mary scowled and stared her.

"What rubbish?" Frank did not like it.

"He told me." Bimla pointed Abdullah with her eyes. "He shares with me all his feelings." Bimla told them.

"Then why're you leaking out his secrets?" Mary stared her.

"I'm not leaking his secrets. I'm telling Max that he's my best fellow." There were expressions of conquer at her face.

Max smiled, Frank and Mary kept quiet and looked to Martha who had almost bandaged the boy. She put the blanket at the boy and moved to the room with her medical box. The children were quietly gazing Martha and Abdullah.

"Everything is fine, Mrs. Wilson," She told rubbing her hand by the cloth nearby and looked down at her who was asleep with her basket at her abdomen. Martha wearily looked and turned her eyes to the children. They were giggling.

"Your friend is fine now." Martha told them with a smile. "What would you like to eat?" Martha asked them. No one spoke.

"Sandwiches," Max loudly shouted. Martha moved to the kitchen to serve the children.

V

When Abdullah opened his eyes, he was lying in his grandmother's bed. With pain, his eyes opened and then closed again. He saw to her left. Something was vague. She was Saira. She was decorating a bouquet of red roses.

"How're you, dear?" Grandmother lovingly touched his cheeks and sat near him. He felt dizziness as he tried to lift himself up.

"Ah", He again put his head at the pillow. "What was happened granny?"

"A vulture attacked you." Granny told him.

"O," He spoke with fear. "It picked me up, granny and threw me down, that monster," Abdullah complained about the vulture. He was almost going to weep.

"I told you to not to go so far. Why didn't you take Saira with you?" Grandmother scolded him and he was quietly listening closing his eyes. "Martha treated you and Mrs. Wilson also helped."

"What? Martha aided me?" Abdullah shockingly opened his eyes.

"Yeah, she aided you, such a nice lady," Grandmother looked to Saira who had prepared a bouquet and started the other. "Look, your sister is preparing a bouquet for both of them," Granny pointed to her.

"O..., O..., O..., I hate it." Abdullah said and put his hand at his eyes.

"What is detestable?" Granny asked her looking to him.

"She the rebellion's wife," Abdullah ostracized.

"Hey, don't say so. She's a nice lady. She saved you." Saira put the bouquets down and made him aware.

"Away, I'm going to sleep." He closed his eyes firmly and pretended to sleep. Saira peevishly went to the table and started the bouquets ignoring his misconduct. Granny stood up and moved to help her.

"What's this flower?" Granny picked up a white flower among other flowers and asked her touching its long green twisted stalk.

"Its daisy granny," She took it from her and put it behind the sunflower and along with hibiscus. "How's it?" She asked granny for appreciation.

"Marvelous," Granny appreciated her with her brows. Saira smiled at the praise of her artwork. Granny was handling her flowers and she was putting them in the bouquets.

VI

When the sun looses its dignity, it sets down to west and when the sky is invaded by the temperate morning, the moon sets to east and the charm of the stars is perished. A month passed and Martha spent this month mostly in the church praying for her husband's safety and the safe arrival. At the dusk, she was returning from the cathedral when she saw a little girl holding baskets full of bouquets of flowers in both her hands. She smiled as she recognized her. The girl also smiled.

"Hey mornin' dear," Martha moved a headscarf down her head greeted her. "Where?" Martha continued. The girl stopped near her.

"Goin' home, No income today," The girl's tone was disappointing but still she was smiling.

"Everything'll be fine." Martha smiled.

"Ok, I'm being late. Granny'll be waitin' for me." Realizing the sunset, she paced faster.

"Goodbye," Martha ambled forward and in no minutes, she reached home. Max was doing his work in the candle light.

"Max, your father'll be arrivin' soon today," Martha looked out of the window with some hope and took a deep breathe. Max was excited after hearing the news. Martha paced to her room. She opened the side drawer of the table and took out a red orange ruby from it. It was glittering. Martha took out a chain from her drawer passed its one side through the hole of a ruby. She strung around her neck. It was looking like a princess necklace. He remembered the time when Oliver gave her when he returned from the journey last time. He gifted this to her and forbade her to show it to any Earthumen or any Sunasian. It was an orange red ruby gleaming strikingly. She was lost in the beauty of the necklace when she heard a knock at her door. It had started raining. The clouds were raging and the lightening was striking the earth repeatedly. The cloud thundered once again and she held her breathe with fear. The door had knocked again. She had forbidden Max to open the door. She quickly removed the necklace from her neck and put at the table. Max was still busy in doing his work. She paced to the window near the exit door.

"Who's there?" She called aloud standing near the window.

"Is lady Martha?" It was a man's voice.

"Yeah, she's me." She removed the curtain and looked out. They were giant looking men wearing uniforms like

Sun's forces. They were dressed in yellow and suns on both of their shoulders. She feared to see them.

"Open the door," The door knocked again. Martha ran to Max and asked him to move into her bedroom. She opened the door terribly. It was raining heavily. She saw the forces in the rain. As she opened the door, the cool breeze came in and she shuddered at once with cold. Her heart was beating fast as she could realize something from their faces. She swallowed.

"Yes, what?" Martha could hardly speak.

"Ms. Martha, Oliver is dead and the King has ordered to arrest you." She could only hear until "dead" and felt lifeless. She was staring the rain unconsciously and she did not know when the forces came and when did they tie her hand with an iron chain and when did they move her away. She was like a lifeless log broken from a spring tree. They moved her into a carriage and she did not know where she was going. The men took their position at the horses and galloped before and after the carriage. It was looking the same carriage in what she sat with Oliver. There were two more men chained with him in the carriage. She could be able to speak.

"Why are you arrested?" She asked.

"Don't know." A man shrugged.

"Perhaps, I've murdered my sister, when she was sitting near me quietly." The man sarcastically replied.

"So, I shall've murdered Oliver." She thought as she was hoping that she would listen something about Oliver. The answer disappointed him and she looked out of the window. She could only see the horses ambling. She had been quiet with eyes opened with fear as she remembered Max. It was raining heavily. She could hear the horses' hooves striking hard the ground and she could hear the lightening, the clouds thundering outside. The carriage was moving fast with the jerks.

CHAPTER 5

☀ The Execution ☀

I

Max remained in the room the whole night. He did not know when the rain stopped, when the clouds thundered when the lightening clashed. He had soon been sleep playing with the necklace in his hand. When he awoke up, he saw the weather outside. It was humid. The sun did not appear. It was foggy but not too much. He felt cold and moved out quickly as he remembered the school. He looked to the big wall clock hung by the wall gifted by Sunasians to his father. It had struck ten am. He was shocked to see the time. Nobody came to awake him up.

"Mama," He ran out shouting. He moved to kitchen, to other rooms and at the end, he moved out. There was sludge gathered out his house due to rain yesterday. He warily moved at it gazing the fields looking for her mother. He could not find her anywhere. He ran hastily backward, he slipped and fell down.

"oops" He exclaimed. No one was here to get him up. He madly went to different houses of the town to know about her mother but he could find her nowhere. He spent two days, weeping, crying, sobbing and running after others alone. At last, he was tired and he sat at heaped clay at end of the street with a protective top of wood. It was again raining today and was going to stop. He observed all the stages of rain. It started slowly, then at its peak, again it slowed down, again it was at its peak and it slowed down and stopped. A curvy wave of seven colors was visible beyond his touch. The children at the end of the street gathered and were overjoyed to see the seven colors. They were laughing, kidding, jumping and flying. The children were flabbergasted to see this spectrum. The rainbow had seven colors. He learnt it in the institute. He was gloomily gazing the joy of the children. None of the child came to console him. He was alone. Men and women had also gathered to view the beauty of the nature. Children were making paper boats and floating them in the water. A competition of first arrival had started. Some people looked to him and asked him to join the joy but he did not give any answer and to some he rebuffed rudely. He wanted to cry once again. He was missing his mother and father. He took out the sapphire from his pocket and looked it. He was feeling the smell of his mother from it. Therefore, he had carefully put it in his pocket. The public was enjoying the damp in the atmosphere and the moist smell of the sand when they heard the horses' hooves. All of they feared and moved back in to their houses. They were the Sun's forces with the drumbeater. He was striking the bloated sticks on to the drum to make people attentive. It was a sign of any announcement as it happened when Sunasians had to announce. He was beating the drum and the people were gathering around him. Mostly were male and old women. Mrs. Wilson also gathered among the crowd. People had worn dresses according to their religions, customs and traditions. The Muslim women had head scarf around their head and a long gown of different styles and different colors, Hindus' women were mostly seen in saris and Christians in long gowns, skirts and shirts. Men of all the religions were in the same dress. Max also moved to the crowd and making way in between the crowd he reached the man.

"Listen Earthumen," The man standing with the drumbeater started as the people had gathered around. The crowd was encircled by the armed forces. "There is a special announcement." The drumbeater continued. "There is capital punishment of the three Earthumen in this evening for the crimes committed. One murdered his sister, Hamid Hamid, the other killed the two Sunasians, Raja Ram Singh and the third is Martha Oliver Beck hem as she killed her husband." The words fell like a heavy stone at his head. The crowd was astounded for these baseless blames at the innocent people. They were quiet. There were no smiles and no tears. They were normal but Max was extremely tensed. "Those who do such sins have no other sentence but only death." The drumbeater concluded his announcement. The Sun's forces pulled the reins of the horses along with the drumbeater and ambled to their places. The crowd dispersed conversating the announcement. Nobody could believe that it would have been happened. All were cursing the Sunasians. Max like the one, a toddling child staggered to the heap. He repressed his lips, as he had not eaten for two days. He was finding her mother and she was prisoner and was going to die tomorrow, his father had already died. He had never thought that his family would separate so unruly. People were entering into the streets feeling pity at him. As the day welcomed dusk, he stood up and moved to his house. The weather was cool. The night overcame the sky as he reached home. He entered the house and moved into the quilt.

"My mother can't do this. My father is dead, what is dead? What is death?" He was asking himself. He was a child of ten years for asking these questions. The warmth of the quilt could not comfort him. Someone knocked the door and it opened it self. She was Mrs. Wilson.

"Max," She called aloud. Max moved down and ran out. In emotions, he hugged her.

"Stop baby, don't cry," Mrs. Wilson consoled her.

"Come on; let's go to meet your mother." Mrs. Wilson consoled the dejected boy. She held her hand and moved out of the house. Pacing, they reached the place of execution. It was crowded. There were two partitions. Sunasians had been dressed with great pomp and show. Women had jeweled from head to toe. On the other side were Earthumen. They were disappointed. In between them had been the gallows. The place, where all desires were ended, heads were cut off and the people were dismounted. Max was staring the gallows. A fire had been kindled near the gallows. Near which three people were standing.

"Mama," Max mumbled as she had speculated her mother, but her face had been covered by black veil and her long hair were fallen at her back. The faces of the other two men were also covered by black cloth. Sunasians were throwing tin packs, dirty covers and rotten eggs. Earthumen were moving back to save and some got the spots and small cuts. King had not arrived yet. Sunasians forces were standing in between the two nations. As they saw a carriage jolting, the Sun's forces made the way. They departed apart and left an outsized gap in between them. King's carriage stopped under the protection of armed force. The carriage was lined with crushed jewels of different colors. The door was decorated with the red flowers and four brown Arabian horses were hauling it. Two men stayed outside, one was controlling the carriage. King had stayed inside with his queen. As the carriage stopped, one of the men moved down and opened the door. Sunasians hooted and raised slogans to see their king. The King, with proud and arrogance moved his steps down elegantly and the queen followed her with a wicked smile. She was in black dress and the same cat was wagging its tail in her arms. Sunasians' excitement was having no end. They threw the flowers at them. The two to more carriages followed and stopped after it. As the queen and the king had reached the stage and had taken their golden large chairs, the door of the next carriage opened. Prime minister holding hand of his wife moved smilingly, greeting the public moved to stage and took seat with the King and his wife sat with queen on the other sight after bowing. The last carriage door opened and a big black man with a thick heavy sword in his hand ambled down the carriage. For some moments, there were muffled cries from the Earthumen and the Sunasians were quiet. The man crossing the way had reached the stage but he went to the gallows in front of the stage. Max was scared to see the big black man. He imagined the man cutting the head of her mother. He was too much frightened. He started crying. No one looked to her as Mrs. Wilson was busy in talking to the lady. The crowd hooted again as they came to know that this man is not for them. The drumbeater who came out from the carriage with the black man moved in front of the gallows. He turned his face to the public and beat the drum. The crowd was quiet, as they knew that there was an announcement. King stood up.

"My people, Sunasians, I am so sorry that I trusted an Earthumen. That woman, whose husband ran away with the diamonds and then she killed her to get them. I have sentenced her to death. I am thankful to Adrastus, who came back safely with the sapphires. He is not here, as he is hurt stabbed by Oliver." The king cursed Oliver. "My men are only Sunasians and only Sunasians." King announced. "The other two men they killed their own men." During the address, the King did not bother to look to Earthumen. Mrs. Wilson was frustrated and her face had been red with fury.

"Let the execution begin," King ordered and moved back to his chair. The queen smiled wickedly and the cat purred. Prime minister, who had stood up along with the King, sat after the King had taken his seat. The man was brought to the gallows. His legs trembled as he fixed them at the stage. His face was covered by black cloth.

"Feared?" One of the men who brought him to the gallows sarcastically whispered.

"Feared of what?" The man courageously asked.

"Death." The man answered sarcastically. Humid chuckled. The man could not see him but he can hear him.

"What death, when I'll be still alive in the hearts of my people, and you are dead, you were dead and you will be dead." The man grounded his teeth in anger. The other man blew him hard at his neck and he was fallen on the wooden frame. Therefore, he was brought to the destination. The black men lifted up the sword, cut his head off and in no minutes, he had crossed the border to other world. Sunasians shouted with excitement as the sinner was punished. Earthumen fell into tears.

"May, his soul rest in peace." Mrs. Wilson with tears prayed. The other boy was brought to the gallows.

"He's my son, he's not done it," One of the women shouted ran to the king but hit by the railings. She was shouting and crying, but none did hear. People were trying to move her back as her hands had bled. "Please, king, have mercy on us," She pleaded. The man passed through the same process. The head was cut off and the mother was fallen down. She was faint. Now was Martha's turn. Max seemed to lost his breathe.

"Mother," She called aloud but no one could hear his voice. Martha was taken to the gallows and she was moving like a lifeless log. She did not look back. Her face was covered. Mrs. Wilson burst into tears and she put her hand at his eyes. Max was sobbing. Her head was cut off and the three heads were brought to the king. In an excitement of Sunasians, Earthumen turned disappointedly to their homes wiping off their tears. Mrs. Wilson lifted Max up and did not let him to look back. Margaret was moving after Mrs. Wilson. The king was busy in engaging with Sunasians. Drinks were distributed and after much show, the king moved back to his carriage. The horses neighed and dragged their respective carriages.

All the three had met their destinations of immorality. Martha left the child alone in this world and the boys left their families alone to get the chance to meet in the other world.

II

Six days, the ceremonies of the execution lasted. The slaughter place remained with crowd. Gaiety at its peak was celebrated on the behalf of the Sunasians. The king had strictly ordered not to provide Max, the shelter. A rebellion's son was found seated on the heap under the shade of wooden shutter. Its roof had splinters at different parts. The children daily came and played but he did never wish to enjoy with them. In some days he moved to the small stream at end of the town and spent his times viewing the waves whirling and the water flowing. He had never thought that his family would be partitioned so unruly. Sitting under the shade of yellow flowers near the stream, he was feeling the most deserted person in the world. He was looking frail and his face was pale. He was thinking to move away from this doom but where to go. He had no transport and neither did he know any way. He was told that his parents would never come back. There will be no mother any more to give him the food or father to sow with him and who will tell him the stories of the past days. He was having little hope that may be the rule of Omnipotent is changed and her mother can have another few years with him.

"Your mother will now act as another mother of any other baby in any other place or in any other world." Bimla told her. "She is alive and she may be that flower." Bimla told her after having a chat with her. Max plucked that red rose bud and put it in his pocket hoping for her mother. He daily took out the flower from his pocket and put it at the heap in front of him.

He was talking to the flower and the passers by were thinking him as a mad boy after the death of his parents. Daily he talked to the flower and told it the stories of his whole day and one day when he awoke up from the sleep he took out the flower and saw its petals falling down. As the petal was falling down so was his heart plummeting. His eyes opened with fear. The color of the rose had changed. It darkened and was no more charming. He rushed to Bimla to ask about the secret of the flower.

"Oh, your mother is becoming old." Bimla told him gloomily standing in the door of her house. Max disappointedly took the flower from her, put the petal and the flower in his pocket and moved away. Bimla sadly closed the door looking him. The next day, Max took hold of her when she was going to her aunt with a basket of honey and butter. The basket was covered with a checkered cloth. Max sadly showed her all the faded petals. Bimla sadly glanced them.

"Nature has its own rule Max. Your mother is again dead. Your mother was a good woman and she will have seven good lives. Bhagwan would have made him something else. She can be that green leaf." She pointed to a leaf at the log. Max left her, climbed the tree and Bimla moved forward. He plucked the small leaf and put it in his pocket of the trouser. The day passed and the leaf faded soon. He wept too much as her mother had again left him. He met Bimla again. This time he pointed to a butterfly waving its wings. Max moved to grab but waving its wings it flew. He cried again sharing his sorrow with the skies who had taken his mother. He was lamenting. Going on a way with the baskets of flower bouquets, he saw Saira. She was going alone. Max rushed to her and told her the whole story.

"O Max," Saira started. "No body can go against the rule of Allah. He who gives the life can take the life back. I am sorry for you, but listen, once a good soul move to the skies, it never comes back. May Allah rest her soul in peace?" Max cried and Saira hugged him. "Calm down." Max was crying when he had cried a lot, Saira looked to him.

"Max, when Allah filches our loved ones, he devotes us with some good relations and the memories of our loved ones never die." Saira was just a baby like Max but she was consoling him like an old woman. Both of they were looking like innocent angels. The basket of flowers was placed on the ground in the mid of both of them.

"Yeah, your mother and father are dead. They will never come back but their souls will remain with you forever and you will always have them protecting you." Saira looked at his appearance. He had not changed the clothes since he fell into the sludge. He was looking too coarse. "You are looking so ghastly." Saira made a bad face. "For how many days have you not taken bath?" Saira continued.

"I don't know." Max voice was heavy due to weeping.

"Hey, look stand up. Change your clothes. I'm to sell the flowers and I want to see you clean in the evening." Saira picked her basket and moved. Max took his way to his house. He was looking all around him to feel the soul of her mother. Patrolling through the town and crossing the pasturelands in the way he had reached his fields. The house door was closed, as he had not returned since the execution. He took bath and changed his clothes. In the evening, he was to meet Saira. He went to the stream waiting for the evening. He sat near the pond. The yellow flowers were flourishing their beauty and touching his cheeks. He stared in to the ponds. He felt his mother smiling and then his father staring him with aspiration and then he felt Saira. Something allured in his heart. He put his feet in the pond folding his trousers until knees. He felt something waving in the pond. He could not understand what that was, but gradually his eyes were able to be aware of something. He looked and was frightened. A big black vulture was flying over his head. It was staring him. Its red eyes were so furious that he panicked. It was coming near him and was about to pounce. He moved some steps back, picked up a pebble and hit it. The vulture made a dreadful scream. Max hit three more pebbles one after the other abruptly. It was screaming dreadfully that Max put his hands at his ears. It had gone far and was soon out of sight. Max feared and took his steps back.

He was sitting at the heap. He ate the coconuts and almonds Mrs. Wilson brought for her. It was his first full appetite since that time. He took the lunch to his full. The children were playing in front of him but he was objective. The day was embracing dusk but the time was looking hard to pass. He was to show Saira his change and he wished to share his day with her. The children playing moved back into their houses and he remained alone sitting under the cracked floor and at the heap. He was disappointing as the velvety night was falling. He went out of his place and looked far in to the air and all he could see the dark, but hoping for her to come. He did not know when the doze had made the way through his feet into his eyes.

The sun had at its peak. The rays of the sun slapped his face and the voices of giggling, chuckling and laughing bashed his ears. The ray of sun knocked his eyes and he opened his. He faced the floor lying down and saw to his right. Children were playing. He moved him up and wiped dust all around his head and clothes. Mrs. Wilson was standing with a rolled paper in her hand.

"Max," Mrs. Wilson called her. "Take your breakfast." Mrs. Wilson put it in his hand when he was lying. "I'll be back soon, Max, I'm to dress Bill up." Mrs. Wilson informed him and moved hurriedly. He wearily awoke up and walked to the pond at the end of the town. He put the rolled paper in his pocket and washed his face and mouth by the water of the pond. It was a clear pond what allured everyone. It was the sink of Max. Max sat near the pond and took out the rolled paper. He unrolled it and took a mouthful of vegetable roll.

"Yummy" He exclaimed and zealously ate it. After finishing it, he corrugated the paper in his hand and threw it taking aim of nothing. It fell nearby him. He looked to the sky and could see no vulture. He went to the children playing and for the first time he was keenly observing them playing. They were playing the game of king and queen. One was king and the other was queen. One was prime minister and they were repeating the scene of execution. It remembered his mother. It made him gloomy and tears fell down his cheeks. He missed Saira awfully. She did not come to meet her the last evening. It made him cry. He was wiping his tears but they were falling when some one hugged him.

"Don't cry dear," Mrs. Wilson consoled him who had been back after finishing her work. "I'm with you dear." Mrs.

Wilson rubbed his tears. "My, dear, look at the children," She pointed to the mob of tiny mischievous monsters. Max looked to the mob. "Why don't you play with them?" Mrs. Wilson encouraged him.

"They won't lemme." Max answered and sobbed.

"Why?" Mrs. Wilson astounded at the children's disobedience.

"Because, it's honorary to've parents and I ... err ... err've none." Max sobbed.

Mrs. Wilson's heart crushed with emotions. She felt like something heavy had trampled her heart. She stood straight and moved to the bubbly children. They were running after one another like pulling the reins of horses and jumping like horses. She sat under a spring tree whose leaves had dried and the branches were drooped. She walked under the tree and the leaves trampled and crunched under hard soles of her shoes.

"You, Abdullah come 'ere." He called him moving his index finger that was playing the role of King at the branch of the tree and at the other side of the tree, at other log Bimla was sitting as queen. Two more children as prime minister and his wife were sitting at the other log. Abdullah who was smiling moved down and ran to Mrs. Wilson.

"Yes," he ran to Mrs. Wilson with an impish smile. He was breathing fast.

"Me think, you need one more actor to end your play." Mrs. Wilson suggested him.

"No, I don't think." Abdullah thoughtfully looked back to his friends with a frown who were waiting for him to come back. "As such, we don't need, but if anyone wants to come than he is welcomed." Abdullah continued like a wise man. Mrs. Wilson smiled at his young expressions at the innocence of his childhood.

"Ok, then," Mrs. Wilson pointed to the cabin behind him at some distance. Abdullah looked back and saw Max wiping his tears. "Hey, Max, come 'ere," Mrs. Wilson called aloud. Max who was staring the squirrel eating nearby him ogled and followed the voice. "Come 'ere," She called aloud for one more time. Abdullah was annoyed at the suggestion.

"Don't resent." Mrs. Wilson scolded him observing his bored stiff expressions.

"But..."

"Sh..." Abdullah wanted to say something but Mrs. Wilson quietened him putting her finger at her lips as she saw Max feebly moving to them. "Haven't your Allah promised to console the dejected ones?" Mrs. Wilson made him think. Abdullah put his head down. "'Why have you forgotten the favor, Martha did with you?" Mrs. Wilson again rebuked him.

"Shake hands." Mrs. Wilson ordered and both of they made them to shake hands. Abdullah did not like Max since the time Max's father got job in the regime of Sunasians and Max did not like him since the time he snatched his paper.

"Come on, let's play with us." Abdullah said and ran to the crowd. He climbed the branch of the tree in no minutes and Max was moving slowly to them.

"Hey Max, how good to see you?" Mary excitedly moved to him and held his elbow.

"Hi, Max," he was Frank. Max smiled slightly in response. All the children climbing the trees moved down. Everyone said Hi to him as his or her leader had accepted him.

"No more theatre game," Bimla announced, as she knew it was not good with Max.

"We shall play hide and seek," One of the chubby cute girls suggested and all of they said yes and they ran to hide as it was Shiplap's turn.

"You need not to hide." Mary with a smile eloquently said him.

"Why?" Max felt strange.

"Because you've already been hidden," Mary told her moving along with her and repressed her smile.

"Hey, haven't you hidden? I'm coming." Shiplap's irritating voice compelled Mary to find her hiding place. She had counted ten but after seeing them unhidden, she had to recount. Max also moved to any hidden place. He found the place at the back of the thick bush to be hidden from the seeker. It had been two hours behind the bush but no one came to see him. One of the boys passed briskly near him. Max smiled to see his playmate but he disregarded and remained his stern expressions.

"What's happening? Why isn't any one coming to see me? Why I'm hidden here?" The questions were bombarding his brain. The night fell but no one came to find him. It seemed as if they had forgotten him. His shoulders shuddered with cold he moved up from there and reached the playground. There was no existence there. The night was whispering silently. The silence was shouting. He looked to his desolated cabin with no windows and doors. There he was spending the miserable hours of his life. He rubbed his hand due to cold.

"That was what Mary talking about," He thought. "What was I hiding for?" He was infuriated at his foolishness.

He tried to stop his tears but when it hurt its throat and he felt suffocated by his snuffle, he cried like a baby but only sky snoop his cries. He paced slowly to the green grass and put his head in between his knees.

"I'm a vulgar idea, a useless thought. Why I'm alive?" Max was enquiring his soul. He was deeply lost in his gloominess and was unaware of it that a big black vulture was staring him with his red eyes. He felt as if the beauty of the garden was mocking at his stupidity. He heard the flowers tossing and laughing, heard the trees chortling at his loneliness, the buds giggling and the silence chuckling. He pressed his ears hard so he could not hear his fun. A big black vulture was revolving at his head.

CHAPTER 6

☞ Prothoplastus Step ☜

I

Black shades had covered the sky. Moonlight had faded. Staring their prey black shades sprinkled slowly and moved to west leaving Max alone again. There were many of the vultures revolving his head but he was unaware. He had closed his eyes. He did not move up if he had heard a dreadful scream. He lifted his head to know the way from where the dreadful scream came. He heard another sound of the fluttering of wings. He shivered with fear to see the big black vulture with red eyes. He was paler and he swallowed hardly. His breathe was held for some seconds. He stepped back a little staring the vulture. The vulture shrieked staring him Max felt his heart was compressed and the blood had dripped out of his body. He took more steps backward. As Max was moving back, so the vulture was coming down to her. It came so near that, it looked him into the eyes and its beak was at distance of two inches from his slender nose. Max felt heat around his neck. Max was about to fall back but he fixed his knees onto the ground to save him from falling. He was panting. The black vulture swiftly fluttered its wings to him but at a distance of one inch, it screamed painfully depicting fear in its eyes and flew backward. As the vulture vanished beyond the bushes, he implausibly stood up and stared the long bushes looking like the posture of a giant. At that time Max realized his held breathe and he took a deep breathe. He could remember it was the same vulture that he had hurt near the pond. He closed his eyes for some moments and opened them abruptly when he heard screams like witches and sluts. He could not believe when he saw thousands of vultures were making his course to him. They were shrieking angrily. Max impulsively stood up and ran fast with a scream. Max was running fast and fast and the vultures were chasing him fast and fast. Once Max dared to look back and he panicked to see thousands of vultures ambushing him. He increased his speed.

"No, help, no," Max was shouting and the vultures were furious. They were shrieking dreadfully. Now, he did not want to look back for one more time. He did not know the way he was following. In fact, he was going to the deserted graveyard where the people had left burying their dead ones. The heat irritated him around his neck. He touched his neck and felt chain glowing and warm like a coal. He ambled opening a small white gate with wooden bars. Touching his chain he hit by a big stone obtruded in the way and fell few miles away. As he stood up, he felt a nightmare. He was fainting to see the panorama. His eyes were closing. A long man was standing with a dry bamboo turned at the top in his hands with big nails. He was in cloak and his whole body was covered. Only a dreadful fleshy hand with the skeletal fingers and long one inch twisted nails, and his long blue teeth with black gums he could see. Both of his jaws were sternly joined together like fixed into one another. Max was to vomit at the sight of his teeth. He saw frightful chortles at his left. The man laughing had taken his seat at a cement grave and his followers were standing around him all covered with cloaks. All the vultures outraged and were fluttering anxiously. The dreadful man stood up and scowled the restless vultures.

"I do not like fracas, you do know." Frightful voice knocked his ears. The man spoke looking to the vultures going to pounce Max. His heart trembled at the frightening sound. He could not understand what he was speaking but the voice was awful. His heart was beating the ribs. "He is frail," The man touched his arm with his long grey bone made stick.

"Oh poor, you can get only a fraction of it. The man sarcastically felt pity at Max. All the vultures screamed awfully. He was outraged and he took out his bony long fingers out of his cloak and faced his long slim palm to the fussing vultures. A big maroon light emerged from his horrible palm and hit the vulture close to him. The vulture screamed and fell down with a cutting log and the maroon fluid was dripping it. All the vultures kept quiet with fear immediately witnessing the death of one. "How can you deny your master? The great master of hundred years, He proudly announced lifting his hands up to his chest and laughed. Max could only understand the horrible laughter. All vultures were fiercely staring him. He tried to touch the boy derisively moving his right foot to his left arm but with a jerk, he fell back and struck badly the cement board of the grave. The cloak at his face was removed and hood was fallen at his shoulder. He was unmasked and his terrible face was exposed. There were no eyes instead the two hollow pits and thick steady pupils inside them. There was no flesh at his face instead were the bones joined together to make a skeletal face and the blood was clotted at the bottom of the jaws. He was so horrible that the man passing by the beautiful stream on his horse galloping uniformly holding firmly the reins of the horse. He pulled the reins of the horse and horse neighed in the moon shinning in front of him at a mount. He saw the fearful face. The horse neighed again with fear. Max was lying down with fear and had not the courage to look up. The ground was hearing his heartbeat. The man hardly controlled his horse what had been looking mad with fear. Winston stood up swiftly, his followers were gazing him fiercely. Winston picked his hands up to the sky.

"Flee back, you filths. He dreadfully shouted and flew in to the skies. The vultures and his followers were also running after him. The man dismounted abruptly to save the little child. He was young and a muscular man of twenty-eight years. A scabbard had hung by his clothes. He was looking warrior as if returned from a big battle. He hurried to the boy and hunkered down near him. He seized his face in his hands.

"No, boy you are to live. Open your eyes." He had leaned at him. He picked up the boy's face in his hands and moved back to the horse.

II

Bellatrix was a very beautiful child sitting in the bed holding a book lying in the bed with a green red blanket at her. She was holding her shinning blonde curly lock in her hand and curling it. There were exemplary collectives in her room. There was a desk at one side of the bed; at the desk was a topless lantern whose flame was flickering in a glass-case. She yawned and turned over the page. Her room door knocked. She weirdly looked the door. He was his brother having a glass of milk in his hand with mischievous expressions. He moved to her. Her eyes widened and with a scream of "no" she put on the blanket and hid her face inside it.

"It can't save you." Her brother called roguishly with a mischievous smile.

"Go away, just go away," She shouted in the blanket.

"No," He answered her sister shouting.

"Listen, my dear sister," He cunningly started sweetly. "Milk makes our bones strong." The boy continued. He turned his muscles but she had covered her face.

"Get up," He shouted and pulled the blanket and Bellatrix put on the blanket again. "It is very beneficial." He again subtly started twinkling his eyes. "Milk will make us energetic because it has vitamin A in it."

"Stop, your didactic lecture," She shouted in the blanket. "Go away," She shouted holding the blanket tightly.

"Hey, it is some kind of an earthquake," Clarke horrified her waving the delicate wood of the bed. Bellatrix after realizing her bed moving impulsively moved out of the bed and grounded her teeth in anger when he saw her brother moving the bed. He slapped at his back and he moved out of the under the bed.

"Oh you…" Before completing his words, a woman entered the room with red face.

"What's up here?" The woman gnashed her teeth. "There guests outside." She rebuked them and swiftly moved outside.

"But mom she is not taking," He said helplessly and the girl ridiculed.

"You, idiot," He mistreated her and dropped milk at her face. Some milk got into her mouth.

"You..." The girl shouted in fury and hurried to the washroom. The boy was laughing. She sprinkled water at her face and cleaned it with a cloth hung at the wall.

"Hey, I was to inform you about one more thing..." The boy came after her near the washroom.

"Move out, Clarke, You have informed anything." She shouted with rage. "Idiot, you are a stupid." The girl came out rubbing his face with the piece of cloth.

"Stop this rubbish," The boy seriously spoke and then showed his teeth foolishly. "Mrs. Burney has come to meet you." He giggled. "She wants to meet you but mother is not letting her to meet you." Bellatrix stopped rubbing her face and the news shocked her.

"Why?" She frowned at him.

"Let us listen to them," Clarke whispered and gave a playful suggestion.

"Let us go," Bellatrix, answered and both of they moved out of the room.

"What are you talking about? Why are you insisting?" Ashley looked irritated. "I have told you earlier. She is sick. She is sleeping."

"I am not deaf Ashley, I have heard her now." The woman replied normally. "You must understand, Ashley, Tomorrow I am moving back to Agra. It is important for me to meet her. I want to finish this work." Mrs. Burney tried to convince her. "It was my late husband's wish." She put her hand at her lips and stopped her tears in her eyes.

"What can I do know when she has been slept?" Ashley made another excuse.

"Ok, then I shall wait for her till it comes morning." She answered sternly.

"Idiot," She cussed her disdainfully. "It is not fair." She kept quiet for some moments. "Ok, then wait here, if you can." She hatefully turned but heard a scream.

"Hello, Mrs. Burney," Mrs. Burney looked and was glad to see the attractive little girl whose front locks were wet and water was dripping down her face. Ashley was stunned.

"Oh, My dear," Mrs. Burney moved to her and hugged her. "I want some words with you." Mrs. Burney asked her.

"With me?" Bellatrix confirmed and looked to her mother.

"Up to you," Ashley moodily shrugged his shoulders. She stared Mrs. Burney scornfully and moved from there. Mrs. Burney disregarded and smiled to see Bellatrix.

"Perhaps we should sit here." Mrs. Burney held her hand and moved her to the soft velvety settee and both of they were embedded in it.

There, when Ashley moved, she went into the room.

"You stupid, you told her," Ashley was outraged in low pitch. She leaned at little chubby boy.

"W... err what?" He was confused in trouble and he cried.

"Be low, you idiot," Ashley rebuked him. He was about to cry.

"Now, go and listen to what does she say?" Ashley gnashed her teeth and pushed him out to the common room.

In the common room both of, they sat in a bi-seated futon. She had taken her hand in her where she saw sun sign.

"Sweet Bellatrix," Mrs. Burney lovingly started. "Have you not ever thought about it?" Mrs. Burney looked to the sun sign.

"What?" Bellatrix was confused and she stared into her face.

"Do you not feel it a little faint?" Mrs. Burney put her hand with her. Bellatrix looked to the hands. Hers was a little faded and Mrs. Burney's was shinning bright and was hotter than her. Bellatrix frowned.

"Yeah..., It... is." She was lost in thought. "Because I am younger," She found the answer and boldly replied with a smile. Mrs. Burney laughed lively at her innocence and touched her chin lovingly.

"My dear, you will get it soon, but still I am to tell you something." Mrs. Burney faced front. A mirror was hanging.

"My dear," Mrs. Burney started after some moments.

"My husband died some years ago. He was murdered leaving a son in my lap and a wish for you. I married an Earthumen. He belonged to Hindu religion. My brothers killed him for he was an Earthumen. Few years later, I lost my son." She stopped and gulped. Mrs. Burney stared into her eyes. "Eighteen years have been passed." Mrs. Burney was doomed. "I spent eighteen years alone. I did not marry any Sunasian." She faced her right and wiped her tears. "Perhaps, I should not beat about the bush." She held her purse and searched something in it.

"I fancy your purse." Bellatrix admired her bag with pearls around it.

"I know you like such garbage," Mrs. Burney smiled.

"Garbage," Bellatrix stunned and frowned. "My choice cannot be garbage." Bellatrix said.

"Thanks dear, this is your love," Mrs. Burney was finding something in the bag. Bellatrix was looking her stern expressions. Gaiety covered her face and her eyes exposed it. She took a red velvety box with yellow golden ribbons tied around it.

"What is it?" Bellatrix asked her gazing the six inches box.

"It is..." They heard a scream before Mrs. Burney would complete. Both of they looked back quickly. Bellatrix rushed to back of the settee.

"It bit me, it bit me," Clarke was shouting as he saw Bellatrix. Mrs. Burney looked Clarke's foot where a small insect had bit him.

"It bit you; it did well, what were you doing here?" Mrs. Burney asked her.

"I did not, I did not, she was mom," She was answering abruptly. "She had sent me to..."He got a slap at his head.

"You foolish," Ashley scolded him and he cried. Ashley pushed him to the room. Mrs. Burney was silently witnessing the fuss and Bellatrix was confused.

"I am giving you five minutes. Finish with her or get out." Mrs. Abrahamus ordered and insulted her. He pushed Clarke who was sobbing. When they had gone, Bellatrix moved back to Mrs. Burney and sat close to her.

"I am sorry Mrs. Burney for my mother, she just speaks like that," Bellatrix looked embarrassed.

"Do not say so. I know her better than you do. She is penurious like her grand ones. Be perfunctory." She said and handed her the red box. "Take it. Trust it. Tackle it. Don't show it to your mother ever." She advised her and took her bag at her shoulder. "Good bye now. My five minutes are complete." Mrs. Burney smiled and moved to the exit door. She stared the red box and returned to her room. Looking the empty room, she got the chance of opening the box. She unlocked the iron padlock and lifted its upper part. There was white paper and a ring placed at its either side. It confused her. She took the letter and unfolded it. It stated;

My sweet Bellatrix, (Bellatrix)

When my eyes are closed, I see your innocent hand touching my eyes. When they are open, I feel you smiling near me and innocent giggles making me anxious to have you in my arms. When you feel pain, I feel the dual. I miss you dear and I will miss you. I wished to name you Bellatrix but your father named you according to his customs.

Take care and beware of your mother. She is not your real mother.

My daughter, do not loose fate. Do not trust your near ones. Read the other papers when you will cross yours sixteen.

From your mother

Rose Beck hem

"Mother" She mumbled. "Then who was this Ashley?" She thought perplexed. The only point he could get was that she had stepmother or a she was a foster daughter. She was confused when the door opened and saw bloated eyes of her brother. He was wiping his tears. She could not bear and she quickly hugged him. She let him sleep in her bed and lovingly caressed his hair. The letter was still in her mind. She was awfully missing her mother. She closed her eyes and the she again witnessed the letter in her imaginations. As she finished letter she heard something struck by the window. Her heart pounced and she jumped up to the window. Removing the curtain, she saw a vulture staring him furiously. Fearfully she covered the window abruptly and immediately hurried to her bed to save from the vulture. She put her leg on the bed but stopped. A whisper echoed in the room and knocked her ears.

"*Prothoplastus Step*"

"*Prothoplastus Steps*" She mumbled to look back but there was no one.

III

Silvery moon light piercing through the window was nourishing Abdullah's face. Saira was sleeping with her grand mother. His black hair were fluttering with cool breeze coming from outside. There was peace and calmness in the whole atmosphere when he heard something hit by the window. The ice was broken. Everyone had slept deeply. The weather had changed into the thundering clouds and light raining and the light raining was turning to heavy rainfall. The room door opened with a jerk and it hit the back wall. Abdullah opened his eyes with the bang. He looked to the door and saw a horrible posture. There was a black shade with the bleeding teeth visible. His eyes were not visible but he felt the shade was staring him. His heartbeat was fading. It was raining heavily in the courtyard.

"Boy, come out," Abdullah heard a terrible voice. The voice was dreadful like a single manly voice accompanied by dozens of shrieks of the witches. "If you want to see your family unscathed," He disliked the unpleasant voice. "It's radical otherwise." The man pointed his long bamboo stick to his grandmother. Abdullah frighteningly stood up to the man.

"No," Abdullah shouted.

"For what No, come out," Winston roared and turned to go out. Abdullah wore his shoes and reached the door. He was about to faint to see the large number of the same devils. In the meanwhile, a large number of the vultures reached him and started revolving around him. His pupils were rotating with the rotation of the vultures.

"Flee back, you filths". Winston raged pointing his finger to the vulture. The same dark light appeared and hit one vulture. It fell like a broken log in the steps of Abdullah. All the vultures feared and stared him.

"You can get only a fraction of him." He said and roared into laughter. It was so dreadful and noisy that Abdullah put his hands at his ears.

"You have rancor." He stepped a little closer to Abdullah. Abdullah opened his eyes and stepped back.

"W... err what ...err... do you mean?" Abdullah stammered.

"Nothing, only that I shall kill you, my special guests will eat your meat as they had eaten ours and you will be our comrade later." He clumsily roared in to laughter. Abdullah swallowed hardly. It was raining heavily. Abdullah had wet. The devil was pacing to Abdullah. The distance of one foot left. The devil pointed his bamboo to Abdullah; the door opened with a bang along with the horses hooves. Abdullah who was about to faint swiftly looked to the door. Winston was infuriated at the interruption. All the devils headed to the bang and the vultures shrieked. The rain had stopped. Light flashed exposing the horse with a man in the door.

Both of they wrathfully saw one another. Winston roared into laughter.

"Come on dear Ali Hamza, My guests had just been waiting for you." Winston sarcastically announced and the vultures excitedly screeched.

"So, you have taken your first step on earth. Ali growled disregarding his arrogance."

Winston sternly answered.

"What do you think; killing two boys can make you win. Ali Hamza growled furiously. Vultures screeched gazing the muscular man covetously and the saliva leaked down their beaks. You can never win until the last blood is shed, the last soul is slaughtered and you know the souls can never be slaughtered. Ali Hamza stopped.

"*Ali* Hamza, my guests are anxious. Winston told ignoring his emotional nationalism."

"Lets play a game, I will treat mine, and let treat theirs. Winston mocked and pointed the vultures to Ali Hamza. The vultures assaulted Ali Hamza leaving Abdullah with their horrible shrieks. He briskly took out his sword.

(Touch him, if you can). Ali Hamza roared.

The vultures had reached him and circled around him. The cloud raged, Winston laughed dreadfully and vultures were shrieking. Abdullah closed his ears and shut his eyes. The vultures surrounded him and Hamza waved his sword in the air slaughtering many of them. He was trying his best defense. A vulture bit his neck. He moved his sword back but the vulture was enjoying the piece of flesh at a distance from him. Abdullah dared to open his eyes. The light flashed illuminating the vultures biting and Hama was cutting them as he got the chance. Some of they sprinkled with fear and some bit horse's legs. The horse fell down with Ali Hamza, but he swiftly stood up to compete the demons. Hamid picked up the piece of log. Winston was heading to Ali Hamza. Abdullah aimed the vultures and three more fell down. The vultures assumed it a rearward attack and flew into the skies with fear. The other piece of log was in Abdullah's hands. He was panting. Ali Hamza had wounded head to toe. He couldn't resist and fell down at his horse and the blood was dripping from each part of the body. Winston stared him and his little monsters. He returned to Abdullah after the view.

"One is gone, let us see you the brave one, the boatel, and mine boatel". Winston was infuriated at the death of his comrades. As he headed to Abdullah, he threw the branch of tree to him. It hit him at the head. The hood fell down and his skull fell hanging his back. The sight was horrifying. It seemed the skeleton of any dead one. Soon, he heard a terrific shriek and then he heard the cries of witches and sluts. The skeleton in the cloak moved upward slowly and into the skies they vanished. Abdullah took his held breathe and looked to the man lying on the floor. He rushed to him, checked his pulse and heart beat. He was breathing slightly. He looked into his eyes, they were closing and opening with pain and the pupils were still. Abdullah ran out. IN no minutes he came with Dr. Shahab and in the way he had told him the whole story. Doctor Shahab was considering it a nightmare in the way but he had to believe looking at the prints on the ground and the wounded man with the wounded horse. Doctor Shahab checked his heart beat and pulse which he could not hear. He checked the cuts and injuries in the light of lantern Abdullah had brought. They were very deep into the skin and the flesh was oozing out. The blood was contently flowing out. Dr. Shahabad touched the hand, it was ice cold. He looked to the brave tiger eyes what was still and then he looked to Abdullah.

"Sorry son," Dr. Shahab closed the eyes of the man. Abdullah put his head at the chest of the man and cried. Dr. Shahab patted his back.

Soon they were moving to the graveyard with dead body at the shoulder of Shahab and Abdullah was holding light in his right hand. He was wiping his tears.

"Be brave boy," Dr. Shahab consoled him. He was sobbing. "Don't tell this to anyone. This should be a secret and don't tell these secrets to anyone. You are really the brave boy." The grave yard had come. They dug the grave and put the man inside it and prayed.

"The men like you are never dead." Dr. Shahab murmured. The night was falling down. The sky had been clear. In the mosques azan could be heard. People had got up for prayers.

"Let's pray son," Abdullah had wept a lot and was sobbing. Dr. Shahabad stitched off the lamp. Abdullah held it and they moved out. They saw the horse dead and wounded outside the grave yard. The flies were sitting at the eyes and into the nostrils. Abdullah looked it and Shahab glance it. He sobbed withe eyes swimming into tears.

CHAPTER 7

⧉ Hexane to Octane ⧉

I

The sun was smiling today. People were basking in the sun. At the end of the town was a thick forest. Near the thick forest was a grey-brown pavilion. There were five people sitting in a circle taking their lunch. There was meat in one try, stew in the other and fish in one tray. They were eating their respective meals, as there was silence among them except the birds chirping, the crows crowing and the cuckoo, manna singing. Sometimes they could hear rustling, and the animals grazing.

"It's really considerin'", Tom the youngest one of twenty-eight years broke the ice and took a little piece of pig meat in his mouth.

"What?" Hamid his age-fellow asked busy in his eating.

"I'm talking about Alberic and the technology ball." Tom replied taking another bite.

"Not your head-ache at this time of delicious lunch," Arjun took a piece of fish. Everyone was quiet for some time.

"It's the head-ache of every one." Mr. Peter the older one of forty-three years sternly gazed Arjun. Arjun was embarrassed at his liveliness.

"The ball is worthless without Alberic as he knows his use." Abdullah looked to Mr. Peter and Mr. Raza.

"But the question is where Alberic is?" Tom looked to Mr. Peter and Mr. Raza for the perfect answer.

"Alberic and the ball are the later problems." Mr. Raza replied cleaning his hands with a bandanna and put it near the tray. He had an Islamic beard. "First of all we're to find any safe place for our survival, so that we could live and we could start our campaigns." Mr. Raza continued with dignity. "It has been heard that the ball is in the confines of mortality and Alberic lives at any other secret place." Mr. Raza looked Mr. Peter. Tom was lost in the loving personality of Mr. Raza and Hamid was lost in the accent of the words.

"Peter, I'm to say prayers and then I'll take some rest." Mr. Raza stood elegantly with dignity and moved to the pavilion. All of them were staring Mr. Raza.

"Conclude quick guys," Mr. Peter immediately ordered as Mr. Raza was out of the sight. They gathered the pots and heard the rhythmic movements of horses' hooves with rustling of the bushes. Observing danger, their eyes met. They stood straight. Tom and Arjun were holding spears and bows aiming the direction and Mr. Peter and Hamid were directing at the other sides with swords. They were attentive and active. Mr. Raza listening to the horses' hooves stopped near the camp. They were prepared to face the attack. The three brown horses appeared behind the bushes.

"Stop", one of the men eyes widened to see the assaulters. He shouted lowering his veil and laughed. Tom, Arjun and Hamid also laughed to see the man's face. Mr. Peter and

Mr. Raza smiled. "It's me Shiva," The man moved down the horse.

"Shiva, you we just thought that you'll have gone," Arjun ridiculed putting his bow and arrow back into the case.

"Gone where?" Shiva squinted his brave eyes gleefully.

"Gone to God," Tom spoke and all three of they laughed. Shiva smiled.

"No," Mr. Peter scowled three of them. Mr. Raza stretched wide his arms and Shiva moved into his arms.

"After so many days, my son," Mr. Raza enquired after separating.

"Yeah, the work was extended." Both of they smiled to look one another. Mr. Raza looked to the other two men of the horses. The men had moved down the horses. Shiva headed to the boys.

"Well, he is Dave and he is Chon Li, the new members." Shiva introduced them. Mr. Raza welcomed them with the smile at the lips and the love in the eyes.

"I don't doubt your choice. Shiva," He patted Shiva's shoulder. Both of they moved to Mr. Raza and shake hands. "What about our friends? Where are they?" Mr. Raza asked. Shiva put his head down. "Dead," he replied without looking into the eyes of Mr. Raza.

"What?" The group was shocked.

"What about my brother?" Tom was shocked at the news. He grabbed Shiva's arm and faced him.

"Oliver was murdered during the journey. He was going to run after finding the gems but Martha killed him." Shiva narrated the story.

"What?" Tom was not going to believe. "Where is she now?" Tom was tensed and restless.

"She was slaughtered by Sunasians for the sin she committed." Shiva was telling him and Tom seemed like a fish out of the water.

"And where is Max?" He anxiously asked.

"Roaming in the streets," Shiva replied sternly. Tom gloomily looked to Shiva who did not dare to look into his cute sad eyes.

"It's a fake story. Martha was not like that and nor my brother." Tom left his arm and moved back. He fell it the ground and held his head. Hamid moved to him and put his hand at its left shoulder to console him.

"Ali Hamza?" Mr. Raza enquired with a little hope in the eyes.

"Vultures killed him." The group was lamenting at the news. Tom was weeping. Arjun firmly held Shiva's shoulders to make him calm.

"My friends and Sons," All of they looked to Mr. Raza. "Yesterday, we were eight but till last evening we had been six." Mr. Raza glanced Tom who was in mourning and staring the ground. "And today again, we are eight. The time will pass and we shall deceased and exceeded simultaneously. One day we shall be uncountable." He moved a little forward. "My dear fellows, One day we shall build a nation. The tips of the spears will batter our bodies and the swords will bleed us but we shall be firmed." Tom stood up firmly to look Mr. Raza.

"And I'll quench the thirst of my revenge." Tom gnashed his teeth in anger and his fists were unconsciously closing.

The sun feared to see the courage and valor as it was hiding behind the clouds. The flocks of birds had gathered into the skies to witness bright chapter of a human history. Once again, the man had started to step up the mountains. As the man was mounting them, the hills and mountains were growing large, larger and largest. The flowers were twinkling and the cloud was shading them to save from rain but he could not control and the first drop of rain fell.

"Ooooops," The girl in red shirt and black skirt murmured.

"How romantic?" A girl in the couple excitedly told the boy holding his arm. The little moved her pupils peevishly and smiled at the couple passing by. She down took her red hat with a white flower at it. She was invariably seen with a matching hat at her head. She was moving zigzag crossing the people in the market. A bouquet of red roses was in her right hand. There in this area, Sunasians and Earthumen could both be seen. Her dazzling eyes were gazing the crowd as if trying to find her desired person. She at last reached the shop where Frank was bargaining about a pair of socks. She stood nearby and patiently stared both for five minutes. She looked to the shopkeeper, then the boy and then ladies' socks.

"Mr. Shopkeeper," At last, she shouted. "Would you please like to sale your socks for the money he is suggesting?" The girl infuriated at the wastage of time. "So that you can have another customer?" The girl ordered, Frank looked to the girl favoring him and then to the shopkeeper. Frank nodded and the girl put on her hat.

"Yes, yes little girl," The man left both and turned to her. "I've more beautiful hats than yours." The shopkeeper swiftly moved to the cabins and took two to three bundles of hats packed in a transparent envelope. He put them in front of her.

"First release the boy," The girl sternly replied. The shopkeeper indecorously took the price from the boy and gave him the socks.

"Thank you," The boy triumphantly saw the shopkeeper and whispered in the girl's ears. He went out quickly.

"Yes, did you like the hats?" He was going to open one of the transparent polythene bags when the girl put her hand at the transparent bag.

"My name is Bellatrix." She did not pick her hand and introduced herself boldly. "I am a Sunasian." She showed him the faded sun sign. The man was confused and worried. "Prime minister's daughter," The man was stunned for this time. "I jus want to know where Mrs. Burney is." The girl enquired. The man came to senses; girl removed her hand from the bag and stared into his eyes.

"Well, Mrs. Burney has left the city." The man replied obediently.

"What?" Now the girl was shocked. "When?" The girl shouted. Her dazzling eyes dazzled more than before.

"Just she was asking from me about the piece of a cloth," The shopkeeper informed her.

"It means, it is not late yet." She hastily moved out. He looked here and there to find anyone. There he saw the same boy moving into the crowd.

"Hey, hey, listen," The girl called him from back. The boy turned and saw the girl running to him. He saw her from head to toe. She was looking like a little princess. Frank got impressed.

"Mr. ... err... err," The girl was panting as she reached near the boy.

"Frank," The boy answered frankly.

"O yeah, Mr. Frank, Would you like to inform me about Mrs. Burney?" The girl asked proudly.

"Mrs. Burney?" The boy repeated. "She has gone. Over there. Look at her cart." Frank pointed alarmingly to a far away wooden cart jolting on the path. Bellatrix looked back to the cart. It was very far away. She could not grab it even if she ran. Bellatrix desirously looked to the cart. It was looking like a small dot into the atmosphere. His bouquet lowered down, some roses fell and smashed under the feet of the passers by. One of the men seemed to be fond of flowers, picked one rose and handed it to the girl standing nearby him. He sat on his knees and gave it to the girl. The girl put off his shoe and struck the man's head. Bellatrix looked to panorama and could only smile as she had lost some thing very significant. Frank was busy in looking at the girl and the flowers and he did not know why the people in the crowd were laughing.

"Saira works so hard." Frank said. Bellatrix looked to the boy staring the bouquet.

"Saira, Who?" The girl enquired confusingly.

"My, friend, Abdullah' sister. She is a flower maker. She prepares the bouquet and sells them." Frank was looking to the roses and Bellary was looking to the boy with a scowl at her face. The crowd was laughing at the man rubbing his head and the girl had moved away from the market.

"You should ask her to learn to tie them." Bellatrix proudly answered ignoring the girls' hard work. She returned to the cart. "There is no use of them now." Bellatrix gloomily spoke.

"Why?" Frank was still gazing the flower. He picked some flowers and put them in his pocket stealthily.

"Was there special commitment?" Frank asked her.

"Yeah, it was." The girl turned and both of they were moving side by side. "My life looks incomplete now." She sat on a stair outside the shop of pullovers and covered her face by the palms.

"Oh, it's really worrying," Frank sympathized with her. "You are too young and you had a crush, I am so sorry you could not get what you desired. I am with you."

"What?" The girl's shout was astonishing. Frank was astounded who was seriously condoling her. "Listen boy, I've no crush. I think you have crush, holding these ladies socks." The girl pointed to the pink socks in her hands.

"These," Frank was ogled. "No," Frank chuckled. "Not at all," Frank abruptly put them in the pocket. "These are Saira's. Today is her birthday and it is a gift for her." Frank was confused. "She is just like my friend." Bellatrix laughed loudly.

"So you are gifting her socks." Bellatrix chortled again.

"Yes," It confused Frank.

"Isn't it funny?" Bellatrix was smiling now.

"No, actually, her previous socks were torn. Winter season was coming and she needed them. That's why I bought them." Frank told the story sadly. "Do you know?" Frank was excited now. "We friends gather money and then we present gifts to one another." Frank was sharing his life with her.

"Hey, really," The girl looked interested. "Ok, fine, Look at this bracelet," The girl showed her a white chain in which twelve gemstones of small sizes and different colors had been embedded revolving around her wrist.

"Wow," Frank was impressed by the shine. The girl unlocked the padlocks and moved it to the boy.

"What?" Frank looked confused.

"This is for Saira." The girl smilingly gave it to him. "A gift," The girl smiled lovingly. Frank frightfully took bracelet from her and put it in her pocket.

"From where did you get it?" Frank was stunned at the shine of the gems.

"My father brought it." The girl proudly informed her. "I have many like them."

"Many," Frank shouted and his eyes widely opened with astonishment. Bellatrix chortled.

"Yes," She was laughing when Frank heard a familiar voice at his back. He turned and Bellatrix saw following the direction of voice. Frank smiled to see the upcoming ones.

"Hey, Abdullah, Mary," Both of they had reached him. "He is Abdullah, Saira's brother and she is Mary, my cousin." Frank introduced them.

"The flower maker?" Bellatrix enquired.

"Yeah," Frank nodded.

"Who is she?" Abdullah asked him and stared her.

"She is erring... Err..." Frank was puzzled. "Who are you by the way?" Frank asked her staring her.

"Bellatrix," She replied looking Frank peevishly and showed the back of her hand where a sun signs was visible. All of the three were feared and stunned to see the sun sign.

"Ok, good bye friends," The girl moved up and ran to her right side with a bouquet of flowers in her hand. Mary and Abdullah stared him.

"Had you been talking to a Sunasian?" Mary enquired her sternly.

"Yeah, she called you?" Mary squinted his eyes. "Have you ever seen yourself in the mirror?" Mary mocked.

"Yeah, many of the times." Frank disregarded her taunt. "You are looking so pale." Frank looked to Abdullah.

"Yup, I got temperature in the morning. I wish to take rest now." Abdullah rubbed her head to comfort his pain.

"Where were you the whole day? Aunt was finding you." Mary told her.

"Right now I m going to Abdullah's home." Frank told her the plan.

"Me too," Mary replied.

"And me too," Abdullah replied sternly. He was looking pale and weird with fever.

"You should be at home. Why are you roaming here?" Frank enquired him.

"I came here to take the medicine." Abdullah answered without looking at any of them.

"Hey you look tensed," Frank, asked him.

"No, not really," Abdullah was lost in the deep thoughts.

They had crossed the market were patrolling in the pastureland setting off to the house.

II

Saira grabbed her head after seeing the ten pairs of socks at the table and her twelve friends standing with heads down around a square table. She lamented at the same pink color as well. The door opened and Mary, Frank entered following Abdullah. Abdullah went to the bedroom and both of they moved to the table. They were shocked to look at the socks.

"If you've socks then don't give it to me." Saira requested them.

"B... b... but," Frank was stunned to see the choice.

"I could spend this winter with two pair of socks only and both of they should be of different colors." Saira told them. Granny was smiling as she was putting the pots at the table for the birthday celebration.

"It's not worrying, dear. I knew they would bring the same things." Mary consoled her. She moved her red knitted bag to her. "Happy Birthday," She hugged her.

"Thanks," Saira dejectedly took bag from her, opened the ribbon, and was pleased to see a beautiful pink knitted ribbon to tie her hair admiring the gift with her glittering eyes, smiling lips. She looked to Frank.

"Saira, I know you gave me a beautiful gift at my birthday, but sorry dear," He took out the pair of pink socks with three flowers.

"Frank," She dejectedly shouted and pretended to be fainted. She looked to him. "Thanks," She desperately took them.

"Ok, ok, fine I've something very special to give you." Frank was excited as he remembered something.

"What special? Another pair of socks?" Saira shouted.

"No, no, no," Frank smiled and took out bracelet from his pocket. The group of children shocked to see the glimmering bracelet. Mary breathed hardly and all of they swallowed barely. Saira could not believe and she took it from him.

"This is a gift for you. I was wishing to give you a surprise." Frank gave him.

"It really... really... is..."

"Ok, ok children come to the table, the birthday feast is ready," Granny called all of they. She quickly put the bracelet in the knitted bag and stunningly saw smiling Frank.

"Crush," Frank whispered and Saira frowned.

All the children had gathered around the birthday girl.

CHAPTER 8

⇥ The Annual Fair ⇤

I

"It's not fair Bill". Mrs. Wilson rebuked her bulky son of twelve years who was pinching the back of a feather tip into nostrils of Max. Mrs. Wilson stared Bill furiously. He took the bite of an apple and pinched the feather in his ears disregarding her mother's words and her rage, smiling peevishly, giggling and chuckling.

"Get away you, idiot," Mrs. Wilson shouted with rage and hastily ran to him. Bill turned to look back who was smiling foolishly seeing her mother holding a stick in his hand, he was feared and he hastily went out without loosing any second. Mrs. Wilson was after her and she had to stop when she heard the muffled cries. She turned to the bed. Max was opening his eyes slowly.

"Mom, mom, mom," He was murmuring with pain. Mrs. Wilson's anger vanished. She reached near him and bent over him.

"My son, my dear, how are you feeling now?" Max was still out of senses. He did not know what Mrs. Wilson had been saying and was unconsciously staring her. "Yeah, it's me, Mrs. Wilson" She moved to the pitcher and poured water into a bowl. She put it near his lips. He took two to three sips gazing Mrs. Wilson. "Just lay down, my son." She put the bowl onto the ground and covered the boy with a blanket up to his chin. Max peacefully shut his eyes. Mrs. Wilson finding the boy calmly lay moved to the kitchen. She was singing softly and slowly. The sunlight was piercing through the window at his face. It was disturbing his sleep. He covered his eyes with the blanket. Mrs. Wilson came out of the kitchen. She was still singing and glancing Max.

"Listen," Max called her. She turned to look. "Are you Mrs. Wilson?" Max asked her.

"Yeah, for all but not for you and Bill, I'm your mother." Mrs. Wilson lovingly smiled to console him.

"What was happened to me? Mrs. Wilson?" Max asked her.

"You were fainted in the ground when I went in the early morning to call you for the breakfast." Mrs. Wilson caressed his hair. He was thinking about the incident.

"Yeah, I can remember. Perhaps vultures attacked me." Max told him.

"Vultures?" She was stunned and she enquired.

"Yupiiiiii, I got it, I got it. One more, one more," Bill came in during their chat with a bamboo in his hand and a dead sparrow hung at the other end of the bamboo. He was dancing with joy. Mrs. Wilson was stunned to look the scene.

"You, rascal, one more time you are doing this," Mrs. Wilson ran after him with a shoe in his hand. Max was quietly looking the sight when the sparrow fell down and Bill rushed out. Max came out from the blanket and squatted near the sparrow. He felt dizziness along with weakness. He felt his body breaching with pain but still he wished to examine the sparrow very closely. He reached it and stared it. It was lying dead with its beak opened and one of its feathers detached partially. The blood was all around it. Max feared to see the dead sparrow. He closed his eyes and viewed his mother smiling to see him and at the same time, he saw her face in veil and a black man going to cut his head off.

"It's my fate, so helpless, so poor." He opened his eyes whispering to the sparrow. "One day I shall be like you, unaware of every custom, every law and every prison of this cruel world." He tightly closed his eyes. Mrs. Wilson came in red with rage. She saw Max and ran to the weeping Max.

"He, the rascal one, always doing this," She was blaming Bill for all this. She flung her arms and hugged him. "He is always doing this. Promise, I won't leave you alone ever. I promise," Max was still sobbing. The night Max took rest in the soft bed. He was too much calm and he awoke up at the time when the sun was going down from the peak.

Bill was sitting in the patch of green field outside his house. There were nine to ten sparrows on the green fields and Bill had crouched near them. He was ridiculously staring them with his tongue touching his upper lip.

Max came out. He yawned and stretched his arms. He was feeling much better today and looked to his left. He was stunned to see Bill. Max frowned and headed to him. He was keenly observing the sparrows and Max was quietly moving to him. Bill observed one of the wounded sparrows. It had moved a bit. Bill was furious. He hastily took out one-foot stick. It hit his nose. "Ouch," He screamed with pain and now he was rubbing his nose. Again pointing his stick to the sparrow, "Hey, you, I'll kill you," He shouted and strictly stabbed the sparrow's abdomen. The half-dead sparrow was dead. Max had reached him. He was observing the sparrows standing at the back. He could not know what Bill was doing. He stepped in front of him. Bill saw shoes crossing the dead sparrows. His eyes moved from shoes to stockings, trousers, and shirt and to the face.

"Yew," He shouted angrily to see Max.

"What is it?" Max enquired.

"Oh, don't you see? These are sparrows." Bill fixed his stick into the ground and looked to his face.

"Why do you kill them?" Max frowned.

"I like them, so I kill them." Bill proudly announced.

"The thing you like you kill that. That's unfair Bill," Max answered and Bill laughed.

"These are the sparrows coming from the red line so I kill them." Bill whispered into his ears. Max realized him mad. "Do you know?" Bill laughed. "Yesterday was Saira's birthday. I gifted her dead sparrow and she threw angrily a daisy to me." He chortled.

"Saira's birthday?" Max enquired.

"Yeah. Don't you know?" Bill stared into his eyes.

"No" Max replied and he looked worried.

"Do you want to give him any gift?" Bill asked realizing his expressions.

"Yeah, but..." He looked gloomily to his pockets.

"Well..." Bill knitted his brows and pretended to be in deep thoughts. "You can take loan from me." Bill wanted to help him.

"R..."

"Bah..." Bill spoke into before Max could speak. "You will return me ten percent more money."

"Ok, Ok," Max excitedly accepted the offer but first we shall sign on an agreement.

"Ok," Max nodded.

"Wait, I am coming." Bill ran into the house and Max sat near the sparrows. All were dead and their beaks opened. He moved his index finger to the beak of one sparrow.

"No," Bill shouted. Max ogled and looked to him. He was standing with a plastic transparent box and a paper pencil in his both hands. He sat in front of Max. There were ten sparrows, a box, a paper and a pen in between them.

"Don't touch my sparrow." Bill ordered. "Don't hurt them." He dipped the nib in black ink and wrote something on the paper. He gave it to Max.

"I, Max am taking loan of five coins from Bill and I'll return him six coins." Max read the statement loudly. "Ok," Max accepted and gave it back to Bill.

"No, no," There was a large no. "Sign here."

"Ok... ok," Max smiled and took the pen. He signed and moved the paper and pen to him. Bill viewed the paper and saw *MS* written. He scowled and stared him in doubt. Max chuckled. "Well, my signatures," Max peevishly replied.

"Yes, yes I can see." Bill evocatively stared Max. He moved to Max jumping up the sparrows and put his hand at his shoulder. "I'll help you." Bill whispered. Max returned with a shock but Bill had run. Max disregarded him and saw the transparent box. He could view only five coins opened the lid and counted the coins. They were only five. Max put them in his pocket. He moved out to the cheap market of the city where he could buy anything special for her.

He roamed the market but he could not find anything of five coins. The prices were touching the heights. He liked woolen cap but it was of fifty coins. He was disappointed. He liked a bundle of ribbons but its cost was forty silver coins. He dejectedly sat at one corner on the stairs outside a restaurant. It was a restaurant where came to spend nights and the travelers took rest. He took out the five coins and desperately counted them seeing an old man in front of him at the other side of the road. He was rubbing the back of a horse very keenly. When he had cleaned the horse, a man came and gave him some coins. The man rode the horse and the horse galloped. The old man's back had stooped but still he was working hard to earn money. Soon after some minutes he had not breathed, a carriage stopped near him. The coachman landed down and said him some words. The coachman crossed the road and entered the restaurant ignoring Max sitting at the stairs. The old man picked his yellow cloth, soaked it in water and rubbed the carriage. He was working zealously that the carriage shone. The owner of the coachman moved out, paid the old man, pulled the reins of his coach and soon went out of the sight. Max observed it and soon came to a decision. He moved to the old man who was waiting for a new customer.

"Hey, hi," The old man with his stoop back hardly turned to Max. "Can I have your help please?"

"I am sorry son; I am hardly helping my self." The old man was looking tired.

"O, let's make a deal," Max, explained his wish. "I'll deal the upcoming customer and both of we shall take half." Max suggested him.

"Ok," The old man smiled as he got the helper. "One day you make a deal of life and the other day you make a deal of death." It confused Max but his attention distracted as another carriage stopped near them. The coachman landed down.

"Well, please wash my coach." The man ordered without looking at the old man and moved to the restaurant. The old man handed Max the cloth. Max abruptly took it and rubbed the coach with it. He climbed the top and cleaned and then he moved to the windows and the internal settee. He washed them and they glistened. In a few minutes, he had cleaned the whole carriage. It was shining like mirror. As he had cleaned, he looked to the old man. The old man admired him with his eyes. Soon the owner came out. He paid the old man and ignored the hard work as soon the coach was moving in to another place.

"How many," Max asked him.

"Twenty coins, both of we shall take ten coins." The old man told him in his frail voice and gave him fifteen dollars. Max put them in his pocket. Both of they were waiting for the next customer. Max and the old man waited until evening. Bill was shocked to see Max bathing a horse when he was wandering as usual.

"Hey Max, What are you doing?" Bill shouted.

"I am earning money." Max replied brushing the horse.

"No, you are not earning money. You are earning love." Bill laughed leaving Max shocked. He looked back but Bill had run. He ignored him and again started his work. The moon was shinning. The shops were being closed. The old man shared him the half income.

"Thanks Sir," Max waved him hand.

"Thank you to you son," The old man smiled.

Now, Max had enough money to buy a beautiful gift for Saira. He moved to a shop where he saw the hand made cards and hand made dolls. He viewed all the dolls and his eyes stayed at a gorgeous doll. It had brown hair of woolen thread and it had a baby cut. Her hair was touching the shoulders. It had worn a pink colored dress and the pink curvy crafting at her lips was smiling. The eyes were brown and a puffy nose he could see. It looked him like Saira. He had enough money and he could buy these gifts for her. He bought a doll and a hand made card to gift the girl who consoled him in the time of need. When he had paid, he counted the coins. Only ten coins left. Max held the bag in one hand and put the coins in his pocket. He was too much tired but the excitement of the gift was not letting him to feel. He paced to the house. The market was gradually vacating. He was feeling fear as the abandoned road was coming near. When he reached the ground, he just ran as he remembered the vultures. Max entered the house. Bill was in bed. When he saw Max entering, he jumped out of the bed.

"He has come, he has come. Look, he has come." Bill was shouting. Mrs. Wilson moved out in a hurry and was calm to see Max.

"Stop Bill, I was feared." She rebuked Bill and Bill quickly moved in to the bed. "How are you dear? Dinner is ready. You can take it in the kitchen." Mrs. Wilson saw to the bag about what Bill had already told her. Max tried to hide it behind his legs as he moved the polythene bag. Mrs. Wilson overlooked the action and moved to the kitchen. Max looked to Bill. He had covered his head with the blanket and Max went to futon near the wall.

"Hey what did you bring?" Bill enquired still in blanket.

"Nothing," Max was looking tired. He closed his eyes and put his arm at his forehead. Mrs. Wilson holding a tray of nuggets and Mr. Wilson taking a bite of one came out of the kitchen.

"Max, stay with bill tonight," Max was half slept as he opened his eyes at Mr. Wilson's order.

"No," Bill shouted putting his face out of the blanket. "I'll be only." He stretched his legs at the bed.

"Bill..." Mrs. Wilson warned him. Bill did not look out.

"Go," Mr. Wilson, ordered and the boy went to Bill who hardly let him to enter.

"It should not be. It's again happening." Mrs. Wilson sat in the futon seriously discussing the matter.

"Yeah, I also suggested not starting this again but they didn't listen." Mr. Wilson picked a nugget from the tray in the hands of Mrs. Wilson and put it in mouth. Mrs. Wilson nodded looking to the boys in the blanket.

"Is the annual fair tomorrow?" Mrs. Wilson asked.

"Yup... tomorrow," Mr. Wilson replied.

"The annual fair," Bill shouted in excitement. Max who was asleep awoke up hurriedly. "I'll go. It will be a good day to gift her." Bill whispered in the ears of Max.

"Hey stop. Let me sleep." Max was irritated, as he was looking all-in. He disregarded his excitement, immersed his face in pillow and closed his eyes tightly. Bill disliked his attitude. He irately moved out to his parents and sat in between them.

"What is happened in annual party?" He winked his rounded brown eyes as his eye lashes twinkled. Mrs. Wilson chuckled and kissed the forehead of his son.

"It is a combined event of all the nations to forget their miseries and to enjoy with the live people, this is it." Mrs. Wilson replied and stood up to the kitchen. Bill jumped up to the bed and for one more time Max was irritated. Bill ignored and slid under the blanket.

II

The gala began at ten in the morning, the next day. The stalls arranged transversely in the garden under the shade of trees. Mary, Saira, Abdullah and Frank had worn the jumpers gifted by Lady Margaret. Lady Margaret was standing smiling to a little boy at the stall who was selling apple juice. Mrs. Wilson was standing cheerfully near the stall of apples. Mr. Wilson was talking to the men of his age with beer in their hands. Bimla and Abdullah were walking hands in hands moving from one stall to another. Abdullah was making way in the crowd and Bimla was following her holding his hand. Many of the women had gathered near the stall of palmist. He was observing the hands and telling them their luck. He was telling one woman about his marriage and the others standing nearby were laughing, smiling and joking. One was gone, she paid and the other came. All the women were dressed well and looking gorgeous. Children were giving the impression of being angels. Some women had held their infants in their laps. In fact, all the houses were empty and people were coming to the stall. People who had gathered money arranged stalls and other were buying the stuff at lower rates. Max entered through the decorated twisted bough immersed in the green grass. It decorated with the flowers of Bellatrix and pink roses. He was astonished to see the vista. It was crowded. He had never been in such a cheerful crowd before. His gloomy mood changed to witness the gleeful crowd. He smiled leaving the twisted bough behind. Bill was after him with his bamboo as usual in his right hand and a polythene bag in the other.

"What will it bring today?" He listened an old man's frail voice sitting near the bough. He was rubbing a yellow cloth at a man's shoes. Instead, he was polishing the shoes. He gazed the old man who was the same one he worked with yesterday. The elegant man gave him three coins and went away.

"Every time, a stampede was ready. Now, today I have no idea, what is trampled and how is trampled?" The man with the same nose and the eyes like the old man replied looking to the mob of men taking tea at a stall.

"Hey hi," Max sat in front of the old man whose eyes were down searching for something into his rusted wooden box. The old man looked up to the voice. Bill was standing near him glancing the stalls.

"Hi, boy," The old man abruptly looked to his shoes. They were shinning. "They are clean son, do you want?" The old man talked about the business after realizing him a customer.

"Um... mm... N... No, I am Max. Yesterday I worked with you." Max reminded him.

"Sorry, boy I don't know you." The old man plainly rejected.

"What? B... but I did," Max forced him to remember.

"Son, if you have any deal, you can stay here, else enjoys the festival." The old man sternly replied with his eyes down into the ground. Max stood up quietly as the old man was ignoring him and the young man was staring the boy strangely.

"I did." Max spoke.

"Yeah, me also saw you." Bill assisted him.

"Why is he doing like that?" Max was looking tensed.

"Perhaps he will have forgotten. The person of this age has the disease. Don't worry." Bill made him calm. He was looking to the stall when he saw Mrs. Wilson. "Hey, take your bag." Bill quickly handed it to Max and ran to Mrs. Wilson. Max looked to the bag and he remembered he was to gift some one. His lips displayed a cheerful curve and Max looked into the mob for the girl. Moving form one stall to another he could not find her. Looking to the stall of palmistry, knocked by Abdullah.

"Oooops," Bimla chortled.

"O sorry," Max apologized with a smile and Abdullah did not bother to speak or to look him. He ran holding hand of Bimla. "Bye, bye," Bimla murmured waving her hand gleefully. Max observed her looking happier with Abdullah. The people were passing by and knocking him sideways. He was not interested in any stall but was interested in the onlookers. He caught sight of a girl while looking feats of a small monkey. The juggler was beating his small drum and the monkey was dancing lifting its one leg up. The spectators were applauding, laughing, smiling and chuckling. Some who had enjoyed and wanted to move to other stall threw coins in a clay pot near by the juggler who was busy in making the monkey dance. The monkey had now lifted its arm at his head. The mob was in stitches now. He looked to the girl and he stopped as he had found the destination. She was in a royal blue dress with a blue pullover and had a pink ribbon in her hair. Mary was standing near her in a pink short skirt with white stockings and ponytail touching his shoulders. Max moved to the girl. He squeezed the handle of the bag in his hand and in fact, he was trying to squeeze his perplexity. He was radiant but was confused. She was smiling at the feats.

"Hey hi," Max cheerfully tackled her. She looked to her right and her smile widened to see the caller.

"Hey, hi," She was excited to see the boy. "How are you?" She asked.

"I am fine and you?" Max asked her.

"Me too," The girl replied. Max did not speak anything else and the girl looked to the monkey dancing. Mary was too much involved in the feats that he could know about the arrival of Max. Max looked to Saira and then followed in the direction of her eyes. The monkey jumped and somersaulted. Max also smiled at the cute looking monkey and then he looked to Saira after gathering his courage he seemed himself able to be vocal.

"Happy Birthday Saira," Max wished her. She was thunderstruck as her eyes opened wide.

"Thanks," She chuckled. "But you have been two days late." She again headed to the monkey. It stood straight at its palms. Saira clapped with the crowd.

"I am sorry. I just couldn't know. Bill told me yesterday." Max apologized and Saira was thunderstruck. She looked to Max, held his arm and moved him out of the mob near to the stall of bangles.

"Do you discuss me with Bill?" Saira was infuriated.

"No," Max denied. "We didn't ever talk about you. He just told me that he gifted you a dead bleeding sparrow."

"Disgusting," She shouted lifting his hands up to his ears. "He is... such a... a...," She was red with rage. Max looked to her wrist. A bracelet was glistening.

"It's awesome." Max was wordless to see the grace of the bracelet.

"What?" Saira looked to Max and she realized him gazing her bracelet.

"Well, Frank gave it to me." Saira was normal and she touched the padlocks of the bracelet.

"Its awesome, it's really nice." He dejectedly looked to his bag. "Well," He moved his bag to her. Saira stared it. "Your birthday gift, I can only have...." In the meanwhile, a sharp sword cut the bag into pieces; it fell far away and lost in to the crowd. The back of the horse passed between them throwing them on the either sides. In no minutes, they saw the crowd trampling under the feet of men and the hooves of horses. They saw the screams and the blood. Max stood up abruptly and saw Saira. She was running with Abdullah and Bimla. All around was doom. Max looked down to run and saw three faces apart from their bodies. Max shivered with fear and ran with an unknown power. Earthumen were being stabbed.

"Run, the Sunasian have assaulted. They are coming to cut us. Run, run," The old man in his frail voice was shouting. Max disregarded the old man. When he had moved some steps forward, he heard a frail scream. His running steps stopped. He had heard the similar scream yesterday. He looked back. The old man was stabbed and dead.

"One day you make a deal of life and the other day you make a deal of death." He remembered the old man's words. Max heard the screams and cries and had to leave the old man. The women were running out of the garden. The life embraced some and the death hugged others. The stalls were broken and the stuff smashed. Abdullah's granny had hidden Saira and Abdullah in her arms like feathers of hen. Bimla ran to her mother who scattered her arms and ran out. Max was running when someone firmly gripped his hand. Max with fear looked back and was comfort to see Mrs. Wilson and Bill holding his hand. The contentious and warrior Earthumen had taken out their swords. Those armless picked up the wooden boards and hit the assaulters in yellow uniforms. The contentious Earthumen were trying to escape the babies and the women but all in vain. When the doom approaches it never gives the chance. The blood flooded, carcasses heaped and the slaughtered heads mounted.

All was over now. The twisted bough crushed and the flowers demolished. The old man was stabbed near the bough. Volunteers were zealously bandaging the wounded and gathering the flesh as well as the scattered bones. Every thing had a terror-stricken peace now. Muslims and Christians were shrouding the dead ones, Hindus were smoldering the dead ones and the Buddhists were mummifying their ones. Carcasses were scattered like rubbish. Silent sobbing, muffled cries and tears had overcome the cries and screams. Blue carpet at the green grass was red now. Abdullah was staggering in the ground looking for someone with a bandage at his head. There were two cuts at his right cheek and one at his lower lip. Max was also out with Bill holding a bamboo in his hand after him. They were keenly observing the carcasses. He saw a head with pink ribbon over it. He feared and stepped to it. He saw Saira bent over his dead granny and her pink ribbon was slid from the right place hanging at end of the hair. Her long hairs disheveled. Max heard her sobbing. He hunkered down near her and patted her shoulder.

"Saira," Max called her and she looked back. She had wept a lot. Her tresses were stuck at her wet face due to the tears. She shed into tears and turned her face to her granny.

"Go away; I don't need to talk to any one." She shouted and then cried. Bill stood up and Max as well. Max was doomed and Bill was composed.

"She insulted," Bill foolishly caressed his hair.

"This is not the time for joke, Bill." Max sternly answered and went on. In the way, he saw Abdullah bent over Bimla. She was bleeding and he could hear her muffled cries in pain. The sword pierced into her tiny cadaver. Her eyes were still staring the sky watching the final destiny and the smile at her lips faded. A group of Hindus came, picked the dead body, put down the gathered woods and sprinkled oil. Abdullah hunkered down and saw the sight with open eyes. As the fire was reaching near the girl's feet, a tear fell down. In no minutes where were her legs gone. It soon reached her beautiful face. The fire frightfully kissed her lips and soon the fire liked her eyes and it burnt her. As the eyes burnt, the fire from other side smoldered her forehead and her ponytail. There was no more any one. The woods also turned to ashes. He could only see the fire. The ashes were becoming ashes. Max and Bill quietly standing looked to Abdullah. He was quiet like a dumb child. The fire was now showing wrath at the ashes. Abdullah fell down like broken log at the ground. Max abruptly moved to him.

"Abdullah, Are you fine?" Max squatted near him.

"Yeah," Abdullah mumbled without opening his eyes. "Leave me alone," Abdullah, said them and both of they moved up.

"Let's go to Saira. Her granny would need the shroud." Bill suggested and Max nodded. When they reached, Saira was sitting alone and had put her head at her knees. She had taken the cap of the jumper at her head and her hair was hidden. She was calm and quiet. She was looking tired after weeping.

"Hey where is your granny?" Bill was shocked to see her alone.

"Buried," Her lips opened and again closed. She did not look back and closed her eyes.

"Let's go home Saira," Max consoled her.

"Which home?" She sternly replied. "I've no home." The girl replied and again closed her eyes to let tears to flow.

"Let's go pal," Bill held Max hand but he did not move and stayed standing under the light of moon near the dishearten Saira. She closed her eyes pretending to be slept.

The week people spent lamenting and mourning, wiping tears, condoling and consoling. Every one left with one or two members of the family. Max was sleeping in his old shelter when the sun awoke him up. Bill was standing near him.

"Hey Bill, you," Max rubbed his eyes.

"Yeah, me, mom is calling you. She is waiting for you." Bill informed him.

"Ok, I am coming." He stood up and moved to his pool. He washed his face quickly and moved back. Max saw Abdullah and Saira holding luggage stepping to the lake. He smiled to see his friends and ran to them.

"Hey hi," Max came near to Abdullah and was worried to see their luggage. "Where are you going?"

"Very far," Abdullah replied seriously. Saira was quietly moving looking forward.

"Where is very far?" Max asked looking to Saira who was looking straight. She was looking sad and pathetic.

"It's very far." Abdullah replied carelessly. Max was constantly staring Saira walking with Abdullah and knocked into the tree. "Good bye," Abdullah said him farewell.

"Good bye," Max mumbled and foolishly rubbed his head. He saw both of them moving very far into the forest, as he was depressed.

Next day he saw Mary, Frank and Lady Margaret moving into the forest with a cart of luggage. Max had no friend left other than Bill. Both of they stood at the top of the hills and daily they saw the caravans moving into the jungle. Max had started a livelihood and he stood at the place of the old man polishing and cleaning. He could earn for his own sake. In the evening, he went to meet Bill and both of they would stand at the top of the hills saying good-bye to the caravans.

"They are going." Bill said looking to a caravan moving into the woods. The evening had worn its purple cloak.

"Yeah, all are gone." Max replied wishfully. "Let's go." Max stood up, moved down the hills, and so did Bill. In the way, they were shivering with cold and crossing their arms to feel warmth. Bill was panting as their feet touched the ground. He put his arm at Max's shoulder and the little Max smiled as his shoulder bent a little at his weight.

"Huh," Bill gasped when he had crossed the slope. Max stepped to his ancient shelter.

"Time to sleep pal," Bill pulled him to the street holding his wrist. Max pulled back his hand. He sat on the mud and rested his back with the cracked white grubby pillar. Bill was staring him with his bamboo fixed in the ground in his right hand.

"I am not to go," Max stationed his head with the pillar.

"Why? It's so cold outside." Bill argued.

"I am in my home Bill." Max replied and took out six coins from his pocket. "Take them." Bill caught and counted.

"All right," Bill took out the paper and tore it. "You are sleep here tonight." Bill looked to the dejected Max.

"Yes," Max nodded.

"Good bye," Bill answered curtly and went to the street. Max looked to the street. Bill was pacing to the house and bamboo was striking on to the ground. The day had changed its purple dress and had worn the black one. The silver stars were glittering. He spent the half night wandering in the streets and staring the glimmering, shinning stars. No one came out for the fear of Sunasians assault. He was alone near the pool. It was clear and dark. There were no vultures. He keenly gazed the sky. There were neither the black shades and nor the vultures. He put his hand in his pocket. A necklace woolen rope was in his hand with a ruby glistening in it. He neither shed tears and nor did he sob. He saw her mother laughing in the ruby what widened his smile. He walked to the end of the town and his heart mashed to witness the sight. There were ruins left. There were no railings and the fields were smashed and trampled.

"They will have come to find me and to kill me." He panicked to think the dreadful and his shoulders shuddered.

The wooden shutter was cracked and mounted. He saw a broken wooden board standing upright. Its upper part was fallen near it. He crossed the fields and reached near it. He sat cross-legged near it and realized. It was his room. This time his self-control lost and the tears broke the borders. He was missing the smiles of his parents spent together, happy moments whispered in his ears and the panorama of farewell to his father pulled the tears out. He wiped the tears and hastily paced unconsciously. He reached the tree. The acacia tree was waving slowly. Cool breeze was blowing. He remembered Saira who consoled her and it was the tree, he hit by, while trying to talk to her. He could not gift her. He remembered Abdullah the one who loved the most and he hated him for he was a rebellion. He did not like to talk to him. Mary and Frank were always with every one. They were his friends and at the same time Abdullah and Saira.

"All are gone, I am alone now." The silence whispered. He supported his hand by the trunk of acacia. His head was down staring the ground. He paced back slowly to the colony gazing the stars. When he had tired and he could listen to azan, the sleep patted him and the boy slept.

"Can I ask you the reason?" Next day he was in a serious trial in front of Mrs. Wilson. She was harsh to him.

"No such reason," Max, answered as his head was down. Bill was standing nearby holding a small stick in his hand.

"Why did you not come to the house yesterday? How did you sleep in the cold outside?" Mrs. Wilson was scolding him. "The place is so dangerous." Mrs. Wilson was infuriated.

"It's frightful but it's peaceful. I am addicted to cold." Max answered normally.

"Listen Max," Mrs. Wilson sat near him. "Bill will not be rude to you any more. Both of you will live like brother here. This is also your house."

"You took it totally wrong. I've no complaint with him." Max and Bill looked to one another.

"Then what's the matter? Why do you not want to live with us?" Mrs. Wilson enquired him in frenzy.

"My life is useless and I don't deserve any pleasure." Max seemed dejected.

"Don't say so dear," Mrs. Wilson consoled him.

"Hey Max," Bill put his left hand at his shoulder. "I missed you last night a lot and now you can hope for a brother and a good friend."

Max grinned with Bill and his eyes twinkled with hope and pleasure.

The day he spent working and earning and the nights he spent in his ruins or sometimes Mrs. Wilson would invite him for dinner. At lunch Wilson, family was found waiting for the boy and he often appeared with a surprise having gifts of fruits and dry fruits. At night, he and Bill met in the cafe and he and Bill took coffee. The snow falling started. It was hard for the boy to stay outside and for this reason; he slept at the place of Mrs. Wilson. He was enjoying with life and the life was pacing, swinging and peacefully smiling with him. Max was often helping Mrs. Wilson in staking dishes, buying the monthly purchases, supporting Mr. Wilson in planting, sowing, gardening and helping Bill in homework. In free time, he wrestled and played with Bill. Max bought woods and Bill helped him in building the house. In rainy season, Bill and Max bathed and in snowy season both of, they brought logs and lit fire. They enjoyed basking in sun. Max was apparently peaceful but entirely restless and sometimes he got irritated. Bill disliked this attitude and at this point both of they were quarreling. In the snow nights, he patrolled at the snow in furry woolen jacket trying to find someone and missing someone. He tried to search his past in the woods. At Christmas, he waited for the presents of his dear ones but he could not receive any. At Eid, he missed Saira and Abdullah. Bill and Max often went in to the woods. Bill was always talking foolish and Max climbed the near by branch to escape his foolishness. When Bill turned to look, he found no one. Max jumped down from the branch.

"I was listening, I was listening." He was nodding at the same time. Bill was infuriated. Max would run forward and Bill was running before him with his long bamboo. At every occasion, Bill forced him to sing and he had to sing. He had made a study room in his house and started a job in a shop as a shopkeeper. After completing his job in the evening, Bill had reached, him and both of they were in the cafe taking coffee. He would depart Bill and entered his study room. He composed his symphonies in his books. The Eid came. People brought him outside and forced him to sing and he sang for someone.

> Oh my will Lying behind that hill
> There is a lot to do Some will kill
> All around is thrill And the enemies will hault
> Some days after There will be the scene
> Of the lie to fail And the truth to sway
> Not very far away But near to our gay
> You will see you will see

The crowd shed to tears as they had remembered their dead ones. In no time, Max was famous among Earthumen due to his kindness. Every one wished to be his friend. Max gathered money and bought a wooden bicycle. Bill and Max would ride it in the evening. They both were looking back moving their bicycle fast when Bill could not know. Mrs. Wilson was standing in between the fields, Bill could not control, and he hit her bicycle. Nothing happened to Mrs. Wilson but both of they were fallen. Mrs. Wilson was red with rage. They left the bicycle and ran. Mrs. Wilson rushed to beat them with the stick. She was waving the stick in the sky and both of they were running and shouting simultaneously.

Days were passing fast. The cold season came and Mrs. Wilson held her woolen threads and the knitting needles. She would go into the kitchen to look the food whether it had burnt or not and when she returned the knitting needle would have disappeared. She was shouting and both of they were giggling under the table. Mrs. Wilson looked out and they put the needle back at the table. Mrs. Wilson would hold the needle and confused. The days of puberty had come. They left seven years irritating Mrs. Wilson. He decorated walls of Mrs. Wilson using his best knowledge of arts. She drew a black and white portrait of Mrs. Wilson at her earnest request. Mrs. Wilson was shocked to see her portrait and Max as well as he saw the big moustache at the face. He ran to Bill who was staring with bold ridicule.

"I... err... err... was just trying that if mom would be father than how would she look?" Max and Bill chortled and plundered hands.

Max had drawn a beautiful painting of his childhood where he had made the murky faces of Abdullah, Saira, Bimla, Frank, Mary and Bill. He put at the table as he had completed it and smirked. It seems he was thinking of starting a new journey.

CHAPTER 9

✢═ The Murderer ═✢

I

Max a cool young boy of seventeen years was standing at the hilltop. His blue green big eyes were witnessing the people gathering wretchedness of the annual gala. One more time, people tried to celebrate and to make it memorial but the mounts of havoc wickedly welcomed them. It had been afternoon and people were cleaning the ground. The carcasses were shrouding, burying and mummifying. There were no tears but terror-stricken silence. He was observing the disaster ominously. He had been handsome looking young man with a smart posture. His golden hairs were shinning in the sun and the hair at his forehead was waving with the air. His eyes twinkled as he saw an equestrian galloping hard into the crowd. He announced something loudly and the people left their jobs. The crowd was looking speechless and flabbergasted. He felt depression among the people of the crowd. He knitted his brows and stepped down to scrutinize the affair. The Earthumen had circled around the equestrian.

"Who did?"

"Who told you?"

"How was it done?" The people were asking different questions from the equestrian.

"I don't know. I know just this I have told you."

"What will happen now?" The two women were whispering as Max crossed the crowd.

"A new destruction," The other gloomily replied. Max reached the crowd and made way repelling the people aside. The equestrian was a man of thirty years and the caretaker of Mrs. Wilson stable. He was a good obedient of Max and Bill.

"What happened Sunil?" Max enquired him as he reached near the equestrian.

"Master," Sunil was looking disturbed. He abruptly rode down the horse as a manner of respect.

"King has been murdered." He told him and the news was terrifying.

"What?" Max mumbled who had been stunned.

"It's true". Sunil replied fearfully.

"There will be one more doom." The man viewing the carcasses commented.

"What is the hell with them? How can we kill their king? Let my son to bury. Please request them." A woman shouted with fearful worry and shed into tears.

"No one can stop them." A man answered him passing by the carcasses. Max turned and looked to the man and the woman. She had put her hands at her face and the man was quietly moving out. He could only see his back. Soon the people were lost in fear. After a few time, Sunasians raided the city. Bill listening to the horses' hooves ran to Max and pulled his arm. Both of they ran and hid behind the mount. Sunasians came and dragged the people and passersby. A black bulky man was dragging the girl and the girl was screaming awfully. Max was infuriated. He glanced Bill and stood upright.

"Where are you going?" Bill shouted. Max did not reply. "Come back." He again shouted. Max did not listen to him. Bill was tensed. He felt a prick at his neck. His eyes widened with emotions of fear and danger. "Max," He mumbled and his tongue staggered. He swallowed hard and dared to look back. A Sunasian was standing holding the horse's reins in his hand and a gift of death for him. The man was sneering but he fell down with a scream. Bill was pale. He was stabbed at the back in his footsteps. Bill looked up. He will definitely be an Earthumen. The man pointed him to the back of his horse. Bill followed the silent instructions. He rode the horse and the horse galloped hard. Bill did not know where he was going. Max had reached the man dragging the girl. He sturdily held the bulky black man by the collar. The Sunasian was stunned and exasperated at his disgrace. His nostrils puffed angrily.

"Leave the girl." Max gnashed his teeth in anger. The black man roared into the laughter. Max exasperated and he punched hard the man's set of teeth. He punched again at the same place before he could defend himself. The grip at the girl's wrist loosened and she ran from there. Man was enraged and furiously pushed him back. Max fell down on to the ground. Man abruptly took out his sword from the scabbard. Max realized the danger. His eyes were broadening as the sword was coming near his chest.

"Stop," Max, shouted and the man's sword stopped.

"Won't you like to take the King's murderer alive with him?" Max suggested the man. "I know him." He continued under the tip of the sword. The black man held the collar of Max and jerked him up. The two Sunasians passing by stood to look.

"Mark, we have no time for discussion, just kill him the boy." They ordered him. Max and the black man stared one another angrily.

"He knows King's murderer." Mark gleefully told men. The two Sunasians rushed to him and took out their swords. The tips of the three swords were facing Max.

"Where is he?" One of the men rudely asked. Max had been free from Mark's grip. Two men were standing in front of him with the tips of the sword and the third one was at his back. Max looked around and was helpless now.

"He... errs... err...." Max seemed to be staggering under the fear of death. One of the men pinched the sword's tip in his neck. "Ouch," Max made a muffled cry with pain and he closed his eyes tightly.

"Come on, Speak," The other man rudely spoke and punched him in his tummy. He screamed and bent with pain.

"I saw him coming from the mount. He will be behind it." The two of the men moved from the place and ran to the mount. "No", Max shouted again as he had remembered Bill. He gathered his courage and he spoke.

"He was behind the mount but he is not now." Max turned to them and told them whom steps had stopped. "He is me." Max courageously accepted. The three men looked fearfully to one another. The black man held collar of the shirt of Max.

"Why are you making us fool?" The black man growled. The other aimed the swords. "You are trying to make the way to be safe." The other man groaned.

"How can I be save now?" Max answered discourteously. "I murdered your filthy king." Max spoke like a rascal staring into the black man's eye.

"Gather the forces," The other men ordered. Sunasians stopped stabbing, dragging and followed the command. A large number of swords surrounded him. Sunasians were moving to the horses. The black man was moving with Max.

"If you let me to take that girl, I'll let you escape." The black man cunningly whispered in his ears. Max was enraged and bashed him at the same place. The man cried with pain. The other man attacked Max abruptly and hit his neck. Realizing him a habitual culprit, two to three commanders held him rashly and pushed him in the steps of the horse hooves. It was happening so abruptly that he was not getting chance even to look. He observed the tail of the horse was wagging at him.

"Let's take him to the court and get the reward." One of the soldiers shouted with excitement.

The black man took out the rope, held Max from the back of his collar and tied him with the back of the horse. Both of they were furiously staring one another. Max saw the lips of the black man. It was bleeding hard.

"I'll see you." The black man challenged him and Max sneered.

The soldiers had been riding the horses and no one rode the horse by which Max was tied. The soldiers on the either sides of the horse were pulling reins of the horse and Max was being dragged all the way. He was in a sudden ordeal of pain, death, fear and danger.

His back wounded and his shirt tore from the shoulders. When he reached the palace, the two soldiers held him by the collar and dragged him through the stairs. He was thrown in the steps of the queen. She was patting her furry cat dolefully. She picked her dejected heavy eyes and looked to the boy fallen upside down on the carpet. The boy was groaning. His bleeding back covered with few shatters of his grey shirt, rest of the cloth was lost in the way. The queen looked to the furious looking soldiers.

"The murderer," One of the men told. Queen was enraged. Her fuming eyes attacked the boy.

"Take him away of my sight," The Queen ground her teeth in anger. The maid standing nearby listened to the queen and went to the soldiers. She told them about the order. The soldiers held him by the collar and dragged him upside down at the carpet. When the boy had gone, the queen sneered wickedly and the cat purred.

CHAPTER 10

The Prison

It was a dark room. Only sun could peek into it through the iron bars near the roof. He was lying upside down at the hard stone bed. He was fainted with pain and a bandage covered his body. A young man was sitting near him. He heard the padlocks unlocking. The man attended to it. The old man entered holding a tray. The man smirked to look the old man.

"So you have got a new comrade, Hamid," The old man sternly spoke. Hamid stood up and looked to the boy lying on the bed. He sneered and the old man put the tray in his steps.

"Huh," Hamid yawned. "How boring is this prison hood?" His muscles stretched as he widened his arms to soothe his vertebrae. The old man laughed.

"Every time I listen this," The old man spoke gleefully. "But now you have got one of the new companions with you."

"But I've been addicted to silence now and the presence of someone seems to me boring." Hamid explained and sat near the tray. He took a mouthful of food.

"Hey," The old man came near him. He was chewing the food and ready to take the other bite. "She wants to meet him," The old man whispered in his ears and winked.

"Who, she," Hamid was confused.

"The new king's daughter," The old man whispered to explain.

"Why?" The piece of bread was hung in his hand and he whispered like the old man.

"I don't know," The old man shrugged his shoulder. The drumbeater was beating the drum.

"Why so? I cannot help. It would be a new trouble. It can lose the boy." Hamid gave sincere suggestion.

"Yup, it can but he is to loose one day like you," The old man told a bitter reality. The man considerately looked the old man.

"Hey, have you given him the food?" The jail keeper realizing the danger of conspiracy asked in frenzy.

"Y... Yes, I've given." He turned to the door and locked the padlocks. "He was asking for water." He told the jail keeper standing near. The jail keeper suspiciously stared the both and the old man went away.

"Prisoners are not allowed to talk here." The jail keeper stared Hamid, quietly chewing the bread and furiously staring the jail keeper. Both of they daily play this game of staring one another furiously but did not say any word. The drumbeater was now striking drum. The beats were now louder. Max had to open his eyes by the noise. He groaned and Hamid left the bowl on the floor. He abruptly sat near him and moved his down side up. Now he saw his face for the first time. It was hard for Max to open his eyes. Hamid poured water in a mug and again went to Max. He was groaning still yet. He took the mug near his mouth and he took a sip of it. He again lifted his head up and took another sip. Hamid put his hand under his head and the boy was slowly taking the sips of water. The boy puffed.

"Ah, enough," The boy murmured. Hamid listened and put the mug aside. Max was able to open his eyes now. The drum was beating louder. Max looked the room as far as he could see. A net of fog was hanging in his eyes therefore, he could not see clearly. Some of the water was fallen out of his mouth at his shoulders. The man stood up the stone bed and peeped through the iron bars. He tried to look down and was succeeded. The drumbeater was striking the drum hard and the people were gathering around him.

"Tomorrow is going to be the Coronation ceremony outside the royal palace in the royal garden." The drumbeater was shouting. The people were gathering and departing at the same time. The voice was inaudible as the drumbeater was moving away from the prisoner's cell. Now only the drumbeater was visible and he could see his lips moving. He moved his eyes up and realized that the cell where they were in prison was hanging at a height between the skies.

"Huh," He moved down the bed. Max had opened his eyes and now he looking Hamid.

"Hey young man," Hamid smiled. "Feeling better?"

"yeah, much better," Max tried to move up and Hamid helped him. Max groaned and put his back with the wall.

"Take the food," He moved the tray to him. Max was about to vomit as he looked the food. The man chuckled.

"Don't worry, dear! You will take this food daily. You will have to be addicted to it." The man suggested him as he was sitting near the bed at the ground.

"But what is it?" Max pushed the tray.

"This is the bread and water. The prisoner's food is of this type." Hamid informed him. "They give us the food they have wasted into the streets and garbage." There was no more smile at his face.

"What?" Max softly showed his shock.

"Yeah, we have a wretched life here and worst than the dogs. Do you know the queen's cat eats in the golden plate?" The statement of Hamid shocked Max.

"What?" He slowly asked and squinted his eyes. He was too frail that he had taken the first bite. He closed his eyes and swallowed the food.

"Disgusting," He swallowed the bread piece and did not bother to look at the mashed carrots with spices in it. He took one more bite and finished the bread in no minutes. The jail keeper was constantly guarding the prison cell.

"Hey finished," Hamid attended him after furiously staring the jail keeper.

"Yeah," Max drank water and took a deep breathe. He did not motion a bit.

"I saw her with her cat," Max told.

"Hey really, how did you see her?" Hamid was astonished.

"Yeah, I saw her and her cat. It was beautiful." Max wearily told him.

"and the queen?" Hamid asked

"She was wicked, like slut and she was very beautiful." Max told him.

"Isn't it a paradox?" Hamid was confused.

"Yeah, but it was so. If you will see you will also realize." Max told him.

"Ok, fine, tell me one thing," Hamid asked him. "Why did you kill the king?"

"I didn't kill." Max closed his eyes with feelings of pain.

"you didn't?" Hamid was shocked. "But I've heard that you've accepted it openly."

"Yup, I did, but I didn't." Max was fainting. Hamid moved to him.

"Hey boy, Are you fine?" Hamid had bent over him.

"Yeah, I just want to take rest." Max wheezed and fell into deep sleep. Hamid let him.

The sun was going to set. The old man unlocked the padlocks and for this time, he came with a lantern. Hamid sidetracked at the voice. The old man smiled to see his friend.

"How are you boy?" The hands of the old man were trembling with weakness and he moved the unlit wooden lantern to Hamid. Hamid held it and sat near him.

"Fine, alive and happy," The man shouted with excitement.

"I know." The old man smirked and looked to Max. He was fast asleep. "Sleeping or fainted?" The old man asked.

"Sleeping," Hamid, answered softly.

"Hmmm," The old man sat in front of him. "How poor," The old man mentioned in his flimsy stumbling voice.

"Any news," Hamid changed the topic.

"Yes, I was passing by the golden street and in the way I saw some children, making stuffed toys. I looked the sun sign. It was glistening. Their smiles were beaming like the sun. Can we call these children angels?" The old man was confused.

"The difficult question, what would be the age?" Hamid asked the old man. The sun was setting. Now they could hardly see the faces of one another.

"Ten years or it can be eleven only," The old man's frail voice was stumbling in the jail. Hamid was in deep thought. He did not give any answer. "What are you thinking?"

"Nothing," Hamid replied carelessly.

"Looking them making stuffed toys I realized there would be any ceremony. I moved forward and entering the street, I listened the drumbeater. Therefore, I came to the point of the coronation ceremony. The queen had taken the decision."

"Has she married?" Hamid asked.

"No, I didn't hear any news like this." The old man was scraping the sun sign at the matchstick.

"Then who will be the king?" Hamid frowned trying to think something.

"I don't know." The old man shrugged his shoulder.

"Han, fine," Hamid held the lantern the old man threw matchstick to him. "No, not yet, I need it today for whole night." Hamid said and threw it back. The old man smiled and could not catch it due to her shivering hands. He picked it up.

"O poor week old man," The old man talked to himself and smirked. "Huh, I'll leave it here. The lantern has the oil for only few hours. It won't work the whole night." He informed Hamid.

"Ok," Hamid replied and lay on the floor with his arm under his head.

"Lantern has the light and the men have the eyes. The flame flickers and the tear beams." The old man was speaking.

"Yes, it happens." Hamid agreed at the point.

"This boy will be slaughtered one day after your execution." The old man lowered his voice a little bit more.

"What?" Hamid was shocked. "But he is too young." He was exasperated.

"Who will see? Yesterday, ten years old boy was executed for throwing a wrapper outside his house." The old man narrated.

"Sunasian he would be," Hamid asked in confusion.

"No one is innocent than Sunasians in this world." The old man spoke. Hamid was dejected at the news. "Yesterday the golden plate of the queen's cat lost and she cried a lot. In the evening, she found it but it was broken. Funeral was arranged at the night time." The old man grinned but Hamid was serious.

"Can you help me to let this boy escape?" Hamid asked him.

"I can't dear; if I could then I would escape you first." The old man answered. Hamid closed his eyes deeply and helplessly took a sigh of restlessness.

"Can this boy murder the king when he has not the nerve to bear the pain?" Hamid asked the old man.

"No other man can know other man internally; even a person can not know himself. The stamina of nerve changes every place and in any time. It's abrupt. Aggressiveness brings it and the death ends it. We are helpless in front of our nature and the rules of nature created by Omnipresent." The old man was speaking and Hamid was quietly listening. The dark was entering the room. The room was quiet for sometime.

"Don't be quiet, Sharma. It's good to listen to you. I am enthusiastic to talk at this time." The old man liked and he laughed. His dull eyes twinkled for this time.

"Yesterday, some people saw the dark shades. The vultures bit some people." The old man told him news.

"What?" the news shocked him.

"But they won't hit you," The old man tried to make him calm.

"Why?" Hamid asked.

"Because you have no days left with you," The old man dejectedly informed him.

"I am doomed." Hamid sneered.

"He has come." They heard the footsteps striking hard the ground. The old man abruptly stood and moved out. Hamid lifted his head up. He could not see but he could hear him unlocking the padlocks and moving. He heard the hard steps. Hamid was calm when he realized the old man had gone. There was hell dark in the room. He felt relief to talk to that old man. The night had fallen. The vultures flew near the iron bars but he could not look them nor could vultures enter the bars.

When Max awoke up, there was hell dark. He groaned, as his eyes could not see anything. Hamid moved his hands all over the place to find the matchstick and he found it. He lit the lantern. The room elucidated. The man headed to Max. The padlocks again unlocked. The old man came, silently put the food and went out.

"Are you fine, boy?" Hamid asked.

"Yeah," Max could hardly speak.

"Water or food," Hamid asked and Max vomited.

"Nothing," Max panicked and Hamid laughed.

"Dear, now you are to eat this daily." Hamid told him.

"I think I would die before my death." Max answered him wiping his mouth.

"What's your age?" Hamid asked Max who had put his head at the loose pillow underneath.

"I'm 20." Max answered.

"You are too young." Hamid admired.

"And what's yours?" Max closed his eyes.

"30," Hamid answered briefly. "I was twenty when I came here and ten years I spent in ten cells and now is the last stage. I fought for life and defeated death but now death is going to succeed." Hamid was narrating his story.

"Were you prisoner at the age of ten?" Hamid enquired.

"No, I was arrested on Sunday." Max asked.

"What?" Hamid was shocked. "How could it be? You are directly shifted here." Hamid asked.

"Because I killed the King." Max replied.

"O yeah, you are hero. The lions would have feared from you and the tigers would have scared." Hamid chortled.

"What lions? I haven't faced any lion ever in my life." Max told him carelessly.

"Do you know I fought lion?" The man smirked.

"When?" Max asked.

"In the last stage," The man replied.

"What last stage? What are you talking about? I can't understand." Max was ensnared. The man laughed.

"When I was twenty, I was taking my mother to the hospital but in a way she was enslaved and they arrested for murdering the treasurer's who was shocked. I had neither held any sword and nor seen the face of any such girl. I was brought to the cell. That was a big hall on the ground floor.

Hundreds of young prisoners were there, enjoying the life gleefully. They daily woke us up early morning and we were to clean the garden of the prime minister, treasurer and the King. We were also to sweep the palace. One day I was sweeping the palace when a girl came in front of me. It was nighttime, the messenger of the prisoners came to me, and he told me about the tomorrow's competition. We were to run as far as we could. The next day we were running before the wild dogs. The wild dogs were chasing us fast and we were running. The destination was above the mount. We were hundred and hundred wild dogs were chasing us." The man closed his eyes with fear. "Now I am master of them." The man smiled to look Max.

"What happened then?" Max was curious to know.

"Then I succeeded in such wars." The man sat down.

CHAPTER 11

⤐ The Coronation ⤏

The three elephants with red palanquins immersed in them entered the earsplitting crowd. They were maddening with joy welcoming the new king. The queen was in the palanquin at the first elephant. The two elephants were following him. Queen was patting his furry cat and did not bother to look the crowd. In the next, the elephant was swinging Prime Minister Abrahamus and his wife Ashley. Their smiles were glistening with the glistening of their dresses. They were waving hands in response of people showering flowers. The children were dancing rhythmically with the presentations of the stuffed toys, picking their toys up the head and then putting it in front of their tummy. The people were clapping gladly at their similar acts. They were smiling and showering some flowers at the children. Ashley was looking more graceful than the queen was. In the subsequent elephant, Bellatrix was sitting with his seventeen years old brother Clarke. She was looking gorgeous in her off-white cocktail dress and the both were smiling to see the crowd and one another. The fancy gloves had covered until elbows of Bellatrix and Ashley. People were yelling to welcome the new king. The Queen moved down the palanquin and went to the throne with proud and dignity. She sat on the chair with big back in between the four chairs. Prime Minister Abrahamus and Ashley sat on the either side of the queen. The queen was still caressing her cat. She did not look to the crowd roaring with joy. Abrahamus and Ashley were waving them. Bellatrix sat with Ashley and Bill with his father. The whole family settled on the fancy iron made chairs with triangular backs. The throne was arranged three feet above the crowd and the chairs were of five feet. The colorful stairs matching the chairs led to the seat. Everything was comfortable. The two men from front came holding the crown on a silver board. The crown was shinning by the glitter of the twelve gems in it. The velvety red fabric covered the golden structure of the crown. At the top, the twelve gems arranged spherically. Diamond was glittering in the middle among the twelve and the rest were shinning with the shine of the diamonds. The tiara taker had crossed the stairs and reached the queen. They bowed in front of the queen. Queen sternly looked to the crown instead of them. The crowd was noisy. She looked the drumbeater and the drumbeater realized the order. He struck the drum hard and there was silence. She moved down the stairs and took the crown from the tray. She was very tall woman of five feet and eleven inches. Her pendants were glistening in her five fingers, wrist, ears, neck and head. Her bracelet moved circular as she picked up the crown. Proud and arrogance were displaying from every feature of her face. Queen looked to Abrahamus and showed him her wicked smile. Abrahamus moved up and Ashley encouraged him with her smile. Abrahamus, a man of fifty years proudly moved to the queen holding a crown in her hand. He came near and the queen with a wicked smile put it at his head. The crowd applauded forcefully with excitement. Ashley and Bill clapped but Bellatrix was quietly viewing the crowd. There was not any excitement or gaiety on her behalf. She saw the crowd and took a deep breathe. The new King lifted his both hands up in response of the audience excitement. The King was smiling. Only Sunasians were invited on the coronation ceremony so no other gloomy face could be seen.

"King Abrahamus, Can the audiences have your words?" The queen in her heavy voice spoke in the noise. Only Abrahamus could listen.

"Make them quiet," The queen ordered the drumbeater in her clumsy heavy voice. The drumbeater started without being late and the crowd kept quiet. The queen looked to the king for the address.

"My people," Abrahamus started and the Queen moved back to the chair. Ashley looked to her with a friendly smile but she did not bother to look her. Bellatrix was looking to her father and Bill was excitedly looking the crowd. The queen's cat jumped to her lap. "Today I am addressing you and tomorrow someone else can address you. However, I promise you until the time I am here, I will try my best to soothe you in any difficulty and I will help you in every time of need." The crowd was applauding and the king was silently appreciating by lifting his both hands up. "The Earthman, the killer will never be forgiven." The King's tone changed. He was enraged and the crowd was infuriated.

"Yes, he is filth."

"He should be sentenced to death,"

"The filthy worm should be dead at the spot."

"He should be the food for the dogs."

"He is a devil,"

"He is demon," The crowd was cursing the murderer. Bellatrix's heart plummeted and she was worried at the slogans. King smiled and raised his right arm pointing the crowd to be silent. The drumbeater struck the drum and there was silence. The queen was caressing the cat and wickedly looking down to it. She did not look to the king for one time and neither did she seem to listen to the King.

"Soon, the day of execution for the killer will be decided." The King announced.

"May the king live long!"

"May the King have many lives?"

"May the King remain King forever?"

The crowd excitedly appreciated the king. The queen looked to the drumbeater and drumbeater struck the drum. The crowd was quiet now. Bellatrix was looking worried while Ashley and Clarke were looking happier.

"Abrahamus," The queen called and moved down the stairs. Abrahamus looked back. Queen was landing down with proud and the cat was wagging its tail behind her. The queen and the furry cat had reached Abrahamus. Abrahamus bowed. "Conclude quickly," Queen spoke slowly and with dignity. "We are to move to the killers soon." The queen winked and smiled wickedly. She turned abruptly and with proud moved to the chair.

'Yes," Abrahamus bowed again and then shifted his attention to the crowd. Bellatrix was looking tensed more. "My nation," King loudly spoke. "Show me your mark," The King lifted his right hand, and showed the fists to the regime where a sun sign were visible. The crowd looked to the sun sign and so they lifted their hands of the sun sign. Ashley also lifted her hand and so did Clarke. Bellatrix looked to her faded sun sign and looked to the crowd. She was confused and embarrassed. Her pupils were moving as she was looking onto the ground.

"We shall rule the Universe," The King with proud announced his next ambitions.

"Yes," The crowd liked the aims and spoke at once loudly. This time queen also lifted his right hand and made a fist with a leer. The crowd opened up the bottles of drinks and make rash sounds of hooting. The crowd was looking as if the universe was in their fists. The sun signs of the crowd were up. They were jumping and tossing. The queen stood up and moved down the stage. She was looking very serious and infuriated. The King followed her and the family as well. They sat in their respective palanquins and the crowd warmly said them farewell. The queen was looking too much serious and sad. The crowd was looking mad. They were dancing with joy showing their sun signs to one another and were happy in their activities. The queen glanced the crowd and this there was no more wickedness at her face. She was missing his King. The elephants were moving passively and the palanquins were jolting at them with the movements of the elephants. The queen shed some tears quietly what fell at her cat. The cat purred and wagged its tail.

CHAPTER 12

⊷ Tale of the Prisoner ⊶

"I was to reach above the mount. The dogs were chasing us. I did not know how many of they were bit and how many of they died. I just heard the cries of pain, the footsteps running after me and the sounds of people panting. I had reached my destination and I almost fell down. I could run but now I could not, because I was tired badly and they had given me the words that they would release me. I was confident and happy. I succeeded but later I realized that they had pulled the wool at my eyes. I was shifted to a new cell. They told me that I had crossed one-step to take freedom. My freedom can be after second step. I was anxiously waiting for the next competition. I was hopeful for the next competition will be soon. We were eighty left and rest of the others died. The dogs pounced at them and tore them into pieces. In this cell, we were given the task of sowing the seeds for the vegetation to be improved. The food was good and edible here. We were given the fruits in the morning. The fruits were rotten but to some extent, they were edible. Thirty baskets they would give us in the early morning and we would finish it as quick as possible. The days went by and all of we were waiting for the next competition. What horrible havoc would be that? We spent our days in thinking this. All of the Earthumen were contentious and warrior. Each one of us wished to live. In the daytime, we were given the same food and in the evening, there was no food. It was not a big room and we eighty would sleep at one another. We were eighty and more than fifty guards were guarding us. They had tied our feet with the chains so that we cannot be in the fugitives. I would daily awake up early in the morning and say my prayers. They daily see me like that and one day they beat me hard for I was performing my religious obligation. The whipped I with a lash and then I had to start it furtively. When was the prayer time, my friends would stand in front of me and made me hidden. I could be able to do this. One day they told me that I would work in the palace of the treasurer. I was to clean the whole house for there was happened to be any of the wedding ceremony. The guards threatened me that if I tried to escape I would be slaughtered at the spot and what I decided was somewhat same. I went their with a dozen of luggage at my back. My back stooped and it pained a lot, before I could relax, a woman handed me a broom and I was ordered to clean the house until evening. Moreover, I was told that I was to stay here for one week, as the wedding ceremony would last until one week. I was happy that I had a good chance to escape but the guards did not let me escape. They remained with me for the whole night. The wedding last for one month and I swept the house for one month. One day when I was sweeping the garden, I realized someone behind me. My sixth sense warned me of the danger. I swiftly turned. I saw a man going to stab me with his sword. I had no time to fear, think and tremble. I abruptly crouched and grabbed his legs. He fell with a jerk and the sword fell far away. I scampered to grip the sword but fell down by the man's leg, which he intentionally set in my way. He also did neither want to die and nor did I want to kill him. I fell upside down, my nose badly hit the ground, and the pain pinched me. When I was rubbing it, the man took hold of the sword. The fear of fatality forgot the pain. I quickly erected up and grabbed his hand of waving sword. I was infuriated at the man's act, both we were staring outrageously one another and both of us were panting. Both of us had the fear of being lost of this world and both of we were gathering courage to beat the other.

"What do you want?" I was wet with sweat. My eyes were closing with weakness and my gallantry was dismissing. I asked furiously. The man was scarlet red and he was loosing confidence and gallantry more than I was. He fell down and sword fell in his steps.

"My life," The man was panting.

"What do you mean?" I asked the panicked person.

"They suggested me to...." The man screamed and his neck rolled down at one side. He died before he could complete. I was shocked as a spear was pinched in his heart. I was confused that from where it came. The soldiers of Sunasians came galloping and cordon me. It baffled me.

"I...err... didn't err... kill him." The situation stammered me.

"We have the proof." The soldier pointed down with his sword. I looked to my right side. There was a bow and three spears in a spear holder in my footsteps. Thus, I realized the conspiracy. The scheme was awesome to trap me as I was going to succeed in the second stage as well. I was going to be free but the scheme did well. I could not do anything except to stare them. They jerked me and held me with the collar. The pulled me like animals. I was a murderer once more. They presented me in front of the king. I did not speak any word. The King infuriated to look my face and he sentenced me to death. I was shifted to the third cell. Now, along with my feet my hands had also locked in the chains. I mesmerized by the scheme. On the way to the new place, I was bare foot. The pavement between the prison cells was flinty. My feet blistered but the pain did not hurt as I was sneering at the plan. They pushed me into the new cell and I fell in between the many prisoners taking lunch. This is was a broad flinty room. The walls were rough and the prisoners had written their stories at those walls. I did not talk to any person in the cell. I was quiet and still could not believe at the situation. I neither wished to eat anything. At last, I lost the patience and I sobbed. The tears did not inform me that they are going out. The prisoners all around were chatting and enjoying their lives. My half-forgotten grief was renewed. I spent the whole night sobbing. I missed my mother and for the first time I wished to die. I wished the instances from the death of my mother until today a nightmare. Every thing awful in life looks like a nightmare. I slept and wished this nightmare to be ended when I awoke the next day, but nothing was so. Perhaps I was still sleeping. The prisoners were taking breakfast. I had not prayed for many days. One of them came near me and gave me my share of food. The clean fresh bread astonished me. There was one benefit in this jail that I was having the fresh food. I grinned at my contemplation. Soon I mingled with them. Eight months of this year passed waiting for the new test. One day I picked up the black coal and wished to write something and I could not write any thing. I threw the black stone desperately. One day the rumors informed me about the incident in the tenth month. He was the man who was ordered to kill me and if he will kill me, he will be free. He was also an Earthuman. The treasurer's daughter in the murder of whom I was accused was found alive near the valleys and for this very instance, they had to make a solid proof for the murder. I was to die either or the other person. The news did not tense me, as I could never appeal for the freedom. They trapped me very finely. The third year went by. On the last day of the third year, the King called out all the prisoners.

"The one who will win will breathe in the open air," The drumbeater announced the king's order. This time once again the desire of the freedom twinkled in my heart and I promised to do or die. They blindfolded us and brought out. After one year, I felt the free atmosphere but could not see it. They loaded us sixty in a carriage. I can feel all seated scared like me. The journey went on. We were weary of sitting. We could feel it a confined place and feel us jolting with the transport. We did not have the idea that what type of the vehicle was it? It was taking us away. At last, we felt the slow speed of the carriage and it had stopped. They ordered us to move down. Every one of us hardly moved down as our hands had tied. They stood us straight in a line and untied our hands. We could feel they were at our backs and they were more than we were. The hands of all of us were untied at the same time.

"Run, if you wanted to save your lives. You are free to run." I was at the front and we were shocked but the gaiety of freedom did not let us to think. Somebody pushed me and ran so did I also. Soon, in no minutes I heard the screams and cries after me. Some screams and shouts I could hear before the other and me at my back. I did not know that what was happening. I was also running madly. The people were coming and hitting into me. I could hear weeping and crying. I also felt my steps had mashed some bodies. I also kicked some and stumbled, as I was blind. My foot slipped and with a cry, I was going deep into something. There was no hurdle in the way where my feet could adjust themselves and nor was any snag. I was waving my hands in the air to take hold of something and at the end, I succeeded. My left arm was feeling heavy. I gripped the support with one hand and opened the blindfold with other. I twitched my head to bring myself to senses. I compressed my eyes hard to look. When I was able to see I saw an arrow pinched into my sleeves. I was shocked and I realized the bloodshed. It was a thick rope. It was moving me up. I looked around. It was a cracked Alberic into two pieces. I looked down and underneath was the river flowing. At once, I wished to leave the rope and jump into the river but I was fooled once again. It was taking me up and I reached the top. I climbed the stony path. My clothes torn from front. I lifted my leg up and saw the Sunasians forces all smirking at me. I looked down and witnessed thousand of corpses lying straight and upside down. Their eyes and mouths were open. The sight wept me. I cried in front of them. I squatted near my dearest friend who brought me the food for the first time. I cried like babies. The forces were laughing at me.

Once again, I was shifted to the new cell. My hands and feet were tied with one another. There were small cells. Each one was given a new cell. A person could only sit or stand in them. There was no place for lying. Miracle, it was that I was saved from the previous one but why was I saved. As was I moving to the new cells, I was facing new hardships. My back was stiffened and I would yawn to comfort it. A year I spent here. Daily I could see, anyone dragging at the path either going or coming. The person in my front cell was a woman. I daily saw her weeping. She just ate her food and wept. She was a very old man. I smiled to see her but she did not change her expressions and she was quiet. At last one day, I was succeeded and she smiled back at me. She became familiar with me. One day when I awoke up for namaz, I saw the back of the forces of Sunasians outside the old woman's cell. They had stooped at something. Soon, somebody brought the cot and they laid the woman at it. Her eyes were opened and I could see she was dead. I wanted to cry but some thing like that hung in my throat and my heart wept. I was alone as my partner was lost. The front cell remained empty and the next day I saw another dead body going. I said it a silent farewell. One day, I saw them dragging a young beautiful girl. They were all drunk. It was nighttime. I wanted save her but I could not even move my feet and hands. I lamented at my restlessness. The fourth passed like that and this time they shifted me to another cell without any trial. It was the fifth cell a somewhat better. I could lay here for sleep. A month passed here and I could perform my actions easily. Once I was offering the duhr prayer, some men entered unexpectedly. I was prostrating and my body trembled as they whipped me hard with a lash and picked me up with the collar, but I was reciting Quran silently. They were beating me at my uncovered back. I returned in a pain and they threw at the hard stone bed.

The next day I was brought to the palace and they keep me busy so I could not get the chance of performing the religious obligation. I was to take care of the royal animals and they give me good food at the end of the day. I was rubbing the back of the horse in the garden when I saw a young woman moving to me. She had the same wicked smile like the queen.

"So you are for how much time?" The woman asked proudly.

"I don't know," The woman smiled and went back without any word. I was perplexed. When I returned under the shades of swords to my cell, I was shocked to see the same woman in my cell. She smiled to see me.

"Hey I am queen's daughter." The woman introduced herself. "I think it would be enough for today," The queen said and moved out. I heard the door locking and I quietly sat down. Next day, I fed the cat and went to the stable. Today she was looking too much beautiful. She had wicked sharp looks.

"Can I have your time?" The woman asked me.

"What?" I hardly swallowed.

"You are very brave." The woman admired me and came very near me.

"I'll see you in the room." She went away. I was shocked and considering it a new trouble. At night, I was in my room and saying prayers. She came in and infuriated to see me. When I had completed and turned. She slapped me hard. I was enraged and I strangulated her. She was shouting and screaming. At this time, there was no one in the prison cell who could hear her screams. The blood dripped out of her mouth. I was strangulating her harder and harder. She scratched my hands with her nails in order to survive herself. The five years volcano of rage had erupted. She had stopped resisting now and her eyes were now closing slowly. I left her. She was almost dead. I felt her pulse. It stopped. The fire of my revenge snuffed out. I was feeling satisfied. I was sitting at my bed staring my feet unconsciously and she was lying dead near me. It was the first murder I did. Next day the search for the queen started. My one year had ended. I had hid her under my bed. No one could know that where was she gone. Before her corpse started decaying, I was shifted to the new cell. The corpse was found under the bed and the new prisoner was called responsible for it. I felt pity for him. I had the nerve to accept the crime but I enjoyed murdering the Sunasians and I wanted to murder more and more. I was satisfied now. In this cell, many other prisoners were with me. All of they became my good friends and one day like before they ordered to gather out of the cell. The queen was sitting chair at the arena. She was wickedly smiling and her cat was wagging its tail in the legs of the chair. She was in her black dress. We were ten now. One prisoner sat at a large distance form the queen. The Sunasians and we ten crowded the arena standing trying to understand the situation. His hands were tied and a gemstone was put at his hands. He was ordered to put his tied hands at his head. His back and legs were tied with the back of the chair and he could not move a bit. The queen picked up the bow and the arrow and took aim of the man. It hit his eyes.

"Boohoo," The crowd yelled. "Does it again, do it again," The crowd encouraged queen. The man was writhing with pain. His feet were trembling but he could not move. The queen took another aim and it hit his hands. This man got ten spears pinched in it. The crowd was worrying at the missing aims of the queen not for the pain of the man. At last, the man was motionless and was turn for the next. The next was ready to die. He was normal and he knew it was a new trial. All of we were about to cry. The Queen's could not take the right aim and she pinched six spears in the man. He was soon dead. The next man came and he was dead. The forth man came. This time queen succeeded in taking the right aim. The arrow directly hit into small gemstone. The man was saved. The crowd gleefully made the slogan and raised their hands admiring the queen.

"I enjoyed the game," The queen was smiling wickedly. We were stunned at the way of practice. In the gaiety of the taking, the right aim. The queen announced to spare the others. The carcasses were picked up and taken away. We were moved to another cell. This time at the end of the year, we encountered lion. All of my friends died. The lion tore them and at the end I tore it." The man stood up and went to the corner of the room. The night was falling and the room was darkening. Max could hear the man sobbing. Max was stunned.

Both of they remained quiet for some moments. "And what about your rest of the six friends.

"the lion ate three and the tiger swallowed the other. I am saved in this death of race." The man replied who had been better than before.

"When I came here in this jail, the King addressed me and I told me that they had given me a lot of the chances to escape but I didn't." The man gloomily told Max.

"What chances?" Max gasped.

"When I reached mount, no one came to me. I should run and once when i hung by the rope I should jump into the river."

"What?" Max was shocked.

"Yes," Hamid nodded and sneered. "Yet, this is not the all I told you but I've been tired of thinking."

"And I'm afraid to listen." Max told him. They were quiet now when they heard the locks being unlocked.

The queen and the new King entered. The queen smiled to look Hamid.

"It's really good to see you, Hamid," the queen caressed his cat. Her expressions changed to look Max. She was scarlet red with rage. She called her pointing her index finger. Max moaned and went stumbling to the queen. As he reached before, he could straighten himself, the queen slapped the little boy and he fell, as he could not control himself. Hamid impulsively stood up. He felt pity to see the pain of the little boy.

"just kill him, arrange the ceremony and just slaughter him," The queen was outrageously staring Max who was healing the pain of his back. The cat jumped put of her arms and out of the open bars. The queen came close to him and spat at him. Max was too much feeble for the reverse attack. She moved out in rage and the king followed her quietly. The servants also followed them.

CHAPTER 13

⊷ A Hope ⊶

The Coronation ceremony was over, the punishment of the murderer was decided and the day was being determined. Every Sunasian was happy for the new King and the reign of the Earthumen across the redline was vacating. Sunasians were not aware of it. They were thinking one of their achievements.

"Don't you have any hope for life?" Hamid asked him pouring water in to the bowl.

"Have you any?" Max had stayed his back with the back of the wall. He asked carelessly.

"Of course, I should not have but I shall have until the last moment." Hamid took a sip of water.

"What do you think? Again for this time, you will escape," Max, asked staring the ground.

"I am astonished at the thinking. Staying in jail, I do not want to live for one second and when the trial encounters me the desire for freedom arises and I pray for the one last chance." Hamid shared his feelings. Max looked to Hamid with a slight beam.

"Every time you are luckily saved," Max smirked. Hamid chuckled.

"And I am hopeful that I'll be saved tomorrow." Hamid told him.

"Tomorrow," Max knitted his brows.

"Yes, they have ended my days of life, but I have the hope." Hamid looked to him and shrugged his brows.

"Such a belief in hope," Max felt gloomy.

"The belief," Hamid took another sip of water and swallowed. He stared the wall. "I have not in hope, I have in Allah." Hamid puffed. "And you should have as well," This time, Hamid looked to Max.

"Bah... for what to live, to die day by day, to see our beloved ones dieing of hunger and thirst. It's the pain and it will never let me to live for one moment even." Max considerately told him. Hamid laughed off.

"Pain," He grinned. "You see a child crying and you can not quiet him, you see a person withering for thirst, but you can not give him water and you witness a man dieing of hunger but you can not provide him food." Hamid was sternly chatting. "You call this a pain?" Hamid looked to Max and put his bowl of water on the floor. He was infuriated. "You felt pain when you were dragged and the bandage soothed you. Have you ever tried to soothe your inner pain?" Hamid frowned. "No," Hamid answered himself without listening to Max. "No," Hamid answered himself. "Have you ever found any tonic for your inner pain? The pain is more pinching than the physical pain. I think if you will bring the thirst child water, it will soothe you. Instead, if you are fond of spectacles, the pains will really a fun. I think you feel proud in being an onlooker." The mocked and moved to the iron bars. The guard passed by the iron bars and smirked to look Hamid. Hamid was standing holding a vertical iron bar and his face stuck by bars. He did not look to the gatekeeper who was constantly looking him passing by him.

"Huh," Hamid puffed and moved back. Max was silently staring him. Hamid smiled.

"I am not an onlooker," Max was a little angry. Hamid laughed.

"I was an onlooker, a frightened onlooker, whose fate was to be decided on the scale of death. I was saved every time and every time I wished for death."

"Going back yesterday?" The jail keeper asked and Hamid turned. The jail keeper was standing with a smile. This time, this man did not stare him.

"Yeah," Hamid grinned. "Tomorrow,"

"Bye than, have a good journey," The jail keeper mocked.

"Of course I'll have dear," For the first time in a year both of they smiled to look one another. He looked to Max. He had moved to the stone bed. "This time I wish to live. During the reigns of my prison hood, I became the King of the prisoners. When I won the battle with the tiger, I was awarded the reward of the King of the Prisoners. I was standing on the wooden board, tired. There were cuts of tiger's nails scratching at my face, a deep wound at my left arm and I was panting. My body was shivering. The two bald bulky men came near me and put a so-called tiara at my head. It was the queen's cat golden plate. The crowd was laughing at me and I was staring the dead tiger near my steps. I couldn't believe that I had done it." Hamid was quiet for some moments. The dark was also looking gloomy. "Now, it has been unavoidable for them to kill me. Because, they have been afraid of me.' Hamid continued.

"What do you think? Tomorrow would be the new game?" Max asked him.

"May be, instead it must be." The man smirked. "If I got the chance, I won't loose it." Hamid told him.

"Listen Max, tomorrow, you will not find me here. However, be careful, they will never spare you. Do as what the old man would suggest you." Hamid was looking sad now. He sat with Max. Max looked to him who was staring the bottom.

"Are you really going tomorrow?" Max asked him desirously.

"Yes," Hamid was first time so brief. The burnish of hilarity at his face was fading. "They have prepared the gibbet." Hamid told with a murky voice.

"Did they do every time?" Max asked.

"No," Hamid replied and Max was thunderstruck. The man was quiet and Max as well.

"Don't worry, I'll join you soon." Max compressed his shoulder with his right hand.

"No," The man shouted. "You are to live." Hamid stood up. Max was restless. He was awakening until midnight. He did not want to loose that man. At the mid night, his eyes closed impulsively and he did not know what was happening. He was in a deep sleep. When the padlocks unlocked, Hamid lit on the light. The old man came in free handed.

"How are you dear?" The old man closed the door tightly after him and talked to him in his frail stumbling voice.

"I'm fine, just fine." Hamid was not warbling today. He did not enthusiastically to the old man. The old man smiled to know the situation exposed from his face.

"Disappointment," Sharma sat in the same place likes before and gazed him.

"No," Hamid replied.

"Fear," Sharma enquired. The man moved his head right and left. "Hope," The old man again enquired. Hamid did not answer.

"What about the plan?" Hamid disregarded the questions of the old man.

"It's perfect." Sharma answered.

"It should be." Hamid replied.

"Are you ready?" Sharma enquired.

"yes," The man answered. Sharma grinned.

"When a man can not face himself, he wishes to die." Sharma glanced him and Max.

"This is not so. I am ready to die for the reason that I should die." Hamid told him. "I murdered three men and a woman in life and now I wish to murder one more Sunasian." Hamid shared his wish.

"Don't worry. I'll give you the chance before the execution." Sharma laughed off.

"I'm serious. Before I die I want to cut off that queen's head." Hamid clutched his fists with anger.

"I wish you could." Sharma grinned.

"Is that girl agreeing?" Hamid asked him.

"Yes," The man nodded.

"Don't hurt my soul." Hamid requested.

"It won't ever be." Sharma replied. "Sleep now, take rest," Hamid answered.

"Who can sleep under the curtain of demise?" Hamid replied. "I am not at all sleepy. Tomorrow is a long siesta to start." The man grinned. Sharma came near him and gripped the man's hands.

"I'll miss you." Sharma stuck his tremulous lips with his hand and wept. Hamid was quietly looking the old man. The lamp light was fading and the dark was trouncing. Max was in a deep sleep. The next morning came. Hamid was at the gibbet and his head was in the rope of gallows. The surrounding place was crowdie. Sunasians were hooting at Earthumen. Hamid put his head down and the black man, the executioner picked up the thick sword and cut his head. The blood flowed, the crowd roared and the queen soared with joy. She was looking very wicked. Her red eyes were erupting flame and fire and the smile was emitting disgust. She finished her drink and threw at the cut off head of the victim. She was wobbling with joy in the stink of the drink and Max awoke up with a jerk. He swallowed hard and felt crowd roaring. He was panting and dunked in sweat. He compressed his eyes and looked around the room. There was no one. He was alone. The rays of the sun were peeking through the iron bars. It was morning, he had seen a horrible dream, and the dream was going to be true after a few minutes. The padlocks unlocked and the old man entered with the tray. He was disheartened and down. He put the tray of breakfast and was going to go out.

"Where is he?" Max asked impatiently. Sharma looked to him and moved out of the door. Max could understand his silence. He was dead. He was quietly looking the room when he saw a white paper placed near his bed. He picked up and unfolded it.

Dear little friend,

I have not the nerve to awake you up, else I wish you to see me last time. Remember, when a strong fragile rope will entrap my neck, when the panel will be pulled away from my feet, the terrific mask will cover my face, I shall hear the screams of my nation repressed by the screams of Sunasians, when my body will be hung like a rope, motionless, helpless, when I shall feel the hand of angel pulling out my soul, I shall be dreaming of one thing. It will be hope, which will lead you to success, the bright future of Earthumen. Never loose hope and be straight. Fight them and tear them away. They are filths. I have planned something, the old man will tell you. Just follow him and let you be saved. Be hopeful. Remember, hope and faith never leaves you, unless your valediction.

From a dream, just like a wave
Of air
Hamid

The letter ended and he remembered her mother. The executioner was same for both of the time. He wept a lot. He could not stop himself. He did not look out for many times. Sharma daily came and performed his duty and they did not talk to one another. The days went by passively and passively the grief was reducing but the pinch of the incident left its mark at the hearts of the both.

"Why was it happened every time? The person he loved would leave him." He thought. He put his head in his knees.

"I'll never leave anyone." His lips were quiet but his mind was deciding. He felt the pain of the lashes before execution. He felt blood dripping down his body. He clutched his fists and closed his eyes firmly.

"That's the pain and the hope." Some one whispered slightly in his ears.

II

The royal garden was in full bloom. The flowers were twinkling, buds were smiling and the fruits were tossing at their puberty. On the green damp grass in the fading blue dawn, Bellatrix was walking bare foot. Her long fancy cloak was waving slightly with the cool breeze. The moist of damp grass crawled through her feet and passed slowly and smoothly near her neck. She took a deep breathe of freshness, but she still felt herself restless. She was cordially thinking of someone. Her dazzling eyes dazzled and twinkled as she thought something horrible and what feared her.

"Can I have some steps with you?" He heard a gentle voice at her back. The voice impressed her. "Clarke, he would be," An idea guessed his mind. "But Clarke isn't so gentle," Another thought tried to guess the voice. He abruptly turned back but was shocked to see a new face. He was a young man smiling.

"Can I have your introduction?" Bellatrix knitted her brows with a princess' proud.

"Servant is called Leonardo." He bowed slightly with a smile. Bellatrix frowned.

"Who are you?" Bellatrix asked in frenzy.

"Really a servant," The man smiled again and looking her confused laughed lively. "I am the prime minister's son. I was astonished the last night that the three members of the royal family had come to meet us and the fourth one was absent, the one for whom I was most anxious to meet." Leonardo stared into her eyes. She was in a dilemma of what to do and what not to do. "Why did not you come to meet us?" Leonardo asked after some minutes of silence.

"I was sleeping." She justified and looked to hibiscus flower where a little daisy was pinching its beak and Leonardo got the chance of looking her face more attentively.

"You should be, and if you should not have been perhaps I would have forgot to look the moon." It stunned Bellatrix and he stared the man.

"Clarke," She saw Clarke coming and she ran to her disregarding the man. Leonardo chuckled. He looked to her long wavy hair what was moving at her back.

"Hey Mr. Leonardo beautiful morning," Clarke greeted him.

"Morning," Leonardo said and both of them shacked hands.

"It's a good day, today," Clarke continued the chat looking to the trees of blue berry.

"Yeah, it really is," Leonardo eloquently motioned his brows. Clarke was busy in looking the beauty around and Leonardo was staring the path deep into the space where Bellatrix had disappeared.

"Our forefathers taught us to clutch the world in our fist." Clarke diverted the attention of Leonardo. Leonardo chuckled. "I think we are damn idiot following our forefathers." Leonardo was astonished at the comment.

"Why so? The world is under us." Leonardo stated.

"Yes, it is but we are taking its support to stand erect." Clarke said normally.

"No, we are not, they need us, we don't need them." Leonardo shrugged his shoulders.

"We are arrogant so that's our thought." Clarke grinned and Leonardo frowned.

III

"Oh, Mr. Max, So alone... This is the worst time of a man's life when he knows that something like death is near to him." Max looked back to see the speaker and was shocked to look the three forces' men standing side by side. The man standing in between the two was smiling to see him. Max turned and put the letter in his pocket. The iron bars' door was opened and there was no one except the three. "My heart fears when I think about your punishment. The King has chosen the cruelest punishment for you. Such type of punishment has not been given to anyone." The man pretended to be shivering with fear.

"But it's not my execution today." Max baffled and frowned.

"Of course, it isn't. But King has called you for the last wish." The man had put his hands in his pockets and he was chatting softly and with dignity to him.

"Last Wish?" Max was stunned, as Hamid did not talk any thing like that.

"Yes," The man nodded. "I am Jesse, instead Captain Jesse. I work in the Navy forces but here I've come to help my friend Bellatrix." Jesse smiled.

"Bellatrix?" Max frowned.

"Yeah, Now move, we have no time to waste. King wants to have a chat with you." Jesse Informed and moved out. The two soldiers remained there for him to come. He moved his steps and slowly and both of they moved after him. He saw the place for the first time. There was no other room and no man in this place. At the end of this forsaken place were broken and shattered stairs. Jesse warily moved down the stairs due to the week construction. The stairs were shaking as the men were moving down. They had stepped down the stairs. Jesse was moving passively with the dignity of an officer. He was a tall and a young looking elegant man of his age. He looked polite and courteous by his manners. The first man of any Sunasians impressed Max. Max was looking to his cadenced gait.

"Come on quick, gentle man," Jesse spoke without looking back. Max paced to him.

"I've such sympathies for every prisoner." Jesse told passing through the dark hallway. The old man with the lantern in his hand had also joined them. "Switch it off." As they crossed the hallway Jesse ordered, the old man and the old man switched it off with a puff of air. "A little bit tough," Jesse murmured. There was still dark and the men could not look to one another. "Wait," Jesse slowly answered. He moved forward and peeked into the hallway. There were cells of the iron bars, many of the prisoners were hidden on either side of the iron bars. Jesse peeked into the hallway. A soldier was patrolling with a thick lash in his hand and guarding the prisoners. As he came to him, Jesse quickly moved back and the others as well. They hid behind the wall. The sound of the shoes smacking the flinty floor was coming nearer and they were sliding backward slowly. The sound was now moving far. Jesse slowly peeked through the wall and saw the guard-moving going backward.

"Move," Jesse whispered and the old man with the lantern move first following Max and then the other two with Jesse moved crossing the entrance of hallway. At the end Jesse moved. All of they safely reached and moved hiding behind the wall. "It's over now." Jesse whispered moving with Max.

"What?" Max frowned.

"The dangers, the people in these iron bars are prisoners for life. Neither they are allowed to die and nor they are allowed to live." Jesse explained Max nodded. Crossing the back yard, they rode him in a carriage. Sharma, Jesse sat with Max. The coachman pulled the reins and the two horses carrying the carriage galloped. The men of the forces rode the horse and galloped along with the coach on its either sides.

"Can I ask you that what's it all about?" Max asked him as the carriage had taken its speed. Jesse grinned and looked out to his friend's horse. Jesse took cigar and puffed. Max looked to the smoke whirling.

"King has called you. I've already told you." Jesse carelessly replied.

"Then why were you hiding from the guards?" Max asked and it confused Jesse.

"CRAP ... Mm... It was erring... just... err a ..."

"It is something more important than the King's meeting," The old man assisted Jesse who was perplexed.

"Well, what is it? Tell me, if it is all about me." Max was infuriated.

"Listen boy," Jesse threw cigar outside the window and closed it firmly. He stooped a little and put his elbows at his knees. "We are going to take you to a place and if any trouble happens you are to compromise with us." Jesse sternly said.

"So, you are going to kill me." Max was looking angry.

"No, son, it is not like that." The old man said in his fragile voice. Jesse was rubbing his head with his fingers trying to answer him logical.

"Just keep quiet." Jesse sternly ordered him looking him into his eyes. The old man squarely looked to Max and the window. There was no more chat in the carriage. The carriage was jerking, jolting and bumping at the road all the way. Starting the journey in noon the carriage stopped in front of a mesmerized and fascinating palace at the midnight. Jesse took a deep breathe and moved out. The old man was looking out of the window removing the curtain and Max was quietly staring the old man. Max looked out of the window. Jesse was talking to the men on the horses and the coachman was standing near them looking all around. One of the men moved away from there and vanished behind the bushes and the other three looked him going and vanishing. Jesse was looking in a serious tension. He was displaying the expressions of worry. Max looked to the old man looking out to the window of his side. Soon after some minutes of serious nervousness, the man came back. He told something to Jesse standing in between them. Jesse nodded thoughtfully after listening to his non-stop conversation. Max saw his lips moving. The coachman nodded and stepped to the carriage and rest of the three entered through the backward door of the palace.

"Come out," The coachman ordered. Max dropped the curtain and came out. "Everything sets." The coachman told the old man when they were walking side by side. They also entered the backward door. The hall way was glittering with diamond and the riches of all types. The stepped over the velvety stairs and reached the first floor. Jesse was standing with his friends in between the corridors. One of the friends saw them and they moved forward. Jesse was moving at the front, the old man, Max and the coachman were walking after him. In addition, his friends were following them. There was complete silence. Crossing the corridor, the sight stunned Jesse. All of they had crossed the corridor and turned right. Jesse abruptly moved back and thumped him at his face. Max moaned with a painful cry and fell onto the ground. The old man with fear moved back. Jesse kicked the lantern in his hands. It struck the wall and its glass smashed into pieces. His friends held the old man firmly by collar with rage. The old man was shivering with fear. Before Max could stable, he received another blow. His head knocked into the pillar nearby and he was fainted for some moments.

"Can I ask you the reason of misleading that old man?" Jesse growled. Max had held his hands and for some minutes, he had lost his senses. The forces' men standing at the right hearing the fuss reached them.

"What happened?" One of them said.

"He is the King's murderer, what is he doing here?" The other man identifying him thoughtfully asked.

"I don't know." Jesse shrugged his shoulders. "I was just passing by when I saw this old man groaning with pain and I realized the situation. He must have misled this old man." Jesse ground his teeth in anger. He stepped to the old man and pulled the frail poor old man mercilessly with the collar. He lifted the old man two inches up from the floor and angrily stared him into his eyes.

"I... err... didn't do.... I...I no, no...." The poor old man was stammering and stumbling simultaneously. Jesse smacked him down and the two friends held the stumbling old man by the arms.

"Take him to the king," The forces' men growled. The two men mercilessly dragged the half-fainted Max kicking him in the hall way and across the stairs. Jesse looked to his friends helplessly rubbing the hands.

"What did you see?" Jesse angrily looked to his friend and thumped his hand strictly into the pillar nearby. "Now what will happen?" The old man was shivering. Jesse ground his teeth in anger.

IV

Max was sitting in front of King at a wooden chair with a bandage at his head. The King was furiously staring him and the queen was standing near the king gazing Max wrathfully. Max had his eyes down. There was queer silence. The forces had surrounded the room the cell.

"Why did you kill the king?" The King roared.

"My hobby," Max shuddered. The executioner was standing near Max and grabbed his disheveled hair. The eyes of queen protruded with rage. Max moaned as the grip was stiff.

"Why did you try to run?" King asked another question.

"Every prisoner does." Max told as the executioner left his disheveled hair and his head jerked forward.

"So you tried to escape and you could not be fugitive and you could never," The queen stood by putting his arm at the table and spoke in her grave tone.

"You speak so ghastly," Max moved his eyes up but head still drooped down and stared the queen. He showed his great wrath. The queen was stunned. The soldier standing near by the chair came and kicked the boy hard in his abdomen. Max moaned awfully. The executioner again grabbed his hair. The king was also shocked.

"Stop," The queen shouted. "Arrange the ceremony tomorrow of his execution and make his death as miserable that people will even fear to think of King's murder." The queen gnashed her teeth in anger and spluttered like a serpent. Max grinned. She held her waving hand touching the ground and the ruby at its either sides flickering. She irately stared the prisoner and moved out in rage. The King stood up and followed the queen. The soldiers unlocked the doors and moved ahead leaving him alone. He was again in the same iron bars and was in a deep thought. The old man standing out side stealthily looked outside and opened the door with the keys. Max looked and was stunned. His anger aroused but the old man smiled.

"I know the reason of your attitude but I won't mind." The old man grinned and sat in front of him where King was sitting. He moved the bowl of water to him. "Relax and drink. Flee away your anger." The old man said him in his flimsy voice.

"What is it all spat?" Max scornful asked and pushed his hand with a jerk. The little water dripped as the old man held it firmly by both hands. The old man giggled.

"Now you are laughing, making fun of me?" Max scornfully outraged. "You befooled me." Max was speaking and the old man was giggling.

"Ok, Ok., Ok, Stop," The old man put the water bowl down and accepted defeat showing him his palms. "Listen Boy," The old man started. "The princess wants to meet you." The old man whispered coming very near to him. Max was shocked.

"Isn't it a new trouble?" Max was tangled.

"No, it's not. She wants a special chat with you." The old man whispered.

"Does every prisoner have it before the execution?" Max frowned ad he asked.

"You are lucky." The old man leered.

"Are you feeling well?" He could hear the same steps and the voice he heard before. He looked to his right. He was Jesse with a lively smile at it. Max was filled with wrath and he turned his face from him.

"Fine, I'll deal with it later." Jesse disregarded his attitude. "I think we have no time to waste." Jesse told him. Max looked to the old man who was smirking. The old man stood up and pointed Max to move out.

\ All of they again crossed the same route and reached the palace. This time they succeeded, as they had looked the path very carefully. Stepping up the velvety stairs, they soon reached the door of the room. Max was staggering all the way, as his leg was wounded. Jesse knocked the wooden door with red shinning lining at it. He knocked for one more time. The door opened.

"Hey Jesse, you," Bellatrix looked excited to see the man.

"Yeah," The man agreed on the smile.

"Where is he?" Bellatrix whispered.

"Here," Jesse turned back and moved him in. He locked the door behind him. Max entered the room. It was bedroom. The paintings of warriors had hung at the walls. She was impressed to see the works. In the room, Jesse was standing side by side him and Bellatrix was standing in front of him.

"Max," Bellatrix was excited to see him and smiled but he was grave and offended.

"I know what's going in your mind?" She softly smiled. "But it's really good to see you here. I feel myself in you." Max was tangled by her discussion. "My joy knew no bounds to see you." Max frowned. She looked to Jesse who was staring her.

"What about the plan?" She whispered politely.

"Every thing is ready, Bellatrix." Jesse answered her.

"Dad comes to visit my room next day in the evening and mom in the noon. Tomorrow the institute is off. I think we'll be back before noon." Bellatrix asked him.

"Yeah, but I think we should be before noon." He suggested.

"Ahab, Fine," Bellary agreed.

"Let's move then. We have no time to waste." Jesse advised. The door opened with a jerk and the coachman came in. He was panting.

"Leonardo is coming to your room." The coachman warned the.

"O no," Bellatrix grunted.

"His filth," Jesse was outraged. Max was still entangled.

"Calm down," Bellatrix held his arm. "Do some thing." Jesse pushed and roamed in the room for the hiding place. Bellatrix also looked around. At last, they succeeded. The door knocked and Bellatrix opened the door. The matter had settled. "Yes," Bellatrix asked the man proudly standing in the door. The man cunning looked to the girl.

"I just came here to say you good night and have sweet dreams." Clarke with a smile told him. Bellatrix nodded thoughtfully.

"Yes, good night, I'll have," Bellatrix sternly replied squarely looking his face and his captivating dress.

"Take care," Leonardo shrugged his brows and stared into her eyes.

"Fine bye," She angrily closed the door hard. She was scarlet red with rage. She sat at her bed. After waiting for some minutes, the door opened with a jerk and Bellatrix abruptly looked to the door.

"He's gone." The coachman informed. She ran to the window, released the curtain, opened it and peeked put. Jesse and Max were standing at the small place stuck to the wall holding the hands.

"Come in," Bellatrix said.

"Bellatrix, we are coming by the wall." Jesse hardly spoke. "You take all of them with you." Jesse said and Bellatrix closed the window.

"Right," Bellatrix murmured and looked to the coachman.

"Let's move." The coachman said and they moved out. Soon all of they met at the back of the palace. Jesse and Bellatrix were sitting side by side and Max and Sharma were sitting side by side in front of them.

"Where are we going now?" Max was tangled. Bellatrix smiled.

"I'm pretty sure that you have not murdered the king." Bellatrix frankly told him.

"Lady, I did," Max sternly replied. The carriage stopped.

"Ok bye, Jesse, Good luck Max," Sharma moved down. "Have a nice trip Princess." Bellatrix smiled. Max had frowned.

"How would you feel when you will see your mother," Bellatrix enquired him.

"Don't try deceiving me. She is dead." Max told while staring out of the window.

"But she is not, Max," Bellatrix told. "I am taking you to your mother.

"My mother isn't a joke." Max shouted with rage and Bellatrix eyes opened wide.

"It is not a joke for me. Do not be tensed Max. She is fine." The girl told him.

"I don't want to discuss her any more." Max was offended.

"Ok, Take this," Bellatrix gave him a red box and Max thoughtfully hold it.

"What is it?" Max asked.

"A past of your and mine," Bellatrix sadly grinned and looked out of the window. It had started raining. They could hear the splashes and the clouds roaring. Bellatrix looked down. His feet and hands were locked in the chains. "Hey Jesse unlock him," Bellatrix was worried.

"Oooops, sorry, just forgot, the coachman has the key. We would do it near the house."

"Fine," Bellatrix agreed.

"Listen Max, you are going to meet your mother soon," Bellatrix, informed him. He astounded.

He frowned and the deep feelings of love touched him. He felt he was hugging her white haired mother, wrinkles at her face and she would have been weak at his loss. The carriage stopped in front of nicely cut long bushes. The carriage stopped. Jesse moved down. The coachmen came in and freed him of the chains. He was astonishing at the gratefulness of this girl. The girl went out of the coach and he followed her. He stood nearby her Jesse was not present and rest of the other were there. He looked to her. She was beautiful young girl and looking good with Jesse. Soon Jesse came out with a woman. He had held him by his right hand around her shoulder and left hand in his hand. She was smiling and her face was showing excitement. She was stumbling and looking to another direction instead of forward. Max saw her and was stunned. The vague image of his mother came to his mind. She was looking dazzling than before. She had changed. She was dressed in jewels. The sight made her furious.

"Miss Martha," Bellatrix respectfully shouted and moved to her. The name was also the same. Max was offended."

"What I was expecting was totally different!" He chewed his teeth lips in anger and clutched his fists. Now Bellatrix had held her. Jesse came with Max.

"Your mother," He told him.

"No, he can't be," Max mumbled and Jesse stunned.

"He is," Jesse told him.

"My son," Martha moved his hand up in the form of a lap.

"He is not," Max, growled. "To get riches, you left my father. Therefore, the story was true. You murdered him." Max shouted in rage. "To get the gem stones," He swiftly rushed to the carriage wiping his tears and moved in. Everyone was thunderstruck. Martha's hands widely spread for lap were moving back. Bellatrix rushed to the carriage and opened the door. Max was sobbing like a child.

"Max," She softly started. "You are taking it wrong." Bellatrix sternly told him.

"No," He shouted,

"He was disloyal to my father. She cheated my father. The statement was true. I was and I am a rebellion's son." Max raged with fury. Bellatrix helplessly closed her eyes and repressed her lips. She looked to him again. He was wiping his tears. She closed the door and moved out. Jesse was coming out. He had left Martha in the huge house. They took back their seats and the journey started. The mood of everyone was off.

"You did not behave well." Bellatrix harshly said.

"Who are you to speak to me like that?" Max was tensed and he did not know what he was speaking. Bellatrix was quiet and Jesse did not comment. The carriage was moving faster. There was silence. After a journey of two hours, the carriage stopped near the mount. All of they moved out. Jesse and Bellatrix leading Max were going up. Jesse's friends and the coachman remained there.

"Keep both things with you," Bellatrix was advising him and he was quietly moving up. The wounds and the pain in his whole body were uncomforting him. He was hardly moving up. Jesse held his hand and soon they reached at the top of the mound. A man with a turban at his head and his face covered by a veil was standing alone. The girl rushed to the boy. Jesse and Max stayed there. The moon was shinning in the skies.

"How good to see you?" The girl smiled lovingly. The boy nodded. The girl turned and went to Max.

"Go, your friend is waiting over there for you," Bellatrix told him and the boy could not understand the situation.

"Go," Jesse forced him. Max unconsciously moved up the steps.

Jesse and Bellatrix was looking him from the back. Her eyes showered and the tears flowed out.

"Bellatrix," Jesse called her as she saw her weeping.

"Thanks Jesse," The girl wiped her tears.

"The least I could do for my best friend." Jesse said with a comforting smile and the girl hugged him.

"Thanks," She was sobbing. Jesse saw into the dark. Max was going into the dark and had been invisible now.

"Why the girl did this mercy at me? Why did she do this to me? Who is my friend coming to take me?" The questions like that were entangling him and he was confusing. He was hardly pacing to the river as the wounds in his ankles, heels and elbows were hurting him but he was struggling to achieve his new destination. Whom was the man waiting for him?

V

Down the mount, he saw a man standing with his back to him. He was patting the horse and a horse was at his back.

"Excuse me," Max started after a little hesitation. The man turned. He had a black turban at his head what had covered his face.

"Max," Man called.

"Yeah," Max answered and the man uncovered his face. The features were familiar to him but he could not remember well.

"You," Max asked thoughtfully.

"What have you been told?" The man smiled.

"Probably an Earthumen and want to help me." Max tried to guess the riddle. The man laughed lively.

"Not probably but surely," The man stooped his head a little and peeked into Max's eyes. He took out a paper and gave to Max. He unfolded it and was stunned to see the paper. The mind visited his past and he was finding the same paper lost eight years ago and boy took it with him. The feeling of joy watered his eyes. He looked to the man. The maturity was evident at his face. He had been young and this time he came for his survival.

"Abdullah," He murmured. The man hugged him warmly. Max with joy closed his eyes. "Can you trust a rebellion?" Max asked implausibly after being departed.

"No, but I can trust a well-wisher," Abdullah smiled and slapped lovingly at his shoulder. Max nodded to look him. There were smiles of joy and gay at both of the faces. "The way is too dangerous and too far. Take your horse and let us move. We are to leave the area before dawn." Abdullah gave him instructions and both of they without being late rode the horses. The horses walked and soon entered the forest. It was a thick forest. They were pacing calmly.

"Where shall we go?" Max asked holding the reins of the horse. His horse had been at the distance near the shoulder of Abdullah's Horse.

"Hexane men Colony, It will take a day to reach." Abdullah had covered his face with veil. There was queer silence in the forest. The owls were hooting and the howls of the wolves could be heard with the passage of time.

"What is it?" Max asked confusingly.

"The Colony of Earthumen. Six men started and now it has become a reign." Abdullah explained him.

"Hmmm" Max nodded. "You took a great risk," Max started after some pause.

"No, I don't think so. I've taken the greater risks than this." Abdullah said.

"What do you mean?" Max frowned. Abdullah chuckled.

"How is Saira?" Max asked him.

"He is well and fine." Abdullah replied normally.

"Any news about Mary, Frank, Bill," Max looked to him.

"All are good, free and independent," Abdullah boldly answered.

The horses paced through the thick forest and reached almost the end. The horses, now trotted, ambled and galloped tearing the mid of the forest. The sleeping wild animals scared and opened their eyes. The owls were hooting and the wolves were howling. The moon was hardly peeking into the forest.

On the other hand, the carriage was moving fast. The two horses were galloping harder at the either sides of it. Bellatrix was doomed. Both of they were facing one another in the carriage.

"Thanks Jesse," Bellatrix started.

"The least I could do for you, it's nothing for you," Jesse looked at her face. She was looking too much sad.

"How good is it? We spent the educational eras together and still you care for me." Bellatrix slowly admired her and Jesse smiled. "Martha would be too much gloomy. She would be doomed and dumped."

"I'll take care of her." Jesse tried to release her tension.

"We should meet her before going to the palace." Bellatrix looked to Jesse.

"No, we have not enough time. You should be in your bed room and I should be at my place before the velvety dawn will aware of the first ray of the sun." Jesse advised her. "I'll see her and provide your every info about her health." Bellatrix nodded and looked out of the window through the curtain.

"How did she get blind?" Bellatrix asked him curiously.

"The very first of wedding, when Jensen came to see her. She pushed him and ran to the stairs but her foot slipped and she fell down the stairs. Her sensitive part was hurt and she was blind. I was sleeping in my room and the scream opened my eyes. The scream still awakes me up just like a night mare." Jesse shivered with fear.

"Can't she be fine like before?" Bellatrix asked. The carriage was jolting.

"No, I asked for many doctors but nothing could happen." Jesse told and Bellatrix was dejected.

The next day was like a doom. King was outraged and the queen was furious. In a fury, she stabbed her cat and it was moaning awfully. The queen trampled it under her feet. She was in rage moving in the room. The maids ran out to survive from the cruel consequences of the rage. The king was roaming in the courtroom and the security guards were proving themselves right. On that day, the small towns of the Earthumen colony were burnt and smashed. People came out crying and shouting, cursing the king. The infants were stabbed, the young men were stabbed and the small children were cruelly murdered. The ropes hanged all the guards of the Jails and the servers of the prison hood were killed. Along with all the servers, three spears hit in the heart of Sharma. He was cold at the spot. The King sent his forces after the prisoner in every corner of the world. Bellatrix was sleeping calmly in her room as she was tired and Jesse was saving his reign at the shores of the sea. Jesse stabled his cap at his head and looked far into the seas. The ships were roaming in the seas for practice.

"Sir," A man came near him. Jesse looked to his right and the man saluted. "I have an order from the king." He was a soldier of Sunasian's forces.

"What?" Jesse turned to him. The man gave the rolled paper to him. He unrolled it and read it. He looked to the man.

"Ok," Jesse replied. The man struck his foot by the ground made a salute and marched back. He saw the man going to his horse and soon his horse galloped. His friends came near him. He grinned to see them and stared the sea. He tore the paper into small pieces disdainfully. He squatted and flowed it into the sea. Both of his friends understood the matter and they saw the paper scraps drowning into the sea. The currents of water swapped the bits and they soon were vanishing.

"The sea admonishes the garbage." One of his friends in the same uniform like him spoke. Jesse looked high into the skies. The black clouds were gathering and hiding the sun. A raindrop fell at his left hand.

"Stormy," Jesse looked back. The other friend who was silent was staring the three stars at his left shoulder. Jesse frowned and his friend was constantly staring them.

"Alan," Jesse called and he ogled. He squarely looked to the stars and his face. Jesse smiled and Alan had to smile. The cool breeze was bowing and the grey dark was covering the city. The calm sea was going to shout. The ships roaming on the surface of the sea were moving back to the seashore. Jesse inhales the cool breeze and it soothed his brain.

"Let's have a nice lunch at the muddy day," The boy standing with Alan invited loudly all the captains landing near the seashore. All of they moved to take their lunch.

VI

"I shall have forgotten you having the post of minister's wife, you'll think. The birth of my daughter increased my fear and the tension of Abrahamus. He was not suspecting it, but Martha believes me, I and my daughter would not be able to escape. Being Oliver's sister they sold me because of the crime my brother did and I am confident that he will not have done so. I will always miss you and my brothers. I'm

hopeful Tom would also be fine and enjoying the days of life."

Yours heartedly,
Rose Beck hem

However, unfortunately the letter could not reach her, which I stealthily hid in my drawer. The days went by and one day I got the bad news of the arrest of my brother's wife in the murder of my brother. I can never forget the day. She was calm and quiet and a soldier had held her from the hair and threw her in the palace in between the onlookers. Her beauty impressed the hall and she was standing in front of the people for the auction. Jensen paid the highest price and she was fainted. Jensen ran to her, picked her up and went out.

The problem for the king was to execute Martha but she was sold. In this way, I was a trash now for the prime minister and she sold me in front of the king. I was slave and I thanked God when they sentenced me to death. I was auctioned five times to new customers and this time I was going to be sent to God. Before my death, I only heard that Martha got married at the condition if the Sunasians would not do any harm to his son. I was satisfied about Max that he will be safe now. Living the last day in my prison hood, I was happy for tomorrow getting rid of this cruel slavery but I am worried about my daughter.

"May she be saved and may she find her real destination."

The words on the paper ended and Max folded it back. Abdullah entered hastily and was tensed to see the face of Max has faded face. He was looking dejected.

207

"What happened?" Abdullah enquired and Max quietly handed him the pages. He quietly sat down with his head drooped down. Abdullah read it and looked to Max.

"Don't worry. The history of Earthumen is full of such ordeals. None of the Earthumen is saved from their trials. It's a miracle that your cousin and your mother are alive." Abdullah consoled him. He handed him the paper and moved out but hastily returned. The faded Max was active now. "The King's forces are out, wandering." Abdullah informed him nervously.

"What?" max was shocked.

"Let the dark to fall completely and than we shall move out." Abdullah silently instructed him and Max nodded wisely. The soldiers shouting, neighing of the horses' hooves and their hooves striking the ground was coming nearer to the cave. They were sliding back and back. At once, Max's foot hit by a flinty stone and he fell down backward with a jerk. The red box opened and the dazzling white light illuminated the cave.

"What is it?" Abdullah reprimanded him.

"I... I don't know." Max stammered and confused.

"Switch it off quick," Abdullah ordered him strictly. Max moved his hands here and there and a very small circle came in his hand.

"Something like a loop," Max told him.

"Whatever is it, just hide it," Abdullah ordered strictly.

Max quickly put it back into the red box and locked it. There was again dark in the room. Max and Abdullah heard the steps coming nearby. The men peaked in. There was hell dark. They entered a step and both of they hid behind the stone. There was no one.

"Move out," One of the men shouted.

"Faster," the other one abruptly growled.

Both of they moved out when the voices perished. Abdullah moved out sticking to the wall and slowly slid to the entrance. Sticking to the wall, he peeked out. There was no one. The forest underneath and the water was flowing peacefully along with the mountains. Abdullah took a deep sigh of relief and closed his eyes for a little instant to make him calm. Max also came out behind the Alberic.

"Everything sets," Max, asked wiping the dust at his shirt.

"Huh, Yes," Abdullah nodded and turned to him.

"Fine, what about the next plan?" Max was feeling comfort now.

"Hey, first tell me what was in the red box in your hand?" Abdullah asked curiously.

"I.... I... really do not know. Bellatrix gave it to me." Max explained.

"Bellatrix," Abdullah knitted his brows. Max was stunned at his naming her like Jesse.

"Yes," Max nodded.

"Fine, show me," Abdullah asked him and Max gave it to him. Abdullah opened it. The room again dazzled. The room was illuminated but the light was too much that both of they could not look at one another. The light started to fade slightly and it ended utterly. There was no light in the room. He saw Abdullah wearing ring in his middle finger and gazing it astounded. Abdullah moved his eyes up to Max. He quickly removed it from his ring.

"I think it is the one, she once told me about," Abdullah thoughtfully told staring the ground. The ring was glittering in the finger of Abdullah. He removed it and again the room illuminated with a dazzling light.

"Take it, and put on it."

"W...Where are you?" Max hardly finding the way moving his arms here and there was trying to reach him.

"Be forward from the place where were you standing." Abdullah guided him.

"Fine," Max replied. Max grabbed Abdullah's wrist and Abdullah gave the ring to Max. Max put on it in his middle finger. The light was gain fading and at the end, the ring was shinning in his middle finger merely. Max looked directly to ring and Abdullah. Abdullah and faced him fully.

"This is not merely a ring." Abdullah told him and Max knitted his brows with a question mark at his face. "This ring belongs to the King of falcons. The birds have their own lives at the skies. We are unaware. Every creature has its own kingdom. This ring will help us soon." Abdullah said. "Keep it on your finger." Abdullah advised. Max looked to the red box and checked it. He was successful in finding a paper along with the letter.

> The races will be
> The hurdles will resist
> The stampedes will come
> The assaulters will halter
> The only claim you say
> The name **Falconee**

He read the words of the letter loudly. Max and Abdullah frowned thoughtfully. Max put his finger at the word Falconee and what they saw. Many of the falcons came and revolved around the cave. They were screaming as if going to kill some. Abdullah held the bow and an arrow and started taking an aim of the revolving falcons. Max ran to him and strictly grabbed his arm.

"No" Max shouted and Abdullah looked to him astonishingly. "Stop, Wait," Max raised his finger up and made the fist of his hand. "Falconee," He shouted loud and all the scampered falcons were moving back slowly. After some moments, there were no more sounds of the falcons. "It works," Both of they were rejoiced and hugged one another happily.

"Think it's the time to move" Abdullah suggested.

"Yeah, me too. I want to reach my land as soon as possibly; I want to see my own people." Max shared his emotions.

"You will," With a smile, Abdullah slapped his shoulder and paced out. Max held tight the red box and moved out. The horses were calmly trotting.

"There they are, the filths," They heard a voice behind them. The sight was stunning. They were moving out of the bushes one by one and their horses were galloping to them with the spears and the swords. Both of they looked to one another and without wasting their time, their horses galloped harder. They were fifty. They left their spears at them but luckily, it saved, as they were moving in a zigzag manner. They were galloping harder and harder and the assaulters were cursing them and following them harder.

"Fast, move fast," Abdullah, shouted as he felt Max at a little distance from him. Max pulled the reins for one more time and horse held its speed. One of the forces' men leading the group threw an arrow at Abdullah finding the short distance but luckily, it pinched in his turban. Abdullah puzzled for some moments but after realizing the situation, he was calm. The leading man lost his control and he fell down. The other group mates trampled him unconsciously under the horses' hooves. He was chopped and smashed brutally. Abdullah at the scream looked back and saw the man. He felt pity but abruptly he looked forward. A vulture flying in its full speed struck in his arrow pinched in the turban. His claws in front of his mouth were trembling with pain. The blood was dripping down from the vulture. He quickly put off his turban and threw the vulture along with the arrow and the turban. He was unveiled. The forces trampled the vulture and the arrow as well.

"Good, it's gone," Max, shouted.

"Fantastic, the enemy had created the safety itself, Hurrah," Abdullah shouted with joy. Abdullah looked back and a long distance was in between them and the forces following. Their horses were galloping harder and harder. "Leave as much distance as you can," Hamid instructed Max. The horses sped. Their horses neighed and both of they helplessly looked to one another. The forces after them and a huge sea with endless water in it was flowing waving its currents forward and backward. They saw the sun drowning but could not find the way to reach that sun. The horse's feet struck the ground hard.

"What do you say now?" Max asked hurriedly.

"Where is your ring?" Abdullah abruptly replied. Max quickly raised his right hand and made the fist.

"Falconee," He shouted. As he shouted, many of the falcons came with wooden backs at their boards and drowned into the sea.

"What's happening?" Abdullah perplexed. Max was also looking them confusingly coming down into the sea.

"Come on," Abdullah suggested. "Allah O' Akbar," He raised the slogan and put his horse hooves into very deep sea. Max followed him. Miracle happened and only the horses' legs dipped into the water. The horses galloped harder at the same speed. Sunasians were stunned at the sight but they blindly followed them. As they put their horses in the sea, they were drowning at the same time. The Sunasians looked their men drowning, feared and panicked. They retreated.

"Follow the detour," One of the men shouted.

"Leave them, we can't reach them," The other man shouted. The captain came near the fearful man and cut his neck.

"Move," The man shouted. The carcass with the live horse remained there and the other followed the outrageous leader.

Max and Abdullah's horses were galloping hardest. Their horses were panting and they decided to take rest in the sea. As they moved down, they were half sunk in the water but their feet touched to something hard. They were in the mind of the sea. It had started to rain lightly. The moon was hiding behind the clouds.

"We should reach before dawn," Abdullah instructed.

"I think, we should move now," Max said. "There is no place to sit or to lie down," Max observed.

"Yeah, let's start again," Their horses once again galloped harder and harder.

Until dawn, they had reached a place. The sun was rising at the peak. The horses stepped at the sand. Both of they looked back; a falcon was going into the sky. They fell down the horses. Max was lying upside down and Abdullah was facing the sky.

"Peaceful," Abdullah murmured and both of they took a deep breathe. Abdullah saw up. The eagles were flying back into the skies.

"Good news for you Max," Abdullah started staring to the sky.

"Hamm," Max was tired, he groaned.

"We've reached our place," Abdullah announced. Max closed his eyes and felt the moist of the sea.

"Is it the end of the sea?" Max hardly asked.

"No, but the end of our trouble for this day." Abdullah grinned. "Remember the sea has no end." Abdullah continued and closed his eyes. He was also tired a lot. They were slowly going into the deep sleeps. The sea was waving and the falcons were going home. Their hairs were disheveled and the horses had slept near them on the either sides.

CHAPTER 14

⊨ Native Gayness ⊨

I

The horses were grazing nearby in a pastureland. There was no more sunlight. The part of the sea was shinning by the moonlight. The slight puff of air was waving their hair at their foreheads. The sun with a farewell to them, the moon and the grace of the world was lost to any new place. Abdullah, from a deep sleep awoke up and glanced the sky thoughtfully in the first sight. He knitted his brows in amazement. He move up, rubbed his sleepy eyes and gazed Max. He had turned his right and was fast asleep. Abdullah looked around. The horses were grazing peacefully.

"Max," Abdullah slowly spoke and trilled his shoulder. Max moaned, glanced him warily and again turned at his right to sleep. Abdullah again trilled his shoulder; this time a little firmly he grabbed his shoulder. "Awake, up Max, we are to move now." He forcefully said and Max unconsciously looked him. He was gazing him with drowsy eyes as he was gazing any stranger. He was gazing the slender attractive features of Abdullah instinctively when he heard neighing of the horses, horses galloping harder and harder, the Sun's forces following them with spears and swords, the currents of the sea going to gulp them but the falcons and soon the falcons flew back in to the skies. In a few seconds, his memory had displayed the wretched instances passed a few hours ago.

"Abdullah," With a sigh of hope, he murmured.

"Yeah, me, Now, come on, let's move, we are to move back before sunrise," Abdullah abruptly instructed.

"Yeah, fine," Max caressed his disheveled hair and rubbed them hard to let go the sand from them. Abdullah picked up his case of bows and spears and hung them at his back. He took out the sword from the scabbard. He wiped it until its tip by the tips of his fingers. He waved it upward n downward in the manner of a warrior and again put it back in the scabbard. Max had reached his horse, he yawned and stretched his arms to comfort his back and pulled the reins of the horse. He had taken his seat at the saddle and was stable. He looked to Abdullah putting his sword in the scabbard.

"Let's go," He shouted and Abdullah looked up to him who smiled. He paced on the moist sand and reached his horse. The horse had understood his master gait. It let its master to move up. "Turn your horse backward," Abdullah guided.

"Where are we going now?" Max enquired.

"What?" Max got shocked with terror by the name and Abdullah laughed loudly.

"Don't worry. It's not at all difficult." He looked to Max. The horses were trotting. "We have left our warrior and contentious men to cope with the Sunasian. Most of the Sunasian have been shot dead." Abdullah carelessly answered and stooped down viewing a horizontal log of a timber tree. The leaves under the hooves were crunching as they were moving forward. The night's howls were echoing. "Sunasian have called this place as the confines of mortality because anyone goes there never come back." Abdullah added. "I have green flag. I'll show them and they will know."

"Fine, that's an awesome security." Max appreciated. The moonlight was filtering though the spaces between the leaves and the boughs. They were passively and quietly moving.

II

The hardly left one man was panting in the palace.

"All died near the confines of mortality," He announced.

"Out of my sight," The king outraged.

The queen was without cat sitting in the royal chair in front of the courtiers at the throne. The sat near the queen and gnashed his teeth in anger.

"I think both of they will have killed near the confines of mortality." The General stood up, he bowed and suggested thoughtfully.

"Did you see them?" The king asked.

"No, how could I?" The General giggled.

"Then, do not speak," The King roared. A man came in. He bowed in front of the king and fearfully spoke with his eyes down on the earth.

"My majesty! I've asked about him. He was the son Of Martha Beck hem and Oliver Beck hem. He lived beyond the red line and was arrested from there. He, himself claimed that he was the murderer of the king." The man constantly informed.

"Son, of Oliver and Martha," The king thoughtfully asked and looked to the King. "I want him alive or dead. I want to gift his head to his mother at the coming Christmas Eve." The king grounded his teeth in anger.

"We are to think about it, we should give time to this affair very thoughtfully. Every prisoner runs away, why?" The queen suggested and ordered them. "Take your seat," The man shivering with fear sat among the courtiers at the left side. "What about Jesse? Was there not any security at the sea shore?" The queen asked.

"No, I didn't see any. They were going running their horses into the sea and in no minutes they had reached very far into the sea. Our men were drowning as they were going in." He told queen.

"Hmmm," The queen nodded considerately. The queen and the king looked to one another. "When will Jesse come now?" The queen asked. "Jesse is the son of Jensen, Charles," The queen grounded his teeth in anger. "And Martha is Jensen's wife." The queen explained him and the King had to think a lot.

"But how could he do so, when he has never met that boy? The sympathies are not aroused for the sake of strangers." The King justified Jesse and the queen cunningly looked to the courtiers.

"I want this matter to be solved as soon as possible. Prepare the swimmers, prepare the warriors and arrange the battle near the confines of mortality. There are no spirits; they are filthy, coward Earthumen." The queen roared with rage and the courtiers unbelievably looked to one another. The King was also stunned at the exposure.

"How could it be?" The King asked.

"It is, Ponder on the circumstances and you will know. I want the forces geared up till this evening." Queen ordered and moved out to go. The king looked to his courtiers and every mind had the cunning ideas and the thoughts in his mind.

III

Bellatrix closed the window and looked Jesse who was sitting in the chair staring to her papers.

"They will have reached," Bellatrix predicted.

"Yeah, sure, they will have," Jess answered looking to her papers.

"For the first time I time I've been indulged in this mutiny, just because of you," Jesse pointed with the felt tip. Bellatrix smiled. Jesse with a powerful smile gazed her. She was in red long frock with broad laces at the end touching her feet. She was looking a fairy queen. Bellatrix smiled and moved to her bed.

"Fine, this is called friendship," Bellatrix boldly said and giggles. Jesse also giggled. "What about the plans of the new reward," Bellatrix said looking to the three stars at his left shoulder.

"I am hopeful, now the right shoulder will not be left vacant." Jesse confidently admired his talent.

"I am too hopeful, you were position holder in the school life too and for my lecture, I was always to depend on you." Both of they laughed off. "I think, this time, Earthumen would also reward you," Bellatrix boldly informed.

"O, I hate that nation," Jesse scornfully said and starts writing on the paper.

"Why?" She was perplexed and she asked slowly.

"The land is ours, and every day I've to kill hundreds of Earthumen crossing the borders illegally through the sea shores," Jesse was acting like a professional.

"But they say this is theirs," Bellatrix informed.

"They are liars, filth liars," Jesse assisted his point. Bellatrix kept quiet and she looked to him writing something on the paper. There was silence in the room.

"When I was young," Jesse broke the ice. "My grandfather told me a story about this earth. He said many years ago, there were men who were having the vehicles with some types of electric shocks in it." Jesse laughed.

"Electric shocks," Bellatrix laughed off.

"Yes," Both of they were in stitches.

"What is this monster?" Bellatrix eyes had filled with tears. She wiped her tears and asked.

"I asked grandfather and he told me something having connections in between two points and these connections were maintained by the circuits." Jesse explained her.

"And where were these monsters gone?" Bellatrix shrugged her shoulders.

"Those filthy Earthumen urged the fight and the electric shocks got angry." Jesse told.

"Really?" Bellatrix mocked.

"To some extent, Grandfather told." Jesse nodded. "Often I saw grandfather working in the room at different project. He was the teacher of the nature at higher level. He had much knowledge. When I asked him what are you doing? He would say bringing back the annoyed light." Jesse ended and Bellatrix smiled.

"He has been successful?" Bellatrix asked peevishly.

"NO, he got annoyed by the light. One day I went to his room, something was beaming and I was dead near it. I ran out to call Martha. He checked the pulse and he was dead. After the funeral I again went to his room. There was no beaming in the room. Everything was calm." Jesse shared his story. Bellatrix was looking impressed by the story. She admired it.

"Why not we start this adventure?" Bellatrix said.

"No, No, No, I don't want to be dead at this young age," Jesse pretended to be panicked. Bellatrix grinned.

IV

Till dawn they had crossed the confines of mortality. The atmosphere was peaceful. There were no signs of danger and trouble. They were pacing at the roads and the horses were walking behind them with the reins in the hands of the masters. Soon he heard the sounds of children giggling and chuckling. Max diverted his attention and looked here and there. At last, he was successful in finding the group. They were running after one another. Abdullah looked to him and understood his feelings.

"This is our reign," Abdullah with a smile told him. They were passing by slowly and the houses at the either sides of the roads were built in two lanes. At a far distance, he saw the young women coming in saris with red clay goblets at their heads. He tried to identify them.

"Hindus," Abdullah squarely looked to him and the women. He answered his emerging question before asking.

"Hmmm," Max said. They had reached and passed steadily near them with a smile. Max looked them Turing his face. They were ten and the goblets at their heads were arranged without any support and they were pacing with elegant gaits. They were giggling and chuckling with one another. He looked forward to Abdullah, he was quietly walking. "Hey," Max abruptly called him as he remembered something. "Do you remember Bimla?"

"The painful thought," Abdullah was gloomy.

"She once fought with me for you," Max grinned.

"She would be in the skies now playing with angels." Abdullah dejectedly looked to the sky and Max followed his eyes.

"I wish her peace and heaven." Max prayed for her.

The streets had started now. Max following Abdullah turning through diverse streets. Some stood to see Abdullah and embraced him, some just smiled and some hugged him. Soon they reached, crossing the streets and dealing with people. Abdullah opened the door entered.

"Come, this is my house," Abdullah told and went to the kitchen. He brought two bowls and a pail of water and both of they drank in single sip. They finished one bowl and took another one. In no minutes they had finished the container. Taking the last sip he put the bowl I the pail.

"It looks to me a dream, just a dream; I can't believe that I'm back." Max thoughtfully said.

Abdullah picked two cushions from the futon and moved into another room-Abdullah put them on the bed and lay on it. Max followed him and lay at the pillow near Abdullah.

"Abdullah, Is it really you, the boy who played with me?" Max was in doubt about his freedom.

"Yes," Abdullah nodded, moaned and closed his eyes.

"Today was my execution and I'm alive today. The fate of human changes as a coin changes its side during the toss. Everything going is change soon. I'm so happy to live independently among my own people." Max closed his eyes with delightful thoughts. "I am back." Max murmured.

Soon both of they were slept after exhaustive voyage and exasperating crossing.

CHAPTER 15

✦ Back With Friends ✦

She crossed a stair and was amazed to see that the door was not locked. She thrust opened the door and entered in. There was no one in the front room. The bedroom in the lounge was ruffled at one end and the empty pail with two bowls was placed near it. She knitted her brows thoughtfully, squinted her black thick shinning eyes piercing through her long eye lashes, her thin lips pressed against each other and she paced calmly to the bed. She removed the layers of her scarf from her head and threw it at the ruffled bed sheet. She took a deep sigh of breathe and free her hair of the ribbon.

"Who will have come?" She talked to herself and threw her piles of papers along with the scarf. She stooped and picked up the pail, bowls and put them back into the kitchen. She opened to wooden cabins, tried to search out any edible by opening the lids and covers of the pots and utensils. She sighed sadly and moved out of the kitchen. She moved to her room and she screamed to look the two men lying at her bed. She was standing shocked and both of they awoke up instantly at her scream.

"Salam, Siso," Abdullah was half sleep and moved down the bed, put on his chapels.

"Who is he?" She asked who was looking stunned and filled with rage.

"Max," Abdullah yawned, he turned his face to Max. "Max, Saira," Max had stood up the floor. The name of Saira filled his face with a joy.

"H...Hi," He giggled with joy.

"Hi," She said and took her hands off the door. He was staring her constantly, she was puzzled and she looked Abdullah. Abdullah was coming to the door. She gave him the way to move out as she punched him at the back and ran after him.

"Where were you the last night?" Saira shouted at her. "I was worried and now you have entered the home with a new boy. Who is he?" She forced him to tell. He had entered the kitchen, squatted near the other pail of water, gargled and washed his face. She was standing near him with a hand at her back, ready to fight while he was satisfactorily performing his acts. He stood, held the thick cloth and rubbed his face hard to make it dry. He turned to her who was staring her like a hungry lioness.

"He is Max, remember our friend, the one whose parents were slaughtered whom we call the rebellion." He told Saira and hung the towel by the peg.

"What?" Saira was stunned and infuriated. "Bah... You told me the last the days that he was in prison you brought him from the prison cell," Saira was looking tensed.

"Yes," Abdullah calmly nodded.

"But, Mr. Raza stopped you already and you are again doing this," Saira reprimanded her. Abdullah shrugged his shoulder and moved out without the answer. She was not going to believe the situation. "Huh," She shrugged and went out of the kitchen to talk to her again. As she reached she saw the exit door banging. Both of they had gone out.

225

"Listen," She shouted but both of they had gone.

Both of they were going. Abdullah was laughing and Max was smirking at the thought of the girl he saw with the hair falling at her shoulder going to touch her back. She was awesome. The very thought of the girl standing in the door with nervous eyes was coming to his thought. Her innocent face was stunned and her lips were wide open to see both of them lying on her bed.

"She is always ready for the tiff," Abdullah grinned. "And I like this, she continues speaking and it is always good to listen to her." Abdullah continued.

"What does she do?" Max asked lost in the deep thought.

"She teaches students about some tips of arts, probably, I'm not so sure," Abdullah said.

"Hmmm," Max nodded.

"Perhaps, we have not eaten for two days, Max," Abdullah smirked.

"Yes," Max grinned.

"Feeling hungry," Abdullah caressed his tummy. Max nodded as he was looking to the passers by. "Let's go to any hotel, because Saira will not do any mercy at us." Abdullah pretended to be gloomy. Max laughed lively to look him.

"I've heard you laughing for the first time," Abdullah was blended with the mixed emotions of surprise and happiness. Max with a contented face looked to him.

"And I haven't seen the true face of liberty in my life…. But today, when I have it, I can't believe it. The people are moving independently. If I go few days back, I saw the people there dumped under the heaps of fear, wretchedness and flame of revenge. I witness disappointment in the past and in the present; I think I'd never like to look back." He wiped his tears of joy.

"Ok, buddy, there is the hotel," Abdullah diverted his attention to a grand building. Max was mesmerized to look it. It was just like the same hotel he first ate the food after a long hard work. The only difference was that the owners were of different nations and the food here would be of cheap rates. The buildings here were well built and he was feeling that the men of the earth are going to rise again. Stepping up the stairs they reached a hall. The tables were arranged orderly and filled with men and women. They chose a table and sat face to face at it. They sniffed the silent smell of the smoke. Abdullah looked to the country. A waiter came with a piece of paper in it. Max was getting more and more stunned.

"Do you know who the owner of this hotel is?" Abdullah took the paper of contents from the waiter and moved it to Max.

"Who?" Max asked taking it from Abdullah.

"Lady Margaret," Abdullah abruptly replied.

"Really," Max was amazed.

"Yes, if he would know, he would let to take the charge free of cost for your sake," Abdullah smiled and Max smirked.

"Why not, let's taste Chinese rice," Max suggested and Abdullah nodded.

"Two plates," Abdullah ordered making the sign of victory by his fingers.

"Once I ate at the hotel of a Sunasian in the market, I saw two earthumen to be pushed even after paying. UI quickly hid behind the chair with my piece of a single pancake. I was sobbing but they found me, checked my right hand, there was no sign and threw out of the hotel at the stairs. The stony stairs hit me hard at the skull. I hardly reached home with a bleeding head. From that day I left going to that hotel," Max told the story. The waiter had brought two trays of rice and put them on to the table.

"This is our own land now. We shall never sell it at any cost and never harm it. We shall live happily here and shall never harm Sunasian. Mr. Raza has said it." Abdullah said.

"Who is he?" Max asked putting a spoonful of rice in his mouth.

"He is the man in real who decided to put the foundation of this colony and where we are living happily and independently. He left some men at the borders and allowed them to stab any stranger at the spot. He is a very sacred person, Mash Allah," Abdullah said.

"He seems a very wise man," Max gave his opinion.

"He is," Abdullah said and again thrust his spoon in the ice. In no minutes, the hungry men ate the rice. They ordered for tea. They took tea and went out.

They stepped down the stairs and saw a girl stepping up. She was looking in a hurry as she had held her skirts touching hid knees and straightened her shirt. She looked up as she reached Abdullah.

"Hey Abdullah," She said and stepped two more stairs. Frank was also coming in a hurry after her. "See you later," She said and moved ignoring the man standing with him.

"Mary, Mary, listen," Called Abdullah from back. She stopped, puffed in and looked back. Frank also stopped. "Hi, Frank," Abdullah moved to him. Mary also stepped down to him. "Look here," He touched his shoulder. "Guess who is he?" Abdullah asked gleefully. Both of they saw to the boy standing with him. Frank frowned and Marry tried to guess touching her curly brown hair. Her green eyes were trying to conclude the boy's personality.

"Who?" Frank frowned.

"Max, our child hood friend, do you remember?" Abdullah asked.

"Max," Frank shouted with a joy. "You," Frank impulsively hugged him. Mary was also rejoiced.

"Max," She also shouted with gay and hugged as Frank gets departed.

"Today in the evening, I'm inviting you in the hotel. There will be a party; there will not be any customers, only friends will be there." Mary said joyfully.

"Yes, there will be Max, Be present with us today night," Frank pated his shoulder.

"Yes, sure," max smirked.

"And don't forget to bring Saira, Abdullah," Mary ordered him.

"Yes, yes, sure why not,"

Ok, Mom has called us. We'll see you later in the evening," Frank said and he hurriedly stepped up the stairs. He put his woolen white cap at his head.

"Ok, bye," Mary with a smile waved her palm and ran up to the building.

"Everything is set here. There should not be any fuss now." Max said contentedly.

"Life is so difficult to live in, we can't live without troubles." Abdullah said.

"But if you consider the trouble a trouble," Max said wisely.

229

Chatting and giggling they ad reached their house. They knocked the door but no one opened the door. Max looked down and saw the bed sheet and a piece of paper at it.

"Don't try to come in before you've washed it" Max read aloud.

"What?" Abdullah shouted.

"Yes," Saira answered from the window.

"This girl," Abdullah helplessly held it from Max." You stay here." He said and went from there. Max sat outside the door onto the ground.

After washing the bed sheet they went in the evening to the hotel. Max joys knew no bounds to see Mr. and Mrs. Oliver, Bill, Mary, Frank, Abdullah, Saira and Lady Margaret together merry making. He hugged them and all of they hugged him merrily. They were eating, drinking and playing independently. Soon some more friends of Mary and Saira came. They went to welcome them. They hugged them and met them happily. Everywhere he could feel the gaiety. The people of all the nations were merrily sit together and there was no more anger or fight.

Max looked to Saira. She was chuckling, giggling and chortling with her friends taking sips of almond shake. He looked to her and then to his friends. They were laughing at jokes and taunting one another. Max smiled and giggled. The freedom was here.

Let the skies to lean on me
My friends! Be gathered forever for me
Your sweet smiles and fragrances
With your gaits and twinkles allure me
Hug me, sit with me, and pat me
Stay with me forever, live for me
Let the skies to lean on me
My friends! Be gathered forever for me

CHAPTER 16

╼ The Exposure ╾

"There is no perfect physician of internal loss than time. It is a big dealer and a soft healer. Time makes us firm as the memory of shabbiness is vanished. In fact, it is not vanished but is lost for some moment. It comes back when the healer itself is sick." She grinned at her thought. "How will be he? I want to see him, how will he be? I wanted to go with them, but there would probably be the biggest storm, if I will go. My father would be mad after those Earthumen and he will kill them one by one, but he is killing the. What to lament at! When you can not speak," She looked dejected at her thought, looked to the sea and narrow her eyes her eyes to see far into the sea. Everything was calm; there were no signs of storm or rain. The ships were roaming at the sea level guarding the borders against the enemies but where were the enemies? They had never permitted any other to live. Then who were they guarding. Where will have they both gone? I wished to move too. I am doomed. She closed her eyes and lowered down her head in dejection.

"Its' good today," Jesse stood near him. He saw directly the sea and the sun. She was startled at the sudden arrival.

"Yeah," She nodded with a grin. "How is everything inside?" She gasped.

"They were asking from me about the Order papers," He almost murmured and Bellatrix gave her full attention to listening him.

"Hmmm," She mumbled.

"I had torn them the day when I got them. They are doubtful about me." Bellatrix was startled at the Jesse's exposure. She gazed him in surprise. "Don't worry, I'll handle it." He tried to comfort her.

"What will you handle now?" She apprehensively asked her.

"Be slow," Jesse almost whispered. "King asked me and I said I gave the paper to the guardians and now the guardians would have lost it."

"Ahem," Bellatrix nodded thoughtfully.

"Everything is set," Jesse peevishly looked back to the office. The entrance door of the hall way was opened and there were no signs of anyone coming out.

"I feel sorry for Sharma," She dejectedly said.

"Me too, it was happened in my absence, else I would save him at every cost." Jesse sniffed.

"How could you?" Bellatrix mocked. "Well... leave it, how is my aunt?"

"She is good." Jesse explained looking to the sun.

"Don't you fee l pity at her?" Bellatrix asked dejectedly.

"Yes, I do ever and anon, "Jesse gasped.

"Then... why not help... her to go to her son," Bellatrix fiercely said.

"What..." Jesse was shocked. "Bellatrix, let this matter to settle down," Jesse dissuaded her and Bellatrix kept quiet. Jesse peevishly looked back. The King and the queen were coming out of the hall. Jesse quickly turned, went to the captain standing near by the ship and pretended to be talking to him. Bellatrix was confused at his act.

"Bellatrix, Come on," Bellatrix looked back at the voice of her mother. She turned and saw her mother standing with Clarke. King and the queen were standing at a little distance from them. They were talking to the two Captains. She stepped to her mother and brother.

"Let's go," Clarke said and all three of them moved to move to sit on their carriage. Jesse looked back and saw Bellatrix moving out.

"Mr. Jesse," He heard from behind the voice of Alan.

"Yes, what?" Jesse distracted to her.

"King is calling you," Alan whispered coming near to him.

"Ok," Jesse nodded thoughtfully as he knew what he was o do now. He reached near them, they were doubtfully staring him.

"Fine, Mr. Jesse, It was a good visit at you place, When are you going to fill your left shoulder?" Queen asked him with a smile. Jesse grinned.

"I'm hopeful it will be done soon," Jesse said.

"Me too," Queen sneered, King gazed him critically, and he smiled lively.

II

"When I and Saira moved out of the reign of Sunasian, I felt sorry for you. We came here and lived in a camp along with other people. But with the passage of time, we were able to steady ourselves. Daily the calamity-stricken people would migrate here with broken families and broken hearts.

The magma of revenge was boiling in my heart day by day. I missed my granny a lot and Bimla, my secret friend. I tried to find both of them into heavens. When the snow came, people lit fire and in the fires I tried to find her. Sometimes I saw her smiling, sometimes, laughing at me and sometimes she was crying, calling me for help. I would consciously move to the grate to help her and the people would push me back. They called me insane and Saira was too much tensed for me. Time is a big healer, I was better as the time passed. We ha made a new house of woods for ourselves. Saira started the business of flower selling. She was master in them. She was fond of gardening as she made a small garden at the back of the house. I hated the king. One day, with a firm plan I awoke up when Saira had slept. I galloped my horse to my previous land. It had been long time and I did not know the right path. At last I reached there after four days. When I reached there, I remembered my granny, little Bimla and my house a lot. There was no change; there were same people, the scared ones the panicked ones. The wretchedness of the life could not stop me and I burst into tears. I wept a lot. The innerness of mine was washed and my heart felt relief. It was daytime, I hid behind the bush as I was waiting for the night to come. You passed by me. Bill was following you and calling you by name. I was glad to see you alive. I wanted to talk you but the severity of my plan warned me. You and bill were giggling and chuckling talking about the new fair. I crossed the red line boldly with my horse. They thought a Sunasian as I was looking like them and I had painted a sun sign at the back of my hand. At the night I reached the King's palace. I was not so sure but I estimated it the King' palace. It was full dark.

There was no one around the palace. They were fearless as they could not expect any Earthumen about this conspiracy. The palace was tall captivating building. There were three buildings alike for the assaulters to deceive so I had not any idea which one was of the King. I put my foot at the outer wall of one and climbed it. I reached the mid of the King's palace. I opened the window with a jerk. It was delicate and the curtain was jeweled. I abruptly jumped in. The fate was fully supporting me. I was astonished to see the king fast a sleep in front of me. The queen was not there and I was to do before the queen's arrival. I quickly closed the window at my back, took out my sword and slaughtered the king's neck. I was succeeded. I wiped it, put it back into the scabbard and started to scratch the sun sign at the back of her hand. It rubbed to some extent. I had no fear of being dead as I had completed my plan. The door opened softly and the queen entered. She saw the slaughtered body and I came to her sights standing confused. She chortled.

"So you made it easier," The queen mocked. I didn't answer and jumped out of the window. I fell at a shutter near the window and I was not hurt. I was climbing down quickly and I had known that King was not sleeping, instead he was dead. Queen had planned it before my arrival.

"Guards," She shouted when I jumped out of the window. I had reached the ground and ran to my horse. It neighed and galloped in no minutes. Realizing the guards after me, I tried to find any place to hide. I left the horse and ran to another palace in the way. I climbed backwardly and jumped into the terrace. It was a white door. I opened it pushing my body against the door. The door opened with a jerk and I fell in. I was panting. I saw some vultures shrieking fiercely to me. Abruptly, the sword came out and I was waving it hardly against the vultures. Two to three vultures cut down. The girl, who was slept, awoke up by the shrieks. She rubbed her eyes and was shocked to look a horrible scene in front of her. She briskly ran to her case and took aims of the vultures. Many of the vultures were dead in the room. The vultures shrieked and flew out in fear. She fixed her arrow at me and I surrendered. She was dazzling, impressive and captivating to look at. Her dazzling eyes inspired me more.

"Let me go, these vultures were following me. I didn't mean any harm to you," I sternly requested her. I got impressed by her boldness and bravery.

"What is the blood on your clothes suggest me to think?" She grounded her teeth in anger. She was looking too much precarious about the situation. She did not move her eyes even for one time away from me.

"The vultures, I killed them, who are you? I mean, I don't even know you." I asked in confusion.

"Prime minister's daughter," She introduced herself in her ardent voice.

"Your name," I dared to ask.

"What's your concern? Tell me what were you doing here when you are not a Sunasian?" She glanced my right hand. "Tell me quickly; else I'll call the guards." She warned me and gripped her bows and arrow more firmly.

"Well…" I sniffed as I was intending to tell the king about the incident. "I murdered the king." I boldly announced looking into her eyes.

"What", she shrieked and the arms fell down of her hands.

"Yes," I slowly but firmly faced her. I could feel she was not infuriated instead was angry.

"Why, when you did it?" The girl asked.

"A few hours ago, the king's forces are after me and the queen saw me." I told him. My face was covered in veil; even she could not see me.

"Who are you?" She sat at her bed nearby.

"An Earthumen, I came here from the colony and intended to kill the king and I've done it. Now I want to go," I told.

"But the King's forces are after you." She memorized me. "How did you dare to think of it?" She was stunned.

"Just a revenge of my granny," I was contended.

"Sit," He pointed to a futon nearby the door of terrace.

"First lock It," As I was going to sit in the futon she said me. I locked it firmly and immersed in the cushioned soft futon. In my whole life, I had never sat in such delicacies. I smirked.

"Have you any face?" She mocked.

"Oops yeah," I grinned and unveiled myself. She gazed me through her dazzling eyes.

"Your name…" She asked after a little pause.

"Well… Abdullah," I told her. Both of we stared one another for some moments.

"How could you do so, I still can't believe." She was staring into my eyes. My eyes were heavy with sleep and in no minutes I fell into deep sleep. The next day when I awoke up, there was no one in the room. I thought the girl had trapped me. I rushed to the door of the terrace. It was locked from outside and then I rushed to the entrance of the room. It was also locked. I was confused and perplexed. I quietly sat at the futon in the room. After few hours, I heard the door unlocking and the girl came in. I restlessly stood up to look her.

"The King's murderer is arrested." She informed me as she came in. I frowned as I couldn't understand her. "His name is Max." She told me. "Who is the real murderer?"

"The queen," I announced boldly.

"What?" She was stunned.

"Yes, the queen told me herself." I told her.

"You play with queen that she will tell you," The girl mocked.

"No, No," I said and I told her the whole incident.

"Right," She thoughtfully said.

"I want to go back now." I said.

"The danger is now over." The girl informed me.

"In the evening I'll move from here." I told her the plan. "But Max didn't do this. He is a good friend of mine." I was tensed and then she promised to help. I asked her the reason of helping me and she told me a story. I was feeling myself very close to her. My horse was dead and she gave me a unicorn.

"A gift," She patted the back of the unicorn. We were standing in the stable at the either sides of the horse.

"Thanks for it," I said.

"Take good care of it, it is not the common one, The Sunasians had these two powers and for this reason they defeated the Earthumen. I wish you to join you soon because you are my people." The unicorn was walking after us and both of we were coming out of the stable. I saw her; she had dazzling colored eyes, and a long nose and a round face with a prominent chin. I gazed her she was looking the moon. She patted the horse once again.

"Keep informing me about you Abdullah, I'll miss you," I saw the tears shinning in her dazzling eyes. She turned her face. I was mystified for her. "Come on, now move." She hugged the unicorn by the neck. "Don't misguide your master", she caressed him and moved at a side. Abdullah climbed it. She looked to the girl. The girl moved her hand to him.

"My name is Bellatrix," The girl gloomily told her and both of them shake hands.

"Come with me, let's go to our world together," I offered her whole-heartedly.

"I can't, it's difficult. But I'll come there one day." Bellatrix said and gloomily slid back her hand from my hand. She was looking dejected.

"Take care of Max," I advised her.

"Don't worry. I'll do my best." She smiled for first time. "Good bye," She said and patted the back of the white unicorn. It lifted its front legs, neighed like a horse and galloped harder and harder. It had the speed many times faster than the horses. I reached my home in on day as I was missing from the house.

"So it was you who killed the king," Max put down the mug of tea at the breakfast table.

"Yeah, me," Abdullah giggled.

"Huh," Max gasped.

"We are happy here in that piece of Earth. Mary works in theatre. She writes and gives the stage directions. Frank works with her mother; I am learning the skills of fighting so

I've a warrior heart. Bill teaches in the institute with Saira." Abdullah told him.

"Fine, the life is good." Max sniffed and Abdullah bobbed.

"Yeah it is, well today, we are to go to tell Mr. Raza about all this."

"Ok and you will find some one there, your own," Abdullah smirked at the scowl of Max.

"Have you finished?" Saira came in from the kitchen.

"Yeah, we have," Max said and Abdullah stood up to the window. Saira stabilized her head scarf at her head.

Max was staring her when she was picking up the pots of breakfast. Abdullah came out of the hallway with a folded paper in his.

"Wow," Saira shouted and Abdullah smirked to look her. He went into the room.

"What is it?" Max asked Saira.

"Letter from Bellatrix" Saira said and went into the kitchen.

"What?" He was amazed. "Really," He wanted to believe it. "How?"

"Bellatrix's pigeon, it brings the letter." Saira pointed to the pigeon and went into the kitchen. Max looked to the pigeon. It was standing quietly in the opened window. It was a white pigeon with black eyes. Soon Saira came out with two bowls.

"Let's feed the pigeon," Saira also offered. Max hastily picked up the two chairs and put them on the either sides of the pigeon.

"O thanks," Saira giggled and sat in it. Max sat in front of her. Saira moved the bowl to the pigeon's beak. Pigeon gulped water and put its beak in the grains. Max gazed her. She had covered her head with a blue scarf and a knitted flower had gathered the cloth of the scarf to abstain from falling.

"She will be writing now." She carelessly said. Both of they were giving the food to the pigeon and Abdullah in the writing a letter to his friend. Every thing was peaceful and quiet.

CHAPTER 17

⇥ Concealed is revealed ⇤

In the council room the prominent members of the society had taken seats and pondering on a serious issue. Mr. Raza nodded as heard the arguments of Shiva. Shiva took her seat as he finished. Tom stood up and looked to all the members sitting and at the end he looked Mr. Raza. Mr. Raza was quietly sitting down lost in the deep thoughts.

"Mr. Raza," He started. "For what to fight, when we have no arms, we have no ships to protect the sea, we have nothing with us except passion, we are armless, and we are helpless. We are happy here living our own life according to our own customs, traditions and rules." Tom sat down.

"You are right Tom, but think about those who are still suffering the hardships," Shiva tried to convince him.

"Listen Shiva, We shall loose this battle, we shall be defeated. Take some more time and make yourself strong. We have neither much armaments and nor much territories."

"Why not think of taking a chance?" Shiva tried to persuade him.

"If you take one chance, it means that you will never find the time to get the next chance." Tom said. During the argument they heard the door opened. Abdullah and Max came in one after another.

"Asslam-o-alaikum," Abdullah loudly and boldly addressed them.

"Hi," Max was confused. All of they saw the new comer stunningly.

"Walaikum-us-salam," Mr. Raza replied and the Muslims sitting in the hall also murmured.

"Hi, good evening," The abrupt replies from the Christians and Hindus were heard.

"It's good to see you Abdullah," Mr. Raza smiled to see him.

"Thanks," Abdullah a little lower his head trying to thank him.

"Where were you in the last five days and who is he?" Mr. Raza asked sternly.

"I went… err…erring to bring him… he lives not very far…, just beyond the confines of mortality," Mr. Raza got shocked and he stood up.

"Just… beyond… the… confines… of mortality," Mr. Raza wisely repeated the words. The other members giggled.

"Yes, the… they… had arrested him in the murder of the king," He was stumbling.

"You are always creating fuss and luckily you are saved." Mr. Raza was seriously talking to him. "You know, these things can create great troubles for not you only but all of us." Mr. Raza advised strictly as he knew the delicacy of the matter. "We have nothing to protect us, nothing," Mr. Raza continued.

"But, we have," Abdullah said.

"What?" Mr. Raza scowled. Abdullah looked back to Max who was quiet listening to the ordeal of Abdullah. Max came forward and stood equal to Abdullah.

"The falcons and the Unicorns," Abdullah explained-raised hand of Max equal to the eyes of Mr. Raza and Mr. Raza gazed the glittering ring in the middle finger of Max. He was stunned.

"Friends and fellows," Mr. Raza loudly addressed them all. "Hence we are succeeded in attaining for what we were struggling, for what we sent our men at the posts of Sunasians, for what our friend like Oliver sacrificed." The hall was stunned and quiet. Frank sitting at the end of the left row to Mr. Raza stood up and moved to them. He held his hand in his hand to see the ring more closely.

"Oliver," Max murmured as he listened the name.

"Do you know him?" Mr. Raza asked.

"Yes, he was my father," The hall was shocked at the exposure.

"Your father," Tom repeated in astonishment.

"And he was my brother," Tom quickly ran to him and hugged him. Both of they wept a lot. "I missed my brother and sister a lot. Where were all of you?" Tom was sobbing. Abdullah patted Max's shoulder to comfort him and Frank patted his other shoulder. "Where is your mother?" Tom asked after departing from him.

"She is in the custody of Sunasians," Max told him by wiping his tears.

"And you left her alone," Tom asked him.

"It was a misapprehension," Max looked embarrassed.

"Nothing like that, we shall bring her soon." Abdullah covered the matter. All the others stood and hugged Max whole-heartedly. After the emotional moments of the happiness and tears all had taken their seats. Max was sitting with Tom and his friends were sitting with him.

"The sacrifice of Oliver wasn't in vain. Before his death, he had stretched the net of a very complicated conspiracy," Mr. Raza thoughtfully said.

"Mr. Raza," Abdullah started. "We have come here to ask from you about these two," Abdullah pointed to the ring with his index finger and abruptly with the thumb outward. Mr. Raza smiled and he looked to unicorn through the window standing out.

"The earth is very minute piece of this world. We live here enjoying our life but are unaware of it that there are certain other worlds like us. The birds have their own world, the animals have their own kingdom and reptiles have their own. The lion is the King of animals but there certain sub-kingdoms. In every sub-kingdom, there is a proper sub-system. The ring you have in your middle finger is of falcons, they live very far above the clouds. They have their own King and their own Kingdom. The ring in your hand from centuries was in the custody of devil but now you have got it. They have their own life, their own system but now they are under your order. They will do and rule their Kingdom as you will say. They wish for freedom but never give this ring back to the King. If you gave he will conquer you." Mr. Raza stopped for some moments and looked out, where he could see the horn of the unicorn shaking. "The Unicorns are the animals with medicinal powers in their horns. It is very faithful to its owner and it will never deceive."Mr. Raza stopped for some moments. There was silence in the room. "Now prepare for the battle," Mr. Raza announced and all of they stood up.

II

It was again her birthday today and she wished to gift her something truly unexpected. He was going out when Tom called him.

"Yes uncle," Max turned back.

"Going where?" Tom asked.

"To Abdullah, just to meet him," Max said.

"Ok, dear I'll see you in the evening. Your aunt will come soon. She will be excited to see you. Take care,"

"Ok, bye, take care," Max did farewell and paced to the home of Abdullah. As he reached in, the birthday celebrations were ready. Everyone was there with gifts and presents. Lady Margaret had prepared a delicious cake in the cooker and it had taken a day. That was the gift he received from her. Saira cut the cake and all of they clapped. "Happy birthday to you," There were clapping. All of they ate the cake, drank the juice and took dinner at the house of Saira. At the end of the celebration, all of they went out. Abdullah went in to write the letter. Saira was picking up the pots to wash. Max also helped her.

"Listen," He called her when she was staking dishes.

"Yes, what?" She turned who was standing behind him.

"I want to see you in the evening near the lake, it's something I'm to tell you," Max said her.

"Is anything important?" Saira knitted hr brows.

"Yes, something like that, see you in the evening at the lake." Max said and went out. He paced to the outer area of the city where there was a lake above the mount. Its water was clear and it had inspiring gleam in the moon light. The evening was prevailing. He squatted near the lake and waited for her to come. Soon, he saw a loop of light coming underneath the mount. It was moving up to him and at a little distance he was able to comprehend the shade. She was coming up and had taken the layers of scarf at her head. His heart palpitated with joy to look her.

"Hi," He said and held the lantern from her as she had reached the top of the mount.

"Hi," She was panting. "Now tell me why did you call me?" The girl asked. "I was tensed about it from the time you said me." She hunkered down by the lake and Max squatted at a distance from him. "Huh," She gasped.

"Thanks for coming," Max thanked him.

"No problem," She smiled.

"At your every birthday, I wished you to present you something, but every time I couldn't. But this time, I'm giving you the most important thing of my life." Max put his hand in his pocket and took out an orange red ruby with a thread passing through its holes. "Happy birthday," She moved it to her. She was shocked to look such a mesmerizing gift. Her eyes wide opened.

"Marvelous," She murmured as she saw it. "Thanks,"

Max grinned and gazed her. She was staring the locket in her hand. There was no moonlit today, the lantern was placed between them.

I wish you the thousands birthdays like that
I wish to wish you the thousands of times
When God beautifies the lonely stalk with
    a flower
When God hurls water to our land like a
    shower
When the water mixes in the seas and rivers
    and hover
When the water trickles making the shutters
    lower
May you blossom with every bud twinkling!
May every drop of rain water flourish you!
May every drop of sea encourage your talent!
May the shutters be strong to save you!
I wish you the thousand birthdays like that
I wish to wish you thousands of times.

Saira read the paper when she reached home what Max gave him along with the locket. Abdullah was fast asleep. She was also feeling sleepy. She felt he was with Max flying high above the clouds. Her hair was waving with the cool breeze. She was chuckling, giggling and chortling with him. Again she saw both of them standing in a garden, where a lot of the fairies were all around them. They were moving hands in hands with one another and the fairies were showering flowers at them. The flowers buds were twinkling in the garden and they were running to catch the fluttering butterflies with joy of the man following them. The butterflies peevishly ran from one place to another and they were running after them. They were sitting on ground of Earth and a basket of flower was in between them and they were staring into the eyes of one another. Her soul wandered the whole world with Max in one night. She was going in deep smile with a curvy smile.

When Max reached home, the woman sitting in the chair was shocked to see and he was also shocked to see him.

"You," She was stunned.

"What happened? He is my nephew, Max," Tom introduced.

"Yes, and he is the same one who saved me from the forces." The woman was now glad to see her and she hugged her. "My son," She kissed his forehead in gratefulness. "You know, I wept a lot when the Sun's forces were dragging you." The girl patted her lovingly.

"He is my nephew after all," Tom proudly stretched his chest and the woman giggled. Today he was very as he had met the girl who consoled her for the first and who got the first place in her heart. He could feel the charm at her face. She was not at all angry. He knew. He with a smile slept for his first successful meeting.

> The days of Past
> Why are you so fast?
> Let the moments stop
> And the words go on,
> To express my feelings
> To display my emotions
> Let me give the chance
> To fix my soul with her heart
> Let me to be lost in her eyes
> From where one more time
> I could take the life at start

The next morning she awoke up very early in the morning with azan. She was restless and confused. The decision about a non-Muslim seemed to her a flaw. She performed ablutions and prostrated at the land of Allah. She wept a lot to release the confusion of her life.

III

"Bellatrix, today I came here for a very important decision. I want your opinion and without this I won't take any step." Jesse was looking excited. "Martha is agreed when I talked to her and she will talk to my dad herself, she has said."

"About what," Bellatrix was tangling.

"Bellatrix," He held her hand. "This time we have reached at the stage where we are to decide about our lives."

"Yes," Bellatrix nodded thoughtfully.

"Bellatrix, I want to end up something now. Instead, it's the confusion of my mind about which I'm not so aware, what should I decide. In this, I need your help." He pressed her hand hard. "I... I want to marry the princess of earth," He completed. Bellatrix flabbergasted and she pulled back her hand impulsively. She saw him stunningly. "Bellatrix, I always felt about you, since my childhood and you were first girl in my life. I don't want to loose you." He explained more. "Bellatrix, I know it would be unexpected for you, you will need the time to think. You can take the time as much you want. I'll come next week; at the end of this week I'm going to the award ceremony about what you are most hopeful about me." She was quiet and stunningly gazing him. Jesse turned abruptly.

"Listen," Bellatrix called him sternly. Jesse turned in amazement. She lifted her eyes filled with tears. "You hate a nation, you call that nation a filth nation, you call that nation a lie, you call that nation a deceiver, and you curse that nation disdainfully." Her voice was stumbling with tear.

"Bellatrix," Jesse was perplexed to see her like that.

"I am of that nation, I am an Earthumen not a Sunasian," Bellatrix was outraged.

"What?" Jesse was stunned and he quickly moved to her right hand, gripped is its back and gazed it. "But you have a sun sign,"

"Yes, I have," She pulled her hand, slid backward. "But it's cool and faded than yours," She showed the back of her hand. Jesse looked to his sun sign. He had never attended to it ever. The sun sign was truly faded.

"An Earthuman gave birth to me in this land of Sunasians and this true. You hate a filth nation and you will never wish to marry filth, disdain and an ugly nation." Bellatrix wiped her tears.

"Fine," Jesse nodded in rage. "He was me... in a deception... the princess Bellatrix Charles... will never like to marry a mere traveler's son. If you had decided something about the prime minister's son Leonardo, then you should have shared me." He was outraged and the tears were falling out of his eyes. "There is nothing a greater deception than the refusal in love." He briskly turned.

"Jesse," She harshly called. "You've taken me wrong. Listen carefully; I've decided such thing like marriage about a filthy Earthuman." Jesse briskly turned.

"What? Who? Max," He gnashed his teeth in anger.

"No, Abdullah," Bellatrix threw the last knife of words at his heart.

"Bellatrix," Jesse couldn't believe.

"Stop, it's over now what was between you and me," Jesse was disheartened at Bellatrix's decision. He didn't speak and went out quietly. She heard the beak of the pigeon and turned. The dark gloominess of her heart disappeared in no minutes. She giggled to see the letter tied around the neck of the pigeon. She gleefully wiped her tears with back of her palm. She gasped-untied the letter and unfolded it.

Jesse had gone into the deep dark like a helpless person. The horse was slowly walking after him and he was quietly pacing on the road. The dark was looking darker to him. The pain of this refusal he would never be able to forget. He didn't know where he was pacing. When he was tired he unconsciously rode his horse and the horse galloped himself. He did not know where he was going.

CHAPTER 18

⊷ The Immortal ⊶

Queen was standing in front of the tusks of the elephants. She had pressed her hands against each other. Her eyes were closed. She opened her eyes and prostrated. The maid standing outside came in as the queen moved up from the prostration. She had a bowl with blood in it and the little gems were floating in that blood. She flowed the blood at both the tusks of the elephant.

"This time, our tusks have demanded for the blood of a virgin, an Earthuman virgin," The queen sneered and gave her the bowl back. She fearfully held the bowl. "Call the King, I need to talk him." She ordered and the maid went out fearfully. The queen went to a covered object at the corner of the room. She released the curtain, there was mirror, she gazed it. She said some charms and there appeared some water waves in the mirror. The currents furiously struck against the mirror and there was dark. He soon saw a piece of blue-black cloth in it.

"How are you?" She heard a roaring voice.

"Everything is good here and you," She replied.

"How are the Earth people?" The man in the mirror spoke.

s "I am killing them day by day," The queen informed.

"How are your people?" The man roared.

"I am dominating them," The queen replied.

"We can't do it without Alberic," The man roared.

"We will find him," The queen's voice echoed.

"The time is not much, you can't find him, and if you find him, you know the Earthumen and the worlds in the universe, they will never let you sway, as they are against us," The man's roaring voice echoed in the room. "You are to trap the earth people in the net of sincerity and dominate the minds of your people at the end of what you will get the thing you desire, immortality. You will never die and the world will follow the rules of Satan." The roaring man chortled and the queen chuckled. "He is coming now, go," The man ordered. She quickly threw the curtain at the mirror-stood in front of the animal tusks like before. The king came; she opened her eyes cunningly as she realized the man at her back.

"My majesty," The king called her. She turned with a subtle smirk. The king bowed as she faced him. "You called me," The king said.

"Yes, sit" The king pointed to a wooden chair and sat in front of him. "The time has come and I've thought that I should marry now," The queen announced what shocked king.

"But whom would you marry, Queen, I'll find the man for you," King obediently said.

"Tomorrow, you and me are going to marry," The queen said and without listening or looking at him went out. The king felt silence jeering at her but the King was excited as he was going to marry the most beautiful queen of the world.

The life of Earthumen was at peace. Everyone was happy with his luxuries and the goods. He was happy at whatever he had.

Max with a bouquet flowers knocked the door of home of Abdullah. Saira opened it and ignored his excited face. She gave him the way to come.

"Abdullah is not at home," She curtly replied.

"OK, I know. He is in mosque for prayers" Max grinned. Her hands gripped the table cloth firmly as she knew he had come to meet her. He gloomily closed his eyes.

"Why did you come here?" Saira asked curtly. He moved to him and leaned a little over her.

"This is for you," Max put bouquet in front of her. She abruptly turned back.

"Listen this is not right." She sternly addressed him. "Listen carefully, w two belong to two different religions, what you think is impossible." She said. "It should be ended now." She said and went into room. She came out with the locket in her hand and put it in his hand.

"No," Max was flabbergasted. "Fine, whatever you say is right, I respect your religion and I respect your feelings, but this was just for you free of any voracity, and I'm so sorry for I hurt you," He went out abruptly. He was dejected and worried. Saira looked him from the window. He was pacing slowly. She held her heart as she was sad. She gazed the locket at the table and held it. She hung it around her neck. It was looking awesome in her neck. With the locket she slept down. She was sleeping fast in the room when in the midnight she heard the man and the woman in his room. The man's face was the whole body was covered in a black cloak and the woman was visible. She was staring the girl with her sharp eyes.

"When no one can cease the first step, there does not come the time of its death ever. Adam was thrust out of the heaven into the earth because he tried to be alike to my Lord but his realm could not even care for itself. It was cursed again and again. I obey my lord and I'll never let you the life of your will." The man's roaring voice echoed in the room.

"Girl, you don't know what's in your neck. It's some that will make the riches to bloom, the reserves to flow out and the rains to shower. These are your grieves what will bloom like riches, flow out and tease you like reserves and shower like ran." The woman spoke in her heavy voice.

"W… Who… are y… you?" The girl asked as she was stumbling. She was panicked and scared.

"I'm devil's servant, Winston and I'm devil's supporter." The woman spoke in her heavy voice. Her eyes were closing slowly and she again slept.

"Man compete devil…, the immortal one…, and he did not know… he is dead all the life fighting with devil.., but the devil remains alive. He is never dead and will never die.

"Evil is the heart of devil…, to kill devil you are to slaughter evil…, but you men are helpless," The man roared into laughter. She was sleeping but she could hear the man. His laughter made her heart pulsate. The woman standing with man sneered to look the sleeping girl. "Devil is, devil was and devil will always live…." The man roared into laughter.

"Just give this back," The woman asked pointing to the ruby gemstone around her neck.

"Little girl, just give my thing back to me," The man whispered and he moved his skeletal hand to him with long bony fingers. His hand was moving to the girl's neck and the woman was leaning over her to help him. The nails were very near to the girl's neck. She gathered her nerves and screamed. Her eyes opened. There was no one in the room; the locket was in her neck safe. She was shivering with fear as she went out to look Abdullah. His bed was empty. She was panting and the sweat was dripping down her body. She sat in the corner. The woman's wicked face was coming to her mind and the devil's hands he felt pouncing at him. She closed her eyes firmly and trembled.

Max had gloomily moved to his home, when Tom told him a bad news.

"What?" He shouted worryingly.

"Yes, the vultures attacked Frank, he was badly injured. Dr. Shahab is treating him." Tom took a sip of tea. For some moments, he forgot the girl.

"Where is he and how is he?" Max asked abruptly.

"In his home," Tom informed taking a shirt hung by the peg.

"Ok, I'm going to see him," He hastily moved out.

"Come back, soon, the vultures are roaming in the city," Tom shouted aloud. Max rushed out to see Frank.

Frank was moaning. The physician was checking him disappointedly. He bandaged his wounds and helplessly looked to Abdullah.

The next day the queen was dressed in her traditional bride costume. She was always seen in the black dress but today she had changed looks. She was looking more than a queen in her light yellow dress. People all around the city had come to see the beauties of the queen. People showering flowers at them and she was standing proudly with her hand in the twisted arm of the king.

Ashley was depressed and she was in Bellatrix's room. Bellatrix was consoling her. Clarke was sitting near Bellatrix. He was staring her mother quietly. He had no words to comfort her mother. She was crying constantly and Bellatrix was making her quiet. The ceremony of the marriage went on. The queen took aims at the Earthumen in the merriment of marriage, she freed some and murdered, slaughtered others.

"She is the queen from centuries, since the time the Sunasians came to this land. When will she die and let the other to join this place." Clarke said restlessly. "What is she?" Clarke was tangled.

II

Max was quietly sitting at a stone thinking about the past circumstances. He was throwing pebbles into the water and was worried about his friend, Frank, who was badly wounded. He looked to the finger gleaming in his middle finger. He was looking worried and tensed.

"Max," Someone called him from the back. He turned at the familiar voice. He was astonished to see the girl. "I need to talk to you, Max," She said as she had mounted near the lake.

"What?" Max asked.

"About this," She opened he fists and showed her the locket gleaming in it.

"Listen, I am not taking it back from you," Max squarely looked to the locket and the lake.

"And I'm not giving it to you." She abruptly said. Max stunned. "Listen, Max tell me, from where did you get it?" She asked.

"Why, what happened?" Max frowned.

"Last night, I couldn't sleep well. It was in my neck and I saw devil, he was trying to snatch it from me." Saira told her the dream.

"What?" Max was perplexed.

"From where did you get it?" Saira asked again.

"It was my mother's. My father gave it to her and I kept it in my pocket as her memory." Max explained him.

"Just believe Max, it isn't good," Saira advised him. Thoughtfully she looked to her finger, where the ring was listening. Saira turned round and squatted near the lake. He clutched his fist.

"Falconee," The boy shouted aloud. Saira abruptly looked to her.

"Yes, my master," Soon he heard a voice at his back. Saira was stunned to look at the back of Max. A fascinating girl was standing with a falcon shell covering her back, front, knees; only her legs, face and hair were visible. Max turned. Her eyes and hair were fascinating like a falcon.

"I know, my master you are worried about your friend. The person bit by the stings of the vultures is never saved but my friend fairy, she lives in the fairyland, and she can help you." Falcon spoke. Max nodded.

"How many days will it take?" Saira abruptly asked coming near Max.

"It can take fifteen days, lady to reach her," The falcon explained them the story. Max nodded.

"Let me take," Max said abruptly. "Saira, take care of Frank, I'll be back right after a month. Take care," He gazed her. The girl turned herself into a large falcon. Max hastily sat at his back. It flew high into the skies. Saira saw them vanishing into skies. It had reached very high at the top. She looked to the locket in her hand and dejectedly squatted near the lake. She wished to cry but and two tears fell out of her eyes.

On the other hand, the marriage ceremony of the queen ended and the next day they heard dreadful news. Ashley squatted in grief, Bellatrix was stunned and Clarke cried.

CHAPTER 19

⇥ One Second Voyages ⇤

Max tied his arms tightly around the neck of the falcon which was flying swiftly above the clouds. He had closed his eyes by the pressure of air in the opposite side as the falcon was flipping his wings as fast as it could. Max hardly opened his eyes as he heard a giggle, the eyes twinkled itself.

"Did you say something?" Max loudly said to be audible for her.

"No," The falcon chuckled. "I just laughed at the human history."

"What history?" Max was confused.

"First you lived in the Stone Age; you could hardly help yourselves, then you people shifted to the reign of mechanics and techniques, then you lost your land, the era was again same for you but the people was changed and now you are going to enter into a mesmerized world of captivation." The falcon seriously ended.

"What mechanics and techniques?" Max frowned.

"It was the time when you had never to do the work. You had the machines for all this. You were to order and they were to act." The falcon told him.

"Was it so ever?" Max grinned.

"Yeah, it was," The falcon nodded. It was briskly nodded its wings into the air as it had started raining. Max looked above, the clouds were pouring water. Falcon moved above the rainy cloud.

"Wow," He exclaimed in amazement.

"Yet I'll show you a lot," The falcon excitedly told and dived into the sky. Its speed was more than before. The falcon was swiftly flying. Max looked down and he could see the bulbous cotton as he looked up, he saw the sun shinning bright. The rain was underneath the clouds and the sun was shinning above it. He was enthralled by the distinctive canon of nature.

"Now, close your eyes," The falcon distracted him to her. "Just close them." It had been slow now. Max looked forward. There was black whole in between the sky. Max frowned as he looked it.

"What is it?" Max seemed curious to know.

"Just close your eyes, quickly, hold my neck tightly and don't move, don't even try to open your eyes," Falcon sternly ordered her master. Max gripped the neck of the falcon firmly, closed the eyes forcefully. Falcon raised his around his both sides and joined them at the end. It made triangle shape around Max. It dived again into the black hole. Max felt himself in dark, he felt him moving down and down at the fastest speed and he felt himself in a narrow dark tunnel, there was nothing except dark and flints. His heart was beating to break his ribs. He wished to open his eyes but did not dare to open them. He got a jerk.

"It's over now," He heard a sigh of relief from falcon. "Open your eyes," He instructed. Max opened his eyes. It was not the same. He looked up. The sky was very far from him and the sun was shinning at a very height. He looked down and saw the golden grass rustling at the ground. The falcon raised high and high again to reach this sky. He looked down and saw lions moving orderly. A man was standing in between them. He had covered his body by the skin of the lion and there were wooden shoes in his feet. He was talking to lion and he felt lions smirking, laughing and gurgling with the man. He knitted his brows in wonder.

"What is it?" He asked in surprise. The falcon grinned.

"A new world, like yours one,"

"It's really, really a wonder," Max was surprised. "A man talking to a hundred lions," Soon he felt falcon moving down. He was perplexed as looked down to the same man waving them hands.

"Have a nice day," The man welcomed as its claws touched the ground in between the man and the lions. The tigers were growling looked like talking to one another. The falcon bowed a little and made his body shake. Max had known what it was trying to say. He looked down to the growling lions. "They won't hurt, don't worry," The man made him calm and his feet touched the ground. The lions did not bother to look him. "How are you here?" The man looked to the falcon now. It had turned into a beautiful girl now. She grinned to look the man.

"I'm going to meet my friend in the fairy terrain," The girl explained and the man smirked.

"Who is he?" The man looked to Max.

"He is my master, an Earth man," The girl told him.

"O," The man sadly said. "I'm so sorry for you," The man looked to Max and laughed loudly. "An Earth man," Max looked to girl and the girl tried to comfort by her eyes. Max nodded. "Very coward people," The man laughed. "Very coward and coy," Man was in stitches. The lions were chatting to one another. Max was nervous and the girl was boldly standing. He laughed so much that his eyes filled with tears. "Fine, boy... I won't let you go like that; you will have to enjoy my feast for today night," The man invited him. He looked to the man from head to toe. He was looking a man of the Stone Age. He stepped to right and the lions made way for him themselves. The girl followed him and Max followed the girl. Lions did not try to hurt them. The man stepped into the cave and looked back. "Come, come," Max entered the cave. It was flinty and rough. "This is my small home," The man showed him. Max nodded.

"My friend is injured, I'm to go back soon," Max told his intentions. Man looked back to him.

"Nothing will happen, don't worry, we shall be there on time," The girl made him calm. He was feeling restless, nervous and timid in front of the man's fascinating and intrepid character.

"So, what are you serving us with," The girl asked frankly and sat at a stone in front of him.

"What you will order, my lady," The man smirked and bowed frankly. The girl laughed.

The night fell down soon. The man had lit fire in front of the cave under the hung meat. It was being cooked. Soon after sometime he served them and both of they ate to their full.

"Now, we should go," The girl and Max stood at the instant. "Thanks for such a dinner," Soon Max firmly held the neck of the falcon and flew into the night sky. The man was waving them hands standing at the yellow grass. The lions were sleeping quietly stretching their hind limbs and forelimbs. The lionesses were wandering and the man was standing in between them at the yellow grass. A lion and a lioness were standing on his either sides. Max took a deep breathe of amazement.

"Who was he?" Max asked the falcon.

"He is Stone Man, the King of lions, He rules here and the lions are his regime," The falcon answered.

"Is it true or a dream?" Max asked surprisingly, "A man ruling the lions,"

"It's true," The falcon seriously said. "All you need to rule the world is to be just and bold. You do not have this attribute, you can't even rule yourselves. The judgment you claim your verdict fearlessly is in fact the timid decision of fiend."The falcon dived up. The jerk was strong that Max had closed his eyes fearfully. When he opened his eyes, he witnessed a new panorama. The scene was changed. The night some minutes ago turned into the day light. He was flying at the ground in under a new sky. He looked down. There were small of houses of only one foot and he saw the very small people moving round about wearing woolen caps of different colors at their heads. The falcon again touched his claws to the ground.

"Hey how are you," It was a small dwarf with a tiara at its head. He excitedly said to see the falcon.

"I'm fine," The dwarves gathered around the falcon.

"Who is the idiot at your back?" The King of dwarves asked. The falcon giggled and Max was embarrassed.

"He is a human of earth, my master," The falcon introduced Max. The dwarves gathered around the falcon laughed. All of them were in stitches.

"Silly people," The King scornfully said. "Ok go now, and come back when you will be alone, my wife has cooked a tasty feast for you," The King lovingly said to the falcon. "Not for this curse," The King abased Max. All the dwarves were staring him strangely.

"Ok, I'll see you later," Falcon said and flew into the skies.

"What was that?" Max asked him when he had gone far away into the skies

"It was the world of dwarves. They are passing their own life peacefully." The falcon was soaring joyfully in the skies. "The dwarf talking to me was the King of the dwarves."

"Ok, fine, he humiliated me." Max was infuriated.

"Yes, he did, but why do you feel it? All you need to be happy is to be wise. To feel humiliated at the disgrace is your folly. You should have the valor. The valor for which you are ready to kill other is not the valor but the nuisance idiocy of imp." The falcon soared into the skies. Max was lost in the thoughts of his words. He was confounded.

"Now, you are going to enter in my land." The falcon excitedly soared.

"But, we were meant to meet the fairies," Max was tangled.

"We are going there, It's a long journey, we will reach soon," The falcon increased its speed. "My father would be glad to see you," The falcon was raising higher and higher. "We reached," The falcon announced. Max looked around. The mounts and the land here were dark brown. Falcons were freely flying, flipping, squealing, yelling and wailing. The falcon raised lower and a stood in front of a big falcon grabbing the log of a tree firmly. A log was at a little distance from him.

"How are you my daughter?" The big falcon soon turned into a graceful man.

"I'm good." She replied briefly. The man looked to max.

"Master Max, I'm really good to see you," The man bowed in front of him. "I was anxious to meet you. Tell me, what should we serve you?" The man respectfully addressed him.

"Y... Y... Yeah..., N... Nothing," Max was nervous. "My friend is injured; I'm to see him as soon as possible." Max said gathering his confidence.

"Ok," The man bowed. "I respect you, my daughter will take you to the fairy and the fairy will help you," The man consoled Max.

"Fine," Max replied. The man whispered coming near to the falcon standing nearby. He soared and soon returned.

"Look back, my master," The man said him and Max turned his face. The falcons at different logs and bushes were bowing before him. He looked down stunningly and the vista was mind-boggling for him. The uncountable falcons had bowed before him. "Your regime, my master," The man informed him. He looked to him. He and the falcons before him were standing with a genuflection.

"Let's move," He could hardly say. The falcon waved its wings, passing between the logs, bushes, moving zigzag between the curtsy falcons it was soaring. Max looked down, the falcons were still bent in respect. Soon, the sight disappeared and the falcons were looking like small coarse dots on any writing paper.

"What did your father whispered to the falcon standing nearby?" Max asked the falcon.

"I don't tell lie, my master, he asked him to call the falcons, for their selfish master has come." The falcon told him.

"What? Selfish," Max repeated the words.

"Yes, selfish…, to be good to others… all you need are faith and sincerity- for your personal gain you mar the needs of others; tarnish the faiths of past and crush the hearts of your truthful ones. Remember… to win the heart of your queen of heart… her inner satisfaction is needed than yours. Love is yours when you want it to be yours." The falcon soared and dived again. Max for the fear of being fallen tightly held its neck. When he opened his eyes, he was staying in front of the unicorns. The unicorn leading the others behind hit had a diamond glittering at the tip of its horn. The claws of the falcons were a few feet above the ground. The unicorns were standing behind their King orderly. Every thing here was white, from a doom to a highest mount. Even the sun there was of white color.

"Welcome to our land," The unicorn sturdily welcomed. He was looking elegant and graceful. "How are you here and who is he?" He had seen animals speaking in his life for the first time.

"He is my master, the man of the earth," Falcon said him. The unicorns roared into laughter. They were laughing, laughing and laughing. Max scowled. The king looked to his scowl.

"The fury diminishes talent and augments sin. You are angry people, the emotional and the egoistic ones." Unicorn looked to his scowl. "I'll see you soon, falcon, say my Salam to your father," Unicorn said her and it soared high into the skies.

"Listen falcon," Max called him abruptly when they had left the land of Unicorns. "Are we jokers?"

"Who, you and me," The falcon said normally.

"No," Max was tangled. "We, the earth people," Max was in rage and confused.

"No…"

"Then why does every one laugh at me?" Max asked it. The falcon roared into laughter itself.

"You are also laughing now," Max asked him in frenzy.

"O sorry, my master," The falcon was embarrassed.

"What was he saying?" Max asked.

"Fury augments fury, he said it." Falcon explained him. Max was quiet. He did not speak any word as he was dejected.

"Now be careful here," Falcon warned him. Max looked forward and what he saw was horrible. There were dark grey clouds. Falcon dived in and there was hell dark. Nothing was visible. As he crossed the clouds, he was in a new doom. There were black clouds all around. There was black marsh around a narrow flint pavement. A man was sitting in flinty chair. His face was dark with protruding flesh at it. He had no eyelashes, ears and his bald head had a deep wound in the middle. Max was horrified to see the posture while the falcon was boldly flying to him. A leather looking mask was stuck to his body and was tattered at some place from where his flesh was visible. He looked to the marshes; he saw the snakes of different races. The man poisonously saw Max and falcon.

"Yes, what," The man hissed scornfully.

"It's good to see you; I just want to surpass your land with him. We want to meet the fairies." The falcon fearfully said.

"Who is he at your back?" The man hissed normally.

"He is my master, the man of the Earth," Falcon introduced.

"The man sneered to see him and scornfully roared into laughter.

"A man of Earth," He repeatedly, "Malicious people," The man hissed disdainfully. "Come," The man called him, pointing by his hand with the tattered skin of a snake. Max unconsciously tumbled down the falcon and walked to him. He stopped at a distance of seven feet from him. The man looked from head to toe. Max was hearing the hisses coming very near to him. The man hissed loudly and the hisses stopped.

"SO you are man, the structure is admirable…" Man hissed admirably. "Ok, go, move on your journey." Max stared him and turned. The hisses were again coming very near to him.

"Master," Falcon shouted. Max with a scream fell down. He was downside up; he lifted his head a little up. There was no man in the chair; instead a Cobra had stung him. It was coiled near him as he could see its hood waving and hissing.

"I'm sorry, it's my nature," The snake hissed and went back to his chair. Falcon flipped to him, held him by his collar through its beak, stared the mocking snake and flew into the black clouds dejectedly. Max was fainting, hung in the beak of the falcon. It was ascending higher and higher, faster and faster. He left the black clouds soon he reached the new land. The mob of fairies saw the man in the beak of

271

a falcon. The kind-hearted fairies were depressed. He threw the man in front of the queen. The queen was puzzled to see the wounded boy. She stooped over him and saw his wound near the ankle.

When he awoke, he saw the mob of small fairies around him. They were staring him with their big and innocent twinkling eyes. The tresses of the small child fairies were waving like a flickering fire. He looked to his ankle. It was bandaged.

"He is awake," All of they shouted and ran back to call the queen. Max touched lovingly the cheek of a small fairy.

"O, he touched my cheek," She looked worried. She picked up a small flowery bandana started to rub its cheek. "You men are very naughty, don't touch me without washing your hands," The small fairy proudly ordered him. Max laughed. Soon the queen entered. The fairy was rubbing its cheeks. The queen disregarded her and moved to Max.

"How are you feeling now Max?" Queen asked, the falcon again turned to a girl followed the queen. Max moaned and stared the graceful queen. She was tall, blonde and soft.

"These are my children," He told about the small fairies. "They were excited to see a human, they were maddening to see you, and so I sent them here." Fairy with a smile talked to him. The falcon smirked. "Hopeful, they won't have disturbed you...." The queen and the falcon sat near him. Max stared falcon with love. She was looking tensed.

"My friend has told me all about your friend, this is your ointment... use it where are the wounds, he would be fine within days." The queen gave him a small golden vessel equal to fist.

"I think, we should move now, I'm fine," He looked to the tensed falcon. Max held the small vessel and put it in his pocket. "Thanks for this," He answered the queen.

"Have a nice journey, you are innocent people," The fairy farewell them. Max at the back of the falcon was soaring high. The mob of small fairies was standing staring them and the queen was standing in between them.

"I'm so sorry my master, I really did not know about the filthy snake," The falcon was embarrassed.

"I Know falcon and I liked you for this. You saved me," Max said him.

"How many days have it been to the journey?" Max asked.

"It has been fifteen days," Falcon replied.

"Isn't it late now?" Max asked.

"Don't worry, master, it won't be late a second," The falcon replied and it flew faster. Soon they crossed the land of snakes. The snakes hissed to see them. Soon the falcon reached to her own land. The falcons looking their master bowed and bent. They reached the land of unicorns. The white sun was rising and everything was dazzling with its light. It took one day to cross them. When the night fell, the day changed into a pink evening and at the end into a purple night. They left the land and reached the land of dwarves. They were laughing and giggling. Nothing unique was there except their heights. In a day, they reached the land of cave lions. He again waved his hand for invitation, but Max did not accept and cave lion farewell them with a smile. At last, he returned to his land. It was day. The claws of the falcon stroke the ground at a distance from the lake.

Max tumbled down and faced. He saw her she was looking tired and doomed.

"Come falcon, come with me," Max said to her.

"No, I'm tired." She tiredly spoke. "I'm to go back to my land," She turned into a girl. Max looked to her arms. They were badly injured, bloated and bleeding.

"Falcon," Max was perplexed.

"I'm to go back, it will be too late," She turned back sadly. Her arms were swelling and injured.

"Listen, stay with me, I'll treat you," Max ran after her.

"Treat your friend," She gloomily replied, turned into a falcon and flew high into the sky.

Max was feeling sorry for her. He unhappily turned and was stunned to see Saira squatting near the lake. She had held the locket in her hands.

"What are you doing here?" Max asked him coming near to her. She turned back and was dazed to see him.

"You didn't go," Saira asked her.

"I went and I'm back after twenty days," Max said smilingly.

"What? Why are you joking? Just go," She forced him.

"I'm not joking Saira," He took out a vessel from the pocket and showed it to her. "I brought this from the fairy. I visited the sky for fifteen days. I crossed six worlds of the black hole at the back of the falcon." Max was telling her. Saira frowned.

"But, you just go by now and you are back after one second," She looked into Max's eyes. He was also bewildered.

"It means it's not late." Max thought. "Let's go, apply it on Max," He held wrist of Saira and they went swiftly went down the mount, Max was stumbling, Saira was assisting him.

"What did you see Max?" Saira was looking curious and Max narrated him the whole story. Saira was shocked.

"How were they all people?" She asked excitedly.

"Cave lions were brave, dwarves were wise, falcons were faithful, unicorns were cool, and snakes were kind. He stung me and he said sorry to me." Both of they looked to the bandaged ankle. "The fairies were proud and innocent." Max laughed to think about the small fairy.

"I can't believe, you saw all that," Saira was mesmerized. Soon they reached the house of Lady Margaret. They entered the house and the scene was thunderstruck. All the people in the room were crying squatted around Frank. He was dead. The vessel fell down of his hand. Saira went to Mary and hugged. She wept a lot. The tears itself fell out of his eyes. He ran out quickly. He was running and running, wiping his tears.

CHAPTER 20

⊷ Meeting ⊷

I

The grief fell at the house of many people of Earthumen for many days. Mary left going to theatre. The institutes remained off for many days. Lady Margaret had locked her hotel. Everyone was deep in sorrow. The people would daily come to her house and console her. Saira cooked food and shared it with Mary and Lady Margaret. Both of they would hardly eat something. In days, Mary had been week. James, her friend and colleague, would daily come to meet her and Lady Margaret. He also worked in theatre with her and had performed in many plays with her. He was his friend but friendship became stronger when he became her healer. She would daily go out with her. He would hug her, made her laugh and loved her to comfort her. When they came back, they would bring a lot of the presents for Lady Margaret. The wound was healed with the passage of time but it pinched when the memory of his son withered her. Mary would also weep with Lady Margaret or ran out to the lake to weep. At that time, she would bitterly weep in the absence of every one. The flower of friendship between Mary and James turned into the flare of love in those days. They would be making love near the lakes and above the mount. James who just came as a condoler did not know himself when this bud burst out of the stalk. The bud burst out in the heart of James, Mary nourished it and at the end it became a blossomed flower. He would miss his cousin but it was no more a sorrow for him. Lady Margaret would spend her majority of time in Church praying to God about the forgiveness of his son or listening to Mary about James. Mary had again joined the theatre. She was again performing well and this time the audiences appreciated a lot. Thus the time came when Mary and James decided to Marry. Lady Margaret neither and nor the parents of James objected. The date of the marriage was decided soon. The news spread to all the friends of Mary. Saira was too much happy. Lady Margaret had unlocked the hotel. Max painted the picture of Frank and Lady Margaret hung it by the wall. He would daily see him and daily wept before the entrance of the first customer. Frank was no more alive in the ideas of people except one woman, her mother. All would praise him in a gathering as he was very kind hearted. The institutions were again opened and Saira joined the institute. Mr. Raza had called the prominent members of the political council for a special meeting.

Mr. Raza was quietly pondering on some important issue viewing the papers Shiva was showing him. Mr. Peter sitting to his right and Dave to his left was looking consciously at the large paper. The matter was critical as the expressions of all of them during the discussions remained stiff. Tom, Max and Abdullah were sitting on the right side of the horizontal bench, Chon Li, Shimer, Hassan and Sidhwa were on the left side of the benches were gazing the four men pondering on the serious issue. All were nodding after listening to Shiva except Mr. Raza. Every one was quiet except the voice of Shiva was murmuring in the room. The voice of Mr. Raza murmured for this time and all of they attentively looked to them. Shiva and Mr. Peter sat at the right side and Dave to right side. The paper was in the hand of Mr. Raza. When all had taken the seats, Mr. Raza put it aside and looked to the boys attentive to him. Mr. Raza cleared his throat and attended to all of them.

"The time has come to rule, to snatch our land back. The danger is wobbling at us. It can be fallen at any moment, but before it we should think of some survival. The queen's intentions do not seem good. She has sent her spies in the seas and near the confines of mortality... but our men defeated them. We are to do something. Abdullah," Abdullah looked to Mr. Raza. "Tom", Mr. Raza attended to him more. "Shiva," Mr. Raza smirked to see the man. "You three will go to conceal the secret of Alberic and the ball. Shiva will be your guide and instructor, just listen to him and start this journey..., Max," Mr. Raza looked to his left. "Dave, you both will get training from Chon Li about taking aims and sword fighting and you will guard the sea. The people are already present in the confines of Mortality." Mr. Raza gasped. "Hassan and Shimer, I want both of you to guard the back of the country and Sidhwa... you will stay with me and Peter guarding the front. Rear attacks would be your responsibility, Hassan and Shimer." Mr. Raza sniffed. "The queen is very clever and she would never let the matter to wander." Mr. Raza stood. "I wish you all luck. Till evening, you would take your posts. I'm out for prayer. Mr. Peter, I'll see you in the evening near the Confines of Mortality," Mr. Raza sniffed. "Shiva," Mr. Raza called. "I wish you a good journey. I am proud of your abilities and I'm hopeful this time you will mar the world, In-sh-Allah," Shiva nodded with a yes. "I wish to see you after the battle are over." Mr. Raza came near them. "Tell me when you would have prepared for the journey." Mr. Raza said and moved out.

"It's Mary' wedding tomorrow, Mr. Raza," Mr. Peter memorized him.

"O, yeah, I forgot.., in the early morning all of you will be back from the posts and would attend the wedding. Lady Margaret would be glad to see you."

II

Both of they were in her room. The locket was placed near her at the bed. The devil and his ally were again standing in front of her. A young dazzling old man was standing besides them in a white cloak. She rubbed her eyes to see them. The devil and his ally were staring her and Alberic was staring they both. She rubbed her eyes to recognize them.

"W… Who are you?" She asked them while rubbing her squinted eyes by sleep.

"I'm dark," The man's roaring voice echoed in her ears.

"And I'm light," The old man in his fervent voice told.

"You know girl, you will see, one day," The devil's ally spoke. "My rule would start," She stretched her arms. Her arms filtered through the wall and she saw her arm stretching high into the city. She was covering the city with her arms covered by the black cloak. As her arms were covering the city, people were loosing control of themselves. They were becoming mad and running to a well. In this well there were thorns. People jumped into it and came out alive with half black face. The women jumped into it with a scream and came out with the wicked smiles. The dark was prevailing. At last in the whole world, there was dark, the half faces of the world were dark. The light was not any more. "So be mine," The woman whispered in her ears. "Give me mine back to me," She whispered again. Saira picked up the locket thoughtfully.

"And you will see," The old man's fervent voice he heard. He picked up his both palms and the light came out of it. It started covering the hands of the woman from the room spread out following the hands of the woman. The woman was standing quiet. "The truth never fails. Illegitimacy will die away under the fire of hell and the heavens hug legitimacy." The light was spreading all around the world. "The spot in the heart would be washed," The people jumped into the well again. This time, there were roses in it. "The people came out and the black spot at the faces was vanished. The woman was screaming. "Where you start the evil, good from there and when you laughter good, the evil is slaughtered there." The light was spreading. The woman was screaming. "Don't give it to her." She put down the locket from she picked up. The woman was screaming. The dark was vanished and the light emerged. The devil and his ally were burning into ashes. The scene changed and she was in an abandoned place. It was a grassy ground. The beauty was admirable but horrifying. There was dead silent. He felt as if the trees were staring her strangely. The flowers were furiously staring. She ran as she felt something running after her. She looked back and struck into something hard. Fearfully she looked. Her heart was beating fast. It was a well and she had fallen near its bottom. The walls were of red bricks and the top of the well was very high. She could not hear any bird even near her.

"Come," She heard an echoing voice at her left and she ran it and she was now in a desert. "Come," The voice came from the mount and she followed the mount. A woman in black was standing at the mount. Her hair was waving at the back. "Come," She heard the voice from the woman standing with its back to her. She reached her. She wanted to speak, but something held in her throat. She was even not able to breathe. The woman was standing still. She turned her face with a jerk. She awoke up with a scream. The wicked eyes, depraved smile made her heart beat faster. Maulvi was saying azan. She closed her eyes and held her sweated head. She was trembling with fear. The locket was near her.

She poured water from the pail in the bowl-drank it to comfort her- went to say prayers.

III

The wedding ceremony was ready. The garden outside was church was decorated; Men and women had reached the church. The people of all the races had gathered together in the church. Max was busy in management. Saira wanted to talk to Max but he was seen busy among boys. He was arranging the chairs and ordering the men for preparing the feat. James was standing at the front in the church waiting for her bride to come. Both were the known men of the city, as all the people went to see their plays. The church was crowded with all the people. Saira was sitting with Abdullah. Max was among the men in the row. Every face was bright. James was stunned to see her bride. She was coming from the entrance. Mary was looking very beautiful Saira smiled to se her. Lady Margaret wiped her tears. She was coming and James was staring her. Mary had reached her and stepped up the stage. Both of they stared one another and smiled. The bridegroom according to the traditions made the bride kiss. The wedding went on. Every face was happy. Mary and James were sitting in the ground among friends after the custom. Saira were looking for Max. The lunch was arranged according to the needs of different religions. Saira looked around for Max and her eyes caught her with the married couple. She ran to her and grabbed his arm. Max looked around in amazement.

"I need to talk to you," She started before Max could speak. Max abruptly stood up. The couple looked to them and was again involved in discussion.

"Yes what?" Max asked her as they reached the corner.

"I again see the same woman, the devil and new old man in the dream," She told Max. Max frowned

"What did she say?" Max asked.

"She was asking for it just," Saira showed him the red ruby in her hand. Max held locket and considerately stared it. It was glistening in the sun shine and nothing mysterious he felt about this locket. "I'm feeling it since the time; it was in my neck, once," Saira explained him.

"I'm sorry Saira, it troubled you, just because of me," Max apologized embarrassingly. Saira snatched it abruptly from his hand.

"I didn't mean this," She angrily turned and went among a group of her friends chuckling.

CHAPTER 21

⊹≈ Princess of Earth ≈⊹

The queen puffed in the cigar looked to the maids standing nearby Bellatrix. The maids understood queen, they bowed and moved out. The queen puffed in cigar again. The maids standing her either side bowed and moved out from her back. The queen was sitting alone in her throne. There was neither courtiers and nor guards in the royal palace. Bellatrix was sitting down the stage at a chair facing the queen. Today, there were no jewels at her dress. She seated calmly wearing a plain simple brown maxi staring the ground. The queen critically stared her from head to toe, blew the smoke to her puffing in the cigar. Bellatrix was quietly observing the gems embedded at the sides of the stage.

"I'm so sorry for your mother, your brother and for you," The queen in her heavy voice subtly started her discussion. Bellatrix sneered. "But we are helpless when we take our last breathe." The queen was looking in a serious melancholy. "Your father and I went to the tusks on the day of the wedding. The tusks got angry by your father and he was dead. I've never tried to violate their rules, so for the very reason, this is my secret of life." Queen puffed, smoke appeared in the form of a whirlpool and soon it vanished. Bellatrix took a deep sigh. "I was very anxious to meet the princess of Earth," The queen smirked. "Instead, the queen of Universe," The queen looked deep into her voice to have a positive reply for her prediction as she smirked eloquently. Bellatrix frowned staring a blue gemstone embedded in the stage. The queen chortled. "How lucky queen I am… to have a princess like you," The queen sneered. Bellatrix tangled stared queen. She was sneering.

"What are you talking about?" She asked confusingly.

"Listen girl…" The queen was stern now. "I know the grief of your father is nothing less… I didn't want to tease you… I've arranged your marriage with Leonardo as soon as possible." The queen like a caretaker told her.

"What?" She shouted in shock.

"I know… you will be puzzled but there is nothing good for you than Leonardo," The queen persuaded her.

"Who are you to think about me like that?" Bellatrix was infuriated.

"The queen," The queen seriously stared her in rage. Bellatrix was outraged. The queen stood.

"Come with me," The queen sternly ordered her. She had to follow her. She wished to kill that woman as she was wildly staring her tall wobbly posture from back. The queen was pacing softly and slowly at the thick carpet. Bellatrix was staring her like a hungry lioness. The queen stepped down the stairs and she followed her. The queen stooped at the carpet. She had seen the queen first time touching the ground. She leaned forward to know the matter. The queen was cutting the carpet with a knife swiftly and sharply. Her expressions were becoming stiffer. Bellatrix frowned. The innerness of her heart spied her about the coming danger. The queen was succeeding in cutting the carpet in the form of a big circle. She scornfully threw it aside and released a rusted, dusty, rotten lid. It was broken at some parts and its tattered parts were looking like sieve. The hallway was vacant. Bellatrix couldn't see any guard prowling and not even any bird chirping. She put the lid at a side and turned to Bellatrix. Bellatrix abruptly stood straight and she stared him. "Come, move in," The queen with a smile asked her.

"What is it all about?" Bellatrix asked her to release her confusion.

"It's all about you for your survival," The queen comforted her. "Move in," She again asked. "It's something about your father." The queen added.

She fearfully stepped to the hole glancing the queen. The queen sneered and turned to the girl. Bellatrix peeked in and saw the stairs going into the dark. Her heart trembled once and she abruptly looked to her. "I'm not going down," She gathered her nerve to refuse her. The queen infuriated but she made she calm.

"Listen girl, It's all about you and your father, if you want to see your father alive, you would have to step down the stairs," The queen tried to persuade her.

"What? Is he alive?" Bellatrix asked anxiously.

"It may be so, if you do as I ask you to do," Bellatrix swallowed hardly and looked again into the mysterious hole. She closed her eyes and put her first step in it fearfully. After putting her first step she had stepped the second stair, third step and she was going down and down. The stairway was invisible but she was carefully putting her feet down. At some distance she observed light and the stairway had taken turn to right into another hole a little smaller. The queen was after her. She moved into the small hole and saw a lantern lightening there. Tiny flickering flame of lantern was hardly helping dark tunnel to be visible. All she could see smell the stench as she pressed her nostrils with her index finger and thumb. The queen had also reached. She couldn't see her face only her tall posture was visible to her. There was mud under her feet instead of grass and thick carpets. The queen was quietly looking to her.

"What is it?" She asked in frenzy.

"Listen girl," The queen tersely said. "Few years ago, I gave my most trusted maid a ring and a four hooded animal and she lost it due to her slackness. She couldn't find it again and I slaughtered her at the spot. Later, I heard of it that princess of Earth is taking good care of them." The queen sneered. Bellatrix was astonished. "Give me them, give them to me, now," Queen shouted. Her soft tone changed into harsh tone and the pitch of her voice into a shout. Bellatrix in a fear impulsively stepped back. Queen moved forward to her. "What do you think? I was bearing you for the prime minister, and the man who later became the king, but died as he got a heart attack." The queen disdainfully cussed. "You have the blood of an Earthuman cursed lady in your veins and I can't bear one drop of blood of Earthumen in my regime. Give me the ring and the unicorn," The queen did her right palm in front of her.

"I don't have," Bellatrix answered curtly. Queen clutched her fists to appease her anger.

"Listen girl, I don't want to be bad to you, I just need the two things, and I've no concern with you,"

"I said, I don't have,"

"Give me them," The queen stepped closer to her.

"I don't have, and if I had, I would never give to you." The lifted her hand up and slapped the innocent face of

Bellatrix. Her hand was like stone. Bellatrix fell near the lantern and her right cheek bled.

"Give me them, right now," The queen shouted again.

"I've never had such thing," Bellatrix shouted with pain and tears flowing out of her eyes mixed into the blood flowing along the cheek.

"Listen, princess of Earth, if you didn't give me, I'll prison you here, and your soul would never think of moving out of here," The queen frightened her.

"Who can stop me? If you are the queen of earth then I'm the princess of earth. I've not only the blood of the woman of earth but also the blood of the man of Sunasia running into my veins. " Bellatrix challenged her bravely. She abruptly stood up and tried to run to the stairs but the two swords stopped her way. Queen sneered. Bellatrix looked at her either side. She could only see the shine of swords at her body and stared the queen helplessly.

"I'll slaughter you, if you didn't give me the…." Queen warned her and hastily turned to the stairs. Bellatrix felt the two sword men passing by her but she could see them as they reached near the stairs. Both of they were the executioners. Bellatrix heard them moving up the stairs and closing the rusted iron lid. A tiny flame was flickering in the room as it was going to be extinguished. Bellatrix touched her cheeks as the blood stuck to her hand, with a cry pain she closed her eyes and squatted near the flickering lantern.

II

The golden chain with a red ruby at its ends was strung around her neck. She lifted her big black eyes and was dazed to look her innocent and sharp features glittering more with the ruby. The young man standing beside her was smiling to see her. "Thanks" She murmured shyly but the voice echoed in the silence of the room and the smile of the man widened. She was running and chuckling with the same man when looking back to the elegant man she knocked into another man. The locket fell in the steps of another man. He picked it up and gave to the girl stunned to look her beauty. Again with thanks the girl took it back. The man smiled to see the girl who was staring the ruby in her hand and some emotions of jealousy filled her heart as he looked to the man smiling to see the woman. "I'm not of the type you are asking for what," The man was saying. "Alberic you are to do it; we'll have the life forever, forever we shall live," The girl secretly told her with a bowl of water in her hand standing nearby a well. "Zeus, don't do it, for what to have a great life forever," Alberic warned the girl. "But I need it Alberic, I want to live till the time this ruby would live, you gave to me, I wish to live with this forever," Zeus tried to persuade her. "For what to live, as much you live, you do suffer, it's a sin, don't do it," Allergic persuaded her. The girl looked into the man's eyes and stuck the bowl of water to her lips. The hand of Alberic hurriedly knocked to the bowl and fell into the well. Zeus could not drink even one water of it. The girl couldn't believe. Her eyes were showing anger and disbelief. "So, you don't like me, it's the entire flirt you do, you don't want to spend the whole life with me," The girl burst into tears and ran. "It's not like that," Alberic shouted after her. He was standing alone near the well. The storm came and everything changed. "I want to live forever, I want riches, I want life," The girl said to the man whom she was knocked. The man sneered and both of they were stepping up the thorns without being hurt. A man was standing hooded in a big cloak with his back at them. Both of they stood at his back. "Zeus," The girl heard a shout. Both of they looked back. "Winston, leave my girl's hand," Alberic shouted. Winston sneered; Zeus disregarded her and looked to the man standing forward. "What's more important for you?" The man in the cloak growled in his astringent voice. The girl looked to the locket in her neck. "This is," The girl whispered and looked back. Alberic was crossing the thorns. His feet were bleeding. She was shocked. "Come back, Zeus, it's a sin," Alberic shouted in pain. "Give it to me, quickly," The man asked standing in front of a statue of black lady. Zeus looked forward, quickly unlocked it and gave it to the man. The man without looking back held it. Alberic was coming nearer. The man held the hands of the girl and soaked it in the fire burning near the statue. She screamed awfully. Winston was shocked and feared and he stepped back in fear. After some seconds in severe pain and burning the man left her and the girl fell back on the thorns. "I've burnt this fire burning ten virgins in it," The man returned the locket to her after a few minutes. The girl looked to her hands they were badly burnt and paining. She was sobbing. "You will have the lives, till you will want, if the locket is damaged, you will be damaged," Man said and vanished up into the air. The locket fell near her steps. Winston looked back to Alberic. He was injured. Winston crossed the door made under the feet of the statue and entered it. Zeus tried to pick the locket near her, as she picked it; her hands were soothing and becoming fine. At the end she got the same beautiful hands like as before. Alberic had reached her.

"What did you do?" Alberic fell near her. The girl looked back. Her innocence was gone. Wickedness was evident. Her big eyes had the proud and the smiling lips had a sneer. "I'm alive Alberic, I'm alive," She shouted and her sweet shrill voice was heavier and bitter. "Stop," Alberic put his hands around his ears. "You are a witch now," Alberic said her. She sat near him. "You know Alberic, it's my desire to live forever and to rule forever," Zeus kissed the forehead of withering Alberic. "And death is must," He was trembling with pain. "It's over now, death is no more," The queen looked to the red-orange ruby subtly. She was excited and joyful. "Give this filth to me," Alberic snatched it abruptly from her and threw under a narrow path. "Alberic," She shouted. Soon she saw a kite flying out of the narrow deep tunnel into the sky with a golden chain in its beak and the red-orange ruby hung at its end. She ran after it. Alberic was fading with pain and wounds but still smiling at her little effort for throwing the evil deep into the tunnel. She was running after the kite. The kite soared high and it soon vanished into the deep sky. Looking it into the sky, she slipped and was going down and down the mount. The storm of sand came at her back. Winston laughed at the man's chat. "Yes, it's true, I can't live for more than ten years in one man' dead body, for this I need any evil imp," The man completed his words and Winston fell down with severe head stroke. He was gone. Zeus opened the door. Carcass of Winston was lying there. "Lord," Her voice trembled. The devil man moved to her. "You want to rule the world, you and I'll rule" The man came near her and roared. Zeus stared into the man's hood. He couldn't see any face. The days went by, and one day came, when her mother became the queen of the earth. She was princess. The woman died and the girl became queen under the supervision of Satan. The devil came in her room and grabbed his forehead by his hand. She was no more the same, a devil ally. The days went by, the wrinkles emerged her face, her bones felt twitching and the hands again burning. She screamed with pain and blaze. The devil came and next day she slaughtered a little child of Earthuman and drank its blood. The pain would appear after every year and she would drink the blood of a young beautiful girl or an innocent child. "I'll rule, I'll rule, give me this, or I'll slaughter you," The woman whispered in her ears and she with a jerk again awoke up. She panted and stood in front of the mirror. The red ruby was strung in her neck. She snatched it from the rope and threw it near the bed.

CHAPTER 22

✦ Farewell for Luck ✦

"It's the time for what we've been gathered here, to fight for our rights, to fight for our land and to fight for the sake of our regime," Mr. Raza was addressing a large population of soldiers dressed with iron shields, armed with spears and swords in the scabbard quietly listening to him. "Remember, Luck will not stab the sword in your enemy if you will not stab him. Luck will not favor you if you will not favor it. You have the courage and you are to show," Mr. Peter was standing with Mr. Raza. The leaders of different troops of commanders were standing before them silently listening to Mr. Raza. Abdullah, Shiva and Tom were standing with Mr. Peter facing the commandoes. Max was also quietly standing behind his leader. "Time will come, when we shall again rule our land, when calamities would be released, and the souls of our old ones would smile in the skies and will shower flowers at our success. That time is not so far." The battalions raised the slogan of success as Mr. Raza ended. "Now, take your posts and face the enemies," Mr. Raza announced and all of they scattered to be ready to go to the posts. The women came out of the houses and hugged their loved one s going out for war. Some stood at the roofs of the houses and showered the flowers dejectedly at them. Saira came out running to the field and hugged Abdullah.

She sobbed. "Have a nice trip," Abdullah got dejected. "I'll be back soon, don't worry," He patted her back. She hugged him tight. "I think, I won't be able to meet you again," Saira cried bitterly. "Hey… hey… don't say it so… I want to see you happy," He slid the scarf at her forehead and wiped her tears. "Be brave, if you are my sister, for the betterment of this town," Abdullah gripped his shoulder tightly and consoled her. She wiped her tears. "I'm not fine, I'm restless," She sobbed.

"I know, you are not feeling good, just pray to Allah and the inner restlessness would be no more," Abdullah hugged her again. "Take care and pray for me," He turned abruptly and joined with his companions waiting. Tom smiled to see Saira.

"Don't worry dear, we shall bring your brother back soon," Saira looked to Tom and nodded. She sighed, rubbed her tears and turned to the house. In a way, the women were weeping and crying hugging their loved ones.

"Who comes back from the war?" The old lady said to his young son who was trying to make her calm and ran inside the house. She repressed her lips in a worry and looked back. The horses of all three of them were galloping far away. She wanted to stop them but she couldn't. She felt her hand gripped tight that she could hardly breathe. A woman knocked into her, covering her face her hand, probably she was weeping. Soon, after hugging the loved ones and the dear ones, the women and the children went into the houses. The streets were abandoned now. The commandoes had moved to South, East, West and North holding their relative positions. She paced slowly to her house and opened the door slowly. It was looking her vacant than before. The

Chinese rice, she lovingly cooked for her brother as the farewell lunch was left untouched. He left in a hurry. She sat at the bed dejectedly and didn't wish to do anything. She looked to the walls of the houses. They also looked to her dejected at the farewell of the master. She put her head at the pillow and closed her eyes. The softness of the pillow made hr comfort when she heard the beak knocking by the window. She abruptly opened her eyes. There was the pigeon with the letter hung around the neck. She quickly opened the window and untied the letter around its neck. She would not open the letter if Abdullah had not asked her to open it. She quickly unfolded the paper.

"Dear Abdullah,

I'm doomed today. Mother is also worried. The queen has married my father as a special obligation for the affair of the state. It's too busy these days. Jesse came to me and he proposed me and I told him all about me with a refusal. Please, I want to join you now among the people of earth. So please, do write me soon and take me with you."

Yours Bellatrix

The letter ended and she was to write its answer. She looked back. The pigeon was gazing her. She moved to the kitchen and when came out put two bowls of water and grain in front of it. After this, she went into the room and started to write on the paper. She was soaking the pen in the ink and it was moving faster and faster at the paper. At last, she finished the letter and tied it around the neck. The pigeon that had eaten to his full flew away as she tied it around the neck of the pigeon. The pigeon was flying joyfully into the sky to reach its mistress with the reply of the letter. The queen with the prime minister and the two executioners was standing in the room of the princess of Earth. The maids were checking the room picking up the bed sheets, looking under the futon and sliding it forward backward and checking the windows, releasing the curtains and the opening the cupboards. The queen was furiously prowling in the room. The executioners were standing holding the swords in the hands and the Jesse with the two officers was standing calmly and silently in the room.

"The girl is a rebellion, she has given the map of war to the Earthuman," The queen blamed Bellatrix in front of them.

"If she has given it, them what are you finding in the room," Jesse was tangled. Queen sharply looked to her. He was really an intelligent boy. The queen admired him and smirked to look him. The hands of the maids shifting the futon stopped with a thrill.

"I'm searching if she had lied" The queen explained and looked to his three stars, the awards of bravery, talent and intelligence.

"Where is she in prison? The details of all the prisons came in my catalogue first, but I couldn't find her name in the catalogue," Jesse asked her another question.

"I shall send the details of the prisoner tomorrow." The queen abruptly replied and went out.

"Ok, stop it," Jesse ordered the maids and they stopped searching into an embroidered bag.

"You can't search a unicorn in the bag," Jesse gnashed his teeth in anger. "Get out," He shouted in rage and the maids went out hurriedly. The executioners were standing quietly in the room. Jesse turned to them.

"Where is she in prison? Tell me, I'm to write the name in the catalogue, I should've the record. The new king can ask me any time." Jesse said.

"In the tunnel," The executioners told him.

"What tunnel?" Jesse frowned.

"In the hallway, the queen had made the new prison, the girls is there." The One of the executioner told him.

"What? Where the girls for the tusks are slaughtered," Jesse wanted to confirm. The executioner slaughtered carelessly and went out. He looked back to the two officers whispering looking at the piece of paper at the futon. Jesse disregarded and went out after the executioners.

II

"How was your first day at the borders?" Marry asked presenting him and Saira a cup of coffee.

"It was good," Max chuckled. Saira smiled. "I didn't know the war tricks, I had no idea about them, and Dave helped me a lot. He was very good at taking aims, sword fighting, he is all in all master in all," Saira looked to Mary who was considerately listening to Max. "It was my first day but still good," Max said. "We saw the ships coming to the beach, we didn't miss the chance and attacked them before they could reach, and the ship was motionless now, I and Dave cagily stepped to the ship, we swam, reached it and climbed it. As we reached the ship, Dave went to the steering and the ship worked. I wandered in the ship all around and was enchanted to look at the soft settees, marvelous beds and the jewels. I removed jewels from the curtains and filled my bags up to the mouth, It was really awesome, we pulled it till the beach our men raised the slogans of success, we were happy at the first success at the last,"

"Hey, I want to see the ship too," Mary was excited.

"Me too," Saira said with the same excitement as Mary.

"Yeah, yeah, why not, Just pray for us to win the war," Max said them.

"We shall," Mary said.

"What about your theatre Mary?" Max asked him.

"It's going well; still they did not offer me any drama in these days," Mary explained and put the empty cup at the cabinet.

"Ahem, What about James, how is he?" Max asked.

"He is good, in the theatre working for the stage directions now-a-days, he said me last day to join the war," Mary told Max.

"That's good, tell me when he will be ready, I'll take him with me," Max said giving his cup to Mary. Saira was quietly trying to scratch the tattoo painted at the cup.

"What about you, Saira," Max gasped.

"Everything is fine," She smiled.

"And Abdullah," Max asked.

"I've no news, since the last time I met him," He told Max and sighed sadly.

"Don't worry it will be over soon," Mary consoled her and Max nodded considerately. She stood up with the cups and washed them at the basin.

"Max, I need to talk to you," Saira whispered as Mary went to the basin. Max looked to Mary and nodded.

"Ok, Mary, I'm to leave now," Max said loudly.

"Ok, fine, has a good luck," Mary replied staking the dishes. Saira was strangely looking to him.

"Saira, come, I'll leave you home," Max offered.

"My pleasure," She abruptly moved up gladly. "See you tomorrow Mary," Saira waved her and both of they went out.

"Ok, have a nice day, sweetie," They could hear Mary's strident voice as they banged the door after them.

"Yes what Saira, Is it the locket?" Max asked her worriedly.

"Yes the same one," Saira turned to him as they were walking side by side, both of they stopped to look one another.

"It was also a nightmare, it was strung around the neck of the same woman, she was young and beautiful and her hands burnt to have the life forever in it," She pointed her neck where the blue cloth of the scarf was waving.

"Who was that woman?" Max asked.

"I don't know, I've never seen her in my life," She explained Max who stared the ground thoughtfully and then looked to her twinkling eyes. He nodded three times simultaneously.

"Give me that," Max did his palm in front of her.

"No," She refused. "This is mine now, I don't want any trouble for you," She persuaded her and stepped forward. Max followed her quietly and slowly.

"But, it's dangerous," Max tried persuade her.

"Whatever is it, it's dangerous in my dreams, and in real she can't even touch me,"

"But be careful," For some time both of they paced slowly to the house.

"So how were you here? I'm so sorry, as I just forgot to ask you," Saira giggled.

"No problem, I came here to meet Mr. Raza, Dave sent me, some kind of the war matter," Max explained.

"How is your life going?

"It's going just like a hung bridge in the jungle, where any wild would step and it will quaver the ropes would be cut, there will be nothing but a distorted bridge fallen in depth of the deadly river…"

"Are you fine Saira?"

"Yes, the life of every one of us in this world is like a hung bridge. One goes out of the life and the other comes into the life, this is the true faith of my religion," She said.

"The biggest hurdle between you and me is nothing but religion," Max said abruptly. Saira stunningly looked to her.

"This is not a hurdle Max, but you are close to a knot which you are to detach," Saira boldly assisted her religion as Max frowned.

"I don't know Saira, What is religion? I jus know, when I was born, I was a Christian," Max answered.

"And when I was born, the lonely thing I knew was that Allah is greatest of all," Saira said and looked to the sky. Max trailed her eyes searching someone in the sky. Both of they were passively pacing to their destinations.

"I wish you luck, Max," Saira said from back.

"Thanks," Max replied without looking her.

III

She quietly picked up the lantern to look for the tunnel where she had been locked. The tunnel was filled with a stink that two times she had vomited and for the third again she was in the state of anti-peristalsis, nothing came out as there was nothing left in her stomach. She put her hand at her nose as a block against the bad odor. She looked up, there was dark. Lifting up the candle she tried to examine up, but nothing she could see except the mud. She stepped some steps forward, the hard way under her feet hurt her. She yelled lightly with pain. There was no day and no emergence of light here. All she could see here all the time was dark and shades of doom hovering around her. The time of cascade when comes, disaster does not believes in the faith. It comes, flows away the wealth and health, but leaves the hope. At the hope of what she was trying to search for the path to move out of this grave. She felt her feet immersed in any murk, "Jesus, yuck," She murmured to herself as she slipped a moment but stable herself. The flicker of the lantern was now fading and dwindling. She felt she had been mounting on squashy slope. Mounting the slope, her feet turned and her body twisted to fall. Her hand erected her twirled body up as something burst and fluid like material stuck to her hand and feet. She lifted the flame of candle and her hand trying to know about the fluid. Her hand was painted red and a tiny piece of flesh hung by her index finger fell to the earth. Her eyes stunned to gaze. She moved the lantern down. It was a carcass of a woman whose face had been eaten and her teeth were visible, what burst was her tummy and the fluid moved out. She was staring her with her brightly opened motionless eyes left at her face. Bellatrix lifted her up abruptly as the lantern was lightening the mount of carcasses as she was twirling up with the lantern. She yelped dreadfully with fear and yelping. Her hands trembled and the lantern fell out of her hand. The flame of the candle extinguished at the instant. She was alone live man among the dark of grave and the mounts of dead bodies. The voice of feet trying to step down the slope was echoing in the room with her yelps. When she fell down in an attempt of loosing balance, she would scream more loudly, but her voice echoed under the murky grave of dead ones. She was screaming louder and loudest. The feeling of smell was no more evident for her.

"God," She shouted loudly.

"Mom," she shouted again.

"Clarke," She was shouting those for help who could not come to her help. She felt the carcasses hissing, the grave roaring repressing her voice and the dark roaring dreadfully at her cries.

She had started sobbing now as after tired of weeping. After a few minutes, there was not anymore of her voice echoing. She was lost, the grave was trying to find her it's dark. The small reptiles were creeping at her body.

CHAPTER 22

✦═ The Conspiracy ═✦

I

The queen was again roaming in her room with the maids turning the objects, throwing them on the floor and unlocking cupboards, the executioners breaking their boards. The room was messy in no minutes but the queen could find nothing. Everyone was quietly staring to his companion and the queen lost in the deep subtle thoughts waiting for the new orders.

"Look out in the Clarke's room. He was his closest fellow." The queen suggested and all of they pacing at the thick carpets, stepping down the stairs elegantly and proudly, the queen was setting off for messing another room. Soon they entered the room of the prince of Earth. He was fast a sleep, probably sick, as Ashley her mother was caressing his head. The room opened with a jerk and the queen swiftly entered as no one was to stop her. Ashley stood up at the instant and was stunned to see the executioners, maids and the Queen in her room.

"My son didn't do anything, Zeus," Ashley sternly guarded his son.

"I know," The queen nodded. "Find it," The queen ordered his followers and all of they looked into the room. "Listen, Ashley, I'm going arrange a marriage of your daughter and Leonardo, hopefully, you will join the marriage soon." Queen told her.

"Who are you to decide about my daughter?" Ashley was annoyed.

"Wife of Charles,"

"You would be but you are not her mother," Ashley shouted in rage.

"Neither are you," Queen sneered and Ashley was bowled over. The maids and the executioners were keenly busy in looking for the objects. Clarke moaned with fever what made the queen attentive to him.

"Check out his bed," The queen yelled and the executioners in no minutes lifted his bed up and the boy was moaning at the ground.

"Clarke," Ashley hurriedly stepped to him. After a great struggle of rummaging around, they could not get the required object. Queen thoughtfully looked to the walls around and stepped out whereas Ashley was trying to move heavy bed up.

"What about the forces at the sea?" The queen asked the executioners following her after the two maids.

"I couldn't hear any news about them," One of the executioners informed the queen. Queen was sternly and proudly stepping up the stairs. The maids weirdly looked to one another and then the queen.

I want to look into the room of that girl again," The queen told them her intentions and all of thy moved up to the room. The maids were now rearranging the room. Queen was sitting at the futon nearby the door of the terrace. One of the executioners, the faithful one of the queen stepped to the window of the room where a pigeon was knocking it's beak with the kerosene lamp to make the princess aware of its arrival. The executioner grabbed it at the instant, the pigeon fluttered as he felt the stone hard hands instead of the delicate soft palms. The beauty of the pigeon attracted the man and he moved to the queen sat in his steps.

"This is a gift for you, hopefully you would love it," The executioner presented it to the queen. The queen held it admiringly and looked to the man with an expression of thanks. She smiled subtly as she was patting her hand at the back and neck of the pigeon when her hand struck by something hard. It was a folded piece of paper tied around its neck. She quickly thoughtfully untied it. As she was reading the statements at the letter so were she startling, gladdening and outraging.

"Stop," She ordered the maids, executioners in the room and they looked to her.

"It's really the best gift you gave me, Sultan," The queen deviously gave the paper to Sultan. The letter read it,

Dear Bellatrix,

> *I was always excited to meet you, to see you and this time Abdullah gave me the permission to write a letter to you in reply of your letter. He asked me to mention something to you. Mary is all right now, as the girl has been married to his love. Lady Margaret just misses her son but she has to live now. But I was to inform you something about Max and Abdullah, Max was on a voyage and the falcon of the ring helped him a lot. Mr. Raza sent Abdullah on campaign*

as he got impressed by his success of murdering the king and escaping Max. If you get any news about Abdullah, do reply me soon and if I would get any news I would try my level best to inform. I'm really glad to see you. Moreover, the war at borders is going on. We've been successful in stabilizing ourselves and soon we shall occupy the land of Sunasia and then we shall get our rule back. Mr. Raza has spread the soldiers on all the four sides of the country. We are safe. All the people of the earth are safe. This was the biggest news Abdullah wanted to tell you and I sent his message. He also said me that after his return from the campaign of finding Alberic and the ball he will bring you back to the land of Sunasia an your brother Max, he is fine and he misses you and his mother a lot. Abdullah has set out for a journey and soon he would be back. The last thing, I couldn't find the chance to thank you for the precious gift you gave me once. It's still in my wrist.

Yours sincerely
Saira

The letter ended and Sultan evocatively looked to the queen.

II

She was alone in the dark of the grave when he felt the affectionate hands at her head. She feebly lifted her upside down head to the person and the bright light closed her eyes abruptly. She could feel they were many.

"Bellatrix," She was familiar with the voice and she briskly lifted her head hoping for is survivor and he was the same for what she had expected. He was squatted near her with a kerosene lamp in his hand. Two kerosene lamps had held the two men standing beside him. She gladly and feebly opened her drowsy eyes.

"It's me Jesse, I'm here,"

"Jesse," She whispered softly.

"Yes, Come on, let's move out," Jesse quickly held her hand and lifted her upside down body up.

"Go away, Jesse, Queen can be here at any moment,"

"She won't, don't worry, just get out of here,"

The two holding kerosene lamps pushed the two men standing at the front and she was moving with Jesse as he was assisting her to step up the stairs. When all of they got out, the panorama was evident for her. She couldn't believe she was out of the grave. The two executioners were motionless under the shades of the swords of the friends of Jesse. Jesse stuck her by the wall of nearby and moved to the friends. He took out his sword and slaughtered the two executioners. The heads of the two were fallen in front of Bellatrix and she furiously looked Jesse. Jesse with his friends dragged the carcasses and threw them into the hole. He put the lid back, covered it by carpet as it was before and them all of they set off. Jesse and Alan were moving and forward, Bellatrix was behind and another friend was behind Bellatrix looking around for the danger. They hid behind the wall and held a bag. Jesse took out a black cloak and gave it t Bellatrix to put on. She quickly put it on and put its hooded cap at her head. The boys covered their faces with the veil.

"I was not to bring the executioners with me, but the fact is that I did not know about the place, So, I had to and they lost their lives," Jesse explained Bellatrix covering his face by a veil.

"You should not kill them," Bellatrix said.

"I should and if I hadn't they would tell the queen, they were her faithful spies,"

"Let's move Jess," Alan returned viewing the hall carefully.

"Come on, let's go," All of they walked sticking to the wall and hiding under the stairs, they were successful in escaping out of the palace. The horses were staying there wagging their tails and waving their heads as the mosquitoes and flies were disturbing them. All of they held the reins of the horses. Bellatrix held the rein of the horse Jesse asked him about. Everything was quiet and silent in the dark. Bellatrix was no more apparent in the cloak, only the black of her cloak touching the ground was rubbing the ground.

"Where are we going?" Bellatrix asked her slowly.

"Bellatrix, I'll cross you the border through the ship," Jesse told her his intentions.

"And you," Bellatrix asked.

"I'll join my office back," He seriously replied with mixed emotions of dejection carelessness.

"Where shall I go crossing the sea," Bellatrix asked.

"To your land," Jesse replied.

"But, I do not know the way," Bellatrix told him the problem.

"Fine," Jesse thoughtfully gazed her. Her face was covered in hood only tip of the nose and the forehead on either sides of the nose was visible in the moonlight. Their shades in the moonlight were waving on the mud. "I'll do something... Haven't Abdullah told you anything about it?" asked Jesse.

"No, he never mentioned, he just told about the hexane men colony where he lives,"

"Fine I'll do something, but first to move from here before dawn," Replied Jesse abruptly. They were moving behind the bushes. Soon their horses were galloping harder in the abandoned streets and crossing the luxurious as well as voluptuous palaces. Their horses were galloping harder and harder one after another as they neighed when they reached the red line. The security guards were standing at either sides of the red line. They raised their swords as they witnessed the veiled horse riders. Jesse rode down the horse and released his veil.

"Jesse," One of the men said looking his face.

"Yes," Jesse nodded. "He is Alan and Mark" The other two also unveiled their faces.

"You people, how are you here? Isn't it doubtful?" The man scared them apprehensively.

"O no, dear," Jesse laughed. "Jackson, I was just going..." He looked to Bellatrix still at the horse with the covered face.

"So, you've no answer," The man abruptly replied. Jesse was quiet. "Listen Jesse, if you've three stars at your shoulder then I've been awarded with the sword of the king." Jesse and Jackson abruptly took their swords out of the scabbard for fight. In the meanwhile, Mark and Alan also took their swords out and the thirty guards at the red line took out theirs. "Jesse, whatever is it tells, me, my men are more than yours," Jesse looked to the guards of the borders ready to attack at the order of their master.

"Still I've the courage to face them," Jesse answered.

"You've the courage to face them but not power to slaughter them," Jackson challenged.

"Let us go, Jackson, it's urgent," The faithful horse of Jesse standing near him was being restless. It lifted its hind limbs up and strokes the chest of Jackson, with a jerk he fell down, lost the grip of his sword and Jesse held him by the collar, he lifted his sword up and threw it to Bellatrix. She caught it abruptly, "So your reward, I'll give to this horse," Jesse murmured in his ears. All the guards ran to Jesse but he warned them of slaughtering their master's head. "Now come, Jackson, the sword of the king," Jesse mocked. He had strongly twisted his arm around the neck of Jackson who was moaning and trying to resist. "If you tried chasing me or informing the queen, remembering your master is with me." Jesse again warned.

The horses one more time galloped harder and harder trying to reach the destination.

III

The contests at the either sides of the borders were continuing. Daily Sunasians would attack by the way of the sea and daily many of their men killed. The Earthumen occupied many of the ships and had increased their power. The queen had called the soldiers back. There were no more ships they could see at the sea. At the rear of the city, the soldiers were practicing, understanding the sword fight, political war tricks and the tricks of bravery. Daily they would awake up early in the morning performed the religious obligations and had started building a wall around the city to save from the attacks of the enemy. Everything was soft and settled. As there were no more ships at the sea, Max went to meet Saira to know from her about the locket. She served him with a cup of tea and snacks with it. Both of they chatted for a long time.

"So how are Mary and James?" Max asked.

"Both are fine and well," Saira told him.

"What about locket? Any new mystery," Max asked finishing his cup of coffee.

"No, nothing new, "She simply replied and took a sip of tea. "What about that girl? The girl of the ring, how is she? You did not talk about her," Saira said.

"O, she," The yes of Max impulsively and he saw the falcon fallen and moaning in the feet of the cave man. He fearfully opened his eyes with a jerk.

"What happened?" Saira asked abruptly.

"Nothing," Max shook his head. The pigeon entered directly onto the table in between them through the window. "O, it has come," Saira excitedly caressed it as the entrance of the pigeon was startling for both of them. She untied the letter hung around the neck of the pigeon. Max grabbed the pigeon and took it to the kitchen to get some feed. Soon he returned with two small bowls and put them at the table. Saira had unfolded the letter and was reading it carefully. Her face was displaying the expression of worry.

"What happened?" He took letter from her. The pigeon did not intend to eat anything. He was constantly staring both of them busy reading the letter. He wanted to tell them something but the pigeon could not speak. It could only shriek, scream or screech. Max straightened the paper and it read;

Dear Saira,

It really was a good day when I read your letter; I'm in a great trouble this time. The queen wants to kill me. Please help me. I am in trouble. Do something. Come and see me, I'll be in the queen's palace.

Yours Bellatrix

"I'll go; I'll never let her to die." Max said.

"I'll also go with you." Saira suggested.

"No, you will stay here, you will never let this locket to be lost, keep it save with you," Max advised her and set out for journey.

"Take good care," Saira farewell him and Max nodded in a worry and hurry. Soon his horse galloped to his old land.

"May Allah help her and may the boy be saved," Saira closed her eyes. Allah is the biggest protector who helps every man. She opened her eyes. His horse was lost in the storm of mud after him. She turned and get into her house.

IV

Martha was standing at the terrace just listening to the birds singing and the air blowing. Jensen was not back from his tours. She was alone in the house, when she heard a knock at the door. The maids went and came back.

"Jesse has come with Bellatrix," The maid told her. "What?" Martha was excited and shocked. She stepped down with the help of the maid and stepped to the door. They four were standing at the door. "Bellatrix," Martha murmured and Bellatrix hugged her.

"I just came to meet you, Lady Martha, I'm going to Earthumen, soon I'll take you with me," Bellatrix consoled her. She almost wept. Bellatrix wiped her tears and soon both of they were gone. "Dear, I can't see you, but I always wished to see you, I've no sight, but still I can feel your features, they are just like Lilly and Oliver, Your Uncle Tom will be there. He will guard you. Abdullah is a good boy, I know him very well, Jesse," Martha called him. Jesse grabbed Martha's hand.

"Yes,"

"Be careful and don't leave her till the danger is over," Martha said.

"Ok, Martha we should go now, pray for our safe journey," Martha nodded. Soon she heard the horses galloping harder and hardest. She was standing alone waving them the hands in her own direction.

The horses were galloping. They had entered the reign of Earthumen. They reached the garden. Jesse moved down and held Jackson by collar,

"Listen, I don't leave any proof," He took out his sword and pinched its sword in the neck of the man. The man moaned. "If you made any noise remember, then I'm cleverer than you," Jesse warned and left him with a jerk.

He stabilized his stumbling body and ran quietly without looking back.

"Is the danger over now?" asked Bellatrix.

"Yes, to some extent," Jesse told. "Bellatrix," He called her taking out a small dagger hung near his scabbard. "Perhaps, you'd have to continue your journey alone. SO, it's just a protection. Hope, there will be no more danger but still I give this to you as a representation of the care," Bellatrix quietly took the sword. She was tangled as she evocatively looked to her. "Bellatrix," He continued more. "The two ladies whom I loved the more in life, Martha who won my heart serving me as a mother, who brought me up when my mother was dead and another who was forever in the heart,"

"If queen had known that I had escaped," Bellatrix asked.

"Don't worry; she would never, because when once she buried the girl in her grave, she never think about her," Jesse was quietly speaking when they heard the horses galloping after them. All of they looked back. Ten horses were chasing them.

"Jackson," Jesse gnashed his teeth in anger.

"Filth," Mark and Alan cussed Jackson. They pulled the reins. Alan and Mark's horses were forward. Bellatrix was following them and Jesse was after her protecting her.

"Bellatrix join Mark and Alan," Jesse shouted and her horse sped fast. Soon her horse was galloping harder than Mark and Alan as she was an excellent horse rider and a sword fighter. The horse riders were coming nearer to them.

"Princess, run as it is and don't look back," Alan shouted and suggested her. Her horse was alone galloping at an unpredicted and undecided way. The horses of Alan and Mark turned and neighed before the ten horse riders. Jackson put his sword at the neck of Jesse. Jesse resisted but the other horse riders grabbed his hands firmly.

"What would you do know Jesse because you are cleverer than me, don't worry, I won't harm Martha but I can never leave you alive." Jackson lifted his sword up to kill him but another sword hit his sword and his sword fell far away. The horse rider was now around Alan. Mark also joined in. The three continued to struggle for their lives and the rest were doing their best to attack them. Alan, Mark and Jesse engaged them into one another and in the meanwhile Bellatrix had crossed the border. She did not know where he was going she did not know where he was; just her horse was taking her to an unknown path. As she crossed the border, Max entered the Earthumen colony to save her.

CHAPTER 23

✦ Helter-Skelter ✦

I

Max entered his birthplace. At the place of his house were mounds left. No one settled there. He paced to the place; there was barren land in place of green fields. Everything mashed. He stepped in the mounds of his house and could estimate the direction. It was kitchen once. Her mother arranged the dishes and cooked the food here. The place where he and his father chuckled and sowed seeds. He wished those moments would be back, but there was neither childhood and nor the life of his father. He was wishing to take her mother back with the help of Bellatrix. He missed his loved ones, with whom he spent some of his memorable and learnable moments of life. Ali Hamid, he would surely miss him every minute and at every moment. "Mom," Something whispered and his heart broke like a sharp noise of any glass broken. As he remembered Bellatrix, he quickly galloped his horse to reigns of Sunasia, to the huge Sultanate of Sunasia where Sun never did disappear. He was to tear the mouth of dragon and to save her sister. In to the mouth of dragon, life could be lost or it could be got. His horse was galloping harder and harder to save the reign. He had covered his face with a veil. When he reached the red-line, no one stopped him. Instead he was fully in the mood of skirmishing. The mouth of dragon looked him kind today. He valiantly passed in between the huge palaces, the giant buildings which would be memorial soon after our victory. Soon he was in a market, where he for the very first started his earning. Errands learnt him a lot as before he did not even know to dress. Soon, he reached the palace. Unexpectedly, the door of the palace was opened. Now, where was Bellatrix? It was his task to find her. He continued stepping forward. The palace was quiet. He went to the stairs to his left.

"Welcome, my guest," He could never forget that voice before. "I had been waiting for you since yesterday, but unluckily the game of life was tripping away from me." Queen proudly went to him. He turned as he had stepped one stair and was stunned to view the tall queen in front of him. "You are looking my king today," She smiled frankly and her taunt pinched Max like a poisonous needle.

"How poor of you, your solely cousin deceived you." She looked pitifully to him. Soon Max saw the tips of swords pinching his ribs. They were four arresting him.

"Where is Bellatrix?" Max sternly asked.

"She is married now to Leonardo, she is happy in her life, she is good, very well," The queen smirked.

"What do you want?" Max asked.

"I want the universe," The queen gazed him. "The two boys on whom depends the freedom of earth; I want to grab the two resilient and brave boys,"

"Take him to my palace," Queen ordered and the men on the either sides pushed him down to make the way for the queen. The arrogant queen proudly stepped up the stairs and

Max after him under the guard of four swords. The queen was moving steadily and the guards were after him. All of they were in the palace. No courtiers. They were alone. The queen proudly sat at her throne.

"Good boy, your mother is in my custody and I would let her free if you do as I would say… As far as the assault is concerned, I know that your leader Mr. Raza has spread the net of his soldiers all around the country, but I've thought for the solution." The queen was sternly speaking puffing in the cigar which a maid standing nearby gave to her.

"I would never let you," Max shouted. She satisfactorily puffed in the cigar.

"Be slow Max," The queen frankly replied. "I'm in a big tension. Listen, the seven kings of the world are after a big pendant, a locket, in which the secrets of the world are hidden. They want to snatch it and rule the world… Listen Max; I do not want the future of both the nations to be ruined. We shall go back to our land Max, but just I want you people to get rid of those seven kings, you visited. You know the way and you have a true friendship with the falcon that would help you." The queen pretended to be gloomy.

"I won't kill any one," Max valiantly spoke.

"Fine, then I would have t o kill your mother," The queen warned softly.

"What is my mother's guilt?" Max asked abruptly.

"I was hoping for Saira and wished to surrender you on behalf of Saira," The queen looked into Max's outrageous eyes. "But unluckily I couldn't find the chance, now I'll surrender Mr. Raza on behalf of you,"

"You would never be successful," Max gnashed his teeth in anger.

"Over to you, you have one night to think about it," The queen said and moved up to the entrance. The sword men pushed him and threw him in a dark room.

II

The thorn pinched her finger while touching a rose patrolling in the garden.

"Ah," She moaned with a soft cry of pain and pressed her finger with the help of the thumb. She could feel the thin flow of blood out of the finger. The garden was quiet.

"Martha," One of the women called her and she moved in. Jensen was standing with a young girl in the room. She could not see her but he could feel the presence of any other person in the room.

"Listen Martha," Jensen sternly spoke and Martha had to be attentive.

"Your time is ended. I've married a new girl and at one time I wish to have one wife. Now you are free. You can go wherever you want." Jensen said. "Go out of my house." He said and took his new wife upstairs. The maids were quietly standing on the sideways.

"Where is Jesse?" Martha said helplessly. "Ask him to drop me somewhere, I'm blind and I can't see," Martha begged as the tears drop out of her eyes.

"Lady Martha, Jesse was dead; his dead body is in the palace of the queen."The news fell like a thunder at her.

"Jesse," She murmured and sobbed.

"I'll do this favor with you, in the evening, I'll take you with me in my home," The maid offered.

"No, I don't want to live with anyone to become a trouble for him. Just leave me at my previous house where I lived with Oliver and my son," Martha requested.

"I'll do," The maid nodded. She held her hand and accommodated her in the futon.

"Jesse," She grabbed her face and wept. Jesse who was the most brilliant and the most gallant soldier on Earth was awarded four titles at a very young age and three stars twinkled at his shoulders, merely at the age of twenty years. He was dead the last night when the dagger of Jackson tore her body and he stabbed it again not knowing why. When the dead body was taken to the palace, he was blamed for the rebellion ship of helping the Earthumen in giving them armaments and fleeing the prisoners. He was blamed for the entire Earthumen colony with his friends. All of his stars were snatched from his shoulder and his dead body was thrown in front of the vultures. Jackson took revenge of his humiliation and disgrace. Alan and Mark were also treated in the same way. The vultures ate the delicious food and quenched their thirst with their blood. Martha went to her old mounds and started a new life with soul of her husband and the imaginations of Max. He felt that his husband would come every night and stayed with her the whole. They would sit, chat and remember the memories of the past. They would squat at the mounds and think about her son. As Martha was blind, he could not see anything, the lonely thing he could see was the soul of his husband coming to the earth to meet her. Sometimes, he felt Jesse has come to meet her. She would stun and she could feel Jesse respecting her like her own mother.

The next day, Jackson was rewarded all the three stars, the swords and all the four titles of Jesse. The vultures were eating the flesh of the Jesse and Jackson was merry making with his friends. He was gifted a beautiful wretched woman of Earth. Everything was helter-skelter all of a sudden. Max was also sent to the palace of the queen and they were ready to attack. One of the soldiers covered his moth, tied his arms at the back and his legs. The battalion was ready and rushed off to the enemies who killed a lot of the soldiers who were killing their people day by day. The journey started under the cunning scheme of the Jackson, the greatest man among Sunasians of that time. They raised their suns signs and faced it to the sun.

"We shall rule the world," They shouted and the people flung off with the emotions of proud and arrogance. They decided for a rear attack. The queen was sitting at an elephant. They had special races of elephants, the vultures were flying above them and they were galloping on the best horses of the time.

III

Shimer and Hassan were taking meals along with the other men. They were chatting and chuckling gleefully. When all of they had been full, they wished to take some rest. Shimer, Hassan along with three commandoes looked deep into path way. They did neither see any army and nor did they feel any danger. Shimer looked up to the sky. The dark clouds were covering the sky and dominating the land of the earth. A drop of rain felt at his hand. Hassan anxiously looked up to the sky.

"It's fine, going to rain," Shimer said and Hassan nodded. All of they went to the camps to have a sound sleep. They stooped a little and entered in. The weather was pleasant and cool. Cool breeze blew and soon all of they went into the valleys of dreams. The dark was increasing. Saira felt restlessness when she was back from school. She felt scorching heat around her neck as she looked up. A jelly like smoke layer of dark was spreading under the clouds. It was 1 pm of the day and the horrible dark was casing the world. The women with the children in their laps rushed out in haste and were horrified to look the sky. The women could hardly see one another. Saira quickly ran to the house as she saw a vulture coming after her. She ran fast and hard. The piles of papers fell off her hands. She ran to the house and quickly stepped banging the door after her. The vulture was now knocking it's beak against the window. She quickly released the curtain.

Mary in the theatre was standing with a flame of fire in her hand. She lifted her leg up and joined it with her right hand; he body twisted and made a circle. People clapped joyfully at the performance of the brilliant actress. The flame in a small clay pot was flickering in her right hand. Soon the dark covered the theatre. The crowd was silent and only a flame of fire was flickering in the doom of dark. No face was able to another face. The voice of the raining could be heard but not any drop of water fell on earth.

"The world is in a serious trouble of danger," Mr. Raza murmured and the heart of Mr. Peter also told him something horrible. The women and children standing in the street quickly got in the houses.

Bellatrix who was running on an unknown way, the dark also dominated there. She was in forest under the shade of dark. He couldn't see the next forest and her horse galloping fast struck into it. Bellatrix fell down. In dark, she tried to search for his horse. It was motionless standing, as something had stabbed in his forehead.

"Who is there?" She asked slowly. "Who is there?" She shouted but she couldn't have any answer. There was hell quiet in the forest. It seemed the animals had also feared the dark. The dark remained for two days. People spent the whole day and the whole night lightening up the kerosene lamps as well as lanterns. The food at the borders for the commanders was insufficient now. The oil in the lamps was also finished.

"It's a fine welcome to my queen," The people heard a screeching voice on that day.

"Be prepared and ready for the battle," Mr. Raza had sent the message at all the posts. "The assault can be at any time."

Everyone at every border was geared up and equipped. The water ended in the wells. The babies shriveled with thirst. They were weeping and crying.

Abdullah who was on a voyage with his companions also observed the dark and they couldn't see one another.

"Where are you?" They were calling and shouting but could not see any one.

"I'm here," They were blindly galloping to one another at the horses. Soon they heard their voices coming from far away and then felt the voices coming from any deep well. They were departed and lost in calm and quiet journey.

After two days, the dark was removing and slowly and it took one day. The night was a normal night. People could see the moon and the stars twinkling and they took deep sigh of relief. The next day started and in the early morning, Shimer and Hassan saw a huge army of carriages, horses with spears and elephants. The next day was a clammy wet day. The horses galloped at the camps in no minutes and slaughtered the people of Earth. They also prepared their swords and attacked the forces of Suns. The vultures were stinging and tearing them. Some were enjoying the dead bodies. The elephants entered and trampled all the camps as well as men. They were not expecting for such a great fight. No one was left saved.

A huge army attacked from the west side and in no minutes killed all. They killed, crushed and defeated each man of earth and at the Sunasians were successful as they were huge in power and armaments. The queen had entered the kingdom successfully and gleefully with the prisoners of war. Mr. Raza came out with his men and encountered her. The queen came out of the carriage. The news of the prisoners and the death of the men of the earth were horrifying for all. The women wept a lot who lost their husbands, who lost their parents and who lost their brothers.

"So, Mr. Raza I admire your reformation," She cunningly smiled. Mr. Raza and Mr. Peter were standing side by side. "How poor of you Mr. Raza! You sent Oliver in our reign to be the resource of your domination and entrance, and check the decree of fate, his son became the source of our entrance." Everyone was shocked at the exposure of the queen. The queen waved her hand and her faithful executioner threw the tied Max onto the ground.

"Max," The queen heard a shout and she looked in the same direction. She was a girl. Both of they looked one another and the girl was shocked to see the woman. She was the same whom she saw in her dreams. The subtle lips were same with whom she would speak odious; the cunning eyes were the same with what she saw her standing at the mount and the hands were the same with which she was trying to snatch the locket. The woman was moving to her with a cunning smile and the girl was in a kind of trance. The people all around were standing quietly looking the helpless Max. The woman moved to her and held her right hand in which a bracelet with gems embedded was tied around her wrist. She lifted her hand up to the girl's forehead and put the index finger between her big black eyes. The girl was in a stupor that she couldn't stop her. The woman's fingers touched her forehead and her eyes were closing. Max was resisting to free himself of the tight knots but all in vain. The girl fainted and fell on ground. Mary ran to her.

CHAPTER 24

⚜ Abdullah on a Voyage ⚜

I

The war was over for some moments. On the other hand Abdullah and his friends lost and departed with another. In dark they did not know in what directions they had reached. Abdullah was looking all around to look for the way when he saw a pack of wolves chasing him in the jungle. He was at his unicorn. It also sped fast and in no minutes he was very far away from them. He was in a serious trouble. He had lost the way, lost the friends and he had no guidance or any way to go back. It was night time and it was raining hard as he was going to cross a stream of water he saw a man in the black horse. He could remember, he was the same man he saw in the childhood in the same hood.

"Who are you?" Abdullah tried to confirm.

"Winston," The man spoke and he could remember the voice.

"So, what brought you here today again?" Abdullah asked sternly.

"Your death, I would never let you to meet Alberic and neither my queen," The man roared.

"And you'll see I'll meet." Abdullah challenged him. Winston roared into laughter.

O poor guy, you can never," Winston said in the manner of persuading him.

"How is your skull?" Abdullah asked. "I can remember, I threw a stone to it and it was hanging," Abdullah told him.

"Yes, it was, I was angry and now is the time to take revenge, for there is no Ali Hamza," Winston said. "It is hanging like as before. Now I'll kill you, when the worms would eat your flesh up, I'll use your skeleton," Winston told him pointing by his bony finger.

"You can never Winston, even if you want it to be," Abdullah stopped for some moments. "What kind of man are you that you can not pass on a life at a single structure," Abdullah cursed him.

"Don't abuse me, I'm no man. I'm Satan," The devil said and Max stunned. Devil roared into laughter Abdullah's shocking face. "The mind of the queen of the earth is under my control for the reason, what she wanted, I also wanted the same. She was mean and I was malicious. So, both of we mesh worked together well," The devil roared into laughter.

"Remember, how much mean and malicious you are, the dark ends one day and this dark is covered by the light of truth and faith." Abdullah said.

"Shut up," The devil angrily roared." Now ready to die," The devil lifted his index finger and pointed its tip to Max. A red blaze emerged and rolled to Abdullah. Abdullah quickly took out his sword. The unicorn abruptly neighed lifting his hind limbs up. Abdullah lost balance and he fell onto the ground instantly. He briskly lifted himself up and was dazed to see the unicorn. It had lowered its head down and the tip of its horn was eliminating a white light colliding with red flames of the devil. Abdullah crouched and crossed the stream under the colliding lights and reached the devil. He climbed the back of his horse at the back of the devil and cut his head off. He heard a loud scream. The skull fell down and the skeleton fell on to the horse. Abdullah lowered his head down to be saved from the beam of light of unicorn. Everything was calm now. Unicorn had stop emitting the rays of light from its horn. Abdullah held the checked inside it. He had held a skeleton by his shoulder and its head was cut off. It was motionless and a bad stink was emerging from it. He threw the skeleton and stepped to the unicorn.

"Thanks," He said to the unicorn as he grabbed its neck to climb it. It has started raining heavily. He and the white unicorn were standing alone under the rain.

"Take me wherever you can," Abdullah offered unicorn.

"It's not so far, your destination. We shall reach soon." The unicorn spoke and Abdullah was shocked. He had seen animal speaking like him for the first time. His eyes wide opened as he dazed to see the unicorn.

"Can you speak like me?" The unicorn nodded.

"I can speak all the languages, but I don't speak much." The unicorn replied.

"Where will you take me now?" Abdullah asked.

"Grab my neck firmly," The unicorn replied and it sped fastest. The unicorn was galloping as hard and fast as it could. It was galloping harder and harder. In the way, it was briskly moving from under the logs that Abdullah himself could not observe where the logs were and where were the bushes. Soon he entered the jungle with the unicorn. It was galloping harder. Abdullah bent and a twisted bough held him by the back of the collar. It gripped Abdullah and lifted it up. He was hanging in between the log and the ground.

"Listen, Listen," He was shouting when girl who looking his dead horse looked to the boy hanging up.

"Abdullah," She saw astounded and laughed.

"Is it unicorn?" She tried to confirm. Abdullah nodded.

"Get down idiot quickly," The girl chuckled to see him like that. Abdullah tried to climb down holding the twisted log and sticking by the trunk of the tree he was moving down. Bellatrix looked forward, bowed her index finger and the thumb towards her palms and put it under her tongue. She puffed in and out, at the ended succeeded in whistling loud. The unicorn stopped. It looked back at its back but could not find his mast. It turned quickly and fatly and was amazed to see his master. Bellatrix patted its face. Abdullah had reached the ground.

"How were you here Bellatrix?" Abdullah was shocked to see her.

"I… I… just lost,"

"I also lost," They were moving passively in the jungle and the unicorn was following them.

"Was everything all right?" Abdullah asked him again. "What's this at your hands as Abdullah had seen the blood congealed at her palms.

"It's on my feet also," Bellatrix explained. Abdullah looked own to her feet. They were also red and looking mucky.

"What is all that? Were you fine?" He hastily in a worry grabbed her shoulder.

"Yes," She dejectedly nodded. "Queen arrested me and buried me in a grave. Jesse saved me." Bellatrix told him.

"You didn't tell me." Abdullah complained.

"I could not find the chance," Bellatrix said gloomily.

"I had asked Saira to reply you, did you receive her message?" Abdullah asked.

"I was arrested on the other day when I wrote you a letter." Bellatrix told him.

"Saira would have written you reply," Abdullah said. "Where would have the reply gone," Both of they thoughtfully looked to one another.

"Don't worry," She abruptly made her calm. "My pigeon does not give my letter to anyone else."

"Fine," He was calm now. "What about your hands and feet and your face?" He was worried as he saw her badly wounded face, the blood coagulated. She smiled.

"Nothing like that, just in the grave there were dead carcasses and they were burst. In dark, I climbed them and the ghastly blood stuck to me." Bellatrix told.

"Are you fine now?" Abdullah again asked.

"Where are you going now?" Bellatrix asked him.

"To find Alberic, We were three, me, Shiva and your uncle Tom," Abdullah answered.

"Was he also?" He was excited to hear the name.

"I truly wish to see him, to meet him," Bellatrix told him her wish.

"Everything would be fine." Abdullah consoled her. "Let's move now,"

"I'll wait for you in the forest, you go," Bellatrix said and Abdullah looked back to her who had climbed the horse.

"Bellatrix, I won't leave you alone," Abdullah said and she looked to her. "I would love to take you with me," Abdullah requested her. She smiled and quickly climbed the unicorn with him.

The unicorn was galloping was harder. She held Abdullah tightly.

"Move down," Abdullah shouted and both of they lowered their heads as there was a horizontal log in the way.

"Up," Bellatrix said as the danger was over. They were enjoying the journey moving up and down. The opposite air was waving their heads back at their foreheads and both of they were chuckling and laughing. The journey went by with the speed of the unicorn when the unicorn threw both of them in front of a mount. Both of they could not stable and fell onto the ground at some distances. They looked to the unicorn.

"My back is tired." It said moodily grazing the grass nearby. They rubbed their clothes and stood erect themselves. The unicorn was grazing itself. They looked to one another.

"Hey tell me dear, what can we do now? Can we take rest?" Bellatrix asked hesitatingly.

"Rest," He said in strange expressions. "Nobody rests at the destination." The unicorn again started grazing the grass. They excitedly looked to one another.

"Where is it?" Abdullah abruptly asked.

"Should I tell you everything?" The unicorn answered. "Find down the mount," The unicorn rebuked them and they sternly saw the mount. Bellatrix excitedly passed by Abdullah.

"Come," She called him and he followed her. They moved all around the mount to find for any place to enter. Trying and revolving around it, they helplessly looked to the unicorn. The unicorn was grazing the dry grass at the ground. He wearily looked to them.

"Now, I'll have to tell you this too," Unicorn moodily said them. "Look under the mount." Both of they abruptly looked down. Unicorn was grazing now again. They looked and were surprised to see a hole at the end of the mount.

"Wait, I'll go and see," Abdullah said and Bellatrix nodded. He crouched at the ground and peeked in through the hole. He observed, a fat man could pass into it but he would have to crawl. Bellatrix was standing near him trying to look into the hole. Abdullah stood up.

"I'll enter and then I'll call you," Abdullah instructed her and she nodded confusingly. He crawled through the hole and Bellatrix heard his scream.

"Abdullah," She shouted abruptly.

"Yes, what," Abdullah hastily replied her normally. "Come, be careful,"

"OK," She nodded and hesitated. She crawled her feet into the hole and his legs entered but she could not find any assistance to put her legs. She waved here and there. "Should I come?" She again asked but did not hear any reply. "Abdullah," She called again but there was no reply. "Abdullah," She shouted and crawled her whole body through the hole. Whoosh, she fell into the mud. She coughed, wiped the dust off her clothes and stood up.

"Crap! The princess fell," Abdullah roared into laughter. Bellatrix was annoyed. She was quietly moving onto the mud. There would be dark if the light through the hold would not have been piercing.

"I think, we are to look for something here," She said to Abdullah.

"But, I can't see anything here." Abdullah replied carelessly.

"We are to find it," She angrily replied. Both of they were passively moving forward. As they were moving, the dark was increasing. "This can't help," She said.

"What should be done now?" Abdullah said.

"Probably, we need some light," Bellatrix told her the solution. Abdullah groaned and nodded. They were moving when they heard the voice of something fallen at their back. They abruptly looked back. Abdullah hurriedly took out his sword out of the scabbard. It was fallen right in the direction of the hole. Due to the minute sunlight they could observe it was a candle lit. Bellatrix went to it quickly. She grabbed it and joined back Abdullah. Abdullah put back the sword in the scabbard, Bellatrix smiled and Abdullah nodded excited. It was like a drowning man catches at a straw. Bellatrix was moving forward and Abdullah was behind him.

"It's your unicorn." Abdullah said to Bellatrix to her moving swiftly.

"Where?" She quickly turned in a surprise.

"Who did this," Abdullah replied normally looking to the flame of candle. She changed her direction sternly and gasped.

"Oops," She shrieked as her foot slid into a narrow hole. It was not trapped swiftly and she could get it out easily.

"What happened?" Abdullah looked to her as she got a jerk in front of him. Bellatrix twisted to look her trapped foot and she viewed a horrible sight. There were holes one after the other. It was the smallest and in the same lane were the big, bigger and biggest holes.

"Be careful," Abdullah stood side by her and he also witnessed the array of holes as he had twisted his to body to move foot Bellatrix out of the hole.

II

"Saira," Mary put her head in her lap. She was fainted and motionless. "Saira," She murmured in worry and looked to the queen. She had turned now in between the crowd at the either sides. Max tried his best to be free of the knot. At last, she ordered the executioner to open the knots. The executioner took a dagger and cut the knots of hands, mouth and feet. He was free now. The crowd was standing quiet. The women in the crowd were moving to the fainted Saira and had surrounded her. Max quickly stood up as he was freed.

"Well... Max," The queen sneered. "The scheme you started is really inspiring, but Bellatrix helped me a lot,"

"Bellatrix is not of that type," Max abruptly defended her character. The queen gazed him with amazement.

"You trust her, not me, who saved you from princess of Earth. She wanted to kill you." The queen cunningly pretended to be very sincere with him.

"Stop this rubbish, I trusted you just and only once, when you blamed my mother and I had almost lost her if Bellatrix did not tell me anything," Max was in a rage.

"And Bellatrix is girl who won your trust favoring your mother," The queen softly tried to persuade him.

"It's not like that, nothing is like that, Remember, the time is going to come when the dark will perish and the light would survive. We men are gathered here, today we've lost, then tomorrow you will see we shall again gather and again our swords will be raised for freedom. We shall never let you to live in peace and one day you will leave this land yourself."

"I know, you are worried about this girl, about your blind mother, all are in my custody, I don't mind your words," She turned her face and smiled cunningly. "For what I do want is… Max I need to have a chat with you, its necessary," The queen said and went into the carriage. The executioner pushed him to the carriage. He resisted but by a forceful thrust, the executioner propelled him to the carriage. Max fell upside down in the foot steps of the queen. She had long nails with black polish at them. The veins of her feet had obtruded and swollen. The executioner tied his hands and feet. He shut the door and his legs impulsively got in. The carriage went on. The forces of Sunasians were standing still holding swords. On the other hand, the army of Mr. Raza was standing quietly ready to encounter them. They were thinking of who should attack first staring furiously one another. Mary with the help of James and took Saira to the home fervently. She laid her at the bed as checked her heat beat. It was beating bit by bit. She saw James who had stooped over Mary to see her.

"What will happen now?" Mary asked in a worry.

"Every one is dead, the army in the east and the west, nothing is left, we shall also die soon," She fearfully looked out of the window. When Frank was dead, I feared a lot. I thought death is just near me. I would fear, scream and ran to the lake for the survival. At night I awakened from the night mares, I would witness Frank yelling and shouting in dark well, and sometimes I would see the vultures hovering on me," Her voice stumbling and fearing. The crowd of women had been scattering. The infants in the laps of the mothers were weeping as hoping for the new danger to come. James held her shoulders standing at her back.

"Everything would be," He consoled her.

"It's not James, it's near, very near, it's the end now, the end of the men of Earth," Mary shuddered with a fear as a tear fell out of her eyes. She closed the eyes and opened them. "Queen would never spare, I always missed Bimla and now I'm going to meet her soon," She sobbed. "I feared death, but now I don't fear as it's very near. When it has to come then for what to fear,"

"Why are you talking like that today?" James asked her.

"Because, it's going to happen." Mary replied worriedly. They heard the door banging. Normally they went to look at the door but were stunned to look the bed. Saira was not in the bed. "Saira," Mary screamed. James opened the door quickly to look for her. Mary ran to the window and saw Saira going very far. James and Mary quickly ran after her. The young couple was running and Saira was leaving larger distance between her and them. Saira had covered the distance till her house in no minutes. Mary was astonished at her fast pace.

"Where is she going?" Mary asked in a surprise as she took the turn into another street.

"To her house," James said and both of they hurried to her. As they reached, the door of the room was opened.

"Saira," Mary hesitantly called her. She couldn't have any reply. "Saira" She called again and entered in. She saw her sitting in a bed with a ruby in her hand. In no minutes, Saira cut her wrist. The blood flowed out. "Saira," Mary screamed but Saira was quiet. She seemed to be unheard of her. At the same time, the queen in the carriage screamed with pain. She held her hand. Max saw her who was sitting down. She held her wrist and saw it. It had burnt. "I can smell her blood," The queen whispered. "I need it, I'll soon have it," Queen whispered. Max was staring her hand. Queen quickly hid her hand under her cuffs as she felt the boy staring her.

Mary squatted near her. "Dear what did you do?" She lovingly held her wrist pressed the cut wound with the side of her shirt. There were no expressions of pain at the face of Saira. Her lips were quiet and silent, and the pupils of her eyes along with the eye-lashes were motionless but she was still alive. Soon, her eyes seemed to be closing and her eyes closed. Mary checked her pulse. It was running. Mary laid her carefully at the bed. The red ruby was in her hand. Mary held it. It's beauty and glitter was admirable. There was a blood-spot at its corner. Mary wiped it with her shirt. She looked to Saira. The blood was clotted at the wrist. James was quietly staring her long eye-lashes of the closed eyes. James took out a bandana and bandaged her wrist. They heard the sounds of swords clashing, men shouting and spears shattering. So, the war was again on. The elephants trampling people were now shaking houses by their force. Sunasians were raising the flags of success in different cities and countries. The layer of dark was again sealing the earth.

III

There was again dark under the mount. The light of the candle was helpful for them a little. They were jumping over the holes warily. Now Abdullah was pacing before him with the light of the candle in his hand holding her hand with care. It was big hole in the way. Abdullah looked forward; there he could see a mud wall. The path ended there. Abdullah looked back to her.

"There is no way," Abdullah turned and unluckily he slipped. Bellatrix tried to grab her hand but she couldn't grab it. Abdullah shouted and fell deep into the big hole. He could hear his scream from any far place. "Abdullah," She shouted two to three times but there was no answer. She was feared and turned to go to the hole in the mount. As she turned she saw an incredible vista. He was a man, her half face was eaten and there was arrangement of bones at the other half face. He had held a blue flame in his hand.

"I think you needed, light," The man offered her.

"Who are you?" She was feared.

"The dark with the light," The man answered hysterically. "What you consider light at the top is the dark in the bottom, you need light and you will have it from me even if you do know I'm Satan, but if you consider the dark is dark, you will not take it from me, but you will take because you need it," The man was moving to her and she was slowly sliding behind.

"No, I won't take it," She turned quickly and jumped into the hole. Before she could complete scream, she fell upside down in the foots-steps of the man. She moaned lightly and lifted her head up and she forgot to breathe. The same man was standing with the light in front of her sneering at her.

"I thought, the princess of earth would need light," The man's terrible voice he could hear. He looked to his black hat at what a snake was hissing. "Don't fear my face; I couldn't get any dead body better than this, this evil man died some days ago, when I entered the grave, the snakes had covered his body. I removed them, but this filth is stinging him still…" Bellatrix stood up fearfully. "You know," He whispered stooping over him. "The soul of this man is screaming wildly as the snake is stinging him. Soon, the worms would eat his body up and I would be have a good array of bones," The man was telling him as the girl was trembling. He lifted his hand up to touch the wounded cheek of the girl. She quickly slid back and took out his dagger,

"Don't come near me, else I'll kill you," Bellatrix warned. The man roared into laughter.

"I don't want to harm you, just close your eyes and listen to the heart of this man, just listen," Bellatrix nerved to go near the man. He glanced his eaten hand with no fingers and the flesh was dribbling out of it. She slowly came nearer looking to the man's terrible face. She stooped a little, closed her eyes and stuck her ears near the heart of the dead body. She heard the shouts and screams and could see a young man just like the body fully structured screaming. He was shouting and the snake was stinging at his head, the snake moved down her shoulder and stung it. The man was shouting and screaming.

"It's not me, it's he," She opened her eyes at the man's voice. He felt he was very near to the man and he could smell the same stink he felt in the grave of the queen. He was a tall man. She looked to her. The man was nodding. "Such a brave girl and a brave boy, who encountered me in the way… I like the men who don't listen to me, but I hate them who don't listen to me," He said it and grabbed her neck from back. Bellatrix screamed. "Look into my eyes," Devil screamed, "I'm Satan, and how can you defeat my queen?" Bellatrix was trying to be free of her. She closed her eyes.

"You would be Satan, but I've the heart of an angel, if you can kill angel then kill me, but you will see, my heart will never be dead." Bellatrix hardly said.

"You talk of angels, when I had made two angels astray and they are passing their days in a deep well in prison," As the devil ended she lifted her hand of dagger and stabbed the dead body. A large flame of fire emitted from the man's body and passing through the hole went out of the dark. There was no more light. She heart the dead body fallen on earth. She sobbed, as she was alone.

"Abdullah," She shouted. "Abdullah" She shouted again. She felt something was crawling at her feet. There was a scream as she remembered the snake at the head of the man. Kicking the snake off her feet she ran quickly to an unknown way. Sh was running when she saw the flame of the candle flickering. She ran to her as she got a jerk and impulsively pushed Abdullah. Abdullah unexpected of the certain rapid arrival jerked, the candle fell off her hand and it extinguished. "Abdullah" She at once spoke.

"Bellatrix," What is this way? You should stay there. Now you have switched it off." Abdullah almost reprimanded. "Just get out of here, there is no use of it," Bellatrix warned her. The candle again lit up. She quickly ran to him with a scream and held his collar with trembling hands in fear. "Get off me, Bellatrix," He removed his hands and quickly held the candle. "What happened? Why are you so scared?" He went to her. She shook her head and wiped her tears. "Is everything fine?" Abdullah again asked. Bellatrix nodded and sobbed. "Look," Abdullah distracted. "This is a slab,"

He showed her in the light of the candle. Bellatrix saw it. The slab needed to be removed as Abdullah had slid it a little. "Take this candle," Bellatrix gripped it. Abdullah was pushing it. He was pushing it harder, when they heard the foot-steps after them. They could hear them commanding and ordering.

"Someone has entered," Bellatrix warned him.

"Perhaps Shiva and Tom," Abdullah excitedly looked back. The excitement appeared at the face of Bellatrix and at the instant it vanished as she heard them more closely.

"They are not, Abdullah, they are Sun's forces,"

Abdullah pushing the slab lifting his head up to he and he made the struggle faster of pushing the slab. He was pushing the slab harder and faster. Bellatrix threw the candle as it switched off and both of they were pushing the slab quickly and at last they were succeeded. The slab fell off. They entered quickly. The voices of the steps were not coming anymore. The room had been illuminated with four candles. There was a bed with the wall someone had slept at it taking the white coverlet till head. It was a small room. A colorful picture of a man in the frame was hung at a side of the wall. He was smiling with slight moustaches at his face. They had seen a man in the frame for the first time. A table was arranged at the other side of the room as a pile of papers were placed at it under the light of the lantern. The small vessel of ink and a pen with blank ink at its top were placed near it. Abdullah went to the table and picked up the pen. He touched its nib and his tip of the index finger became black with the ink. Bellatrix stepped to the bed and observed the coverlet slightly moving up and down. The man was taking breathe and was alive. Abdullah turned; naively his hand struck the lantern at the table. It fell horizontal at the table. The glass broke and papers caught fire. At the instant, he lifted the candle up and extinguished slight fire with his hand. There was still light in the room. Bellatrix abruptly looked back. Abdullah was moaning holding his burnt hand.

"Have you come?" As Bellatrix wished to step to Abdullah, he heard a feeble stumbling voice from the bed. She abruptly twirled her face to the bed. Abdullah also forgot the pain and directed to the voice. "Now, put it off me, I can't help." Again a stumbling, frail and feeble voice they heard from the bed. Horrendously, Bellatrix removed it off the man's face. Abdullah had reached her and stood near him. He was too weak. His jaws had not teeth as cheeks were pressed in. He was looking a live skeleton, with skin at his face and the arm visible and no flesh in between them. "I don't know, who you are," The week and pale lips of man moved. "I've not the power to see you even… but I'm hopeful you would be Abdullah… Come near me," As the man said, Abdullah squatted near him and Bellatrix sat side by Abdullah.

"Yes," Abdullah nodded.

"I should say Salam," The man said feebly and it seemed the lips of the man slightly curved in a smile.

"Wasalam," Abdullah said.

"If I'm not wrong, you are Alberic," The girl asked hesitantly.

"Yes, who are you? Bellatrix, I can guess," The feeble man asked.

"Yeah," Bellatrix nodded.

"I'm really glad to have a meeting with you, yes I'm Alberic," The man said. Both of they gleefully looked one another. "You are very brave Bellatrix, you really did well job, you will rule the world one day, both of you will rule, I can sees" Alberic said. "I've not enough time children," Alberic said. Bellatrix looked to his right hand motionless placed at his heart. He sun sign at his hand was still shinning bright. "I've not much time, and neither have you," Alberic continued. "Eh, Eh," He coughed. "Queen is going to astray Max; he will soon go to kill the seven kings of the seven unique worlds just to save his earth. But the queen wants all this for her rule. She wants to rule the universe. Just go and stop Max. You are soon going to win this battle and if he did, you will see… a war, a great war," They were quietly listening to the old man. Their expressions turned to worry and tension as Alberic was speaking. "I was a doctor, a very renowned doctor of Sunasia but I couldn't stop my people. The life in loneliness and dark made me saint along with the instructor. One day, I heard bang of the slab outside my home and I think many years I've passed without food and water. I just wished to live for this time. Now time is over. I must go now. The ball is under the table. So, I am getting rid of this helpless and wretched life. Have a nice and a fast journey. Go now," The revolving pupils in his eyes were still.

"Alberic," Abdullah called him quickly. He had closed his eyes. Abdullah checked his heart beat and pulse. He was motionless and his lips closed forever. Bellatrix closed her eyes and tears fell out. Abdullah dejectedly shut eyes of Alberic and put on the coverlet at his face. He gloomily turned and took out the ball under the table. He was hoping for the small ball, but it was big and heavy.

"Come on, Bellatrix, We are to stop Max." Abdullah gathered his courage. Bellatrix wiped her tears and followed Abdullah. The reached the top of the hole.

"How to get out of here?" Bellatrix asked him.

"Hold it," He gave the book to Bellatrix. Bellatrix held. Abdullah went into the room and took out a staircase. They arranged it with the top hole and climbed it. The same staircase they used when they reached the other hole and they came out quickly. The unicorn was now freely sitting. There dark out side. There was no moon and the stars. The candle was flickering in her hand.

"Give me back my candle," The unicorn snatched it from her hand through his mouth. "Get on my back quickly," Both of they listened to the unicorn and did as it said. Soon they set off for a new journey.

CHAPTER 25

✦═ The drink of malice ═✦

I

The war was on. Mr. Raza and Mr. Peter were fighting at the battle field. The swords were clashing and the spears were shattering. The Sunasians martyred mosques, elephants destructed temples and churches. The two day quietness of dark turned into a storm. The two races were valiantly fighting to save it, one wanted to have its land and the other wanted to conquer it. The object was same but the desire was dissimilar. The vultures attacked. Soon, they encountered the attack of the hooded men on behalf of the Sunasians. They were moving lifting their feet above the ground. They would fly and attack at the back of any man. Sidhwa, who had killed many of Sunasians, received a back attack from such ghost. Sidhwa died and at the same time fighting with two swords he cut off the heads of the two Sunasians. He fell on the earth in between the two cut off heads. Every one felt the side attacks and they were waving their swords backwards and forward both. They were again defeated in the war of devil and man. The dark was covering the whole earth. Mary had lit the fire at house. She was warming her hand sin the bonfire when James came with bundles of woods. "Mary," He called her silently. "I'm going for war, today at the same time," James said her. Mary surprisingly and fearfully gazed him. Her rubbing hands stopped.

"Fine," She nodded quietly. "Go," She said with dejection. Soon, James' horse was galloping to the battle field and she was waving him hand with a lantern in her hand. The battle field had got one more brave man in the army of Earth. The both nations were clashing the swords in dark. Sunasians subtly retreated without telling them and Earthumen were stabbing their own men. In dark Mr. Peter stabbed his closest friend. He heard his scream and he understood the subtle scheme at the same time. He ordered his men to stop fighting. Soon, the battle field was calm and quiet. There was no more noise in the battle fields. They quickly lit up the lanterns. Their swords were stabbed in their closest friends and with the spears they had aimed at the nearest friends. They felt the fate laughing at them. The battle field was silent but the storm was rising in their inner sides. All of they squatted and crouched at the place where they were standing in grief.

Mary was quietly sitting near Saira when James entered the battlefield. The scene was changed. There was no more fight. It seemed they had won. James came near them and heard them moaning and crying near their men. All of they were weeping.

"What happened?"

"O Lord, Lord of the Universe, Help us," One of the men cried aloud. "We do not want to kill our people any more, it's over, forgive us, forgive us," The man was shouting. The battle field was crying. They heard the horses' hooves striking the ground and they had to surrender. They were hands up. There was no more battle. Mr. Raza was dead. Mr. Peter left of the leading leaders.

II

The carriage jolting and jerking reached at an abandoned place. Queen came out with Max. His hands and feet were untied. The place was dark and its blue ground was shinning in dark. Queen looked around.

"Follow me," She asked and Max went staggered after her as his blood clotted in his legs for some time. The blood started to flow as it got the warm and Max could easily walk now.

"Max, this is my room, where I sleep." Max looked all around. It was an endless room with Blue Mountains at the ground, black sky and a twisted ditched tree. It was black with no leaves or fruits and was dried. The queen was going to the table where some bowls were placed. He followed the queen as he had reached her.

"Look here Max… these six bowls would take you to the eternity… you will have the valor and you will get Saira forever. There will be no more hurdles. Your mother can get back the eyes. So, both of we nations will live peacefully, when there would be no fear of attack of any other," Max was staring the bowls on the black table. They were arranged horizontally. "You can drink, whatever you want," Queen said him.

Max confusingly looked into the bowls. There was stagnant water in black bowls of deep blue color.

"Be quick, Max, I want you to be saved and your mother, soon you will also know about Bellatrix," Queen said suspiciously.

Max tried to grab a bowl. "No Max," He heard a familiar voice with a frown. "This bowl is of lies. When you will have it, you would be having Satan running in your veins. The man who follows Satan is an evil. If you want devil in yourself, drink it," Max left the bowl and picked up the other bowl. Queen was cunningly staring him. Mary turned with a surprise. He looked to Saira. He lips were murmuring but she was asleep.

"No, these bowls have sins in them. If you could get your land, mother and me then all of we should be welcomed to have drinks," Max left it down. Again Mary saw lips of Saira murmuring.

"Come on" The queen again asked her. Max grabbed the third bowl.

"This bowl would fill your heart with greed. You will be the richest man in the universe, but in the hearts of the people you would be the poorest. You will snatch the rights of the poor and will take the throne. You will sleep with full appetite but the people of your reign will sleep on the roads hungry, withering with cold suffering from illnesses. If you want it to be so, then you should drink them," Saira's lips gain murmured in sleep. Max left it and grasped the fourth one.

"No, Max," Mary tried hear her and she could only hear the name of Max. It seemed to hear she was talking to Max. "Don't even think to touch it Max, it's the bowl of fornication. Don't take it, lest you would be addicted to it." Max left the bowl and picked up the fifth bowl.

"No, it's the bowl to speak ill of others. If you want the fires of hell to encounter you and give a warm welcome to you, then you should drink it," Max left the bowl and the last bowl he held.

"Come on, Max you should drink it," Queen forced her.

"No, Max, it has malice in it. It will spoil you and darken your heart." Saira said. He lifted down the bowl.

"Max, do it, do it, now," Queen said.

"NO Max," Saira murmured and the voice echoed in his ears.

"Drink," Queen forcefully said.

"No," He was hearing the two voice repeatedly asking him to do and to not to do. In trance he lifted the bowl to the lips. The voices of No rose higher and queen appreciated the boy with her eyes. At once, he felt a bandaged hand had pushed the bowl from his lips. Mary saw she waved her hand in the air sternly as it stroked her face.

"Saira, dear, are you fine?" Mary did shake her shoulder.

He hardly held the bowl. The water sprinkled and fell at his hands. His middle fingers on the either were burning and they burnt almost. Max moaned with pain. He left the bowl at the table. The queen sneered.

"A sip will do, you have done it," The queen said him. Max sat at the corner impulsively and held his throat. The queen stooped over him. "Go, Max, save my universe," Max stood in a trance. His face expressions changed and his eyes were displaying malice. Max hurriedly went to the carriage and got into it. The carriage was driving him out of the room of the queen and queen was sneering at her scheme. "Be back soon, I'm waiting for you here,"

There was no more war. Sunasians were taking breathing Earthumen to prison. Queen also came to visit the battle field. He saw dead body of Raza. She smashed his hand with his high soled shoe.

"So, your king is dead," She sneered. "What you call a king, kingdom of only few days," Queen said. "See my rule, a forever rule, a rule of the whole world," Queen scoffed. She had hidden her hand under her dress and she was walking in the lane of the house of Saira. Saira withered and opened her eyes at once. She quickly removed off the bandage and ran to find ruby.

"Saira, what happened? Are you fine?" Mary grabbed her tightly. The carriage of the queen was moving faster and faster. She was quiet and she was quietly resisting against Mary. She quickly held her free and saw ruby at the table nearby. She ran to it, held it and her right wrist with another cut. The queen screamed as her other hand also burnt. Both of her hands were burnt till elbows. She hid them, abruptly under her cuffs. The carriage was swiftly moving to her house. The carriage jolting and jerking was echoing in the ears of Saira. The voice was coming nearer. She brutally wounded her hands. This time queen was screamed badly as her nails were burnt and fire was flickering at their tips. She was feeling the same pain as she felt hundred years ago.

"Get back to the palace, quickly," The queen shouted at the coach man. The carriage took turn. Queen was trying to extinguish fire off her nails but nothing was helping. Saira heard the carriage going back. The locket fell off her hand and she was fainted at the floor again. Mary held her. She saw her hands and wrists, they were badly injured. In these, flowers would smell and now these hands were bleeding. She again bandaged her hands and wrists.

"You will never get, what you will want," She murmuring.

"I'll, you filth," The queen roared in her ears harshly.

"The time will come and you will see," Saira challenged her while she was murmuring. Saira had gripped the locket tightly in her right bandaged hand. As the queen entered the palace, she instantly ordered to bring ten pious virgins of earth. Earth had been dominated. Soon, ten virgins were arranged for the queen. The face of the queen was becoming older and the wrinkles at her face were appearing evident.

The unicorn was moving faster and faster in the dark to take them to Max to stop him from the wrong he was going to take. In this state, if both of they tried to stop him, may be they both be killed.

CHAPTER 26

⊰⊱ The Voyage of the Killer ⊰⊱

The carriage left him near the lake. He looked to the ring in his hand. His eyes were red with anger, malice and jealousy.

"Falconee," He raged clutching his fist. In no minutes, the falcon appeared in front of him.

"Yes, my master," It bowed and smiled. He was stern and strict. He was strictly gazing him with drunken eyes. Falcon astonished at the changed facet of Max. "Man is selfish," Her father whispered in her ears.

"Come, take me to the Cave lion, I want to meet his master," He said sternly. Soon, the falcon was soaring into the sky high. Max closed his eyes near the black hole and they reached the land of Cave lions. The cave lion wholeheartedly waved them hands and falcon moved down. Max touched his feet to the ground. Cave lion hugged Max this time.

"O, Max I'm glad to see you today. I was thinking of joining you. I liked last time. I wished to have one more meal with you." The cave man welcomed him lovingly and both of they went into the cave. Falcon had turned into the girl. She was following him. The man like previous time arranged a tasty meal for Max.

"Why do I feel something change in you today?" Cave lion asked malicious Max who was quietly busy taking his meals.

"Last time I looked coward to you… and now I'm braver than you,"

"No, Max you are more coward today" The cave lion replied. Max looked to man keenly. He had a muscular body and his body looked stiff. He observed it was hard to kill him. "I think we should have a walk here. I would take some rest. Falcon, please show my guest my reign," The man smiled and both of they go out after eating to their full. Max was looking quiet and quieter. They were walking quietly in the pasture land.

"Master Max, you did not ask me about my arms, remembers they were hurt last time," Falcon said.

"I know, they are fine so you are with e here." Max said.

"Master Max, I've sent my father to the earth, he is ready to fight against Sunasians for your," Falcon was gleefully telling him and he was carelessly listening to her conversation. "He can easily compete the vultures. The dark layer was obstruction but he has said that he would remove it soon."

"When will night fall?" Max sternly asked.

"Sun is going back soon," She thoughtfully gazed the sun. "It's going to fall. Till what time do you wish to stay here?" Falcon asked.

"Till I complete my job," She felt the tone of Max strange as she frowned.

"What's your job? Master, Can I help you?"

"I would do it myself," Max proceeded to the pasture land where a herd of sheep was grazing. Max reached near them and the sheep restlessly started their, "Bah, Bah,"

The night fell soon. Till midnight they visited the whole land of the cave man. The sheep had grazed and had slept.

"The sheep had a queen. She is like a woman, a very nice, kind-hearted and a polite lady... She seldom comes out," Falcon told him. "It has been night; let's go for a sleep," Soon they motioned their steps to the cave.

The cave man was silently lying in the cave staring the stones of the cave at the roof. A lion had put its head at his right shoulder. The other lion was lying at his left and he has put his hand at the lion lying under the previous lion.

"I think, my rule is finishing now, there should be any other ruler at this place," Cave man was sharing his feelings to the lions. The lions growled. "I know, you won't like it, but it's a matter of fact, one day who comes to live has to go back to live," The lions growled and he felt his right shoulder warm with water. He abruptly looked with a frown. It was lion; he was weeping thinking of the parting of his master.

"What happened? When I'll go you will rule, you will guide your lions, you will help them, you will never think of hurting the sheep and nor will you tease the queen of sheep. The justice and unity, I like and I would be happy to see you like this," The lion growled. "I can understand you... but I'm helpless before the rules of Omnipotent." Lion looked up and was quiet. Max and Falcon had reached. As they entered, the cave man abruptly stood and the lions briskly took their positions to encounter him. The lions roared to see Max as he slid back, before they could pounce at him, the cave man encountered them and growled outrageously at them. The lions kept quiet with a panic and paced out staring the malicious Max.

"Come, Max, they are just annoyed when they wish to sleep with me," Man said. Max nodded. Soon they had slept. Next day Max went out for a walk with the cave man. He had wished to meet the queen of the sheep. They were going quietly, when a cute lamb ran into his arms.

"Look Max, it is my best friend here. My lion likes it a lot," The cave man replied. The way was abandoned now. Cave man was moving passively with a lamb in his arms. Max slid back a little; he took out his sword and stabbed it at the back of the cave man. The lamb tripped off the hands of the cave man. It shouted, bah, bah at Max. He was withering with knees stuck to the ground holding his tummy where the sword had shredded his body. Max quickly and fearfully ran back to the bushes. The lamb was staring his best friend and quietly dropping its tears at the face of the man.

As he reached behind the bushes and found a proper place to be invisible to every one, "Falconee," he shouted. In no minutes, he saw falcon standing in front of him with a smile.

"Yes, my master,"

"We should go now,"

"OK, let's say a farewell to the King,"

"No, I've met him," Max abruptly said.

"Ok," The falcon said with a surprise and soon they both were soaring into the skies, reaching the reign of the dwarves, Max was a little confused. "Let me down," Max said to the falcon and falcon hastily landed at the mount.

The king of the dwarves was reading the newspaper sitting with the queen at the carpet.

"I needed to have a chat with you," Max harshly. Queen scared as he held his dwarf king tightly.

"Yes, yes, sure," The dwarf king bravely answered.

Soon the dwarf king was steeping forward and Max was after him. Falcon remained with the queen at the order of Max.

"Sorry, Max, last time I couldn't offer you a tasty meal, my wife was sick and not fine," The dwarf was speaking frankly and gladly but Max was in the deep thought to kill this dwarf king. He was maliciously staring the cute looking dwarf. Dwarf turned and looked to the giant Max in front of him.

"Yes what, Max," The dwarf addressed him boldly. Max fervently looked around and backward. There was no body nearby. Max disregarding the dwarf took out his dagger and cut the dwarf into two pieces.

"It will be enough for you," He maliciously cussed the dwarf. He cleaned his knife with a leaf nearby and threw it down, then he reached to a safe place where he called falcon and they both were soon soaring into the skies.

"Is your father home?" Max asked him evocatively.

"No, he was deciding for the war. He would have reached the earth now." Falcon replied.

"Ok, then take me to the king of the unicorns," Max abruptly asked her.

"Fine, my master as you will say," replied the falcon respectfully. "Master, Can I ask you, what is it all? You want to meet the kings,"

"No, you are not allowed to ask," Max curtly replied. Falcon kept quiet. In no minutes they had reached the reign of unicorns. It was not easy to kill the king of the unicorns. He was not only cool, but was bold and passionate. He had the mystic powers and the features of a saint. He had the real problem here. He was standing in the shinning crystallized dream of the unicorns. He spent a whole night there.

"So, Mr. Max, we are very glad, you are back with us," Unicorn gently addressed patrolling with Max in the night. Every thing was purple around them. Max nodded. "What id you do to your eyes? I don't feel you well,"

"No, I'm fine," Max overlooked unicorn.

"Fine, I hope, you should... what bring you here?" Unicorn asked.

"My mother and a life of the girl,"

"What's her name?"

"Saira, my friend,"

"But, I think it has been more than the friendship," Unicorn thoughtfully replied as Max frowned.

"No, we are just friends and help one another in the time of trouble," He replied curtly.

"I feel the smell of astray of malice, here around me," Unicorn sniffed. The smell was becoming strong as Max was preparing the plan of killing the king. "It's unbearable," The unicorn sniffed and galloped.

"Come, Master Max, your bed is ready," A female unicorn was standing behind him. He entered into a beautiful cave. The room was bright white. He couldn't distinguish between the bed and the room. While walking he was hit by a bed and fell onto it. So, in this he reached his destination. Warily, he laid at it. He was tired so he soon slept. It was midnight when Max saw falcon standing at the entrance of the room. Max abruptly awoke up. His eyes were no redder. The falcon was staring him wildly. "You killed her," Falcon murmured. The wildness and wickedness at his face was gone. He was the same Max as he was before two murders.

"Who," Max confusingly asked. Now he was looking the same confused Max.

"Come, follow me," Falcon said. Max quietly went after her. Soon they passed the reign and reached the border. Max witnessed a stair-case going into the sky. There were flowers all around the either sides of the stairs. Falcon abruptly stepped the first and reached the middle while Max confusingly stepped first looked up to the endless stair-case immersing higher into the sky. Falcon turned. "Come, quick," Falcon said and Max stepped the stairs. He reached confidently and reached the last step of the stair. Falcon was invisible after immersing into the sky, after that, he entered flabbergasted and soon vanished. Max looked back. The clouds had covered the ends of the sky.

"Look there," Falcon said and Max looked forward. It was a room of glass hung between the skies without any assistance. It was floating slowly in the sky. "Go, quickly, before it goes," Max abruptly moved to the room. He could observe white clouds and papers moving in the room. He peeked into the house sticking his mouth by it. The shadows were flickering and he was able to recognize them. He saw Saira in white maxi holding a bunch of flowers. She saw black hair falling at her back pinned white at the either sides near the ears. She was smiling with white shadows of the women. There were white soft earrings in her ears. All the shadows in the glass-case were chatting joyously with her. At once, Saira laughed loudly and he heard her standing out as his lips also made a curve. Saira holding the bunch of flowers turned to her right. She was pacing as she felt any dark shadow outside the glass-case. She held the handle of the door in front of her and stared his left. Her eyes told him she had recognized the boy. She smiled lovingly to see him. Max felt the birds singing with her smile and the flowers on either side of the stairs tossing. Max tried to enter through the glass case but it was tiff. He punched it harder and harder but all in vain. His hands stopped as he saw Saira opening the white and a dazzling entered. She again saw him and smiled for the last time. The time was over now. She entered the door and vanished. Soon the other girls were also entering with her holding the bunches of flowers. The glass-case was floating faster. It reached very far from Max holding Saira in it. It had now started moving upward and upward.

"Master," He heard falcon and quickly opened his eyes. Falcon was standing at his head awakening him up. His eyes were gain red. He had the same wildness and wickedness at his face. "Master, wake up, its morning," Falcon was telling him. He rubbed his eyes and came out of the cave. Everything again changed from purple to white. It dazzled his eyes for some moments but he was fine when his eyes became addicted to it. Unicorn served him well with tasty breakfast of bread and doughnuts. After taking the breakfast, he was again at a walk with the unicorn. He looked to the glittering diamond at its horn. It impressed him and this time there was the malice of getting this diamond from him. Patrolling at the white carpet Max witnessed a white rope in the way. He stealthily picked it up and hid it inside his pocket. The unicorn was confidently and sloppily walking at the carpet. Max again looked around and quickly sat his back. Without wasting time he tied the rope tightly around the neck of the unicorn. He was strangulating it harder and harder. Unicorn was withering and jumping to get itself free. The blood dripped out of the mouth of the unicorn. His hind limbs and forelimbs twisted and he soon fell on the ground. The cool animal was cooler. Max got off, hit his horn scornfully with his foot. He snatched the immersing diamond at the horn. Diamond was now glittering in front of his eyes and between his index finger and thumb. Max cunningly looked it and soon he reached the land of serpents. He saw snakes hissing and sleeping. The King of the snakes was lying quietly slept on the chair. His eyes were opened and soon he felt him motionless. He took out his dagger, before he could slaughter man quickly transformed into a snake hissing and waving his hood. Max quickly jumped back, snaked slightly crawled to him waving his hood with hisses.

"Master run," Falcon shouted and grabbed his hand. He freed himself with a jerk.

"NO, I need to talk to him," Falcon saw a dagger grabbed in his hand. He lifted the dagger. The snake waved his hood higher and higher to sting him. As snake reached equal to his nose, the dagger came down and hit its head. The dagger was stabbed in his hood. Falcon screamed.

"Master, what did you do," The snake King was lying dead in the feet of Max. He heard hisses snakes and the ground shaking by their crawling. "Master, quick," Falcon cried and quickly turned into a bird. Max climbed its back and soared into the sky.

"What did you do it, master? Your world can be in danger now, you should not do this. If there was any specific matter to be discussed, then you should talk to me," Falcon and he was quiet I the drink of malice and proud. In a few hours they had reached the land of fairies. The queen was glad to see him alive and healthy. He feared to look into his eyes. The small fairies were moving all around him gleefully but he did not bother to look at them. Soon after, all of they were quiet.

"What has happened to his eyes? He is looking brutal today, what's his purpose of coming here?" The fairy whispered in the ears of the falcon.

"The snake king attacked him and he killed him,"

"What?" Fairy was stunned. "Is he aware of the consequences?"

"We should help him, fairy. He is not of that type. He is nice." Falcon requested.

"I would." Fairy said.

"I need to have a chat with you, fairy," Max asked him.

Soon, both of they were walking alone at the mountains in between the trees of juicy fruits.

"Princess, I just want to say you sorry," Saying this, he took out his knife and stabbed her. The innocent delicate fairy fell at his shoulder. Soon he breathed her last at his shoulder and her eyes were motionless forever.

"Let me take to your father," He said as he turned and saw the falcon standing behind him. She was looking hurt and dejected. The fairy was fallen upside down behind Max. Her long shinning blonde hair covered her back. Max disregarded the tears of the girl and the girl knew what Max would do to his father.

When they reached the earth, his father was helping the army of Shiva as rear attacks form him. His warfare matters were awesome. He gathered his army near the sea and arranged their positions at the roofs of the houses. He first ordered the men to hit the elephants. The people of different races took the aims according to their cultures and customs. The Arabs threw Lances, the Christians took aims through spear s and the Hindus had held their swords. They had checked the positions of the elephants, soon after the elephants moaned and they were no more. There was dark and in the dark they had already sorted out the positions. The elephants were dead. In no minutes they had killed all the elephants. They whistled and soon they gathered at a place where they had lit fire. A lot of the ships they had already kidnapped. Soon, they entered the city and killed the hidden Sunasians forces of men. The falcons also came for help and they were fighting with vultures.

"You eat dead and I've never smelled the dead, I catch my prey alive and swallow," There is difference between you and me. The falcons were roaring in rage, as they had torn the layer of dark, when they came to the earth to help people of earth. The falcons were killing the dark shades. They were screaming and the flames of fire emerged and vanished into the sky. Sun could peek into earth now. The father of falcon was fighting a vulture with its beak when falcon threw him had at the ground. Shiva was boldly fighting against Sunasians and Tom was slaughtering those taking aims at forces of Sunasians. They ran to look for their elephants, but they didn't move, all of they were wounded and dead. Abdullah had also reached the war with Bellatrix. Max quickly stood up, held the sword fallen near a dead body, lifted it up to hit the falcon, but the daughter stopped it with her falcon,

"Give me my ring back, master, the spot at your dagger had already caused me to think and at last I had known, but I won't let you to kill my father, you deceived me, you deceived the creature who loved you, just for your sake, just for yourself, if you think of killing the kings, then you are the king of our regime, you should kill yourself," Falcon shouted in rage. Her eyes were staring him ferociously. She lifted the sword and hit his sword and his sword fell few miles away. "Now I should kill you," Falcon lifted her sword high and it was lastly coming very near to Max.

CHAPTER 27

⊹⊱ Court of Justice ⊰⊹

I

Saira had been much better than before. Both of they had come near the lake for peace and fresh air. Today Saira had changed her dress. She was in an off-white Maxi and a black belt was fitted around her slim waist. A scarf had covered her forehead of the same color as that of Maxi. She had held the locket in her both palms and was standing near the lake. Mary was squatted at a distance from her.

"War is on, when it will be off," Saira asked Mary staring the deep lake.

"I don't know, but I feel it's the end of every thing," Mary said scratching the soil with her fingers.

"No, its start, it's going to start. The world would be regained." Saira normally said.

"How are you feeling today Saira,"

"Very well,"

"I suggest you to throw this filth locket,"

"No, I would be incomplete,"

"The war is on; queen is coming to the battlefield. Max did wrong. The three drops of malice are adding to his veins, his blood. His blood is becoming black," Saira said and closed his eyes. He saw the drops flowing down the throat and entering his veins and blood. The soul of Max screamed as it was blazing her good human inside him. The sword of falcon was coming near him, he jumped at a side and hit by the tree. The pointed tip of the trunk scratched his wrist and the black blood oozed out of his wrist. "It's black. It has been black." Saira opened her eyes and shouted hysterically. "The thing you consider light is dark at its back. We are wrong in our judgments. It's not our decisions. It's the Satan who astray us." She was murmuring. "The war is on, it is going to end soon and my time is going to end with its end,"

"Saira, why are you talking like that, I want to see you live, I want to see you happy, I want to see you good, Saira," Mary was perplexed.

Saira slowly shook her head. "When the unknown is revealed to you, you should not be alive any more,"

"Saira," She almost sniveled.

"Yes that is also coming near, you can not escape it." She whispered. "O the vast seas of the world," There was wobbles in the seas of the worlds, "the proud at the tips of mountains," mountains trembled, "erupting volcanoes rising high with fury and rage," the volcanic mounts quivered and the lava flowed, "the springs, the fountains flowing down in the rain forests," she heard springs flowing, " the rivers of seas," the rivers tried to pour out like the water storms, "it's going to be the end, the queen sheep has see the dead body, she screamed to see her dwarf king, the unicorns have lifted the dead body at his shoulders, the snakes are around their master hissing, the children of fairies are weeping, the queen is coming to save his servant, they are coming, it's going to come… human has destructed the peace of skies, it has again bloodshed, Gabriel was right, O Lord of all the worlds, do help us," Her pray echoed in the whole world. Mary stood up wordless gazing her thunderstruck.

"S... S...Saira," Mary called her. She was quietly staring into the sky.

"Today, I'm going, Mary. I'm going; the point where the seas meet is the point of departure,"

"Saira, let's go home," Mary quickly held her hand but she didn't move.

"No, the house will fall, you are to live Mary, you and James are to live life together," Saira said. The lake was quietly flowing. Mary was strangely staring her. The queen has entered the field.

II

After escaping from the falcon, Max hid behind the tree. Bellatrix and Abdullah had reached.

"Stay here Bellatrix with the ball," Abdullah held her the unicorn that was being restless and went to the battlefield raising his sword high. As he entered he had killed the three at the instant. Unicorn fled and Bellatrix saw it was going high into the skies. She hid the ball behind the mount and ran after the unicorn. Max after escaping from the first attack of the falcon hid behind the tree as he was trying to find any armament, when he felt the tip of sword at near his right forehead. She turned his face abruptly. Falcon was gazing him outrageously. "I meant to be good to you and you killed my friend, you killed the guardian of queen sheep, you killed the saint unicorn, you killed the snake for your personal interest, you killed the innocent dwarf, you crushed them into the pieces." She shouted in rage and raised her sword high to cut his head off but his time her sword struck by a strong sword. Her sword fell off and she fell onto the ground. The upcoming fighter was undefeatable. The war was on, at one hand. Abdullah was slaughtering as many people as he could. Bellatrix was climbing up the tree to catch the unicorn vanishing into the sky. "Unicorn," She was trying to call it louder and louder in the noise of the shattering of the arrows, clashes of swords and hitting of lances. Turning to her left, she witnessed a horrible vista. Max standing side by queen, queen was going to slaughter the sliding behind falcon.

Queen was outrageously gazing her when she saw Bellatrix had come in her way in no minutes. She had held a small dagger in her hand.

"The princess of earth," Queen was shocked to see her as well as Max.

"Yes," She nodded bravely and stared into her eyes. "Don't be confident about the sword in your hand and the dagger in my hand. You know it very well, I'm a very good sword fighter," Bellatrix challenged the queen.

"You can never kill me,"

"Yes, I know, you are an evil, a dead evil, Max, come to me, she will kill you," Bellatrix shouted. The girl had soon turned into a falcon and flew high into the skies. Max got tangled to see her wounded face. "Come Max, Come," Bellatrix preceded her hand to him with an eye at the queen and dagger rightly pointing the queen. Queen oared into laughter.

"I know about your all tricks, that are why I panicked once to see you here," The queen sneered.

"Your rule is over now, all the elephants are dead, and I've got the ball," Bellatrix shocked the queen.

"Where is it? Tell me, I'll release you,"

"Forget about it now," She scornfully said. "Think about your past and ask God to forgive you, because your time is over now."

"But I think, your time is over now," The queen scornfully sneered to look a black shade coming to her about which Bellatrix was unaware. She was bravely staring into the eyes of the queen.

"Max, give me the ring," The girl said. Max was motionless, he frowned the girl. "Max just give it to me, be quick," She shouted. "What has happened to you, why don't you understand? Queen has dominated your mine. Max," She shouted and at the same time a black shade had grabbed her neck twisting his around her neck. She screamed and tried to resist. Queen sneered. Max looked to his ring. Bellatrix tried to lift her hand of dagger to kill the dead body at the back.

"Remember me," She heard the same voice she heard near the room of Alberic. "It's me the same one, the devil," He whispered coming near to her ear. Max stared deep into his ring. He was drinking the bowl of malice in the ring. He frowned. He felt something blazing in his intestines and veins. The queen was sneering.

"Go Max, kill the seventh one, and you will get Saira and the eyes of your mother," Queen sneered. Max quickly held the sword in the hands of the queen and rushed to the battle field.

"Max, No, No," She screamed and the devil held her neck tight. The vultures were flying at her and coming nearer to her, the queen was sneering and the devil held her lifted hand of the dagger, when they felt the sky trembling and the earth shaking. Max had reached the battlefield and he saw the falcon king fighting with his sword against the Sunasians. Max rushed at the back and stabbed the falcon. He fell on the ground; the devil lost its grip due to the strong shakes. It slid and rolled down near the river. As it reached near the river, the red flame flew out of it and vanished soon. The queen also staggered and was falling down with the Bellatrix.

"It has come," Saira opened her eyes abruptly standing near the lake. Max fell down at the earthquake. Bellatrix and the queen were rolling down. Abdullah who was going to be stabbed from back was saved as the earthquake moved the man into the deep tunnel. He was screaming there. Everyone instead of stabbing ran to caught hold of anything firm. Max facing the falcon who was seeing his unfaithful master when he had never wished to take back the ring or the kingdom from him. "Do not trust a man; he who attacks at the rear is a coward." Falcon murmured.

At the earthquake, Mary and Saira staggered. The locket slipped off her palms, both of they gripped one another and caught hold of the trees nearby. Max quickly stood up and went to the mounts to grip them. The battle field was empty. There was no live man except the carcasses and wasted swords and spears. Mary flabbergasted, and Saira satisfactorily had held the trees. Bellatrix was rolling down. The sky was shaking harder and harder. The queen was going down. The door of the evil had opened but the queen. Saira caught hold of the stone in mid of the mountain and held the queen's hand firmly. The vultures were restlessly flying.

The water of the seas flowed out with the currents flooding the city. The water of the river come up and both of they fell down into the river. Soon the men of the earth and Sunasia saw a terrible panorama. The unicorns were outrageously running to the battlefield, from other side a huge army of dwarves were coming shouting and screaming holding spears, lances and swords. Soon the lions came roaring and growling with rage. The earth trembled harder that it got cracks at different parts of its surface. The falcons torn the dark layer completely and the dark shed. They were flying and screeching with fury. The battle field filled with hisses by snakes erupting their hoods out of the earth and crawling their bodies at the ground. In the meanwhile, small fairies were flying in the whole earth. The camouflage of fairies attracted the hidden ones as they were wiping their tears and the battle field was dampening as the tears were falling on to the earth. The earth was trembling with the gallops and strong strokes on the earth. The queen had reached the bank of the river and Bellatrix was still swimming in the shaking river. As she would take her mouth out of the water, vulture would attack her and she had again to dip in to the water. As the last snake erupted, Mary got a strong jerk and the knife in her stabbed unknowingly in the mid of the locket fallen on the earth. The queen screamed awfully. The flames of fire erupted out of her body. Her hands were blazing. Saira got a jerk and her knees touched to the ground. "It's over now, Max," Saira whispered and a black liquid erupted from the locket. Max staggered at the mount and fell upside down as Saira fell down. Queen was screaming at the edge of the river. Her hands burnt. The vultures were rolling madly at the screams of the queen. Bellatrix took her face out to have

369

a breathe of air and saw queen. She was no more a young woman. She was motionless and her body was trembling at the surface of earth. Soon she was static. There were uncountable wrinkles at her body and face. He arms were black like a coal. She was looking older and ugliest than Alberic. The stomach of Max gathered the black liquid and flowed it out of his mouth. Max was vomiting and the black fluid was coming out of his mouth. He was vomiting.

The earth was still now. No more shaking. The animals had taken their places. Vultures were finding the places to hide. Max was vomiting. People hidden behind the mounts came out and stood at the top of the mounts. He was out of the state of trance. The recent activities flashed back in his mind. His inner good man had told him his mistake. He looked to his burnt fingers.

"You've lost me Max," He heard the whisper of Saira in his ears. "It's over now, it's the end, the knot is still the knot," She whispered.

"Saira, Saira," Mary grabbed her shoulder. Her eyes were open and her pupils were still. She was ice cold. She checked her pulse and heart beat. It was no more. "Saira," She shouted, the tears fell out as she has lost something. She put her palms at her lips. She couldn't control and sobbed.

"NO," She cried and set her head in her lap. "No, NO," She was screaming and sobbing. "She was calling a motionless girl. Her tears were falling into the bright eyes of bright Saira. The locket was place near them with a knife stabbed in it. The trees were silent and still. The lake was quiet, the flowers of her bunches were faded, the rose bed outside her house stopped flourishing the roses and the roses refused to take nourishment. The leaves of the trees whom she water were still and quiet. There were only sobs of Mary beyond the mount.

III

All the creatures living in the sky had circled in the battle field. The unicorns neighed, lions growled at once with rage, the falcons shrieked, dwarves shouted, snakes hissed and the little fairies were hovering over the outrageous animals with faces in grief and sorrow. The earth shivered at once with their rage. The houses trembled, the rivers quivered and Bellatrix who had almost reached the land fell back again into the water with a scream due to the jerk. She had tired of swimming. She made the last attempt to reach the bank. The vultures were trying to hide. The men of the earth and Sunasia climbed the mounts gazing the scene. The dark layer vanished completely. The moon and the stars were visible to all now. The unicorns, dwarfs, lions, falcons, eagles and fairies stared the men of earth and Sunasia all around the mounts. Lions looked to unicorns and they started.

"We don't need any harm to you, people," One of the unicorns spoke elegantly. Men stunned. Women stayed at the roofs of their houses. "Your man has killed our Kings," Abdullah standing with Shiva crushed with disappointment. "Now, we need only him," Unicorn shouted. Men were silent and exasperated as they were busy in fighting with the one another.

"Who, man? All of we were at a war, we have no idea of you even." Shiva gathered his courage to say.

"You do not have but your man have, where is that filth? Get him out in front of us," Lion roared with rage. "My master isn't a coward and he killed my King at the back," The voice of lion trembled with grief and sorrow.

"Bring out him," The little fairy hanging in the sky fluttering her blue feathers yelled in her shrill voice. "She killed her mother." Shiva flabbergasted looked to Tom and Abdullah. Every one was silent and quiet.

"Which man, of earth or Sunasia?" Jackson shouted.

"We do not know, our master knew, we just want that man," The snake hissed. The scene of the terrible snakes covering the ground was heart-rending.

"I'll bring" Falcon flying over the fairies flew away immediately. As she flew, she saw the dead body of his father lying on the ground in the form of a man. The fury augmented her fury. She soared in rage higher and higher. In the way, she saw Bellatrix who had reached the bank. The dagger was still in her head. She saw the queen moaning and witnessed her old, pale, wrinkled and the feeble body. She scornfully lifted her dagger and stabbed in the dead body of the queen. Her hands and legs withered at once but soon they were motionless. The falcon soared in the sky and soon was back with Max holding him by the shoulders and threw him in the place of the circle. There were no more drops of malice in it as he had vomited all. The lions roared, unicorns neighed and stroked their hooves onto the ground, snakes hissed, eagles shrieked, fairies screamed, dwarves shouted to see the culprit in front of their eyes. The earth trembled again by their shrieks and Bellatrix swiftly caught hold of the Alberic but the jerk was so strong that dagger fell off her hand and she slipped again into the river. Mary quickly held her hand by the tree and Saira slipped off her lap into the lake.

"Saira," She was going down and down into the lake. Soon her whole body dipped in it. Mary preceded her hand to the hand left at the surface. The lake engulfed its princess quickly into it. The flowers at the nearby tree fell by the strong jerk. It seemed as if they were wishing to fall at their queen. The houses trembled; women came out in fear of earthquake and saw the sight. They quickly climbed up the roofs of their houses. The seven worlds had gathered on earth. The shakes stopped after some moments. Sunasians ran to call their queen and some stayed to look the next moment. Everything was quiet and calm now.

"Why did you kill my master?" The lion roared.

"Because I was coward, instead all we men are coward." Earthumen were shocked to see their fellow in the crowd of brutal animals. His head was down. The lion roared with rage. "The wanted kill you the last day, when you entered my cave," The lion growled. "But look the kindness of master. He did not let us, even he knew you. The lion growled. I want to kill you now but, I don't want to bury my teeth in the malicious body." Lion stepped to him and with his brutal paw, it slapped the boy. Max slipped a little with the force of the hand, but soon stabilized himself. The black liquid flowed out of his face.

"Yes, your master was brave, so he did not fear death."

"We shall punish you and your punishment would be nothing less than death." The lion growled. Max was quiet with his head down staring the ground.

"Remember, our master had never let us to slay the goats, but on that day, he did all this for you, and you, you men are coward," The lion roared with anger.

"Tell me, why did you kill my king?" The dwarf queen shouted now. Her eyes were heavy with tears.

"Because, I was silly," Max replied.

"Silliness does not mean to murder someone for none, you brutally cut him,"

"Yes I did it," His head was done staring the ground. Falcon had turned into a girl near her. There was a cut at her face and arms.

"Tell me, I did well to you, I brought you the medicine, I helped, I saved you from the filth nation of Sunasians, but you still killed my father? Why?" Falcon shouted.

"Because I was selfish, I was unfaithful," He replied silently and quietly. Falcon was outrageously staring her.

"Tell me why did you kill my king and where is our crown?" Unicorn neighed and asked him in frenzy.

"Because in emotions I forgot the lesson of kindness," Max sobbed as he saw to his burnt fingers.

"Why did you filth kill my king?" The snake hissed scornfully.

"Why did your master stung me?" Max asked boldly and angrily.

"Because venom is always ready to be out in us," Snake hissed and admired its nature.

"And malice entered in my veins for some instants," Max replied dejectedly. All the animals looked to one another.

"Why did you kill our mother?" The little yelled in grief.

"Sweet fairy," Max looked to her. "I feel the scream of your mother at my shoulder, her eyes closed here. I said sorry to her when I stabbed her but she did not speak. She got annoyed. She was a kind, nice and innocent lady, the scream of her death would never let me live. I'm a killer, a big killer. I'm ready for the punishment. I'm too thankful to all of your masters who served me well when I came to your lands every time. They listened to me well. They served me well. But I did wrong to all of you. It was I who did, who had no control at himself. I got astray. I was wrong. The light which attracts us, illuminates us and filches our faith from us is in real the dark behind at. Pleas forgive me, all of you forgive me," Max wept and cried. He sat at his knees. "I did all this for saving a girl. For saving a girl I took seven lives, but still I couldn't save her. When we try to get anything walking at the paths of thorns we only get our feet wounded. I learnt a lot from this life of twenty three years. I learnt to live without parents; I learn to understand the feelings and emotions of others. I've learnt everything and now I do not wan to stay any more. Yes, you can kill me. Lions you can immerse your fangs in me, unicorns you can stroke, you can kill me in the way I killed your king, snakes you can sting me as many times you want, I wont mind and I'll be saved I won't even ask, Dwarves, you can pinch you swords, dwarves you can stab, fairies you can kill me and falcon," He looked to the falcon who was gloomily staring the ground. He put off the ring of his middle burnt finger and gave it to the falcon. She quietly held it.

"You can do with me, whatever you want," Max said.

"Falcon, it's your now, you are the queen," Unicorn said to her. She sobbed, wiped her tears and put on the ring.

"Now, you can decide about my punishment, I wont beg for mercy, I wont beg for life, you can kill me in whatever way you want," Max said. Abdullah quickly mounted down and warily moving down escaping from the snakes reached in between the circle.

"He won't beg for mercy, but I do beg,"

"Abdullah," Max excitedly witnessed him with some hope, he saw him helplessly.

"He was innocent, he didn't know. Unluckily he drank the malice and he was drowned in the black sea of Satan. Please forgive him, I beg for mercy," Abdullah pleaded.

"We haven't asked him to drink malice." The little fairy yelled.

"Look at your fingers Max, the drop what have bunt your fingers, what would have done to your stomach and throat," Unicorn said. Abdullah looked to his fingers. Bellatrix had also reached them and was stunned to see Abdullah and Max in between the huge crowd.

"He will be punished at every cost," Lion roared bravely.

"WE shall prison him for life till death. He will wish for death but he will not be given." Lion growled.

"I accept it."

"We shall bind him by Earth for thousands of years. He would wish to move up but he will never be let up." The queen dwarf shouted and Max nodded and he looked to the falcon for mercy.

"He will be remained in my prison, as far as I'll want," Falcon said tuned into a bird and joined the other falcons. Max helplessly moved his head down.

"Our King, if he would be alive, he will definitely forgive this man, but still he will be punished. He will remain in our prison for some years. He will not be given any food or any water. You will wish for death and death will never come near to you." Max was quiet at the order of falcon.

"We shall sting him daily," Max' body shivered. "When he will be fine, we shall gain sting him,"

"We shall beat him daily with the lashes," The little fairy shouted in rage.

"Ok, I accept it,"

"And on the last day, we shall kill that man," Abdullah shocked and Tom was quiet.

"Please have some mercy on my son," To hiked down the mount quickly to ask for mercy.

"We shall think over it," Falcon said and stared Max.

"Take him of here, quickly," Snake hissed. Lions stepped forward and Tom hugged Max tightly.

"What did you do my son, what did you do?" Tom was bitterly weeping. Bellatrix had also reached them in the crowd. "What shall I tell Martha?" Bellatrix put her hand at her lips and sobbed. Heart of Abdullah also was trembling and the heart beat was slowing down. Max also wept. Bellatrix grabbed his shoulder with her hand.

"Max," Her voice was trembling. "I am Bellatrix, I was not at all wrong," She was sobbing. Max abruptly turned to her.

"Bellatrix, my niece," Bellatrix nodded at Tom's excitement. Bellatrix hugged Max quickly and both of they were weeping. Tom hugged his nephew and niece quickly. When they had wept, Lions had reached them.

"Give the boy to us, you can't trick us," The lion said.

"How can we trick you now?" Tom sobbed and said to lion.

"Your friend Shiva is thinking of it." All of they saw at the top of the mount. Shiva was counseling among groups. They abruptly slid back as they had taken their positions. Shiva was confused. "I know he is brilliant-minded but he can't cheat us. It's good." Lion said. Max hugged Abdullah as the friendship was going to an end.

The falcon soared down and held Max by the both shoulders. All of they saying him farewell with trembling hearts. The falcons vanished in air. Soon the lions went back, without creating fuss as they had got their culprit, unicorns returned, fairies flew to west, snaked got into the soil and the erupted soil was balanced, dwarves also went back quietly on their small horses and carriages. The battlefield was empty now. Queen was dead. Sunasians surrendered at the mounts. Satan was lamenting at the death of his satanic queen. He could not be successful in his plans.

CHAPTER 28

⊷ Back to Light ⊶

The best swimmers dived away but they couldn't find Saira. All of they were out. Abdullah dejectedly threw bunch of flowers in the mid of the lake. The water waved due to the weight of the bunch of the flowers. Mary had disheartened squatted near the lake. Abdullah couldn't control and he burst into tears. Her lonely kin in the world was ended. He wanted to see her sister laughing with him, chatting with him and fighting with him, but she was no more. Bellatrix who always wished to see the girl whom she had gifted a bracelet, but unluckily she couldn't see her. The next shock was the death of Raza. Many days' people spent in finding the dead bodies of their relatives, lamenting and weeping. The earth was quiet and calm. Abdullah opened the lock of the cells and prisoners fled out gleefully. He went to meet Jackson in the palace with Mr. Peter. Bellatrix stayed with Mary in her house and Shiva with Tom looked after the area. Shiva ordered strict security all around the boundaries. Tom attended to the smashed and cracked houses due to stampede and hits of the elephants. The masons were sturdily mending the buildings. Lake was quiet. Mary and Bellatrix would daily come here and showered flowers at the lake. The whirlpool in the lake was circling the red roses and white lilies.

"How was she?" Bellatrix asked Mary staring the whirlpool.

"Just like an angel, standing here she was talking about the future and her all predictions were right," Mary said.

"Can she ever be back?"

"I wish her."

The trees blew air with some more yellow flowers standing by the lake fell at the lake.

"We can not achieve anything without sacrifices. Saira didn't die in vain, she has saved a lot of lives, killed the biggest evil, the queen." Bellatrix said and Mary nodded. Standing at the mount they looked to the men shrouding, burning and mummifying their dead ones. "We can never forget Max and Saira, on the behalf of what we got this land. If locket would not have reached Saira, then it can never be stabbed by you, then Max would have never drunk all the bowls of evil and thus Satan would have another disciple, and if Max would not murder the kings of the seven worlds, there would not be any stampede and the queen could never be killed. The queen entered her half soul in Saira, but his inner good girl did not accept it. Daily there was fight of good and evil in her. At the end, when the locket was stabbed, Saira wished to be dead instead of being a Satan." Bellatrix was speaking and Mary was quietly listening.

"How could God make such a person Satan, who had always, remembered God," Mary said thoughtfully. "In the last hours standing at this lake, she prayed to Lord for the good,"

"The people like her are never dead."

The masons were whole-heartedly involved in building and designing homes, martyred mosques, churches and the cracked temples. Covering a long distance of one part of the earth to the other part they had soon reached the palace. There were no guards and hurdles encountering them. This time they boldly entered the palce and stepped up the stairs. All the people had frightfully been staring the two men of Earth. Jackson stood. Her clothes were tattered and his shoulder was badly wounded.

"Yes," He staggered to them.

Mr. Peter sat in a futon and asked him to sit in front of him. Jackson quietly sat and Abdullah stood by the side of Peter.

"Jackson, we do not want to hurt you people. Just go out of here to your land," Peter softly ordered him.

"Yes, we shall go soon. But we have no conveyance to get us there, we want some time. We need your help," Jackson begged them.

"We've no flying objects with us, and we have no space for you at this land," Peter admonished them. "Remember Jackson, time passes so quick, it was the time when I was begging of help and you slaughtered my family and now look, I've the authority I can yours In a second,"

"Please forgive us, we shall go back soon."

"I can't bear you at this land for a second." Peter said sternly.

"Please…." Jackson wept,

"OK, ok, we are giving you some time, we shall prepare something for you, till that time all of you will stay in the cells," Abdullah jumped in. Mr. Peter liked his suggestion.

Fine, then now, wait for us in the cells," Peter said and stood up to go.

The cells where Earthmen had been in prison, people of the earth were now dragging the people of Sun. Daily three times the prisoners were given good food and good environment, but they were not allowed to practice or experiment anything. Abdullah went quickly to Jasmine and talked to her about the falcon if they could help us.

"We have deceived them Abdullah and they would never listen to us." Bellatrix dejectedly said.

"Why to try for one time?" Abdullah convinced her. Soon both of they were standing by the lake. Bellatrix looked to the sky. It was calm and quiet.

"Falcon," She shouted raising her face to the sky. "Falcon, falcon," She again shouted. Abdullah hopefully gazed the sky all around. "I know, it was a big mistake, I know it was a blunder, we should not do so, Please do help us, for one more time trust us, Do not punish the whole humanity at the crime of one man." Bellatrix shouted but there was no reply. She disappointedly looked to Bellatrix. Next night they again came and tried in the same way but there was no reply. Sky was calm and quiet. The sky creature had sealed the black hole for ever. At first they enjoyed the life of the people of earth but now they did not even like to see them. The sound of Bellatrix knocked the seal of the black hole and again echoed back to her. Max staying in a hole guarded by four lions could not listen to Bellatrix. Although the prison had no door but he knew that if he took one step out, his next step would be in the mouth of the lion and third step would be in the stomach. He was enjoying the life of prison when one day Falcon entered his hole. She quickly turned into a girl. Max excitedly looked her with a hope.

"I only came to tell you one thing Max, the girl for whom you killed our Kings is dead in the lake, and she was died at the same time when you killed my father. It was not we or our revenge, it was the revenge of the fate," The girl scornfully informed him and flew back into the skies. Max felt her heart crushed. The girl who told him her dreams, he wanted to share with her a dream that he saw her. But he couldn't tell.

"Yes, Saira, she was you, standing at the sky smiling at me, smiling at my guilt, you were gone, the mystic unicorn warned me of the consequence but I was malicious. I could not understand. On the path of sin we do not know where we are going; we are lost and make our personal faiths and beliefs. This gives birth to a foundation of a new religion… the religion of Satan," Max was quiet. "In this religion, lie, murder, adultery, fornication, drinking, back-biting and injustice become legitimate. We feel glad to tease someone. This becomes the faith of the religion. None of we are the true followers of the faiths of a true religion. Saira, the hurdle between you and me was not the religion but devil." Max thought gloomily at the corner. Lions were guarding his hole attentively and he did not want to get out of the hole now as he wanted to open the knot of hurdle. The hole was sealed forever and the key of it's lock was thrown far away that no one could find it and no one could open it. The prisoner was ordered to never let him to be free. Saira was drowning down and down in the layers of lake and the layers of the lake were hugging it with love. Soon, she reached the bottom and the clay underneath opened its mouth and buried her. A grave was made in the lakes. The fish would passively pass at it. The lake was hushed and tranquil. Bellatrix and Abdullah were staring the lake again. They stared it and soon returned to the house.

One day, Bellatrix was shocked. Abdullah was coming holding hand of Martha. She was not dressed like any queen. She was blind but still her eyes were moving to find his son Max.

"He will be back soon," Bellatrix held her hand and hugged her. Tom was glad to see Martha. Bellatrix stayed with Martha and Tom at home. They made a family. Bellatrix would serve Martha. Daily all the time in the day she would ask her about Max. "He will be back soon, mother," She would say and Martha had to be quiet.

Mary was back from theatre. She looked to her disheveled hair and opened the drawer to comb her hair. The cruel locket was in it as the knife had stabbed in it. She tried removing the knife from it, but it was tightly fixed in it. She quickly put it back in the drawer as a remembrance of Saira. The door knocked and she quickly opened the door. A Muslim girl with a scarf around her head was standing. She frowned as she witnessed Saira.

"Saira," She murmured. The girl smiled.

"No, I'm Zainab," Mary shocked as it was her hallucination.

"O, how are you here? Fine," Mary asked her flabbergasted.

"It's card. I'm cousin of Abdullah. He and Bellatrix are going to marry soon," The girl told him. Mary excitedly got the card. James held it abruptly who was rubbing his wet hair with a towel.

"Are they marrying?" James excitedly asked reading the card. In no days the marriage was arranged and they got married according to the Muslim traditions. Bellatrix had followed the religion of tusks for the whole of her life. A month after the wedding, they decided to open the ball. They went beyond the mount and took the ball out of the ground where Bellatrix had buried it.

They squatted at the either sides of the ball encountering one another. Abdullah was pulling it at the both sides, but it was not being broken. Bellatrix took out the dagger and pinched it in the middle. It got a cut.

"Good," Abdullah appreciated her and Bellatrix smiled. She cut the ball into two halves.

"Well done," Abdullah called from her name. She smirked gleefully and her round face and dazzling eyes shone with the spirituality of her change. The ball was cut into halves. There were a pile of books in it. Abdullah frowned and Mary got surprised as they were hoping for something dazzling and illuminating. Abdullah opened the cover of one book. It had horizontal and vertical lines in it and difficult statements. He put the book at a side and opened the other book. There were different formulas in it. As he opened the third book, he found a hard white cover. He picked it up and looked it. It was a picture. Alberic and the queen were glistening in it standing in front of one another. Bellatrix hastily grabbed it from her.

"She is the same... I think he is Alberic with him, they are too young," She got excited to look at the picture. "Abdullah, I'll keep it," Abdullah nodded and turned over the pages of books. It was written in different languages.

"Let's see it at home," Bellatrix said and both of they were stepping to the house.

Shiva looked at the books and Tom also glanced them.

"It would be easier to prepare the flying objects for Sun Asians," Abdullah said to Shiva and Shiva nodded thoughtfully with Tom. Mr. Peter looked at the map and divided the earth into three parts. He gave one part to Abdullah, one to Shiva, the best reformer and the third part to Tom. Shiva soon got married to the daughter of Peter. They became the Kings and queens of their reigns. The Muslim King Abdullah gripped justice strongly and did not let the men to quarrel as the nations are destructed due to injustice. Tom gave the authority of Queen to Martha. Although, the queen was blind but she was pious and kind. She was waiting for his son to return who was staying at the skies opening the knot. There was peace and prosperity. The foods were good, crops flourished well and the water was surplus. In the rain, people enjoyed rain, in the summer people would independently shelter under the shades of the trees and in winter people would bask in the sun without being scared. "This was the dream I always wished for," The just king Abdullah said who once became king of Bimla at the branch of the tree. Bellatrix and Abdullah had a daughter and they named her "Saira".

In the just and peaceful reign of earth, the sun was drowning down. Peter in the church looked it. He was a priest now; he went inside preparing for the preaching. The world was living gleefully and far away in the skies Satan was infuriated at his failure and planning a new scheme.